Star

Bright

By: S.L. Kotar and J.E. Gessler

Ahead of the Press

St. Louis MO

Library of Congress Cataloguing-in-Publication Data

Star Bright
/ S.L. Kotar and J.E. Gessler

ISBN   KINDLE Mobi   978-1-950392-59-9   (ebook)
ISBN   PAPERBACK   978-1-950392-58-2

Ahead of The Press Publishing
St. Louis, Missouri

Table of Contents

Star Bright

DEDICATION

For Johnny Depp.

SLK

And JEG, always

Star *Bright*

CHAPTER 1

Star bright, star light
first star I see tonight.
Wish I may, wish I might
Have this wish I wish tonight.

It was four o'clock in the morning. Unfortunately, the actual concept of measuring time in twenty-four hour increments held little meaning, for it was based on the rotation of the Earth around the sun. Helen Fitzgerald was a long way away from either, and unlikely ever to set eyes on home again.

Encounter, always referred to with a capital "E," had radically altered her life and the two hundred crewmembers aboard *Target,* the star cruiser upon which she served. Only thirty-five had survived the initial devastation occasioned by contact with a ribbon of dark matter. In six short months, or a reasonable approximation thereof, considering they had lost track of time, that number had dwindled considerably, although most had perished in the first two weeks. Nine had died in what had euphemistically been referred to as Sick Bay II; that designation being given when the actual Sick Bay had been rendered contaminated by escaping poison gas. One had perished from a condition called "madness," brought on by extreme isolation. Two had perished in an aborted mutiny. Their service records had been closed with the notation, *"Court- martialed postmortem."*

Six had vanished, presumed missing in action, after the ship was taken through a wrinkle in space. Leaving seventeen souls to brave a doubtful future without the prospect of rescue.

Target, herself, had fared little better. The starboard side, containing hydroponics and nutrition services, recycling and crew's quarters had been torn away and subsequently destroyed to prevent it from exploding and taking the rest of the ship with it into Kingdom Come. What remained was so badly damaged it was patched together "on a wing and a prayer."

"Stop!"

Responding to her verbal command, the lift, known in shipwide parlance as the transport, on which she was riding, cranked to a slow, laborious halt, suspending her 'tween decks, so that she was, physically as well as metaphysically, the human equivalent of *Target*.

Caught between the quick and the dead.

Stifling the urge to scream, not from panic, but from sheer frustration, Helen forced herself to calm. The effort proved difficult. No one would have blamed her had she pummeled the small, claustrophobic walls with her fists, smashing the muted, overhead lights, then pulverizing the dancing digital display of yellow and orange figures on the directional panel.

"I am in control."

The lift failed to react, not recognizing the statement. Her lips contorted into a wry expression that even a communications expert could construe as a simple smile.

"Level Four."

As if to defy her verbal skills, the transport remained obstinate. Her expression went from grin to grimace, to outright contempt.

"Level Four, you piece of space junk, or I'll dismantle you myself."

Although trained in the art of detente, she was equally schooled in the power of a well-phrased threat. The lift shuddered, sunk down several centimeters, halted, then agonizingly resumed its trek. Timing the descent in heart beats, Helen counted twenty-four before the doors finally parted.

Prizing her command voice over her restraint, she stepped out into the gloomy, isolated corridor, just far enough that the perverse door didn't clip her as it sealed.

Having finally achieved her destination, the insomniac confronted the very real fact she had no purpose in mind for traveling to the lowest level of the ship. Level Four housed Engineering, Security and the shuttle hanger where the sole functioning Skip transport vessel and its badly damaged companions were housed. With limited crew available, there was likely only one man on duty. His time would be occupied with preordained checks and balances. Hardly a companion for her solitude.

Stiffening her back, the sense of something about to happen sent goose bumps up and down her spine. The air turned colder, as though some unseen presence had adjusted the temperature. Bringing her hand to her face, Helen exhaled, fully expecting a cloud of vaporized mist to envelope it. It did not, but the sensation persisted.

She moved a foot, setting it down with a firm tread. The long, sinewy corridors, branching out in a "Y" just beyond, echoed with the sound. It tweaked her imagination just enough to believe the short trip on the transport had mysteriously catapulted her into the midpoint of a bottomless cave.

The analogy was apt, for the modern-day equivalent of stalagmites and stalactites grew from floor and ceiling, not really solidified mineral deposits, but the remnants of equipment, torn from their anchors by Encounter. The crew had cleared the corridors of major obstructions, but had left the majority of clean-up for some future period when time "didn't press."

Were she afraid of ghosts, the lurking of *Target's* "dust bunnies" behind severed cables and shattered walls would have given her pause. That, and the lingering smell of blood and corrupted flesh their limited quantity of disinfectant could not completely remove.

"Hello?"

No reply, but the mocking reverberation of her own word.

"Anyone here?"

Had she been standing at Death's Door, she could not have been more isolated.

"Joshua? Jingles?"

Joshua Terry was the captain; Jacob "Jingles" Gingleheimer the chief engineer. Neither responded. There was no reason they should.

It was not a human presence she felt.

Next came the sound of tinkling. Celestial wind chimes. It was a low, musical chorus of perfectly blended notes, registered on a subliminal level.

Stars. The stars were singing to her.

"Impossible."

Less a denial than a hope.

Beyond and to her right stretched the main artery of Level Four. Walking down the port side of the forked corridor would bring her to Engineering. The opposite branch led to maintenance, the Skip hanger and the storage bays. At the point of deviation between the two sat Security. Beyond that, the tail of the "Y" corridor contained the brig and an observatory. To the later area she directed her attention.

Waving her hand across the electric eye, Helen waited until the door fully extended before entering. Darkness enveloped her, the floor-level safety illumination curtailed to conserve energy. Large viewscreens lining three of the walls were also disengaged. When the ship had been fully functional, the Observatory had hummed with life, serving the dual purpose of astronomy and recreation. Since Encounter, however, it had been all but abandoned. What scientific data the crew required they garnered elsewhere. Or, not at all.

Like the room, recreation and research had become obsolete.

Carefully picking her way across the expansive room cluttered with shattered walls and destroyed equipment that had remained virtually untouched by clean-up efforts, her attention was drawn to a sharp point of light emanated from the monitor of a personal viewscreen placed toward the front. The blinking green alert indicated stand-by status, an odd fact in itself, for it should have been turned off. Approaching carefully, the way a traveler, stranded in the desert sidled toward the mirage of an oasis, Helen clapped her hands together. The screen activated to full power.

The last person using this "window" had trained its eyes outward, toward the distant stars. Without reference, Helen had no way of divining which direction her attention was drawn. It did not matter. *It* was out there.

What "it" was, became another matter, entirely.

Space.

Stars.

Planets.

Moons.

Asteroids.

Meteors.

Particles of dust.

Debris from *Target,* ripped from the ship after collision, or portions of the detached half which had been destroyed by laser light to prevent a second and more deadly impact.

A space ship of unknown origin.

Alien minds.

All were improbable. What was impossible, was that her mental contact came from the United Planet Earth's loosely woven fraternity. *Target* was one of only three explorer crafts capable of extended deep space travel. The others were assigned to distant quadrants, blissfully ignorant of their sister ship's fate. Captain Terry had made it clear no rescue could be expected from that quarter. Helen believed him implicitly.

In her former life, she had spent many years traveling the galaxy. Her tours of duty had included everything from stints on semi-developed planets, to chairing conferences on the intergalactic interpretation of the various symbols diverse civilizations used to transmit information. Her pre-Encounter assignment, which explained her position aboard *Target,* had been the creation of a universally accepted form of written and spoken language.

Among her land-locked peers, Helen was affectionately referred to as "Esperanto," after the failed 20th-Century attempt to form one pattern of speech from many Earth tongues. On *Target,* she was referred to as "Catwoman," but that sobriquet was used sparingly and only by one person. To everyone else, she was just "Dr. Fitzgerald," or "Helen." All four suited, although circumstances had altered even so simple a thing as a name.

Prior to Encounter, the idea of her picking up and translating telepathic impulses from space would have been preposterous. Her work, she might have said, only partially tongue-in-cheek, was "down to earth." Evoking both the disciplines of mathematics and the creative arts, her job was to expand the *known,* not to delve into the transcendental.

Yet that did not explain how, with a little imagination, she could hear the shadowy voices of those crewmembers, so recently perished. A twist of her head away from the viewscreen and she could easily envision her friends, co-workers and family, related by space rather than blood, coming into the Observatory, faces radiant with shared secrets.

We just returned from a spacewalk, Helen.

It was wonderful. You should have come.

The stars seemed so close I felt as though I could reach out a hand and touch them.

Were we gone long?

Did you miss us very much?

Yes, she thought, in answer to their spirit-questions. *I miss you very much. You've been gone... a long time. Months. It seems like forever.*

Forever and a day.

Readjusting her position so that her back was to the door, Helen's eyes returned to the viewscreen. She did not want to dwell on the past. That was gone. Beyond her reach. She wanted her attention on the present. And for the moment, her present was expanded by the premonition of some unknown entity watching her.

As she had in the empty corridor, Helen repeated her one word sentence. *Hello.*

This time, however, it was not a question, but a welcome. The irony was not lost on her. With every expectation of receiving an answer, she had couched her former interrogative with inquisitive inflection. Alone in the observatory, without the possibility of human intervention, she stated it as a certainty.

I am a communicator. I would like to talk with you.

The fact that the computer, like all the others on *Target* had been rendered either inoperative, or had their programming corrupted by the influence of the dark matter, bore no relevance to her present situation. She was not actually attempting to speak to another life form via a mechanical device, but rather it was reaching her through the façade of something she understood.

Childlike embarrassment flooded her mind. Only those too innocent to know better spoke to the stars.

I do not believe the stars are talking to me.

Shame replaced discomfiture. She did believe.

Please.

To placate those she had offended.

Without knowing why, Helen held out her hand, gently extending it toward the panorama revealed on the monitor. Stars. Ancient, distant, unreachable.

Alluring.

As her eyes fluttered shut, the images of their light remained ingrained upon her retinas. The doctor, who was not a physician of the healing arts, opened her mind, admitting the possibilities. She began to hum, instilling inside her a calmness she had not felt since Encounter.

Concentrate, she willed, timing the tempo to the pulse in her arteries. *Listen. Identify.*

It came to her slowly, from out of a dream. She reacted too quickly, overshot her mark, lost the rhythm. Desperation gripped her essence. *Be calm. Be careful. No hurry.*

The stars were singing simple words. Not worldly, at all. With the cadence of a poem.

So familiar it brought tears to her lidded eyes.

When self-imposed darkness did not solidify the poetry, Helen reexamined the monitor. The stars were still there. Their song was still coming through on her inner, private wavelength.

The stars? she wondered suddenly. *Or one single star?* Was it just one chanting the lullaby? One out of ten million? Or a chorus of stars?

Probe.

Her brows furrowed in marked attention. To identify where and how the song originated became her one abiding goal.

"Hello," she called, whispering the word softly, lovingly. "I'm here. I'm listening."

I am coming.

The shock of this almost tangible assertion woke Helen from her trance. Frightened at her own foolishness, she drew away, head arched in fantastic disbelief.

"I'm coming?"

Swallowing down the pounding in her chest, she distanced herself from the viewscreen. The muscles in her arms quivered. Flexing them with conscious deliberation, she found they ached, as though having been held under intense pressure.

I am coming?

Had she thought those words, or had some cosmic intelligence put the phrase in her mind?

There was no possible way *she* could "come" anywhere. *Target* was damaged, possibly beyond repair. While it possessed the rudiments of movement, with little more than the facade of forward progression, there was no possibility of it reaching those distant stars.

Not in her lifetime.

I am coming.

Who was the "I" in "I am"? How was it coming? What could its arrival possibly mean to her?

The logical answer was pedantic. Rather than originating from *somewhere,* her own subconscious had answered, responding to her desperate need for help which could only come from beyond. Rather than comfort her, the idea was shattering.

"No. I heard it. It's real."

Prove it.

Rubbing her tired eyes, Helen glanced at the monitor without looking directly at it. The stars were still there, exactly as they had been. None of them were any closer.

How could they be? Stars did not possess the will to travel.

Nor did they sing.

What was the rhyme? She tried to remember, but it was gone. Vanished, as surely as if it had never been sung.

"I'm getting space happy," she diagnosed. "A person, standing in an empty room, is prone to imagining things. I'm lonely."

She might have added "I'm afraid," but did not.

Fear was not precisely the emotion, but it was as close as she did not want to get.

"I shouldn't have come down here."

Her acknowledgment came as a weak protest. She was on her own time, depriving no one of her services. She had sought solace in order to prepare herself for work. Although private, her quarters, which actually constituted a part of her language lab, were cramped. Her motives had been pure, yet guilt persisted.

From out of nowhere, the communicator at her side ironically came to life. It flashed a Red Alert signal, followed by a high-pitched squeal nearly propelling her back by the force of its decibels. Lights on the small device flashed, on-off, on-off.

Danger.

This did not frighten her. Whatever had happened was tangible, recognizable. Real.

It was nothing compared to having the stars sing to her in an old, forgotten lullaby.

The door slid open before she was halfway across the room. The physical need to react, to move, compelled her to hurry.

Red Alert. At that moment, Helen Fitzgerald would have walked, unprotected, into a wall of flame, just to prove her corporeal humanness.

Over the shipwide intercom she head Captain Terry's calm, controlled voice.

"Evacuate Level Four. All hands, evacuate Level Four."

The problem, then, was not far from where she stood. Disregarding the order, she turned down the corridor, running for all she was worth. Whether or not she could be of any help, she would offer her services. And pay for her disobedience later.

To "Meow," the counterpart to her "Catwoman." Who not only commanded the ship, but had been, in their life before Encounter, her fiancé.

The hall was sparsely lit. Running lights, they called them. Emergency light panels constructed into the deck, designed to operate when the main illumination system went out. Since the accident this was all they had. It was enough. She knew her way.

He was standing outside a sealed door, as she knew he would be. A sheen of perspiration covered his brow. His face was taut, under tension. He had ordered the area evacuated but had stayed behind.

The captain was always the last to abandon his post.

"What happened?"

Captain Terry never took his eyes off a small monitor by the door. While the numbers meant nothing to her, she knew he was reading them the way others poured over obscure religious tracts, written in cuneiform.

"Outside bulkhead weakened. This section automatically locked."

Although she knew they were in the Engineering section, she didn't recognize the specific designation.

"What is this area?"

"An equipment subsection."

"What did we lose?"

The veins in his neck revealed his emotion. With a gesture of casualness belying the pressure, Terry ran his fingers through his long, dark hair. Rather than serve to smooth it, he only managed to rearrange the ends so that they stood up at the corners, making his ears appear pointed.

"Nothing, yet." Which may or may not have been true. "What are you doing here?"

"I was in the Observation Room. The elevator locked," she lied. He accepted her excuse on face value. "Who's in there?"

"Sonya Hykowa and Hernando Diaz." He waited a beat, then added, "Jingles." Her world shattered nearly as completely as his. Jingles was their chief engineer. Without him and his two technicians, they were as good as dead. A communications specialist might consult the Med Doc and pass for a physician, and a Technology Specialist could double as a botanist in Hydroponics, but no one could take the place of the man who considered the operational system his flesh and blood kin.

"What are we going to do?"

Not "What are *you* going to do?" In the new world Fate had created for them, the personal had been abandoned in favor of the universal.

"Get them out."

"How?" She indicated the control panel. "Does that mean they're locked inside?" Tightening his eyes, Terry nodded.

"The doors won't open as long as there's any perceived threat to this section. Safety precaution," he unnecessarily added. She understood he said that for his own benefit.

Identify.

Confirm.

Act.

The holy trinity.

"Can you do a manual override?"

The corners of his mouth twitched. She had not meant to find him lacking.

"I could have before Encounter. But those safeguards no longer exist. If the sensors don't detect an 'all clear,' they won't respond to command."

"I should have realized that," Helen hastened to exonerate. It was beyond her power to repair the damage. "Have you been in touch with the engineers?"

"No."

She did not ask if they were already dead. That would be to verbalize a lack of faith.

"What, then? Burn a hole through the lock? The way you freed them last time? After Encounter?"

"Too dangerous. Without knowing the problem, I risk compromising this entire level. If the bulkhead does blow it will take out the inside door. Everything in this sector will be drawn into space by the vacuum." He did not have to underscore that danger. It was one they feared above all else. "There's only one way I know to get them out. Take the Skip and use the lasers to burn an escape hatch through the outer skin. That way, we relieve the pressure in the direction we want it to go."

"But if you do that, won't you be exposing Jingles and the others to space? Their life support will be compromised."

Terry's teeth bared in unaccustomed anger. His emotion was not directed at her, but she felt its stab.

"That's the only piece of luck we've had. They have spacesuits in there. They'll have to put them on. And tether themselves so they won't be swept outward."

"But you said they weren't responding. If they're unconscious –" Her words trailed off and she bit her tongue. The decision was not open to vote. They had been down that path before.

To command – to take ultimate responsibility is your life's avocation. What you sought – what you trained for. As personnel aboard this ship, we accepted that as a given. Such approval cannot be abdicated now. Not ever, so long as we're all aboard Target.

Brother Brian had issued that declaration. His words rang true. Helen Fitzgerald appreciated them more now than she had at the time. Being an absolute ruler was a tremendous responsibility.

"The channel is open. I can only trust they'll hear me. It's that or do nothing."

He was not asking her permission, but she gave her approval. It was all she had.

"You're right. I'm with you." She saw the light flicker behind his eyes and knew why she loved him. "Take me with you," she underscored.

"On the Skip?"

"Why not?"

For a moment she thought he would ask, "What use can you be?" but he didn't. Instead, he smiled.

"Is this for your resume, hazard pay, or logging flight hours toward your licence?"

Helen was ready for him.

"None of the above. For the excitement. Once wasn't enough," she grinned, alluding to the time she and Joshua had spent together on the Skip bringing in the ice blocks they now used for water. He nodded his understanding because she had matched his sentiment.

"You're on."

She saluted him in quasi-military fashion. Unlike his crew, who only pledged loyalty, hers was a dual promise.

To have and to hold. To love and to cherish.

Of all the vows she had prepared herself for, these were the two she least expected to be challenged on. She had been wrong, once. She hoped never to be so, again.

CHAPTER 2

"Terry to bridge."

"Bridge here, sir," came the immediate response. Like her captain, Commander Paula Burbone's voice was tightly controlled. Efficient. Considering the fact she had been an officer a mere six months, rising through attrition from ensign to second-in-command, her conduct was admirable.

"Has Level Four been cleared?"

Checking her instrumentation for confirmation, Paula gave him a crisp "Yes, sir," then added, "All hands accounted for except for the three trapped crewmembers, and..." Her voice dropped an octave. "Dr. Fitzgerald."

"She's with me."

Had he been able to visualize his officer's expression, Terry would have been both pleased and mildly surprised.

"I'm glad to hear it. I thought, perhaps, she had been in Engineering."

"She was down here, but safely away from the danger."

"I'll send the transport for her."

"Negative. She's going out with me on the Skip. To bore an escape hatch from the outside."

Paula ran her mind over the consequences of his statement before rising from her seat. The chair swiveled from the abrupt evacuation, coming to a stop so that the backrest faced her.

"It hasn't been flight tested yet, Captain. Jingles only just reported it fit for trial in the hanger. We have no way to be certain it's space worthy."

"This is how we're going to find out."

"You'll need a co-pilot. I'll join you."

"Helen can guide me. I want you right where you are. In the Captain's chair," he amended, rationalizing she had assumed that position of authority.

Biting her lower lip in annoyance, Burbone glanced forlornly at the useless stump protruding from the uniform sleeve of her right arm. Normally, she ignored the pain from the amputation, but at the moment, it throbbed with insistent intensity.

"I can handle the job, Captain." Only after speaking did Paula realize her mistake. He was not rejecting her because of her disability, but rather from the fact he wanted his most competent officer on the bridge. The ache in her arm vanished. Rank had its privileges and hers was to ride shotgun over the rescue attempt. "I can handle whatever is required from here, sir. I'll monitor your progress."

"Keep trying to raise Jingles. I don't know whether his communications are out, or if they're injured." He did not have to add, *I'm gambling on the former.* She fully comprehended the enormity of the situation. "They must have their spacesuits on before we break the seal."

"Understood. Burbone, out."

Snapping off the hand communicator, still the most efficient way to keep in contact, her lips pursed as she realigned the command chair, slipping onto its black polymer seat before resting her arms on the dual side rests. Motioning with her good left hand, an act she was still unaccustomed to, Paula issued orders from the location formally occupied by Captain George Nguyen.

"Activate the main viewing screen and bring up the peripheral monitors. I want to closely follow their progress."

"Yes, sir."

Ensign Anna Bates spoke from the navigation post. Prior to the devastation aboard *Target,* she had been a quantum physics technician. Like the remaining seventeen, she was being cross-trained. Her new position was as a member of the bridge contingent. The task Paula had assigned required three tries to complete. No one complained. Aside from Burbone, who had graduated from ensign to commander overnight, none of the surviving crew could have responded as quickly.

In their brave new world, having the impetus to perform an assignment was as important as the result.

Turning to Helen, Joshua beckoned with his second and third fingers. "Let's go."

Leading the way, they hurried to the shuttle hanger housing the three remaining Skips. Small, rectangular crafts used for transporting personnel and cargo to and from the large star cruiser, the Skips were their only ingress and egress from *Target.*

Had this portion of Level Four been destroyed in a way similar to that of the starboard side, those left aboard would have been locked inside. Without independent help from a compatible vessel, even the discovery of a habitable planet on which to settle would have been denied them as they would have had no way of reaching the surface.

Of the initial four Skips, two had been crushed beyond repair. One had been stolen by mutineers and subsequently destroyed by Captain Terry aboard the *Arrow,* the last shuttle. In the performance of that nearly suicidal mission, however, the *Arrow* had been severely damaged. Rendered inoperative, it had taken six months to repair, using parts from the ruined craft as well as jury-rigging substitute pieces for the outside shell. As Burbone needlessly pointed out, the *Arrow's* space-worthiness had not been tested. To do so under extreme duress was foolhardy.

And brave beyond measure. Should the spacecraft disintegrate, there was no way to get them back. The only working tractor beams were on the Skip.

Taking the precaution to don their spacesuits, Joshua indicated they tether themselves together. No explanation required. If the patchwork repairs failed to hold and they were forced to abandon ship, one could not go floating off without the other. Helen consoled herself with the idea there was safety in numbers.

As the gull-wing door slowly rose, Helen preceded him inside. A great deal of interior work had been done on the craft since her last mission. That had been to retrieve ice blocks, desperately required as water, from a frozen meteor. As dangerous as it had been, the flightless Skip had been fastened to the hanger floor. This journey would be different.

Although she had been on the 'planet hoppers' before, traveling to and from planet assignments, neither the structure nor accommodations had elicited particular observation. Then, the Skip had been nothing more than a conduit; a small, insignificant transport. It had never crossed her mind to question its safety, or the fact she might one day find herself in the co-pilot's seat. Now that it had become the lifeline to a rescue attempt as well as the crew's sole means of escape from *Target*, the interior appeared cramped and vulnerable.

As originally designed, the middle of the vessel comprised the main compartment. Rows of seats, three to either side filled the space. Lining the walls were a dozen individual monitors, while situated above them were two larger screens for scientific observation. A master computer was placed by the sliding door leading to the cockpit. On routine missions, the door was left open so the occupants could communicate freely with the pilots.

To the rear, also separated by doors, was a small cargo bay. When doing duty as a hauler, the crew seats could be removed, more than tripling the available space. Spacesuits and exploration equipment were stowed there.

Since the devastation wrought by the mutineers, however, much had changed. The entire back of the vessel had been cut away, leaving only limited space to accommodate spacesuits and select equipment. Were it eventually to be used for ship-to-planet evacuation, multiple trips would be required to remove the seventeen crewmembers. Nor did the outside offered a more substantial picture. The power pod had been transplanted from one of the non-functional Skips. It listed downward, as though affixed by insufficient means. Taken together, the *Arrow* promised both a technological marvel and a portal to disaster.

Shaking off her gloom, Helen mused that in her free time she would familiarize herself with the workings of the entire craft. That, she decided, was a better way of spending her sleepless hours than staring into space attempting to recall lost childhood rhymes.

Coming up behind, Joshua gave her a friendly squeeze on the shoulder. Catching his eye, she returned his smile.

"I won't fail you," she promised. "Tell me what to do and I'll do it."

My nerves are steady.

Come what may.

"Strap yourself in," he indicated, taking the pilot's seat. Watching as he performed the deed, she copied his action, bringing the "X" shaped straps across her chest, then fastening them to the side. The buckles snapped into place with a reassuring click.

Routinely, the exit operation of the shuttle would have been handled by one of the engineers, but as all three were trapped in the storage area, Lamar Porteous, the head of security, stood by to do the honors. Having been sent back by Commander Burbone, he worked the controls from outside the hanger, waiting for the captain to give him the "All clear for departure" signal. When Terry issued that familiar command, Porteous called out, "Good luck, sir. Be careful."

Catching Helen's eye to reflect the sentiment that there had been a time in the not too distant past that Porteous had been suspected of harboring mutinous ideas, Terry gave him a thumbs-up. Waiting until the security officer activated the system which would equalize pressure within and without the hanger, he made a visual inspection to assure himself all safety precautions were in place, then reestablished contact with the bridge through the shuttle apparatus.

"All secure; opening doors now."

With the ease of one who could pilot a ship blindfolded, Terry's fingers danced along the control panel, the multicolored lights reflecting across his face like so many tiny strobes.

The ship rose motionlessly from its berth and glided out.

Staring at him with unmasked curiosity, Helen absorbed the essence of Joshua Terry that she had never witnessed before Encounter and seldom as unfettered as this moment. The bridge, his self-acknowledged home away from home, was a place forbidden to those to those civilian-scientists whose business did not pertain to day-to-day operations. While the past months had given her ample opportunity to observe his leadership and courage, only once before had she witnessed this aspect of his command demeanor. And that had been when "flying" the Skip had meant operating the controls while remaining ship-bound in the hanger. Observing him now, alone aboard the small transport, she marveled at the change.

Gone, any pretense of impenetrability. No self-imposed aura protected him from those prying, judgmental eyes of the crew. He worked for himself, by himself, at his own pace. His very actions proclaimed independence and a sense of freedom he could not hope to achieve aboard *Target*.

Remembering a private moment when Joshua had offered a hard-wrung confession that after his service days were over, he would prefer to fly a Skip through space, exploring the unknown without human companionship, she finally absorbed the truth of those words. While he had been born to command, his nature – one part of him, barely acknowledged – longed for the freedom of space, not to the rules and regulations imposed on starship commanders.

The realization brought with it a pang of regret. While he belonged to her physical world; while his human love had been pledged to her, a hidden corner of his identity would always be held back. He would share many things, but not his dream. That he reserved for his private flights of fancy.

A hand, crossing before her line of vision broke Helen from her thoughts. Without making any attempt to form eye contact, he activated the viewscreens, then indicated the series of numbers scrolling beneath.

"Keep your attention here," Joshua advised. "This indicates distance; these chart our velocity. I've directed the sensors," he continued, leaning further past, so even in a spacesuit his body seemed to radiate heat over her, "to display temperature. I'll need you to call it out to me once I begin slicing through the outer skin of the ship."

"While you were repairing the damage done by Radcliff and Marr," she pursued, inwardly shuddering over the names of the two traitors, "did you happen to discover the manual? I understand Jingles said he would have to use it to repair the inner workings. I was hoping to borrow it."

He heard more hope in her voice than teasing.

"No." And then more kindly, "Officers are expected to know their duty before assuming the co-pilot seat."

"I'll write one," she promised, before adding, "for cross-training purposes."

Drawing back and thus taking with him his warmth, his attention returned to his own panel.

"Skip to Engineering, subsection 1A; come in, Jingles. Skip to Engineering. Come in." Helen could not divine from his expression whether he expected an answer or not, yet her own spirits sagged at their failure to respond, knowing it was vital for the three trapped crewmembers to don their spacesuits before they lost life support. Failing to do so, they would perish when the lasers cut through the wall, compromising their environment.

Even though Terry had explained his rationale, failure meant his judgment would be questioned. The chief engineer and his technicians were vital to the survival of those aboard *Target*. Without them, any hope of keeping the ship "afloat," one of the few jokes shared among the crew, would evaporate. It had not taken an official report from Jingles to remind her that the considerable damage done to *Target* left them in a precarious position. One day, with very little warning, it was possible, even likely the vessel would break apart. Lacking Jingles' magic touch and a hefty dose of luck, life, as they knew it, would come to a very rapid termination.

Long-term prospects presented even more dire prospects. If the Skip failed on this, its "maiden voyage," even if it were capable of reentering the hanger, life for the seventeen would shatter. Lacking any way to escape should they find the hoped-for Earth-like planet, they would be doomed to existence aboard a crippled ship until food, oxygen or fraying tempers reached the breaking point. Eventually, fingers would again be pointed toward Terry and his decision to chase the mutineers in a contest that eventually destroyed one Skip and nearly the second. Second-guessing his decision would only add fuel to the smoldering embers of despair. She had lived through mutiny once; she did not think she could endure a second trial.

"Bridge to *Arrow*, come in," boomed a pleasant voice, shattering her gloomy illusions. "We've got you on our monitors. Smile for the cameras."

"Brian," Joshua identified, rolling his eyes. "Who allowed him on the bridge?" Protests to the contrary, she saw him grin and silently thanked their resident cleric. If anyone could break up tension, it was Hardy, affectionately referred to as Brother Brian.

"We're smiling," Helen informed him, noting Joshua had engaged the transmitter for a response.

Before the conversation divested onto other pleasant subjects, Burbone's command voice broke in.

"Steady as she goes, Captain. She looks stable from my perspective. How does she handle?"

"Sluggishly," he stated in a soldier's monotone. "At minimal power. Inside pressure holding."

"That's what I want to hear. No need to push her. This is a trial run. If you start to lose her, turn back."

"Copy," he responded, meaning the opposite. "It's going to take me a moment to get her straightened around."

"Fitzgerald," Commander Burbone continued, changing voices as she spoke to the subordinate officer. "Stand by with the tractor beam. If anything goes wrong you may have a window of opportunity –"

"Yes, sir. I'm prepared. Captain Terry has explained."

Her avowal caught him off guard. Without acknowledging as much, she saw him nod and knew she had said the right thing.

Everything is a test, she reminded herself, not for the first time. It was as well to keep that foremost in her mind. The concept of relaxation had been erased from her personal repertoire. There would be few, if any, truly free moments until they had escaped the prison of their crippled vessel. And perhaps not even then.

Placing the transmitter on standby, Joshua returned his attention to the view outside the front shield.

"Skip to Engineering subsection. Jingles, I'm coming in through the outer wall. Put on your spacesuits and secure yourselves. Repeat: put on your spacesuits and secure yourselves to the inner bulkhead. Depressurize the chamber. Over."

He waited, because that was protocol. No reply was forthcoming. Helen had not expected one. Terry's expression was inscrutable. She decided it was just as well.

Aligning his sights on what had become, to them, the "target," Joshua nodded encouragingly to his passenger. "You all right?"

She nodded.

"I should have asked. Have you reconfigured the controls? Corrected the damage done by Radcliff and Marr?"

She was not frightened. She asked because she presumed he expected such a query. Her job, her former position in life, was as a communicator. To remain mute now was to obfuscate her self-image. It never occurred to her to play the silent hero.

Or that he might appreciate such bravery from her.

They each had their roles to play.

Terry hesitated, then shook his head.

"The only way to be certain is through a field test. We're doing double duty, here."

The fact he included her in his statement sent chills down her back. Determined to live up to what could only be taken as a compliment, Helen's eyes leveled on her console, memorizing the rapidly flashing sequences. When assured they maintained consistency, she stole a peek outward with the intention of assessing their proximity to *Target*. The moment she disengaged her attention, however, the power of the stars engulfed her mind. As though they suddenly represented a gateway to a new universe, an almost physical pull grabbed and propelled her forward. Straining against the safety belts, ears attuned to the silence that inexplicably transmitted the rhyme of distant...

"I beg your pardon. What was that you said?"

He had spoken and she had missed it, barely registering the fact until replaying the sound of his voice in her mind.

"Stand by," he repeated. "We're in position."

With an unconscious jerk of her head, Helen found her attention had been so focused on space, she had lost track of time.

"Yes, sir. I didn't realize –"

He indicated the viewscreen with his gloved hand. Following the motion, she gasped at the proximity of their small craft to the suddenly looming star cruiser.

"You understand what's going to happen?"

"The ship looks so large," she said, fumbling for a coherent sentence.

Fortunately, he misunderstood her confusion.

"It's difficult to gauge size. You're used to seeing things from a different perspective."

"I thought you would... get closer," she faltered.

For the first time, a flicker of doubt rippled across his features, accentuating the lines which had spider-webbed around his eyes and mouth in the last six months. He was thirty-six years old. She wondered when that had happened. To her, Joshua Terry would always be in his mid-twenties, the age he had been when appearing unannounced at her quarters on a planet named Zertan, distraught and embarrassed.

Asking about an outlaw cat and her litter of kittens.

"Meow," she whispered.

"Say again." He had not been following her train of thought.

"Nothing."

Had he changed after discovering his ability to love even so alien a creature as a cat? And then by applying that emotion to a member of his own species? If not, she had entirely misread him. *Odd,* she mused, *how one can miss the obvious.* Prior to their first encounter, she had viewed him only one way: by the exterior he had presented. Career officer, dedicated astronaut, brave ambassador; a man dependent upon no one but himself. One evening had altered that impression. Nothing in the subsequent years of their distant but ever closer relationship had altered that startling awareness.

She wondered again if she knew him at all.

We've all changed.

An expression too often expressed.

"… If I were certain Jingles would depressurize the cabin, I would have gotten closer. That way, boring a hole in the side would be no more dangerous than opening the hatch of a cargo bay."

He was talking and she only partially understood what he was saying. Her mind was engraving the image of a second lieutenant, sitting on the floor of a dignitary's quarters, blowing streams of air onto a kitten's fur, then laughing as the tiny feline made desultory attempts to smooth it.

"Go on," Helen encouraged.

Keep talking. That way, I can remember you the way you were. Your voice hasn't changed.

"If they haven't, then the sudden loss of pressure will propel the atmosphere and a portion of the wall out. We could be struck by a flying missile."

"Then we'll know immediately," she rapidly interceded, "if they've heeded your warning."

"Precisely."

"And if they haven't?"

"They'll die."

Helen suppressed a chill. She was wrong. His voice *had* changed. Like his face, it had been warped by circumstance and experience. Somewhere along the line, she had missed that, too.

If Brother Brian were reading her thoughts, he would have encouraged her to remember the good times. He was always the optimist.

Brian Hardy has changed, too. Because he no longer believed in the power of memory.

We've all forgotten.

She began singing out numbers, forcing her mind to concentrate. Distance and temperature were the only problems which need concern her. Satisfied that he had explained himself, Terry attention returned to his controls. Nowhere on his visage was any indication he had ever been Meow.

"Coming at you, Jingles. On the count of ten." He gave the engineer more time than was necessary. Both passengers understood he was delaying the inevitable that much longer. Just in case. "Ten. Nine. Eight. Seven. Six. Five. Four. Three. Two. One." Each number separated by a pause. *Twenty seconds,* she mentally calculated. Language was a wonderful thing.

God, let him be right.

The laser beam was invisible to the naked eye. The only proof of activation came when a small hole suddenly appeared at their area of interest. With her eyes on *Target,* Helen continued calling off numbers. Although she was not, could have been making them up, they made no sense. Her body steeled for an explosion.

Which never came.

Joshua exhaled, then licked his lips. A gloved hand went to his forehead, forgetting for the moment, he could not wipe off sweat through the spacesuit. His simple gesture reassured her. Not because the trapped men had depressurized the chamber, but because he cared. Deeply and passionately. Her prayer, perhaps more accurately expressed as, *God, make him right,* had been answered.

Meow liveth. What she was now confronted with was the equally disturbing interrogative.

Was the Catwoman still extant?

Averting her head, Helen silently sobbed.

Her tears of joy were short lived.

"I don't see them. They're not coming out."

Biting her lower lip until she drew blood, Helen forced herself to look. He was correct. There was no sign of movement. Nothing but an ugly rent in an already destroyed space ship.

"They have to be alive. There was no explosion," she tried, the timbre of her voice betraying doubt.

"The strength of the laser – I might have –" He did not finish the sentence. The idea of severing flesh as easily as the outside wall was too graphic to articulate.

Moments passed, then one minute. Two. Terry's tongue ran across the inside of his cheek, fist one side than the other in tempo with his disappointment.

"I'll have go in after them. Determine what happened." Resignation was palpable. His mind had already accepted the inevitable. It had moved from "rescue" to "recovery."

To who would cross-train in Engineering.

Another job for the "jack of all trades" crew, none of whom were capable of the assignment.

"Look!" she pointed. "There, Joshua! I saw it!"

"Saw what?" he demanded, straining forward, eyes wide and piercing. Needing to believe.

"A hand; at the opening."

"I didn't see it," came the terse response.

"There it is, again! Look!"

In a split second his head went from shaking to nodding.

"Yes.... Yes, I saw it! Some movement – But I'm not sure. Space debris? Working its way out in the vacuum...."

"Have you lost so much you can't tell the difference between animate and inanimate objects?" she cried, the words slurring across numb lips. "Look again – there it is! Purposeful, directed movement. It's a hand. Waving!"

He laughed because he could not cry.

"You're right. Waving. I never thought Jingles was the type."

She laughed with him, even though it was her prerogative to weep.

"All right, Jingles," he called through the shipboard communicator. "We see you. Stand back. Have you out directly."

Calm, cool, professional. He would not fool her a second time.

Working faster, more assuredly, Joshua cut away a section of wall, making an opening just large enough for a man to slip through. There was no possibility of bringing them aboard the Skip; the crew would have to float out, working their way the short distance to the star cruiser's main hatch.

"Piece of cake."

"With whipped cream on top," she automatically replied.

"Save that for our litter," Joshua joked, relief palpable on his face.

"Litter of what?" Helen countered, wondering suddenly if he had been reading her mind.

One prayer had been answered.

Twice over.

Brian would appreciate knowing God was still in His heaven.

CHAPTER 3

They came, one by one, through the narrow hole Terry had blasted through the outer wall of their prison. Helen waved at them, a frantic gesture of welcome and relief. Joshua started to comment, then raised his own arm and copied her style. Catching her shining orbs, however, he did not fail to point out the flaw in her greeting.

"Hardly military precision, Fitzgerald."

"I am not a member of the armed services," she retorted. "I am a civilian. It is best you do not forget that, sir, for should you ever be rescued in like manner, I will fly to greet you with arms raised. I will make a terrible scene, weeping and wailing; kissing and hugging you. You shall be terribly embarrassed and it will require all your professionalism to keep a straight face."

"I stand duly warned. But I thought we had agreed," he pursued, "that the status of everyone aboard *Target* has altered. You have all been recruited into the Service."

"Yes, that was your understanding. But I think you will find, Captain, that while you have our unmitigated support, we will never march in ranks with the rest of your soldiers."

His eyes flashed but his answer was light and airy.

"Then I'll throw the lot of you in the brig."

"And we'll summon Brian to get us out. I understand, from very good authority, that in your former capacity as commander of *Target*, you were unable to incarcerate him for any length of time."

"Too many stories," he groused, suggestively raising his eyebrows. "I shall certainly include him in your number when I lock you up. He's just as much a civilian as the rest of the scientists."

Helen hesitated before replying. While a jocular answer suited the occasion, she did not have it in her to lie. Instead, she merely shrugged.

"You can't change a cat's stripes. We simply don't think the way you do."

"That's what enlistment is all about." Without giving her the opportunity to reply, he mitigated what might have been a warning by staring through the cockpit window at the three approaching spacemen. "They look all right. None of them seem to be injured."

She agreed, noting Jingles, Sonya and Hernando were appropriately moving arms and legs, and that none were being carried in tow by the others.

"I wonder what happened?"

"I don't know. But I'm going to find out. At least we learned one salient detail."

"And that is?"

"Even an engineer can maneuver into a spacesuit and figure out how to use the directional jets without a manual."

She groaned at the previous reference to manuals, then resumed waving. Hernando, the lead astronaut, now close enough to see through their viewscreen, eagerly responded, moving his own arm back and forth with such vigor he threw himself off course. Just as he floated overhead, Sonya grabbed him by the foot and dragged him back into frame.

"So much for your assessment, Captain," Helen grinned.

"I'll chalk that up to cross-*contamination*," he sourly observed before reactivating the communication channel. "Jingles, do you read? Over?"

"Loud and clear, Captain," came the somewhat muffled but obviously relieved voice. "A dandy little job you did. And with my Skip, too." Underscoring the courage it took to test the shuttle, he asked, "How's he holding up?"

Wincing at the engineer's penchant for male pronouns, Terry nodded.

"Just fine for two. You'll have to make your own way over to the hatch."

"Don't I know it. Sorry for the cramped quarters. Although I don't suppose you and Officer Fitzgerald mind."

Captain Terry ignored the innuendo.

"To be of the safe side, I'll wait here until you're safely back aboard. Stand clear when we re-enter."

"Aye, sir."

With the danger passed and time left for private rumination, Helen once more dared contemplate the future. Proving herself worthy of being his co-pilot, she determined the next time he flew she would go with him. With Burbone holding the bridge and no one else qualified for the position, she saw no reason why she shouldn't train for and assume the position. If Joshua agreed to teach her, she could become proficient at the controls so that she might truly be of assistance.

Share a part of his world hitherto excluded from her existence.

Yet, with that idea she realized they would never actually share the same ambitions. The relative difference between their perspectives was far greater than either had realized. While necessity had altered and brought them closer together on a professional level, she was not a military officer and never would be. That was not her calling.

Calling. The concept was overwhelming and all inclusive. Duty called. Nature called. Men and women were called upon to make choices.

Space called.

But, in her parlance, it did not speak in the same language to her as it did to him. He sought the cold, impersonal, often harsh expanse of the universe, while she looked for the living mysticism that existed beyond his ken.

Space had come calling to Helen Fitzgerald. And this time, she answered back.

Tell me your identity, she silently implored, her words carrying beyond the viewscreen and out into the depths of the unimaginable. *Who are you? Where are you from? What do you want?* And then, more hesitantly, *How can I help you?*

The celestial orbs sparkled brightly. Neither old nor new, they were timeless, and in this state of constancy, she found an answer.

Communication. That was the key. *I am needed to translate; to speak for another an idea or a concept it cannot express for itself.*

The idea had been in her grasp all the time and she had failed to see it. Now that comprehension was upon her, Helen's resolve strengthened. In her career, she had faced similar obstacles, translated more complex means of communication. She would break this code because that was why she was born; why she had ventured into space. Beyond that, why *Target* had been crippled. To set this play in motion.

The enormity of that concept nearly overwhelmed her.

"They're safely back in *Target*," Joshua's voice boomed into her split world. Tearing herself from the stars and their compelling lullaby, Helen offered a sigh of relief before hesitantly inquiring, "Will you show me how to operate the controls as we work our way back?"

"Considering the fact you're my new co-pilot," he agreed, eyes luminous with success, "I will."

Although confirming what she had only hoped, his answer held only a modicum of excitement they might have a moment before. And the words came back to her. Not the amorphous ones whispered by *out there,* but others, less inspiring.

We've all changed.

But, that was past tense.

We're all changing.
A new interpretation of the old.
Bringing back something else Joshua had said.
"I don't know who I am, anymore."
She finally understood the sentiment.

"Very nice, sir. Almost home."
The voice over the ship-to-ship communications sounded young and chipped, a child playing grown-up. With tension dissipated and final maneuvers for bringing the Skip back into the hanger nearly complete, Captain Terry finally had the opportunity of concentrating on Commander Burbone's tones. He was surprised by what he heard.

He had dismissed from his mind how youthful she was. Without bothering to scan the video image transmitted from the bridge, he recalled her unlined features, the darkness of her skin, the intensity of her eyes, uncorrupted by experience. While tragedy had touched her life, as it had all aboard *Target,* she remained what she had been: a twenty-four year old functioning as second in command aboard a crippled ship.

Behind her proud words lay unbridled enthusiasm, an exuberance for danger, a willingness to please. It reminded him of his own first tour of duty, when the summons of space had been so powerful he had been awed by the chance to explore their unknown vastness.

Cheered by her enthusiasm, yet saddened by circumstances which deprived Paula of the opportunities she might have had: moving through the ranks, maturing as an officer, finding her own special path in life, he glanced over at Helen, wondering if she, too, were thinking as he. Instead, he found his co-pilot oblivious to the present situation. She was eagerly pressed forward, eyes glued to what lay beyond the window. While she was not staring at the three rescued crewmen just working their way into the hatch, he presumed Helen was imagining the reception they would surely have and the congratulations she would surely receive for her part in the drama.

That, he realized with a pang of regret, was a separation between them which they had failed to fully acknowledge. She had been right in her assessment. There were differences between military and civilian minds. One, he decided, which would be more difficult to breach than either anticipated.

Returning to his own business, he accepted Burbone's praise with a curt, "Thank you," naturally falling into a professional cadence. "Once I've debriefed Jingles I'll join you on the bridge."

"Yes, sir."

Signing off, he deliberately maneuvered *Arrow* through the hatch opening, signaled the door be closed and life support restored. Emotionally thrown back as the outside view was lost Helen snapped out of her trance, but too late to respond immediately to Joshua's thumbs-up. Surprised it required a moment for her to respond, he shrugged off the delay and being given the green light, popped the shuttle door.

Back to her normal self, Helen followed him out and rushed to Jingles, who was in the process of removing his protective suit.

"Why didn't you signal us? You had us worried to death."

"More to the point," Terry officially interrupted, "what happened?"

The engineer responded first to his commanding officer.

"We were replacing a transducer in the auxiliary subsection and short-circuited it, causing a power surge. That's what triggered the alarm. Their communications blew along with everything else." He frowned and indicated outside. "We might have been in there 'till Kingdom Come and I didn't even have a vending machine to empty." He waited for Terry to scowl, which he did, before continuing. "I thought you'd have to risk coming after us with the Skip. That took raw courage," he added, glancing at Helen. "I'm not sure I would have recommended it, myself."

"If not, what would you have done?" she asked.

"Knowing what you didn't, I'd have blown the door if I was able – which I wasn't. Not being aware of the situation as you were," he added, lowering his voice, "I'd have summoned the good brother to say a few words over us and let us rot."

"While the thought crossed my mind, "Terry stated with conviction, "you're unfortunately too valuable to give up on that easily. But from now on, there's going to be a new rule. No three of you going anywhere together. One always stays in Engineering. It's that way with Burbone and I on the bridge. If something happens to one of us, there's still an office left in charge."

Jingles instantly grasped the significance.

"I think I like the old way better. Having all three of us together prevented you from abandoning us."

"Thinking is the exclusive realm of command officers."

"Aye, sir. I'll remember that." He turned to Helen as she stepped in to ease the discussion.

"How did they know to put on your space suits and depressurize the chamber?"

"I followed the same reasoning Captain Terry did." He tried a grin. "Who would have believed it? A 'command officer' and an engineer on the same wave length?"

"Stranger things have been known to happen," she demurred as he continued along his previous line of thought.

"We'll have to repair the entire substation. That'll put us back months."

"Work on the intraship communications first," Terry ordered. "And see what you can do about re-establishing the manual override. Both are vital to a well-functioning ship."

"What about the communication devices attached to your spacesuits?" Helen asked, determined to understand the accident. "You could have contacted us through those. As it was, we thought you were…"

A flicker behind Terry's eyes revealed the same thought had occurred to him.

"Dead," Jingles finished with a grim look of disgust. "The batteries were corrupted. They should have lasted for a decade or more but the system wasn't operational. Possibly from the effect of going through the eye of the dark matter barrier. They should have been checked, but they weren't. There wasn't any need. Until there was," he finished, guilt hanging heavy over him. "No one's gone through the nonessential checklists since Encounter."

"That's another thing we're going to have to change," Terry snapped. "Too much has been overlooked. Assignments are going to have to be changed."

"It was easier before," she pointed out, refusing to acknowledge the blame he laid at his own feet. "We had two hundred people aboard. Thinking back on it now, I can't imagine how we managed to keep ourselves busy. We must have been tripping over one another."

Joshua started to reply then kept his own council. In the "before time," *Target* had been more than twice the size of the ship that remained. After losing a third of its bulk when the starboard side had been ripped away, then sealing off the entire medical section of Level Three as well as major portions of Two and Four, they had rendered their world small, indeed.

But still too large for seventeen able-bodied crew to adequately monitor and maintain.

"We haven't done enough," he argued.

"This time, Jingles intervened.

"Not that I'm one for defending your scientists, Captain, but they're not the ones who can do that sort of technical work. I think we've come farther than could reasonably be expected."

Glancing at Helen, Terry stared, "'Reasonably' is not a word in my vocabulary." Tapping his fingertips on the bulkhead, he pursued the thought. "Burbone and I will have to do it. We can't afford to ignore maintenance and upkeep. If we do, our oversights will eventually cost lives. Just as they nearly did today."

Because there was no way she could counter his argument, Helen's mind snaked back toward the stars. Was it remotely possible help was on the way? Could that explain why she had been approached by the unknown life forms? Was it possible for there to be a mutual exchange of cultures?

In their experience with alien civilizations, the explorers from Earth had encountered the aggressive and the peaceful; the intellectually advanced and those stagnating from disease and famine. If her contact was reachable – if, in reality she hadn't imagined there was a contact – then salvation from their dire straits might just be possible.

It was, as Brian would say in his endearingly antiquated fashion, "A crap shoot." An idea best stored within the recesses of her heart for the time being. To make promises now would as unfair as they were potentially dangerous.

"I'll begin now," Terry announced, separating himself from the others. "With my post-flight checklist. Helen, you're dismissed."

Slightly confused from his abrupt change of mood, she stepped away from him. And right into Jingles' arms. Throwing them around her, he gave the doctor a hug, then as she turned her head toward him, met her lips with his. She responded to his overture and to the utter amazement of his technicians, the couple completed what might have been a very romantic display of affection. Finally breaking away, the chief engineer made her a slight bow.

"Thank you," she grinned in a breathless gasp. "But, what in the universe was that for?"

"To make up for the Captain's abruptness and to make a confession. For a while there, I thought we were going to die: either from the danger of further short-circuiting that might actually have blown the bulkhead, or by being catapulted into space. And, after surviving the last six months, I've grown rather appreciative of drawing breath." He wrung his hands, only partly for its theatrical affect. "I figured out what Captain Terry would have to do, but I'd have been a whole lot more confident if I knew he'd chosen you for his co-pilot."

The confession was almost as startling as his kiss.

"Why?"

Shaking his head, then glancing upward, figuratively through the sculptured roof of the hanger, he mumbled what might have been an apology.

"All my life I've trusted my own instinct for survival. These past six months I've been forced to acknowledge there are other factors in play. One of them is the reaction and the skills of the people around me. Do you understand?"

"Yes," she confessed, feeling again the unsolicited tingling in her hands and toes.

"Hykowa and Diaz and I never saw trouble coming. We made a mistake. Violated a rule we didn't know we were breaking. I'll have to study what went wrong," he hurried on in a rush. "And I'll find out. But that was for the future. What I had to face was that our three lives were in Captain Terry's hands. I've learned to respect his ability to command but our situation required something on a higher plane than that. Am I talking nonsense?"

"No, Jingles. What you're saying is exactly right. But, I didn't –"

He brushed aside her objection.

"Captain Terry is like me: he understands the known, but when he looks into the unknown it's on a personal level. One he doesn't share. Your mind is open to wonder on a wider scale. You're looking for something to embrace with more than just yourself. When something out of the ordinary happens, he needs a bit of help, but doesn't open himself up to ask. I learned that," he added in an undertone only she could hear, "after Encounter. He's brash and he's determined, but we needed more than that. Someone with… poetry in their soul. Like you."

Flustered but deeply moved, Helen gripped her hands together.

"Now, I don't understand. I just went along for the ride."

"You feel things; your judgments aren't like mine. Or Terry's." Using his hand, he made a sweeping motion, inadvertently brushing aside a loose strand of her hair. Feeling the breeze, a warm glow settled in Helen's body. "It took courage. And more than that." He struggled for the word. "Faith. You cared. Not just because we're vital to the ship, but from the fact we've somehow been incorporated into your concept of family."

"Of course you are," she cried before receiving the full impact of his avowal. "But so did Captain Terry. If you had seen his face –"

She tried, but discovered it was beyond even her powers of language to describe Joshua's countenance. Jingles shrugged it away.

"He had the technical skill, but he was driven by duty. You believed we were alive. Your mind was open to the positive. That's what saved us." He hesitated as he carefully and very astutely appraised her. "If I were an alien looking to communicate with humans, it's you I'd make contact with."

Stunned by his statement which came very close to summing up her own thoughts, she demanded, "Why did you say that?"

Rather than answer, he quietly pulled back.

"Don't make me say any more," came the weak, emotional protest. "You better kiss those two engineers of mine, or I'll never hear the end of it."

Only too glad to oblige, Helen engulfed Sonya in her arms while bestowing a kiss on Hernando.

"I love you all."

"Thanks, Doc," Sonya choked, averting her face to hide her expression.

"But if we're family – even including his lordship," Hernando concluded, indicating Jingles, "then you must be part engine. You'll have to be put on a checklist – to make sure all your working parts are in order. I volunteer for the job."

Laughing delightedly at his innocently risqué joke, Helen reluctantly pulled back.

"We'll leave that for the captain. But if you care to draw up a detailed plan, I wouldn't object. He could use some pointers."

Rejoining them from the cockpit to the sound of lively good humor, Joshua stared at them in confusion.

"What's this all about? Something amusing? Have I missed the joke?"

"Jingles and Hernando were flirting with me. Even an engineer can tell there are more men aboard this ship than women."

"I see. They're staking their claims."

"It's wonderful what an escape from death does for the psyche," she breezily dismissed. "We aren't so far removed from that, ourselves. You ought to keep it in mind."

"I'll banish them to Engineering. But if Brian ever makes a pass at you, I'll flatten him to the deck."

"That's only because you can't keep him locked up," she grinned, relieved to have a way out of the conversation. Not that she wasn't flattered by his sudden jealousy, but from the lingering impression Jingles' words had on her. She needed more time to assimilate what they meant. And what they might portend.

On the long shot that he might have been more correct than even he imagined.

CHAPTER 4

It was not meant to be that easy.

As the Joshua and Helen emerged from the hanger Brian Hardy appeared. After performing a ritual hop, skip and jump, he clasped their hands and thumped their backs with equal enthusiasm. Responding to his displays, both stared as he shoved a teacup toward Joshua.

"Knew it would all come out well," Brian bragged in a hushed tone calculated to be overheard by everyone present. "I read the tea leaves. It's all here."

Squinting down into the nearly drained cup, Joshua's eyebrows knitted into a "V."

"Really?"

"Absolutely. And for an additional fee, I can read your palm. Tell the future."

"Additional?" Helen joked. "You mean we already owe you restitution for what you're telling us after the fact?"

"Safer that way," Brian admitted, staring lovingly into his less-than-crystal ball. "Maintains my perfect record of divination."

"I'm impressed," Terry admitted, grabbing the cup from him with a swift, fluid motion. Small bits of dark remnants floated in a pale yellow liquid, the color of cat's eyes. "Particularly when these aren't tea leaves."

Snatching back his prize, Hardy pouted. "Yes, they are."

"Where did you get them? I didn't think there was any tea on board."

Like most comestibles, the supply of tea and coffee had been lost when dietary, food processing, storage bays, hydroponics and recycling were destroyed.

"My own personal supply."

"Then you won't mind sharing it with the rest of us."

Pretending to be wounded, Brian slunk away, shoulders hunched in an attitude of depression. Not until he was safely out of reach did he turn back, cup clasped firmly between his hands.

"They're *used* tea leaves," he pouted. "No good to anyone but me."

Waving him away, Helen took Joshua by the arm.

"I hope you weren't too harsh on him."

"Never. He has an indomitable spirit."

Abruptly changing the subject, she steered him down the corridor.

"Let's go somewhere and celebrate," she suggested. The color rising to his cheeks alerted her to the fact he correctly interpreted her innuendo.

"Don't tempt me, Helen Fitzgerald," he intoned in a low, barely audible voice, but she was not to be put off. Although their relationship had begun a metamorphosis after Encounter, the past several hours had badly shaken her. For the first time since their engagement, Helen felt her emotions diverted. No longer was the sound of his voice paramount in her consciousness. Unwittingly, it had been replaced by a lullaby from space.

If she were to regain any grasp on reality, it was time to draw him back physically into her life, first as a lover and then as a husband. That was her best and possibly last hope to dispel the mysterious influence woven around her heart.

"I mean it, Josh. After what we've been through, we both deserve a few hours to ourselves. There's nothing of paramount importance awaiting you on the bridge that it can't be delayed. Burbone may be expecting you but she's not going to institute a search party if you don't make an appearance. I love you. We've held off this long, waiting for the right moment. This is it."

Clearly torn by the idea, he asked, "Are you sure?"

"We risked our lives out there. I know you tried to minimize the danger but we both understood the implications. The Skip hadn't been tested. After six months of gluing it back together, there was little guarantee it would hold together. I understood why you had to go. Not just to save Jingles and the others, but to prove you hadn't destroyed our chances of ever escaping this ship. I went with you to demonstrate my faith in you to the crew. We both won our private wars. Now, it's time we did something for ourselves. "

"I'm not disagreeing." Placing his arms around hers, he held her fast. "If I haven't said it enough, especially after Encounter, I love you. But what about the rest? Brian was going to perform the marriage ceremony."

"He can still do that. We can let the crew decorate the ship; use the occasion as a morale booster," she added, without recognizing the bitterness in her tone. "We don't have to explain ourselves, Josh. We're consenting adults. Please. I need this."

"I'm afraid you're over-reacting because of the danger we were in –"

"It's not that," she protested in genuine anger, disengaging one of her arms and placing it on his. "It's something else; something I can't explain. I want you as my own. Now."

"All right," he agreed, shyly smiling.

Although he gave her the appropriate answer, she suddenly stiffened in fear.

"I know we've changed. How I've come to hate that expression. And I'm equally aware I released you from your proposal. What I want is –"

"For me to propose again. To reaffirm my commitment. That, I gladly do," he avowed with sincerity, guiding her down the corridor into one of the partially un-cleared passageways. Once alone, Joshua wrapped his arms around her in a spontaneous gesture of affection, eyelids closing as their lips met. The kiss was long and passionate, warm and sensuous, promising mounting eagerness. "Where shall we go?"

"Somewhere we won't be disturbed."

Looking around the corridor, then shifting his gaze further away, he came up with a solution that would not require them to leave Level Four and thus break the mood.

"One of the observation rooms on Level Four? Not very comfortable, but –"

"No! Not there," Helen objected, pulling away from his grasp in horror. Searching desperately for a neutral zone, she waved away his unasked question. "I don't want to lie on the floor," she lied. "Back in the Skip. There isn't much room in the cargo area, but it's private and we can make do; share it the way two people in love ought to share a bed."

"You make me feel like a teenager, sneaking off from my parent's home."

"Not a bad thought," she countered, praying she had convinced him. "Come on."

"Just a minute." Her heart sank, but a quick wink reassured her. "Stay here a moment and let me see if the path is clear. If we're caught going back, Porteous or one of the others will come in and check on us."

Slipping away, the captain returned to the hanger. Finding it deserted, he retraced his steps, gave Helen the all-clear and they scurried back. Activating the exterior controls, the gull-wing door rose invitingly. Checking inside with the type of look usually reserved for peeking under the bed on a dark night, Helen laughed.

"Josh? You look scared to death. Is the prospect of making love with me that daunting?"

"Actually," he confessed, closing the door and sealing them inside, "I've already done so."

"Where was I?" she suspiciously demanded.

"It was a dream. Not so much a dream as… an alternate reality. I was on the bridge. You can say I was delirious – that is, perhaps what you said when you found me later. The reaction from the concussion I sustained. But, to me, it was as tangible as anything I've ever lived. You and I – that wasn't all I experienced in that altered state, but it's what I remember best. I thought afterwards – what I realized it hadn't been real – I'd given myself the opportunity I'd never actually have."

"When you thought we were all going to die."

"That's one explanation," he uneasily dismissed. Searching the confined space, he took some padding from beneath several containers and spread it over the open floor space. "Other than that, I'm fairly new at this."

Allowing him to put his arm around her, Helen mischievously grinned.

"Me, too." His head arched back in surprise, prompting her to add, "You doubt me?"

"No. I… It's just that a beautiful woman like you –"

"One who's traveled the known galaxy in the company of equally beautiful men? One who was a charter member of the Zertan Officer's Club for three long years? One who has chaired conferences on intergalactic communications, attended by the best and the brightest?"

"Yes. That one."

"If you're asking me whether I've been – propositioned – then the answer is yes. About as many times as you have – Captain." Reaching out with her free arm, she turned off the interior lights, remembering correctly where the control was situated. He nodded approvingly.

"You're a fast learner."

"That's just it, Josh. I have as much to learn here as you do. If I understand you correctly." Helen pressed her body close to his. "I won't say I've never been tempted. But I've never been in love. What about you?"

"The same."

She felt his stomach muscles jump and questioned, "What else?"

"I never thought to fall in love. I didn't think I had the capacity. It was Brian who told me."

"Told you what?"

"I'd find love."

"How did he do that?"

"He was reading my palm. Years ago. But, he didn't say how it'd turn out."

"He wanted you to discover that for yourself," she lied, suddenly nervous and afraid. Confronted with the reality of their situation, doubts assailed her. "I don't want to do anything wrong, Josh. Maybe I'm rushing things. We've just been through a harrowing experience."

"Your adrenaline is wearing off. I know. That always happens. It leaves you sort of... depressed."

"I'm not sure that's it."

"Are you afraid because there's a lot we don't know about each other?" Stepping back, he took her hand in his. "It's odd, isn't it? We've been engaged for more than a decade, yet we've never really spent a lot of time talking."

"What have we done?"

Pressing his fingers to her lips, she kissed them tenderly, then motioned they sit. Shoulder to shoulder they slid to the floor.

"We've played with kittens," he softly began, his words containing the wonder she found so appealing. "We've discussed the arcane rules and regulations of sundry planets we've visited. We've talked about work. We spent a week alone aboard a Rover craft, looking at the stars. Why don't you tell me about yourself?" he prompted suddenly. "The important things."

Leaning against him, Helen closed her eyes, allowing a sense of peacefulness to envelope her frame. To the rhythm of his breathing she began a gentle rocking.

"I don't know where to begin."

Joshua was ready for her.

> "'Bye, baby bunting,
> Father's gone a hunting."
> "'Mother's gone a milking,
> Sister's gone a silking –'"

"And Brother's gone to buy a skin..." Helen continued, greatly touched he had chosen a poem dealing with family. In her present frame of mind, the reassurance was blessed.

"'To wrap the Baby bunting in,'" he concluded in a hushed voice. "We have nursery rhymes in common."

It was not the first time they had quoted Mother Goose to one another, but neither had explored their peculiar shared knowledge.

"Where did you learn them? On your mother's knee?" she began, tentatively probing the waters.

"I was a voracious reader as a child. I read everything."

"Nursery rhythms seem an odd choice for a boy."

"You think so? It didn't seem peculiar to me. I found them a window to the past; a simplistic depiction of a time gone by."

"History interests you?"

"I don't know if 'interest' is the right word," he carefully admitted, reaching across to nuzzle her. She responded instantly by kissing him lightly on the lips. The taste of her, not unknown and yet still new, stimulated his body, which conversely freed his mind. "Somehow, I felt a deep, abiding sense of continuity. That history – at least as it pertains to me – is fluid; connecting time. Drawing it in a circle around me. Past, present and future."

"How peculiar," Helen gasped, snuggling closer to absorb his physical presence, "that you should express that exactly as I would."

"Really?"

"Absolutely. Those children's rhymes were written in the 1700s. While the language has changed – no one uses the word 'bunting' anymore – the sentiments remain constant. As a child, I was compelled to investigate the ancient terms and translate them into more understandable words. When I did that, it gave me a sense of power – a link, if you will – with the authors who composed them. That, to me, was living history."

Reforming herself into the contours of his arms, Helen lowered her eyelids, merging her memories into the throbbing of his pulse.

"The aliens we've encountered aren't so very different from us, if we take away the outer shells. They appreciate life; they raise families. Merging, through the dominion of children, reminds us we're all one great, extended family."

"I like that." Placing a hand on her arm, he gently stroked it as she purred in contentment. "Have you ever thought of having your own children?"

"Yes. I think that's why I never accepted any of those offers of sex. It was too casual, too... transient. I wanted something more lasting than sensual gratification. Does that make me old-fashioned?"

"Of course. But I admire you for it."

"And you?" she asked, holding out her arm so he could massage more of it. His touch, the strength of his fingers, was simultaneously soothing and erotic.

"I didn't want anyone having a claim on me. No matter how casual the contact, it implies a bond between two people. We may think ourselves enlightened, but intercourse is an act of intimacy. We bare more than our bodies. We give away more than fluids of passion. I never wanted to expose myself to that kind of relationship."

That she comprehended to the roots of her soul. Lowering herself down, Helen waited for him to do the same. Then turning on her side so she could stare comfortably into his face, she smiled.

"I do love you, Joshua Terry."

"And I love you, Helen Fitzgerald."

Leaning over, they kissed, allowing their emotional confession to intertwine them.

"Will you marry me?" he whispered into her lips as they parted.

"Are you asking for the first time or the second time?"

"I meant it the first time and I mean it, again."

"What about the stars?"

"Are you asking if they'll bless our union?"

"I think so," she admitted, before immediately regretting her words, for he responded quickly.

"Let's ask them."

Unable to prevent him, Helen watched as Joshua activated one of the small rear viewscreens. Thousands of tiny white gems leapt through the darkness at them. For a moment, sheer numbers nearly took their breath away.

"It's peculiar," Joshua began, the wonder of his voice transmitting his awe. "Most people can dream upon a star, but when it comes to actually going out among them, they're afraid."

"Of what?" Helen intoned, hardly daring to interrupt the majesty she beheld.

"Distance. On Earth, they appear so close you can reach out a hand and touch them. But that's an illusion. They're light years away. As you and I know," he concluded, bringing his head closer to hers so that they touched.

"The stars would never lie," she objected, a tremor running through her body like an angry shiver. "If people misconstrue, the blame is theirs."

"'The fault, dear Brutus, is not in our stars, But in ourselves, that we are underlings,'" he quoted.

"In their ignorance, they blame that which is pure and holy."

Surprised by the vehemence of her statement, Joshua broke his gaze from the celestial orbs.

"The stars, I've always believed, are the true windows to our soul. I never knew you felt that as deeply as I."

"There's too much you don't know about me," Helen blurted, eyes riveted to the screen. "And much I don't know about myself." With effort, she closed her lids, effectively shutting out the panorama. "We've changed, haven't we? In ways we can't fathom."

He winced at the question.

"Survival has altered us, but not our inner core."

Head bowed, Helen sank back on the floor, breaking their nearness. Following her example, he reclined, leaning against his arm to look across at her.

"What I mean is, we're still changing. Nothing remains static. We look at things differently. What I wouldn't have been receptive to before Encounter now strikes me as infinitely wondrous."

"Explain," he pleaded, eyes misting.

"I don't know if I can."

"You're the great communicator. Try. I need to know."

"Yes," she admitted, raising her head into a semi-recumbent angle. "You do. And so do I."

"I'm listening."

"Something happened to me, Josh. Today. Just before the Red Alert sounded. Something unexpected. Unanticipated. I couldn't sleep, so I decided to get up... move around. I heard it first in the Observatory."

"Heard what?"

"A song; or more accurately, a melody. It wasn't until I found myself by the viewscreen, staring out into space that I grasped the music was accompanied by words – a sort of lyric rhythm."

"Were you able to translate it?"

Helen's lips pursed as a sadness descended over her sharply etched features. Staring at her face, Joshua wondered if he had ever truly seen her before, so alien did she look at that moment.

"Not the precise meaning," Helen tried in a distant hush. "But the intent.... Yes."

He blinked, then cleared his throat, subconsciously moving his arm so that it swept past the monitor, temporarily obscuring her vision.

"And that was?"

"I was being enjoined to wait."

Silence descended like a blanket of mist. When he finally found the power to articulate, it had the effect of ripping away their false level of comfort.

"To wait... for what?"

"'I am coming,'" she repeated in such an otherworldly voice he did not recognize it. Nor was he cognizant of the fact her answer was a measure of faith in him.

Placing his hands to her temples, Joshua gently massaged the flesh, hoping, perhaps, to hone in on her thoughts.

"Did this message come from the stars....? Or from some being among the stars?"

In another, the question would have been rhetorical, or worse, grossly skeptical, but not from him. He knew that however she answered, his acceptance would be absolute.

"I don't know that, either. I couldn't identify it. I tried... forced myself to concentrate, but that only distanced me from it. The sensation was so brief, so – ethereal. Yet, I feel it inside me as we speak. It hasn't gone away... just gotten quieter."

"Was it God?" he intoned with dread. "Do you think we're... going to die?"

"I wondered that, too. No," she tried in a firmer voice. "It wasn't God. But it instilled in me the belief in God, if that makes any sense," she avowed, finally readjusting her body into a sitting position. On her summons, they touched shoulders, but did not share the same intimacy they had the moment before. "I don't believe it was a premonition of death. Rather, the contrary. It was the cry of life. Of a loneliness so great it transcended the realms of imagination."

A cold sweat broke out across his brow. Shaking his leg in nervous agitation, Terry unwittingly bit his lower lip.

"That's why you wanted me; to ward off that sensation."

His statement was neither accusatory nor bitter. He merely stated the truth. She sadly nodded.

"Yes." Imbibing the tortured expression on his face, she placed a hand on his forehead, in part to wipe away the perspiration, in part to bestow a blessing. "I do love you, Joshua. That much was truth. What I feel for you will never change. I know that now."

"But you're not sure you want it to be forever?" He bowed his head into hers, so that she would rest her hand on his hair. Helen did so gladly, tousling the loose strands the way a mother would a child, with affection and comfort.

"What I feel for you *is* forever. That much I know from the depths of my being. We've been coupled in an emotional sense since that night on

Zertan. When you came to my home, seeking the cat you had so unceremoniously 'discharged' from your quarters."

With a grimace of pain, Joshua detached himself from her, rising to his full height. In the cramped space of the Skip, he appeared as a giant. For a fleeting moment, Helen grasped how he must have appeared to Miranda, the feral cat.

From Helen's altered perspective, a sense of insignificance, or more accurately, helplessness, washed over her. She was vulnerable, alone and bearing a terrible responsibility, not only to herself, but for the memory of that feline which had touched both their lives so dramatically.

Like Miranda, an unwelcome alien on a planet neither of her choosing or her ancestors, Helen was displaced and homeless. Her security, her mental stability had been brought into question: not by the man at her side, but from within the recesses of her own personality.

Joshua had faced a challenge when ordered to rid himself of the pregnant cat or face serious repercussions. Those were the stoical, unyielding rules of Zertan and not to be disobeyed. He had done as ordered, then regretted his action, for he had abandoned principles greater than the civilization to which he was then a part. Were she to deny the call from space, she, too, would be tossing away perhaps the greatest chance she would ever have of asserting her humanity.

Just as the unwanted stray had found her way to Helen's door, so had the alien song reached her ears. Whatever, or whomever was out there needed protection, a shelter from the storm of universal indifference. The star-crossed wanderer had crept into her world on cat's paws with a plea she could not refuse.

Following Terry's example, Helen stood, stretching her taut muscles by squaring her shoulders and standing on tiptoe. If he likened her actions to those of a cat he did not say so, for his mind was light years away.

"What – are you asking of me?" he suddenly inquired, separating himself from her by pacing toward the pilot's cabin. She comprehended his defensive position. When confronted by an inexplicable dilemma, he retreated toward a place of safety.

One which could also be construed as offensive, for it gave him the opportunity of potential mobility and aggression. Where he would take charge of his fate by assuming the course of its direction, she was content to let the unknown come to her.

That, Helen realized, was the difference between the military officer and the civilian communicator. Rather than stand as their common denominator, the stars were drawing them apart. She would have to be careful how she answered his question.

Rubbing her hands together, she quietly took in a breath.

"I never objected to the fact space was your first love. I accepted that as part of your make-up. What I'm asking you now is to accept the fact I have a new awakening for something beyond my grasp. Although my new affinity came second to the feelings I hold for you, it's no less consuming."

"We're speaking of the same emotion," he protested, withdrawing further into the cockpit so that the gaping entranceway loomed huge between them.

"Are we? I'm not as certain as you. I must try and clarify what I feel... these signals I'm receiving. They may be no more than wistful thinking," she tried, torn between hurting him and expressing what was in her heart. "It's my fault. I asked you to come in here with me. I thought by physically consummating our love, I could... fight my doubts."

"And yet you found you couldn't."

Shaking her head, Helen took a step toward him, then changed her mind. Close proximity would only exacerbate their unease. Reaching her hands over her head, her fingertips brushed the ceiling. Because she could not caress him, she would bestow gentleness on his little spacecraft.

"What I discovered is that these new sensations are not that easily assuaged. I want it to be right between us. I want our union to be pure. I don't want to deceive you. That would be a sin on my part."

He smiled and she had not expected that.

"We're not talking about sin. What's come between us is wonder."

Helen respected the word, the power it conveyed, shooting currents of electricity through her lithe body.

"What does one do with wonder?" she whispered, silently pleading with him for an answer.

"One opens one's mind to the vastness of its complexities. Come with me," he invited, extending his hand. This time, she accepted it gracefully.

Moving aside to permit her entrance, Joshua guided her into the control seat. When she was comfortably settled, he activated the viewscreen by the pilot's chair. Stars twinkled before her eyes. Her breath caught at the *wonder*.

"Sit here. Watch. Listen."

"I'm afraid," she confessed, for suddenly she was terrified at the idea.

"So am I. I don't want to lose you."

"Do you think that could happen?"

The answer was succinct and sharper than he intended.

"Yes."

"Then I won't –"

His hand restrained her from arising.

"You will, because you must."

Helen worked herself into the contours of the pilot's seat.

"Will you sit beside me?"

When he didn't answer, she was compelled to raise her eyes upward, in a similar but not exact duplication of her position when envisioning Miranda's situation.

"No. But I will wait for you."

"For how long?"

There was only one reply.

"For as long as it takes."

"Even if it takes forever?"

To this, he had no ready answer. Only time could tell. And time, it was commonly believed, was cruel.

CHAPTER 5

Informing Commander Burbone he would debrief her after taking his four hour rest period, Joshua accompanied Helen to her language lab. Since moving out of the Command Center where she, Brian and Joshua had spent the first weeks after Encounter, the room also served as her private quarters. He had not intended to stay more than a few minutes, but seeing a note left on a personal computer beside two dinner trays which had been set out in anticipation of their return, he indicated she read it. Helen did so with reluctance.

"It's from Brian. It says, 'Eat, drink and be merry, for tomorrow is a new day.'"

"I don't know whether he's being optimistic or not," Joshua concluded, looking away in annoyance. "What do you think?"

"I think if I ever see another nutritional pill I'll go mad." Pushing away the small plate containing three different-colored pills and the accompanying glass of water, she picked up the tablet and deleted Brian's message.

Inferring from her action her opinion was negative, he prodded for confirmation.

"Is that what he meant?"

Frowning, Helen shrugged her shoulders.

"I think he was trying to be cheerful, but his sentiment came out more pessimistic than he intended."

"Then I wish he hadn't written anything." Taking a chair next to hers, the captain absently pushed his own three tablets around with his finger. He had been hungry a moment ago but her statement had depressed him.

As though loath to be too near him, Helen ill-disguised her intention by getting up and beginning a walk around the room. Familiar objects which had once been a comfort, a reminder of past, present or future, appeared foreign, mere shadows of what they had once been.

The trip from the shuttle bay to Level Two had made her restless. Nothing in the dim lighting, the sluggish elevator, or the stark, barren walls had improved her spirits. To discover Brian's note and the alien-ness of her office only sharpened the sensation.

"Are we going to get out of this?" she suddenly demanded, freezing him as he went to put a tablet in his mouth. With more weight to the action than prudence required, Joshua chewed it before swallowing.

"You mean, will our distress signal be answered? Or that we'll find a habitable planet to settle on where life will resume a sense of stability, if not normalcy?"

She rolled her eyes at his optimism, which, like Brian's, seemed more affected than sincere, although in neither case was her interpretation accurate.

"Before we all go space crazy." He opened his mouth to reply, but she interrupted before he uttered the first syllables. "The truth. Straight."

"We'll survive until we won't," he slowly admitted, guarding his words as though he were sifting gold flakes from silt. "I can't peer into the future, Helen. You know as well as I the dangers we face. We encountered one today: an accident that could have been fatal. No matter how careful we are, we'll never anticipate every contingency. I'd like to say our biggest concern is failing to avoid a meteor shower, or some small piece of floating debris that will puncture the outside skin. But, that isn't necessarily true. A part we can't replace will wear out. The power pods will fail and we'll lose life support. Our lack of medical technology and medications will always be a problem."

"Which falls on me. I'm not a medical doctor. No one is sick right now, but there'll come a time when they will be, either from accident or natural causes." Pulling at the sleeve of her uniform, she made a low, deprecating sound. "We don't even have the capabilities to manufacture clothing. What we're wearing was never meant to last. It's disposable. We're already starting to look like a group of island castaways. It won't be long before we're indecent. And then what?" Aware he had no answer, she resumed her pacing, hands fluttering nervously at her side. "Go on."

Her actions made him less inclined to comply, but to refuse would only worsen her mood.

"We can't expect a rescue ship to come looking for us."

"I know that," she snapped. "Not for two years. Five years. Ever. The UPE won't even know we've gone incommunicado because we're too far from a booster for them to even bother monitoring space for our communications. What about a planet?"

Leaning back in his chair, Joshua crossed his legs, inadvertently blocking her path. Helen backtracked in annoyance.

"That's our best hope. We've never explored this sector; no one has. What we thought we knew was incorrect. Which can only work in our favor. We may encounter any number of life-sustaining habitats."

"But none anywhere near our present position. And we're moving awfully slowly."

"We're lucky we have propulsion at all," he sharply countered before regretting his rashness.

"How long?" He waited for her to clarify, not trusting himself to second-guess her. "Best case scenario before we find a place to settle."

"I can't answer that."

"I'm sorry," Helen apologized, finally taking a seat. "I don't know what's the matter with me. Getting claustrophobic, I guess." Fingering her food, she made a face. "I'm tired of being hungry. I know I should thank..." She paused, feeling uncomfortable finishing it with "God," or "our lucky stars." "I should be grateful you found these nutritional tablets. And I am. But, they're a poor substitute for actual food. You," she accused, pointing to his plate, "just chewed your meal. The instructions are they're to be swallowed whole. But, we're all so desperate for something real to taste, we resort to anything that might make us feel better."

"You're right and I shouldn't have done that."

"Does it make any difference? Probably, but I suspect we're all doing it. If there was any hope for relief I think we could endure it, but our makeshift hydroponics is still in its infancy. We're a long way from harvesting our first substantial crop."

"I'm aware of that."

"And even when we do, we have no way of processing it. Whatever we grow will have to be eaten 'as is.'"

"Yes," he cautiously admitted. "But there's no saying we can't eventually construct a food processor."

"Out of what?" Helen cried in desperation. "Spare parts?" Pushing away her plate, the three tablets on it flew to the floor. Neither went to pick them up. "I'm sick of eating the same thing every meal. I'm so fed up with staring at these walls I'm beginning to imagine things. I'm not a botanist, or a doctor or a command officer. I'm a language expert, and I feel so far away from my avocation. All my life's work... was rendered meaningless by that damned Encounter."

"I think," he began, copying her example by distancing himself from his plate, "we're going to have to shake things up; change our routine." She looked up, her expression both angry and puzzled.

"What good will that do? What should we do – play meaningless games? Or should we all take turns in the Observatory, trying to hear messages from space?"

The sarcasm, directed inwardly, made him flinch.

"Change our thinking, for one. I gave you leave to work on the development of a universal language translator. You put it aside trying to study medicine. I want you to go back to it."

"What use is it now?"

He dared smile.

"You're the one who sensed a communication from the stars. If someone's out there, we're going to need the ability to talk with them."

"I don't think I can... work on the translator. My heart isn't in it. It was meant for use by our space fleets; by thousands of people."

"Does it make it any less valuable if only we employ it? Besides, eventually, someone will find us. Not this year; maybe not next. But eventually, people from Earth will venture out here. There will always be a need for your services. No one's going to develop it without you."

"There are others," she protested, weakening under his argument.

"But none like you. It's your genius which will make it possible."

"But how can I? There's so much to do. You just said it. I'm supposed to be studying medicine."

"As part of your duties, yes. That you'll continue. But it doesn't mean you have to put everything else aside. We've managed to get over the worst; now, it's time to re-evaluate."

"And you?" She hurried on before he had a chance to offer an easy answer. "You were the one who said there are too many checks and balances that have to be weighed. You put the onerous on yourself and Burbone."

"I did say that," he agreed, reaching down and retrieving her tablets. Placing them back on the plate, he shoved that and the water glass toward her. "And you're right. I can't omit myself. Or Paula," he stated, using the officer's first name where Helen had not. "I need to get off this ship. Give the Skip a more thorough test. I'll enjoy that," he meaningfully added.

"It's dangerous," she stated in a monotone.

"Everything is dangerous," he spat before forcing himself to calm. "The Skip is vital to our survival."

"And you're not?"

His hand went up to end the argument.

"Let's not go there. Once I prove it's space-worthy, I'll begin cross-training. Paula, first; then you and Brian, or some of the security guards. That will help the walls from closing in."

Helen drummed her fingers on the table, staring down at the plate.

"I want to be the first."

It was a daring assertion. One, even a scientist-soldier knew better than to make. To his credit, Terry didn't flinch.

"You and Paula can draw straws."

"The way we discussed who goes out the airlock first?"

"Helen," he warned, "you're tired. You've been stressed and now you're feeling alienated from me because we tried an intimacy that didn't work out the way we hoped."

She cried and turned away.

"I'm afraid."

"Of the contact you felt?"

"That, and about everything. I understand the need for normalcy, but it brings with it other concerns. For the past six months we've all been too busy to realize what we've lost. We haven't had time to mourn... either the dead or our own lost dreams. You're talking about years, Josh. Maybe forever, for all we know. Stranded out here."

In an act too reminiscent of taking poison, she grabbed the nutritional tablets, shoved them in her mouth and swallowed them by drinking the water. "I know for a fact half a dozen of our 'survivors' are married; some of them have children. Those husbands and wives left behind will never know what happened to us. We'll be declared dead. Or, what is it they say? 'Missing in action.' Spouses will remarry, children will grow into adulthood. Our people will miss all that. It's horrible to contemplate. When reality settles in, there's going to be serious trouble."

"What are you saying? You can't have it both ways. Do they need more time to themselves, or should I keep them so busy they won't have time to think? That's unfair. It's also unrealistic. Sooner or later, we'll all have to face what we've lost. When we do, we ought to have something to fall back on."

"Painting? Writing stories? Working on universal translators?"

"Yes."

"And then what?"

Moving his head away from the light, Helen saw the deep circles etched into the skin under his eyes. He had been a young man, once. Tragedy had aged him prematurely. She had viewed that one today and dreaded a second encounter, small-case "e," with the encroachment of time.

"We have to face reality. You're right. One by one, we're all going to have to grapple with the fact this is our world. Like it or not, this ship is what we've been reduced to. We can make it more comfortable; we can slowly resume a routine similar to what we had before. We can seek a planet to settle on; we can hope in our hearts we'll be discovered and taken home. What we can't do is change what's happened."

"Do you really think it's that easy?"

His nose twitched in anger before he got to his feet and began removing the trays. He did not speak again until the room was tidied. His voice was tired and deep.

"Ask Brian. He's the one who believes in God. It's his theory that we're being tested for a great and noble purpose. My job is something of the opposite – to keep us alive."

He was angry and bitter and disappointed. Helen was not insensitive to the fact that part of his depression was her fault.

"All right," she decided, interlacing her fingers, then removing them beyond his sight under the table. "I'll work on the translator. Maybe that will help."

But she had pushed him too far, unwillingly proving that even the highest ranking officer aboard ship had his breaking point. Balling up one fist, Joshua struck it into the flat of his opposing palm. The spanking noise reverberated off the walls, returning with a dull presentment of doom.

Steadying herself, Helen waited for the explosion she had ignited. Yet, when he spun on her, she was unprepared for the vehemence of his angrily curled lips.

"Don't pacify me. What you do when you're off duty is your affair. I was only trying to help. You act as though I should be impervious to all this." Pointing toward the empty trays, particles of saliva spewed from his mouth, watering from hunger. "I may be a captain, but I'm also a man. You're the one who's so damned eager to separate the two. But when you do, you reject my overture. Which do you want? Do you know?"

Without waiting for a reply, nor giving any mitigating wave of good-bye, Terry turned and exited, the hiss of the door closing like a slap on her face.

Condemning her linguistic's mind, which rapidly equated the expression "your affair" to its harsher social implications, Helen wept bitterly, ruing the fact she had ever dared hope that a lyrical poem from space might be the answer to hers, or anyone else's prayers.

Like the rest of the crew, Terry's personal quarters had been destroyed when the starboard portion of *Target* had been ripped away. With it went his few cherished mementos; the framed commendation received for conspicuous bravery while serving as a second lieutenant on the *Rutgar;* official notices of promotion, and six holographs of distant stars he and Helen had taken from their Rover craft. Ironically, none of those images contained either one of their own likenesses.

That holiday, taken together, stowed away on the small, leased space explorer seemed years ago. Another lifetime. He had been a different man, then. She had been some other woman.

Leaving her office in an unwelcome rage that had crept upon him unbidden, Joshua stood in the corridor, realizing for the first time he had no sanctuary – nowhere to hide. The idea of lying down was repulsive. Not only would sleep abandon him, he did not want to announce his return to Brian, who used the Command Center as his bedroom, which he would have to cross to reach his own.

Without doubt, the good brother would be waiting up for him. He would be expecting a happy face. When he didn't see one, an explanation would be required. In Terry's present frame of mind, such a task would be difficult and emotionally trying.

Tightening, then loosening the muscles in his calves, he hesitated, debating the best course of action. To his right lay the area designated Sick Bay II. Officially, the numerals "II" had been dropped when the entire Level Three, which had once housed a functioning medical center, had been placed off limits and abandoned. At its height after Encounter, Sick Bay II had held nine crewmembers. None had survived.

Without the services of trained medical staff, all of whom had perished after the ship had nearly been destroyed, they had never had a chance. Each morning's report brought with it the unwelcome news of the patients' deteriorating conditions. He had memorized Helen's recitation by heart. "No change." "Little change." "A change for the worse."

On and on, until they were all gone. Underscoring her words was the tortured confession, "I am not a doctor," and his no less agonized reply, "We all appreciate your efforts."

Like all the other bad news, it had become rote, rendered inconsequential by repetition.

Captain Terry had hoped with the death of the last patient never to hear or reply to that statement again. Yet, like everything else in their grim existence, the harder you wished for something, the less likely it was to happen.

Beyond Sick Bay II were the areas redeployed as "Crew's Quarters." Three converted offices had been set aside for the men, two for the woman. They lacked amenities and, without proper beds, were totally devoid of privacy. No solace there.

To his left, down the main corridor, they had begun a new hydroponics unit. Arguably, it was now the most important area of the ship. Without a thriving growth center they would be reduced to swallowing tablets as their sole source of nutrition until death finally caught up with them. Or, they actually discovered an Earth-like planet. Whichever came first.

With Helen's anger over their sustainable but unsatisfying diet fresh in his mind, a shudder passed through him which he erratically attributed to a draft. Directing his footsteps down the left corridor, the captain ambled slowly down the hall. While he had no particular desire to visit the "water farm," he could think of nowhere else to go. Any location was preferable to none, and if he stood irresolute much longer, Brian would eventually emerge from his quarters. He did not want to hear any archaic banter about his posture resembling a "cigar store Indian."

Swishing his hand across the electric eye from habit rather than necessity, Terry activated one of the few properly functioning electronic doors and entered the vast chamber. Removing walls to enlarge what had been three computer rooms had been a matter of no consequence. Several of them had already fallen; those remaining were either damaged or unstable.

Such awareness did not prevent him from sustaining a small shock as the door closed behind him for he had not yet accustomed himself to the large, open space. Compared to the bridge and the cramped Control Center, Hydroponics was nearly as large as the Skip hanger on Level Four.

Nostrils instantly assailed by the subtle but distinct odor of open water, he paused a moment to assimilate the merry bubbling of the pumps. They had a calming effect, simulating that of a waterfall. In his childhood, he had spent a great deal of time by clear-flowing lakes. Due to the fact he had seldom visited this room, the analogy had never struck. Identifying it now made him realize how tired he was and how narrow his world had become.

"It wouldn't be a bad idea," he spoke aloud, "to have the crew spend time here. Just imbibing the sights and sounds."

"Always working," a crewmember from behind him observed.

He recognized the voice without turning. "You, too," he noted. "You're not assigned to hydroponics."

"I volunteer," Paula Burbone dismissed. "Hanson and Bates came up to the bridge to relieve me. I felt as long as it was quiet, they could use the experience; and appreciate the trust."

"I agree," he stated, surprised and pleased she had taken that initiative. It indicated she was growing into her position as second in command. Six months had altered her from an untried ensign into a commander. "That gives me more time to teach you the intricacies of the ship. Lessons you would have gotten at the Academy in your third and fourth years. You've been cheated out of a great deal."

"Experience is a great teacher, sir."

"As I'm finding out. But, that doesn't explain why you're here."

"Couldn't sleep," she admitted, passing by him so that she could speak to his face. "That was a great rescue you pulled off, sir."

He had almost forgotten. So much had happened to mute their pitiful victory.

"I trusted Jingles. He said the Skip was space-worthy."

"No, sir. He said it might be, but that he needed more time to be certain before it was taken out for a joy ride."

"Then, we both bet our lives on it."

"The three you rescued and that of your co-pilot," she corrected.

"I felt it was necessary."

She didn't probe his open-ended statement concerning Helen Fitzgerald.

"We require more than one pilot for the Skip."

"You first. And then Fitzgerald."

"I think Fitzgerald, first," she replied with un-emotion, opting to use the officer's surname as he had done. "And then Porteous. That leaves me on the bridge. One of us should be there in times of... adventure."

He smiled at her word choice.

"Yes. You would say that."

"Besides," she continued without the least self-pity, holding up her right arm which ended at the wrist, "I'm limited in what I can do. The Skip controls require two hands."

"Fitzgerald. Burbone. Porteous. That's the order."

When she made no further objection, he glanced around the room.

"I was looking for something green," he lied. "I'm forgetting my colors. We seem to be functioning in a black and white world."

"Not much of that to see here," she begrudged, cocking her head to one side to deflect the mental blow. When Terry displayed no disparaging action, she gathered courage to continue. "Some of the seeds have sprouted, but they're not to the leaf stage, yet."

"Take me on the tour."

"With pleasure."

He doubted that, but followed as she walked between rows of low-formed hydroponics units. While he did not bother to count them, he knew there were thirty-seven separate tanks, with as many more under construction. They would have to do much better than that, but for the time being, it was a giant stride in the right direction.

Which gave Hydroponics nothing in common with his psyche.

Seeing Paula was indisposed to initiate conversation, Joshua prompted her.

"Talk to me." She clearly read his actual meaning: *I'm lonely. What I need is the sound of a human voice.*

That, and reassurance. To go with the color green.

"We were really very lucky, sir," she began, discovering it more pleasant than she imagined to converse with the man who had been no more than "Commander Terry" to her half a year ago. "Finding two more Nutritional Dispensing Apparatuses on Level Four was a godsend. Establishing a hydroponics unit wouldn't have been possible," she continued, giving him the background as an excuse for conversation, "if you hadn't identified the ice volcanoes on the meteor and managed to harvest the ice. Once water was no longer an issue, it encouraged us to construct what you see here. We took a vote on whether to divide up the extra meals from the vending machines and eat them immediately, or salvage the viable seeds they contained in an attempt to grow them. It was... unanimous after we discounted Jingles' objections as being incompetent, immaterial and irrelevant."

"What does that mean?" he grinned because the statement sounded like that it was. Silly.

"I read it," she stated, chin jutting out, "in a book."

"A racy space novel?"

"Does it sound like one?"

"No."

"Good. Because it isn't. It's a crime novel set in the 1950s. The lawyer and his gang solve all sorts of improbable murders."

"So, you're a history aficionado?"

"I enjoy clever repartee."

"Oh. I'll remember that. For your yearly evaluation."

"Will I have to stand an examination?"

"No. But it is a two-part evaluation. Past and future actions."

She laughed as he hoped she would.

"How are you going to judge what hasn't happened, yet?"

"I'll leave that to Brother Brian. And his tea leaves."

She suddenly grew grim and he was sorry he had said anything.

"He already tried that on me."

Deciding from her tone he didn't want to pursue the subject, he pointed to the water tanks.

"Walk me through these."

Which is where, he decided, he should have stayed in the first place.

"We have mung beans, alfalfa, radish, tomato, clover, cabbage and several types of lettuce. Those you see here. The meals stored in the 'vending machines' contained multiple varieties of sprouts. These," Paula continued, indicating a separate area, "are sunflower and lentil. We're depending on them to supply bulk; eventually, quantities large enough to provide for salads."

Crossing toward the encasements, Terry's body movement triggered a motion sensor. A computerized growth chart appeared on an overhead monitor.

Pausing to contemplate the multi-colored lines, a separate hue for each variety, he sucked in his cheeks in approval.

"Very nice."

"Janice Miles and her team were able to reprogram several of the computers and got them into some semblance of working condition. Those that didn't go to the bridge or Engineering were distributed among the other researchers. Ensign Carson took one for hydroponics. Aaron Coleman wrote the program you see displayed here. He's not a vegetation specialist, obviously, but he had some familiarity with plants due to his work on atmospheric studies. With it, we can accurately and quickly access growth progress. It also indicates the proper time to harvest. As none of us were familiar with 'gardening,' it eliminates the guesswork."

The red, pink, blue, green and yellow graphs all displayed healthy, upward trends.

"Looks promising."

"Projected servings are in this column, divided by seventeen: the number of crew eagerly awaiting solid food," Paula pursued, although the timbre of her voice deepened. Quickly scanning the figures, Joshua did not have to rely on advanced mathematics to determine the cause. The portions were depressingly scanty, while the time-lag between harvests lengthy.

The graphics changed, revealing a new set of equations. Although the designer had taken care to choose a variety of cheerful colors to enhance the prospects, nothing could obfuscate the dire conclusions.

"We need to eat more than we can grow," he correctly interpreted.

"The distribution of meal size is arbitrary," she countered, but he ignored the optimism.

"Determined by our need for vitamin and mineral intake?"

"Those are supplied by the nutritional tablets. Rather, we view them as a relief from pills. As something to chew and taste," came the reluctant admission.

His stomach growled, prompting her to lift the lid off one of the covered tanks.

"Would you care for a sample?"

"I would," he admitted, backing away. "But I better not. It's late, and the acid indigestion will sour my stomach."

She accepted his falsehood with the grace with which it had been dispensed, realizing he did not want to be accused of favoritism.

"What's over here? They look green to me."

Crossing through a number of intersecting pathways, Terry strode to the rear wall where a number of small, tree-like plants grew.

"Several of the smaller Rec Rooms were preserved from major structural damage. They all had plants in them. We gathered them together and brought them here. Eventually, those without edible potential will be redistributed throughout the livable sections of the ship."

Although he knew the answer, he asked, "Why?" to keep her talking.

"For morale," she replied with the chipped voice of one being examined. "A touch of 'home,' if you will." She did not have to add, *Serving the same purpose they did before Encounter.*

"How many are there, total?"

"Fifteen."

Until she saw him react, the number had held no special significance. Correctly interpreting his facial expression, she grimaced.

Two fewer than the number of those living aboard Target.

And wished neither had drawn that conclusion. It implied they were two lives over the limit.

Shoving the prognosticator to the back of his mind, Terry broke apart his interlaced fingers and rubbed thumb and forefinger over one of the larger leaves. The tactile relief it offered was tangible.

"Before you caught me talking to myself," he slowly began, "it occurred to me that we ought to open this space up to the crew – for morale, as you say. To break the monotony of sterile shipboard sights. But after visiting here – on an empty stomach – I've decided that's probably wrong. Too much temptation. Gathering your trees and shrubs together into another rec room makes better sense. We all need a place where we can get away. That would do nicely."

"Making one large greenhouse, rather than disperse them? I see the advantage."

He noted she had dropped the "sir" from the end of her sentence and nodded approvingly, a tiny grin forming at the corners of his mouth. It was after-hours and neither were officially on duty. To stand on ceremony only exacerbated their separation as human beings.

A loss he was feeling acutely.

"Helen and I were discussing the need to recreate normalcy. Perhaps if the crew has a Rec Room where they're surrounded by living things, they'll be more prone to relax; take up hobbies. Read. Create debating societies; play games. Put on theatricals."

"The idea never occurred to me. In the morning, I'll put together a committee. Unless you think it's too soon," she added, assuming a place by his side as he continued walking.

"The sooner the better. What's going on here?"

Stepping away from the hopeful profusion of green, he stopped in front of an entirely different grouping of vegetation. Unlike the mature trees and the healthy seedlings, these plants were wilted and turgorless. The monitor above depicted a sharp downward trend in brown, tan and yellowish hues.

The lines around Terry's chin deepened as he contemplated the grim picture.

"They're not getting enough light? Or,not the right kind of illumination?"

"The seeds these specimens grew from were discovered in the cargo area of one of the destroyed Skips. They were discovered when we explored it for spare parts to repair the *Arrow*; presumably a consignment meant for the actual Hydroponics unit. Why they were never delivered I can only speculate. It's possible the scientists had no place to store them and would have requisitioned the lot when they were ready to grow. Considering the damage to Level Four we're fortunate they survived at all."

Staring through the plexiglass, he wondered at their good fortune. Aware of her close proximity, however, he chose to voice a different sentiment.

"They're experimental? Biologically altered at the DNA level for a specific purpose? Infused with fatal diseases, by chance?"

Assuming he was trying to lighten the situation, she responded in kind.

"Several specimens were being nourished with human blood; others had been genetically altered to grow into redwoods. Those we left behind."

Clasping his hands behind his back, military fashion, Terry considered carefully before replying.

"Sounds more like they were brought aboard for Dr. Frankenstein. They won't develop into people, will they?"

"I haven't seen any fingers or toes, yet. But we could run a growth projection and see."

"By the looks of them we won't have to," he retorted, the moment fading. "What are they, really?"

"High protein and fiber soy, millet and rice hybrids."

Although already briefed on the type, hearing that salient fact in the presence of the failing plants added an ominous foreboding to the discussion. A low, disparaging growl rumbled in his throat. Wiping his brow with the forefingers of his right hand, Terry stared distractedly at the dampness a long beat before continuing.

"Those upon which we anticipated exchanging with the nutritional tablets for a more normal diet," he reiterated through clenched teeth. "In report... I was led to understand these were our best hope for self-sufficiency. The rest," he concluded, waving an arm in the direction of the sprout farm, "offer diversity of texture, flavor and sweetness, but not subsistence. Which is not to be underestimated, but as a relief rather than a divergence from the pills. "

"Eventually we anticipated harvesting substantial crops... for bread and cereal," she finished on a low note.

"Long term," he snapped. "One we won't get if these plants languish and die. Why are they in such poor condition?"

"I don't know, sir," Paula replied, stung that she didn't have a proper response.

"Does anyone here have the answer?"

Turning to her, he squinted as a ray of overhead light caught his eye. Blocking the beam with a gesture of annoyance, the commander bent over, staring at the plants. Catching sight of his reflection in the glass, Paula chose to stare at that, rather than the back of his head.

"If they do, I haven't seen it on a report."

"Neither have I." As his features contorted, she stepped away, moving around the other side of the plexiglass container so she could meet his gaze directly.

"We require a more thorough accounting. And a diagnosis." Annoyed at the word he chose, deeming it an incorrect one, Terry curled his upper lip, revealing teeth. "Who's actually on duty here tonight?"

"LaTanya Carson."

"Where is she?"

Appearing out of nowhere, the graphic artist-turned-botanist-in-training appeared behind them, seemingly transformed from thin air.

"Right here, Captain."

One look at her face confirmed his suspicion. She was as ignorant of the solution as he. It was a situation which could not be tolerated.

"Has anyone attempted to discover the cause for this wilting?"

"Sir, the instructions which were included in the seed-transport container were incomprehensible to a layperson. I presume the specialists at Hydroponics understood what was required for their growth. That may be the reason they were never called for; the seeds were either experimental and unlikely to survive, or were for delivery to an out-station where conditions were more favorable."

He indicated the graphs on the computer over the water tanks. All revealed downward trends.

"That didn't give you an indication?"

She wilted under the criticism.

"I did discuss that with Maurice. He explained the program he wrote was applicable to known species. These are an unknown variety, sir. He thought what we were seeing might represent a normal stage of development for these hybrids, making his data unreliable."

He silently debated the rationale, then pursed his lips.

"Had you considered giving the data sheets to Dr. Fitzgerald? She's our language specialist. She might have had better luck making sense of them."

Carson stiffened at the charge.

"I would have, sir. If they had been written in code; or, some alien script. But, I didn't consider the fact she could interpret obscure scientific abbreviations and references."

"You haven't had any success researching them in the computer?"

"The tech specialists have tried, sir, but as you're aware, very few data programs survived Encounter. None, that I'm aware of, dealing with agriculture or hydroponics."

"Alert Lieutenant Miles. She's our resident expert. Have her try again. Tonight. If she can't access the main library banks, try searching the intraship logs. They may be filed under alternate headings. A seed is a seed. It should grow into a healthy plant. I want to know why these are languishing. We can't afford to lose them, either through ignorance or negligence."

"Yes, sir."

"When do you go off duty?"

"Three bells," came her succinct answer, using the antiquated system of telling time, initiated shipwide by the late Captain Nguyen, as a harmless and amusing display of flaunting their naval roots.

"If you find anything, I want to know about it. Tonight."

"But it will be late, sir. One-thirty – or past."

"That doesn't matter. I'll be up. Commander Burbone and I will both be up," he amended.

"Where shall I find you?"

She posed an awkward question. One for which he had no ready answer. Nor could he explain the mad fluttering in his heart. Hunger pains came close, but *close,* he remembered, "only counted in horseshoes."

CHAPTER 6

Joshua could not take Paula to his quarters for it would mean waking Brian, who slept in the outside room of the Command Center. Nor, could they go to hers as he had already made that innocent mistake once. One which nearly cost him his relationship with Helen.

"The Observatory on Level Four," Paula decided for him. When he flinched, she failed to comprehend the reason. Reading his military mind was one thing, but delving beyond to the personal was a place she had not been.

"Very well," he agreed, too late to soothe over the short lapse in time.

Paula followed him out, trailing a step behind as they walked the corridor to the transport. His sudden discomfiture disturbed her. If he did not want to be alone with her on a place other than the bridge, she wished he would say so.

There was no way Joshua could explain his feelings, or the sudden trepidation he experienced at the idea of going to the Observatory. That was where Helen had heard, or felt, or detected the lullaby from the stars. It was not that he feared he, too, would fall under the spell. Rather, it was the contrary.

Stifling the urge to allow Paula to enter the elevator before him, Terry marched in, head held high in the attitude of one going to his own execution. She followed and the door slid shut, effectively sealing them in.

"Level Four."

It began its unsteady descent downward. Both reached for the handrail, their hands almost touching before they realized their mistake and withdrew. Acknowledging the inappropriateness of his behavior, the captain's shoulders finally sagged in embarrassed resignation.

"I'm sorry. It's not you. In fact, I was a little too glad to see you in Hydroponics."

It was an opening. One she was not sure she should pursue.

"The Bridge, then, sir," she replied, reverting to formality as the better part of common sense. It was a calculated risk; the memories they shared there were less conducive to work than confession. It also conjured images of the first night they had spent together, trapped with two badly wounded crewmen and eight mutilated bodies. Shattered by trauma and exhausted beyond human endurance, they had curled up together, using one another's body heat to ward away lurking terrors.

"No," he decided without apparent consideration. "We told Carson where we'd be."

"She can reach us by communicator."

"She'll think we've gone to bed. To sleep," he corrected, blushed, then struck out with his foot in annoyance at the unintentional double meaning.

"Maybe we *should* get some sleep. Whatever she finds can wait until morning." He waited for the "Joshua" at the end of her sentence, but it did not come. Neither did she conclude it with a "sir," which only slightly eased his emotional turmoil.

Before the vibration of his kick had died away, the transport door parted. The choice had been made for them.

The path to the Observatory required they pass the brig. The only known member of the ship's compliment to be incarcerated there had been Brian Hardy. He had escaped its confines numerous times until his prowess had achieved legend status. More recently, Terry and Burbone's discovery of the nutritional tablets stored there had been celebrated as the figurative gold mine it was. Although a poor substitute for culinary pleasure, the two hundred cases of pills had saved the crew from certain death by starvation.

Although they had cleared the path which had seemed endless at the time, the walk now seemed short. Too short. Neither had recovered their aplomb before reaching the small, star-studded chamber. Standing by the door as it parted, they paused with a sense of foreboding, finding the room deserted. The viewscreens were off and no light illuminated the darkness, exactly as he presumed it to be before Helen's fateful encounter. Before stepping inside, Terry's noise twitched. His was an animal's instinct, seeking danger before traversing a wide, unprotected field.

The air was clear, without obvious odor. No physical danger lurked within. Neither sheep nor wolf, nor wolf in sheep's clothing. Unable to decide which of the three categories he fit, Terry crossed the threshold. Not until he was inside could he make that determination.

It was not Paula's place to activate the overhead lighting. Therefore, she remained a step behind the captain, allowing him the decision of whether or not to illuminate the area.

Instead of activating the overhead lights, he utilized one of the monitors. Immediately, a scan of space jumped into view, dominating their enclosed world. Placing a trembling hand against the screen, he waited, imbibing the impressions. Those he sensed were recognizable, understandable, familiar. Nothing out of the ordinary; no alien presence to draw him forward.

Relief, tinged with regret, prompted him to sit. He did not, however, face the panorama, but maneuvered the chair so that his back was to the stars. Paula followed his example. When he did not speak, she finally assumed the initiative.

"I think we can begin dispensing the sprouts to the crew soon. To supplement our diet."

As if he had forgotten their intent in coming to the Observatory, Terry's head jerked up in surprise. Watching his eyes, she saw them slowly clear. The effort was palpable.

"It didn't look that way to me. Besides, there has to be enough for everyone. I don't want to pick five crewmen at random every week to receive their treat. That's too much like... drawing straws to see who goes out the airlock. We went," he added with effort, "from fear of starvation to hating the very tablets that removed that fear."

"Yes, sir. I see your point."

Which left her nothing else to say.

Terry crossed, then irritably uncrossed his legs. To delay his next comment, he reached out and picked up a small, hand-held tablet, a forgotten relic of what could now be looked upon as their innocent youth. Turning it on required no effort. Studying the unfamiliar shapes and characters, he clicked his tongue in puzzlement before awkwardly turning the screen so Paula could view it.

"What is this?"

She finally grinned in good-natured skepticism.

"You don't know?"

"No," he admitted so readily she had to believe him. Taking the object from his hand, she quickly punched in a code. Instantly, the images changed into human countenances. His intake of breath increased her mirth.

"That's my face! Why is it on the screen?"

Withholding the device so he couldn't snatch it away, Paula suggestively raised her eyebrows.

"I didn't do it. Whoever played this last programmed your likeness into the scenario. It's a mystery – or, rather, a detective game," she corrected. "The player, or players, have to solve a crime, using whatever clues they can uncover. How these detectives go about their task – either solo, or by joining others in a group effort – is a part of the challenge."

She worked the small computer, bringing up other characters, but none had recognizable faces. "Any number of crewmembers can compete," she continued. "Some drop out along the way, or press charges against a suspect they either can't prove, or are in error, and they're eliminated. You can either play against the game: that is, have it assume the character of the criminal, or one of the players choses to play that role. Whoever determines the correct outcome wins. If no one solves the puzzle, the criminal gets away with his crime."

"How did this… come about?"

"Actually, Janice and Maurice Kincaid developed it. Not as a game, actually, but as a test of the computer system they were trying to repair. As it started, they knew the answer and challenged the software they were writing to break the code, or sequence of clues. If it did, that was one checkmark on the positive side. If it didn't, they hadn't repaired the problem caused by Encounter. It took a great deal of effort, and as you're aware, most of the systems were unsalvageable."

Joshua stared in fascination at the depiction of his own body, dressed in a wardrobe he had never worn, asking questions to a man he had never seen.

"What am I? A detective or the criminal?"

"I don't know," Paula professed in a tone meant to imply otherwise. "I'd have to get further into it to see."

"Do I solve the problem or not?"

"Whoever started the game hasn't finished it." Staring up, she winked. "I'd say you were still a work in progress. Commander," she added, alluding to his former rank.

Grunting in annoyance, he shook his foot.

"It sounds like identity theft to me. I don't want to be a character in that game."

"Even if it means you turn out to be a brilliant detective?"

He paused, considering the alternatives, then sighed, conceding the point.

"I wish I were. I wish I could pull a rabbit out of a hat. I wish...." What else he wished remained unspoken. "Who did it belong to?"

"I don't know."

He started to make his own identification, then abruptly held back and reverted to their original conversation.

"If I permit the crew to rotate through hydroponics they'll see the dying rice, millet and soy plants. That's depressing. It depressed me. Counter to the point of relieving their stress."

Dropping her gaze, Paula went back to the game.

"We could separate them from the rest."

"I'd like to do that but it's too difficult. The tanks are large and fragile. Besides, word will eventually get out and we'll be in a worse situation."

"Dashing hope that we're making progress toward self-sufficiency," she finished, her attention still fixed on the frozen image on the game console.

"Yes." His fingers drummed on the armrest as his ire increased. "Why does that game work when the computer banks throughout the ship have either been wiped clean or corrupted?"

"Janice never explained to me. I suspect it was in a protected area less exposed to the effects of the dark matter; this observatory, for instance, which may explain why it's still here. It doesn't work anywhere else."

"If that's the case, it may be prudent to bring more of the computers here."

"I'll suggest that to Miles and Kincaid in the morning. Are all the computers in the Observatory working?"

"I haven't been in here since Encounter."

Paula stood and walked to another of the viewscreens. Attempting to activate it, she found it failed to respond.

"Nothing, sir."

"This one will," he announced, activating the monitor immediately to his right and by doing so seemingly going against his assertion he hadn't been in the Observatory in months. With a litheness she hadn't anticipated, he fluidly adjusted the image, bringing up a different vista of space than the one revealed on the first screen he had activated. "It responded to my input." Without losing a beat, he demanded, "What do you see out there? Think before you answer. Open your mind."

Paula did as ordered, without question. Immediately, her brain filled with swirling emotions.

"I see mystery; the unknown. I envision vast depths, incomprehensible wonder. Challenge."

"More," he whispered. "Listen."

"I hear the stars; the planets."

"What are they saying?"

Leaning forward, the hand-held computer clutched in her left hand, she spoke, but it was obvious her words were the result of past, rather than present tense.

"'We were here before you were born. We shall be here after you die.'"

"No!" The sharpness of his statement startled her. "Don't make it up. I'm serious." Peculiarly, the request was as pitiable as it was sharp.

"Thoughts," she hesitantly admitted. "Mindless impressions. Ageless."

"Nothing... newer?"

"Perhaps. I don't know." Finally tearing her gaze away, Paula directed a question at him. "What do *you* hear?"

"The same as you," he replied in a barely audible whisper. And then stronger, "Nothing."

Shivering under the tone, Paula replaced the game on the table, allowing her eyes to shift around the room, acutely aware how barren and cold it was. The sensation augmented her insight. Not of the stars, but of herself. No one, she imagined, would use her likeness to represent a great detective. Not after she had lost her right hand during Encounter. Famous characters were always perfect: tall and handsome or clever and beautiful. To her knowledge, none of them were ever cripples. The awareness cast an ever greater pall over her suddenly depressed spirits.

Using what few clues he had given her, the detective's "best friend" tried to piece the puzzle together.

"Do you think there's something out there? Have we been contacted?"

Terry shrugged, the fingers of his right hand balling into a fist.

"I... don't know. Not officially. Not through channels."

"Brian? Has he been seeking God, again?"

She hadn't meant to be sarcastic, and shuddered at her word choice. If Joshua picked up on her regret, he gave no indication.

"Not Brian."

And then she knew. It was as clear as though their new game had played itself without her active participation.

"Helen Fitzgerald."

"Yes."

Directing her attention back through space, Paula tried harder, opening her mind to the possibilities. Her failure was acute.

"I'm sorry, Captain. I'm not picking up anything else. What did she say?"

"It was what she didn't say," he continued, maintaining a low tone. When he could think of nothing else to add, his hands, palms upward, went out in resignation. "Maybe it's nothing. Wistful thinking. A need to believe we're not alone."

"Leave it at that." The statement was quiet, strong. They were no longer attempting to solve a mystery. Paula's world reverted back to reality. That was something with which she could identify. "Imagination."

"Thank you, Paula."

His tenseness and disinclination to believe tugged her back. If he were not through playing, she wouldn't abandon her post.

"It might have been any one of us; Helen's not the only one susceptible. Left alone here for any amount of time, I have no doubt we'd all hear something. It's no reflection against her. On the contrary, I think it shows how badly she wants to help."

"But she was frightened of it."

"Was she?" Paula leaned closer, stared at him a moment, then averted her eyes. What she wanted was a different perspective. One far more alien to her than the idea of communicating with space. Placing herself in Helen's situation, it required courage to demand, "Was it the supposed contact she was frightened of? Or was it your reaction?"

Twitching like a live wire, the captain came to attention. With an angry gesture, he turned the monitor off. The stars disappeared so fast they might have been wiped off Creation's map.

"There's nothing out there! Nothing!" Rising from his chair, he pointed an accusing finger at her. "You've changed."

Paula's eyebrow shot up questioningly as she debated how to answer.

"Yes. I suppose I have. But not in ways you can possibly know."

Rebuffed by her statement, he was not yet ready to concede the argument.

"Why not?"

"Because you never knew me," came the unadorned reply. "Half a year ago, I was an ensign on the bridge; a command trainee. When my tour was completed, I was going back to the Academy to finish my courses. In your career, Captain, you've interacted with scores of ensigns. They've come and gone and most you never gave a second thought to, unless they were later reassigned to your ship. What did you really know about any of them?"

Seeing he was not going to reply, she continued.

"You instructed them on bridge protocol, lectured them on tactics, carefully exposed them to danger, graded their performance, then dismissed them from your life. If *Target* hadn't been struck, I would have meant no more to you than the rest."

There was no point denying her allegation, for it was true. With a flush of less than righteous indignation, Terry ran his hands through his hair, stood up and walked around her, coming to stop when he reached the back of her chair. She did not bother craning her neck to stare up at him.

"So, what's this all about?" he demanded, leaving her to interpret the vagueness of his interrogative. She was equal to the task.

"You're jealous."

"Of – what?" he gasped, nearly struck dumb by her words.

"Of what Dr. Fitzgerald felt out there."

"You just got finished saying she didn't feel anything; that she made it up because she was lonely."

"All right," Burbone readily agreed. "You were jealous because she was lonely. Whatever you two have meant to one another wasn't enough to stave off her disquiet."

"No."

Without moving her head, Paula got up and glided away from him, carefully positioning herself between Terry and the viewscreen, so that her upper body was obscured by darkness.

"Where did you two go after you rescued Jingles, Hykowa and Diaz? I expected you to report directly to the bridge. You never came."

"Where do you think we went?"

Her own heart leapt, which she silently damned herself for.

"Somewhere private."

"For what reason?"

He could not see her face but he knew she was smiling.

"To reaffirm your commitment to one another. Was it Helen's idea? I suspect it was. What happened? Did you accuse one another of 'having changed'?" Not until she sensed his deflation did she continue. "You're pushing things, Joshua. Both of you. Your assignation didn't work out as planned and you panicked. Helen's mind was somewhere else and now you're striking back at whatever's out there." Pointing a finger upward, then making a circular gesture to convey the vastness beyond her grasp, she sighed from a conflict of emotions. "You don't want to believe Helen was contacted by an alien presence because she's also drawn to it."

"I never said that."

"You didn't have to. Perhaps," she concluded with a sad smile, "I divined it from the stars."

"The hell you did," he cursed, out of character. Picking up the computer game, he flicked it on. The screen immediately filled with unidentifiable symbols. In petulance, he shoved it under her nose.

"Look at that: things aren't as they seem. One minute my face is on the monitor, and the next I'm replaced by – fill in the blank." He wavered and she finally relented.

"I see your point. What we're dealing with is an unknown factor. If some intelligence exists, we have no basis to determine whether it's good or the contrary."

"What do you propose we do about it?"

"Keep an open mind. We sure as 'hell' can't go to it; it has to come to us. If and when it does, then, and only then, will we be forced to render a judgment."

The advice was as sound as it was emotionally unrewarding.

"I want to know, now."

"No more than Helen does. But you'll both have to wait."

Thrusting the game into her hand, she accepted it willingly.

"What do you want me to do? Play it out? Are you that curious to see whether you're the great detective?"

He finally relented, relief obvious on his face.

"I believe I am."

"All right. I'll take it with me."

Cradling the computer in her one good hand, Paula started for the door.

"Where are you going?"

"To hydroponics. To tell LaTanya that you'll review her findings in the morning. After I've had a chance to play 'Commander Terry' and you've had some sleep." Walking to the door served the effect of severing a bond. "Good night, Captain."

"Paula –"

His use of her first name affected her, but the former ensign did not respond. She dared not, for his mood was too conflicting to trust. Whatever demons raged inside could not be pacified by her presence. They could only be greatly scrambled in the wrong direction. Just as the computer game had reverted from a recognizable likeness to an obscure set of figures, so, too, was it possible to divest his interest.

He was correct that a challenge confronted them. Whether it proved to be actual or fantasy, a positive or negative force influencing their lives, only time would tell. The sole way she had of giving him those days was by departing.

Had he said "Burbone," instead of "Paula," she might have let it be otherwise. But he had not. The vulnerability and possibilities behind his word choice was best left unexplored.

In that, she was certain, Helen Fitzgerald would agree.

CHAPTER 7

His original intent had been to walk with her to the transport but the idea of riding up two floors in the close confines suddenly overwhelmed him and he backed off.

"I'll meet you on the bridge at the change of shift."

Accepting that as a dismissal and realizing it was probably for the better, Paula hesitated, then saluted Terry before walking away from the Observatory. Ill at ease from her honest but perhaps too open analysis of his confrontation, Paula reached the transport and found it waiting for her. Stepping inside, she struggled under dual responsibilities, uncomfortable with the idea she had not handled the situation properly. In fact, as the roundabout moved upward, doubt assuaged her. The poor prognosis of the plants in hydroponics, the game, Helen's telepathic link with some outside force and Terry's own conflicting emotions had all seemed strangely unreal. She had been prepared for none of them, and while she prided herself on being equal to any situation, this had rapidly gotten out-of-hand.

Nothing progressed as it should have, beginning with the error, if such it had been, of allowing the newest members of the bridge contingent to man the command chair by themselves. She had never done such before but when the sudden *urge* to report to hydroponics had affected her, the decision seemed a logical progression of their responsibilities. The fact Terry had not objected didn't serve to lessen her guilt. When the captain failed to report, she should have stayed. That's what she had always done before, no questions asked.

Although she had implied she often volunteered for duty at the "water farm," such was not the case. Like him, she relied on reports from the staff working there for updates. Allowing herself to be enthused by the progress of the sprouts, she had willfully failed to adequately address the failure of the hybrids to thrive. The captain's reaction had revealed two salient details: he was the more attuned of the two, and had not been adequately briefed as to the situation.

His reluctance to go to the bridge should have warned her that whatever was troubling him required a mature, measured response, yet she had not been equal to that task, either. Annoyed by her own speculations as to why he hadn't reported after the successful rescue of the engineering crew, it had not been her place to analyze his emotional turmoil. Worse, she suspected her tactless response had more to do with her own feelings than his. Knowing his attachment to Helen Fitzgerald, she should have backed away from any discussion of jealousy.

The game, too, had bothered her. Immediately drawing the conclusion it belonged to Helen without proof, she had been nearly as upset as he, but for a different reason. After opening it and finding the story had been developed around the captain, she should have claimed all further innocence, rather than prying into the specifics. That would have ended the irritant before it started. More complicated was the discussion of the extra sensory revelations Helen had received. Rightfully troubled by them, he had sought her interpretation and instead, she had dismissed his concerns rather than delving into the significance. If true, which she had too lightly dismissed, it bore a relevance she, as a command officer, should have responded to with a serious debate. Instead, she had turned his confusion into a matter of insignificant speculation. Although undoubtedly accurate, her unconcern was both unprofessional and deeply troubling, making Paula question her own values.

She had no right and no reason, she debated, to harbor any feelings for Captain Terry. Yet, six months working daily, almost hourly with him, had provided a latitude she would have never dreamed possible. That he sometimes reciprocated the changing relationship was not enough for her to pursue it, much less allow it to affect her judgment. Altogether, the startling events of the night had not done her credit and she felt relieved he had opted not to follow her to the bridge.

Resolved to do better, she dismissed Hanson and Bates more sharply than intended and settled into the commander's chair, resolved to put her attention on more salient matters. The fact she failed to do so was indicative of the complexities of their complicated lives aboard the "floating hulk."

Giving Paula a five minute start, Joshua lingered outside the Observatory. Unable to control his agitation, he finally abandoned the idea and walked down the corridor. Coming to the branch which led to Engineering and the transport he suddenly hesitated and changed his mind. With a deep-rooted sensation of matters spinning out of control, he took the opposite route to the brig.

Long unused in its original intent, the confinement area had served a far better purpose, for that was where, eons ago or so it seemed, he had stored a cargo destined for, but rejected by, colonists on a distant outstation. Remembering it only after tragedy and near starvation had brought the crew to the point of death, he had rediscovered the two hundred cases of the nutritional tablets they now used as their sole means of survival.

Such sustenance had solved the issue of "food," but had failed to satisfy the inner craving for "meals." The project of establishing a limited hydroponics plant had been the answer to achieving normalcy and diversion. Finding the plants they anticipated supplementing and eventually replacing their diet on the verge of death had triggered a deep-set unease. Coupled with factors simmering below the surface had only increased his anxiety to the point he was drawn to reassure himself all was well on at least one front.

Slipping through the unlocked door he stared with undisguised reserve at the stacked boxes. Counting them for no better reason than it served as a mindless exercise, he had nearly satisfied himself and turned to leave when a gnawing in the pit of his stomach compelled him to take a closer look. Stepping inside, he reached for the nearest case, shook it, then exchanged it for one closer to the back. Lacking the proper tools, he ripped open the seal and inspected the contents.

If the anticipation of horror had not become part of his everyday life, he would have lost control.

Hands shaking, he stared at the contents. They were not what he anticipated. Instead of neatly packed bottles of nutritional pills, he saw what appeared to be farming implements. The original cargo the late Captain George Nguyen had been assigned to deliver. Mislabeled as nutritional tablets.

Tablets the remaining survivors of *Target* depended upon for life.

"No," he muttered aloud, as if denial would somehow alter the inevitable. "It's not possible."

One box, possibly two were incorrectly marked.

Surely, that was the answer.

They had counted on sixteen years of high protein, high fibre, vitamin and mineral-enriched pills. Sixteen years to find a habitable planet and settle there to establish, if not a normal life, than one as close to it as possible.

"No," again. Followed by the more logical acceptance. "All right. We'll need these to create a farming community."

Put on a happy face. Fool the gods into believing they had dealt him a hand he couldn't win and then turn the tables on them by making the best of the situation. If they didn't have sixteen years, then surely they had ten. Or five. Long enough to dispel despair.

The boxes they had already removed were properly labeled. They had contained nutritional tablets. The bulk of what was left were surely the same.

"Surely" was a word that should already have been stricken from his personal vocabulary. In six months he should have learned nothing was sure.

Nothing but worst case scenarios.

Another lesson taught by Encounter. He would have to tell Helen. She was the language expert, after all. She would find a way for them to survive with one fewer word in their collective dictionary.

Carefully placing the box of instruments aside, he opened another. After the third box, he cursed. And began to sweat.

He would open them all. And then, he'd know.

Four of them had assembled: the ranking officers of the star cruiser *Target*. They were a ridiculously small contingent. In other times, better times, when the captain summoned his "heads of ship," twenty representatives from the various disciplines would have reported. Each on time, and each prepared to respond, instantly, to whatever situation required emergency handling.

In one of his more blithe moments, Brian Hardy might have observed, *The big wigs on Target have gone from 'observing' to 'reacting.'*

He was the acknowledged wit aboard ship.

Under present circumstances, no one would have found his observation amusing.

But then, the statement would have been more caustic than humorous, and Brian's feelings would not have been hurt at the stony silence.

It was as well for the present contingent he kept his own council.

Preliminaries were dispensed with and the duty roster for the day posted outside the Command Center. No addendum was attached, warning the crew not to disturb the officers during report. None was needed. Among the uninvited thirteen, it was well understood a crisis was pending.

Even Jingles Gingleheimer, the chief engineer, felt that, and he was not a man famous for deep insight into the workings of human beings. The fact he had not been summoned to the conference broadcast louder than words that the danger under consideration was not related to any mechanical or structural breakdown.

What comfort the crew took was highly individualistic.

"Good morning," Captain Terry began anew, meeting the gaze of his officers with cold detachment. Each, in their turn, met his. "Commander Burbone, Dr. Fitzgerald, Dr. Hardy." He spoke their names the way a man might recite from a list of the dead with whom he was familiar but not intimate. Captain Terry had had practice. "None of what we're about to discuss leaves this room. Is that understood?"

"Yes, sir," Commander Burbone acknowledged for the whole.

"Before you is a summary of the plants currently growing in hydroponics. It was assembled by Ensign Carson last night on my order."

He nodded to Burbone who took up the subject.

"Specifically, it concerns the hybrid, high-protein plants which were developed from seeds recovered from the cargo area of a destroyed Skip. Originally meant to be delivered to the main hydroponics sector, the consignment was either overlooked, or, like the nutritional tablets, were stowed there until called for. At this point, we have no way of knowing since all the computer records were wiped out after Encounter."

Terry proceeded with the lecture.

"Five hundred seeds were obtained. Fifty of them were placed in a water tank; thirty-three germinated into seedlings. It would not be understating the issue to say that they represent, to a very large extent, our only chance for self-sufficiency."

Brian raised his hand and was given the floor. He indicated the report.

"This is very technical work. Where did the data originate?"

"Included with the seeds was what appeared to be a data sheet, but it was written in complex scientific jargon not easily translatable by uninitiated civilians. Carson originally reviewed the information, extracting what she felt was a basic series of instructions." He hesitated before concluding, "Apparently, that was not the case."

No one cared to explore this admission of guilt.

"What brought about the sudden interest?" Helen inquired.

"Last night I observed the plants were... languishing," Terry concluded for lack of a more appropriate term. "Wilted. To an untrained eye, they appeared to be dying."

"Why didn't we hear about this sooner?"

"The condition of the plants was originally believed to be normal for their specific species." Terry dismissed further discussion as moot. He was not there to remedy the mistakes of the past. It was beyond his power.

"I want all of you to read the text. Thoroughly. We've made too many decisions lately without the proper facts. I will wait while you do so, now."

Under ordinary circumstances, the captain would leave the room, allowing the initiated to digest the data and discuss it among themselves before demanding coordinated answers. That was a luxury he could no longer permit. Scrutinizing their expressions was equally important as listening to their conclusions. One would be useless without the other. Officers were trained to present best-case scenarios. He needed truth.

As a language professional and thus better versed in scanning intricate dissertations, Helen finished before the others. Her pursed lips and paled complexion relayed to Terry she had correctly absorbed the implications.

Brian read more slowly, lips moving in silent pronunciation of unfamiliar words. Several times he paused to dictate a note to himself on his personal audio recorder, question a reference, or to make some obscure correction in the text. His respirations increased from fifteen to thirty a minute. Completing the report, he began an intense surgical operation with his teeth, extracting a hangnail from the longest finger of his left hand.

Paula read the material once, then reread it a second time. She was the last to finish. Her head bobbed slowly at points of interest, or shook in mute denial at others. At the termination, she was the only one to meet his gaze.

"Very well, sir," she began with deliberation. "Professing my ignorance of the technical aspects, may we summarize the data before debating specifics?"

"We could all use that," he admitted. Lacking a conference table, he was seated before a small personal desk, while the others were spread out of chairs, making a semi-circle around him with Helen to his right, Brian to his left and Paula in the middle. They had fallen into this configuration naturally. It served protocol as well as the social amenities, wordlessly representing the military-non-military mix of the crew. "Does anyone want to begin?"

After a respectful pause, Helen raised a finger, indicating she would speak if no one had objection.

"This report will have to be broken down into manageable sections," she began. "There's too much information, assembled in a desultory fashion. We must translate it into a workable manual – a guideline for the botany section that is understandable to even the most untrained crewman.

"That said, if I've managed to make the correct interpretations of their 'technical jargon,' which is by no means clear, the gist of the records, submitted by the researchers who hybridized the plants, is fairly straightforward."

Brian waited for her to pause before rising from the table. Indicating she continue through his action, he brought a pitcher of water and four glasses, distributing them as she spoke.

"The plants are exactly as we hoped; high protein, fiber, high vitamin and mineral content. They were developed as part of the UPE's program to colonize sterile planets, allowing the population to become self-sufficient by growing crops which would provide adequate nutrition. Rather than supplement their diet, these versatile plants would form the basis of their food supply."

"In that manner," Brian took up the thread, "they wouldn't have to be dependent on cargo ships. If I understand correctly, the intent was to seed these sterile but aqua-rich lands, maintaining only a small crew to tend the crops. Once the plants were thriving on the surface, they could then bring in the colonists. An admirable idea."

"These hybrids – those which we now have growing in our hydroponics unit – are the prototypes. Once they were fully developed, I imagine Captain Nguyen would have received orders to settle a party of botanists on an appropriate planet and leave them to set up the operation," Paula concluded.

"Yes," Terry agreed, sipping water from the glass Brian had provided. "That seems reasonable."

"Logically, therefore, we ought to be able to duplicate that goal on *Target,*" Helen pursued. "The plants are low maintenance and reproduce prodigiously. The problem is, in the early stages of their growth development – which, I conclude, is the stage they're at now – the vegetation requires high doses of liquid nutrients to fully develop. Our plants are 'languishing,' Captain," she continued, nodding toward Joshua, "because we have not provided that growth medium."

Leaning forward in his chair, fingers crossed, the commanding officer searched the faces of his advisers. They were pinched and grey.

"How do we rectify the situation?"

Squaring her shoulders, Burbone assumed responsibility for half the answer.

"Level Three is sealed. The structure is unstable and without capacity to sustain life support. While it might be possible to traverse the corridors in protected space suits, seeking IV fluids that may be used as a substitute fertilizer, I don't recommend it. Not only would it put the 'search and rescue' crew in jeopardy, we 've concluded, and I believe accurately, that the gas which contaminated that level has penetrated everything. Rather than solve our problem, we're more than likely to poison the plants."

"Agreed. What other options do we have?"

Inasmuch as Helen was the officer in charge of nutrition, she assumed responsibility for the answer.

"The obvious suggestion is to take our own vitamin and mineral tablets – the ones comprising the bulk of our present diet – and dissolve them in water. That ought to make a solution rich enough to stimulate plant growth. It may not be optimal but it should help."

"An excellent idea," Paula agreed. "We have more than enough to spare."

It fell on Captain Terry to answer.

"I think not."

If he meant his statement to shock, he was not disappointed.

"But, surely," Helen protested, "we've hardly made a dent in our supply. If we use some for the plants, what harm? We're only cutting our time estimate by a year. Perhaps less."

He had been waiting for just that word.

"'Surely' is a word we are no longer going to use."

He felt a sense of satisfaction by making that pronouncement. He had been waiting all night to use it.

"I don't understand."

The statement was disingenuous, for the speaker had already inferred a very dire problem. One she could not readily comprehend.

Captain Terry tightened his already tense muscles.

"Last night I went to the brig and examined the remaining cases of our nutritional support tablets. I opened every one of them. Nearly the entire lot was mislabeled."

Brian spoke in the ensuing silence.

"What does that mean?"

"They were filled with farming implements; the bulk of the original cargo we were supposed to deliver. The crates we did bring to the planet contained mining equipment. Which was totally inappropriate. Captain Nguyen and I presumed there had been some error in Logistics. We never thought to look in the boxes marked nutritional tablets." His voice hardened. "Why would we? When they, too, were rejected, we took them back aboard and I stored them in the brig."

"But, we've opened dozens of those boxes," Brian weakly protested. "They all held what they said they did."

"Obviously, they were stored together. When we opened one, we presumed they all contained exactly what was written on the outside. We were in error."

"What does this mean?" Burbone demanded. "What is the current status of our food supply?"

"I've only done a rough estimate. Based on the requirement of three pills per meal and taking into consideration the amount remaining in the brig with what we have here in the Command Center. Without a rate of reduction, I estimate we have no more than one month's supply."

"One month?" Brian gasped, the grey of his skin turning a sickly ashen green. Wrapping his arms around himself, he started forward then abruptly collapsed, as though his legs had already been sapped of strength by malnutrition.

Paula was the first to react. Instinctively thrusting her right arm out to support him, her bandaged stump grasped nothing but air. Crying in frustration, she turned aside, abandoning the man on the floor. That left Joshua and Helen. As their pained eyes met across the table, both transmitted a silent cry of anguish, reminding them their physical ills were only one facet of the impending crisis.

Responding to their respective disciplines, the captain went to his officer, while the civilian hurried toward one of her own. Tucking her hands under Brian's armpits, Helen lifted him to his feet, steadying him against her body. Terry guided Paula across the room so that her distress would be less apparent to those she outranked.

"It's all right," he began, dictating her return to emotional solvency by employing his command voice.

"You saw what happened!"

"All right," came the terse interruption. "You forgot."

"I'm nothing but a damned cripple! I can't face the fact." Raising her voice into a shout, Paula ripped off the bandage, revealing, for the first time, the absolute reality of her loss. "I want my hand back! I want to be whole again!"

With his eyes riveted to the ugly, puffy scars, the extent of which he had carefully chosen to avoid imagining, Joshua swallowed the lump in his throat. While his pity for her was acute, it did not tax his sensibilities to transpose the image to his own arm. Or that of Helen's.

As fleeting as emotions rose, they were absorbed by discipline and training. Forcing his taut muscles to respond in a natural, flowing movement, the captain placed himself between Paula, separating her from Helen and Brian.

"We all want that." Paula's nostrils flared, but she held her tongue. "But, we're dealing in reality. You've coped with your disability. You'll continue to do so. Right now, I require you to face a different crisis. One which involves us all. Take a deep breath and consider. Are you able to deal with that, or do you want to be dismissed?"

Bitterly ashamed, Paula stared down at her stump a long beat before responding. To her credit, tears did not choke her words.

"I am ready to participate in the conference, Captain."

Without answering, Terry led the way back to where Helen and Brian had already reseated themselves. The minister was the first to break the awkward silence.

"I beg your pardon for my outburst. I assure you such will never happen again."

Terry set his face into rigid immobility.

"The question under discussion was nutritional support for the hybrids. It has been put forward that our vitamin/mineral tablets be solubilized into plant food. Who will address that under present circumstances?"

"I will." All eyes turned to Helen. "The idea has been rendered impractical. We don't have another source of food to replace those nutrients in our diet. Nothing currently growing in hydroponics is adequate to sustain us."

"Although we've gone over this before and thought never to do so again, be more specific."

"Without the tablets providing 100% of the nutrients and fiber we need, our bodies will immediately begin to draw nourishment from tissues, muscles and bone. Our blood will become anemic, affecting our thought processes as well as depleting energy levels. Bones will become brittle. Our internal organs will fail."

Changing her position in the chair so that she could easily face all three of her listeners, Helen delivered the hard facts as she knew them.

"Starvation is a slow process. With adequate hydration, which we didn't have the last time we went through this horror, it will take weeks, perhaps months to bring about death. However," she underscored, gripping her hands until her knuckles drained of blood, "even if we were to use some of the tablets to nourish the hybrids, even presuming that will work as anticipated, it will take considerable time. Over the course of which we'll grow steadily weaker. While we might survive until the first harvest, it's problematic whether it will be of sufficient quantity and quality to reverse the damage done. It may do no more than keep us alive at the lowest possible level. And considering that the best case scenario, we can't possibly replenish the supply fast enough to live on indefinitely. That requires months and months of surplus."

Brian wiped his hand over his nose, then sniffed, hesitant to proceed. Terry urged him on.

"Which doesn't even address the issue of losing what mental stability we still have. Hungry people are irritable and irrational. Workloads will have to be reduced. Mistakes will occur and go uncorrected. We may not starve, but it's just as probable we'll blow ourselves up. We've already had a taste of that in Engineering."

His expression of grim resignation, although unplanned, sealed the discussion.

Terry rose to his feet, symbolically blocking the exit, making the point no one was to leave without forming a plan of action.

"That statement is noted. What options have we?"

The mood in the conference room deepened. Paula's gaze held on Terry, while Brian ducked under the table to pick up a microscopic fibre, invisible to the naked eye. Helen re-knitted her hands, setting them on the table in an attitude which was neither prayer nor attack.

Both, the captain reasoned, would come later.

Everything in its own time.

"Let me state the facts," Terry began, "as we know them – for the record." The comment was unnecessary. As with most formalities, digitally recorded briefings had ceased with Encounter. "We have hybrids in our hydroponics unit which will either die, or fail to grow properly without supplements. Before we discovered the loss of nutritional tablets, the hybrids were looked upon as a welcome change of diet that would eventually supplant the tablets. That dynamic has dramatically altered. They now represent our sole hope for the future. Which is to say, the immediate, as well as the long term survival of this crew." He paused, opening the floor for objections. None were forthcoming.

Again, silence. Hearing the equation expressed in cold, hard words brought no further clarity.

"Options? Suggestions? Rebuttals?" No one moved. They might have transformed into statues. While their quiet was not damning, it was damnable.

Leaning back on his heels, Terry hooked his thumbs under the waist of his trousers. The attitude was not meant to convey relaxation. Those watching him with eagle eyes understood it to mean they were not going to be let off the proverbial hook.

"It's been six months since Encounter. We've faced more than our share of crises. We've also had several serious discussions on the duties of command." Without moving his head, Joshua made eye contact with Brian. "I'm not going to require any of you to make a final decision. As captain, that is both my prerogative and my duty." Images of dictators – inglorious, infamous, power-mad men – passed through his mind. "Whichever way we go, the burden weighs on my shoulders alone."

Helen parted her fingers, prefatory to making a comment, but he shook her off.

"Let me finish what I have to say. Then you may all speak." *That is an order,* his expression conveyed. "I will take into consideration what my advisers think. That is the purpose of advice. Once a conclusion is reached, I will make a final and absolute determination which I will transmit to the crew."

Paula shocked everyone by slapping her good left hand down on the table.

"Why?" she demanded, eyes steady. Her attitude left no doubt of her feelings. "The captain does not have to explain himself."

Terry's head dipped toward her in acknowledgment.

"Correct."

Which drew the attention back to Paula.

"No matter which way you decide, rationing is inevitable. I wouldn't tell them the truth. Beginning immediately, I would issue two tablets instead of three. If they object, I'd say we have previously been in error: two is the requisite number needed to sustain life. More than that provides excess nutrition."

"That would be a falsehood," Helen objected. "When they discover the truth, which, of course they eventually will, it will destroy their faith in… us. I suggest we tell them in a way that won't instill panic."

"Yes," Burbone remarked, running her tongue under her teeth. "You're the language expert. You know how to use words to their best effect." Helen cringed but did not back down. "Put it any way you will, the end result is the same." Adjusting her position, she faced Terry. "Suspicion is better than outright certainty. They can put two and two together, but their own fear may stop them from adding the numbers up to four."

"That's right." This time, it was Brian. "You want to give them an 'out.' It might be better that way, Josh."

"No 'outs'. Not this time. I can't take the chance."

"Of what?" Helen asked, voice hard, yet cautious.

"Mutiny."

He had come to fight a battle and found himself in an entirely unanticipated war.

CHAPTER 8

Terry held up his hands. While he pantomimed the action of calling for peace, what he was actually doing was putting an end to the discussion.

Being a dictator had its privileges.

"Enough!" And then more harshly, "Lower your voices."

"Yes, sir," Paula officiously replied, straightening her shoulders, then adjusting her posture in proper military fashion. True to form, Brian slumped back and Helen reunited her fingers, although this time she hid them under the table.

Joshua's first inclination was toward anger; his second was to offer an apology. He rejected both alternatives.

"We were discussing the critical shortage of supplies," he began tersely. "We can make no decision on what comes after, until we have that issue resolved."

"Isn't that like us?" Brian tried, tapping the tip of his nose with his finger. "Putting the cart before the horse?" The company cringed, waiting for the inevitable, *What's a horse?* When no one asked, the tension was inadvertently relieved.

"Thank you." The officers did not inquire whether the captain referred to the cleric's statement, or the ensuing silence. It was enough the mood had been broken. "I stated that each of you would have the floor. The time has come. Commander Burbone?"

Paula stood, fixing her eyes on a point over Terry's shoulder.

"Sir. Continuing to issue the nutritional tablets on a rationed schedule has an end point. When the pills run out, we starve. Attempting to use some of them to support the hybrids offers us a chance. Granted, a slim one, but its outcome is less certain. Therefore, I support the idea of informing the crew what I suggested earlier: three tablets are not required for a sustainable meal. We take one third of what we have left, dissolve them in water and feed them to the plants."

She paused for breath, sweating profusely. A stream of salty fluid rolled to the edge of her jaw. No one moved until it dropped. "I believe we'll know within a short time whether the nutritional fluids will improve the growth of the plants. If it does, we germinate as many more seeds as we can, creating more hydroponic units to hold them and continue the process.

If we detect no obvious success, we declare the project a failure. Only at that point would I explain the situation to everyone. We then move into an entirely different realm: that of how, or if, to divide the remaining tablets. The discussion of the limited survival of the many versus the more prolonged survival of the few has already been placed before the crew once. In the name of humanity, I suggest at that point, you do so again. "

Acknowledging she had verbalized her opinion, the commander retired to her former position. As she sat, the seat cushion made a small gasp, as displaced air strove to escape.

"Thank you. Father Hardy," the captain continued. "The floor is yours."

Copying Paula, Brian stood. Unlike her, he paused before speaking to stare into the strained, taut faces of his companions. He would not play at being a soldier, for he was not.

"You evoke the name of humanity, Commander Burbone. I agree. Humanity is the issue. We're talking about life and death. Not a 'good death,' versus a 'bad death,' but pronouncing a sentence of execution on innocent human beings. I agree, feeding the planets, although it limits our predictable life expectance, is our only viable chance for continued existence. But, if it fails, to ask for volunteers to willingly sacrifice themselves? That, I cannot condone."

Shifting his weight from one leg to the other, he made his plea. "Not so very long ago, you made a confession to me, Joshua."

"I remember."

"I won't divulge the nature of that confession, but –"

Dismissing him with a violent chopping motion, Terry stood, both legs planted so that he appeared poised for a fight.

"The time for secrets is past." He stiffened his back, preparatory to divulging his sin. "Immediately after Encounter, I confronted a situation very similar to this: the starboard portion of our ship which had blown away, was drifting precariously close to Target. Were it to strike us, the collision would have terminated all life aboard both halves.

"I didn't know at the time – I still don't know, and never will – whether any crew were alive on that... floating hulk. I made the decision then to blast it away from us, thus... termination any aboard who might, conceivably, have been saved. It was not a decision I made lightly. Nor do I regret that action, though I will carry that burden of guilt with me the rest of my life. My confession, such as it was, was a plea never to have to face that life and death decision again. In that... 'god' has forsaken me. Which is why I stand before you now, listening to what you have so say before I, alone, make the final determination on how best to utilize what resources we have."

I already bear the responsibility for murder. To do so again releases all of you from so heinous an act.

From where she was sitting, Paula noted his irises appeared horizontal, rather than round. She recalled Helen's nickname for his was "Meow" and marveled at how apropos it was.

"Just a moment!" Helen interrupted, rising to meet him at her full height. "I was under the impression this meeting was open for discussion. If your mind is already made up, then Brian and I will leave now, and damn you for not hearing us out."

Without uttering a word, the captain gave his permission. Brian Hardy, the worse for wear after his brief interlude from speaking, shuddered noticeably. The fight, if not the argument, had gone out of him.

"I'm sorry," the cleric began, awkwardly rising with head bowed. He let the apology stand for his previous professional indiscretion. "I'm upset. We've already had enough bad news; I can't face more. Not coming from your direction," he added, alluding to, but not facing the captain.

Wanting to sit but feeling loath to ask permission, he steadied himself by leaning both arms on the back of his chair. Unintentionally, the posture served to augment the impression he was speaking from a pulpit.

"We shut down life support on Level Three and portions of Level Four. We all participated, whether actually or vicariously, in the hunt for, and destruction of, two mutineers; two of our own who had turned against us. So, we have all made life and death decisions."

Finally wearying of his physical stance, the minister drew back the chair and sat in it, not in his accustomed place in the semicircle but at a distance away.

"What I said earlier – about evoking humanity. I stand *by* it, but not *with* it. Not to the degree you may have assumed. My suggestions are these. One: we make very sure there are no ships in our vicinity. I know the long-range scanners are non-functional. But we increase the frequency and velocity of our distress signal. Two: before we begin rationing, which can only lead to a lingering death because I believe time is against us, I suggest we give ourselves forty-eight hours to man the viewscreens, visually scanning the heavens, looking for help.

"Three: At the same time we look for any inhabitable planet; not an ideal one, but one which conceivably holds out the possibility of life. Once decided upon, we head in that direction with all possible haste. If it's too far away, we approach it at impossible speeds, accepting that inherent danger. If we find the planet in any way satisfactory, we send out an exploratory party and make a determination whether there's any eatable vegetation. If there is, we put the ship into orbit around it and settle. If not, we've come to the end of our journey."

Hanging his head, Brian closed his eyes. Long locks of dark grey hair fell over his brow, mercifully covering his face. The effort had cost him much.

"Thank you," Terry said. Unlike Hardy, his voice had mutated into a unemotional tone. "Dr. Fitzgerald?"

It was Helen's turn to speak. She did so, her eyes bright, her resolve firm. She had not expected to stand alone, but the numerical superiority she faced did not dissuade her from voicing an alternative.

"We all know the legends... and the historical facts," she began, leaning forward to bring herself nearer. "Of people placed in similar situations. Of commanders or planetary leaders faced with the decision of dwindling supplies. Who to save, and how many? How to decide which are most necessary; most valuable? The governing body, or the populace? The soldiers or the poets? The men or the women? The lame or the healthy. The black," she added, staring at Paula, "or the white.

"In these 'historical precedents,' the people making the decisions have often chosen the survival of the few over the many. In others, they have resorted to cannibalism. A subject," she grimly added, "We haven't yet touched upon. In those notorious cases we know so well – the ones we're taught in ethics class – help has occasionally arrived. Too late to save those who were sacrificed, but before any need have died. The leaders were prosecuted for their perceived crimes against *humanity* and convicted.

"How many of us disagreed with those convictions?" She waited but no one spoke. "Hindsight has a wonderful way of enlightening the situation. Judging someone placed in an intractable situation is wrong, yet as a civilization, we have done, and will continue to condemn. Our 'Code of Morality' demands restitution for the dead, no matter how unfair that is to the living. In such a case, we avenge a perceived wrong with a willful wrong.

"Like Brian, my considered opinion is that several, possibly a larger number of the crew, will suffer acutely from reduced rations. Both mentally and physically. Putting them through that torture is not only counterproductive, but it instills false hope. We know nothing about those plants. None of us are experts. The very nature of their being hybrids means they're experimental. Attempting to save them is irrational. And even if they were to eventually thrive, how many of our fellows will we have lost to malnutrition and... suicide? For, let's not humor ourselves. None of us want to face the prospect of starvation again. A quick death may be preferable."

Helen paused, inhaling deeply, then prepared herself to deliver her denouement with the resolve of one who knew, present company excluded, they were not alone.

"As one, and possibly two of you already know, I received a communication from space. Not in words, or in any recognizable speech, but enough to convince me there is intelligent life out there – possibly, and understand I have no means of stating this with any certainty – coming to our aid. If this proves accurate, we need not take any drastic measures at this time."

Terry attempted to speak, erroneously assuming she had finished, but a slight shake of her head silenced him.

"If I'm in error – if no rescue ship from the stars arrive – then I will support the conditions Brian laid out."

"I said forty-eight hours," Brian whispered, greatly astonished by Helen's revelation. "Is that enough time for you to – substantiate your claim?"

The answer was verbalized before she had time allow emotion to overcome what she perceived as fact.

"How can I say?"

Terry shook his head.

"We don't have forty-eight hours to waste. I've heard you out and gained your insight. Your points are well-taken and insightful. But, I respectfully disagree. My decision is as follows: we begin rationing immediately using Burbone's argument. Only two tablets are required for proper nutrition. The remaining third go to feed the plants. We germinate as many more seeds as possible and continue that until we determine success or failure. If we fail, that is the time I explain to the crew our actual situation. No one volunteers to walk out an airlock. The tablets are dispensed until there are no more left. Thank you for your honesty and your support."

He was the first to leave the room. Paula was the only one who followed him. Not until the door slid shut behind them did the other two move.

"God help us all," Brian intoned, reverently crossing himself.

It was a far cry from a prayer for hope.

Lights flashed across the circular circumference of the bridge, indicating activity. Terry registered them peripherally, through the corners of his eyes, registering, subconsciously, the inner workings of *Target*. Janice Miles sat at navigation, her concentration so enmeshed in the sundry controls, a less knowledgeable observer would have thought her at work, busily plotting in a course change.

As if she were a part of the instrumentation and not a crewmember at all, the captain paid her no heed. Whatever she was doing bore no relevance to his moment.

At the lower, right-hand corner of the central viewscreen ran a series of ever-changing numbers. They chronicled the passage of time. It was there he fixed his attention. By his expression, it might have seemed his very existence hung in the balance of passing seconds. Only four people actually understood it was death he was counting down.

Not until the elevator doors slid open did he avert his gaze. Immediately identifying the interloper, Joshua's face registered shock. He had expected Brian Hardy. Whom he was about to receive was Helen Fitzgerald.

She approached rapidly, neck rigid, eyes fixed with determination. What he read in them was not what he hoped to see.

Seven steps brought her to the command position. With hands behind her back, she was the epitome of an officer, reporting for duty. If he had believed that, the sinking in his heart would have been drastically reduced.

"I should like to speak with you. Privately. If you have a moment."

He nodded acceptance and stood. Directing his gaze toward Burbone, he snapped, "Hold the com," and followed her into the roundabout.

"Level Two."

The pair spoke no more until they had settled into Helen's private chambers. It was only then she began to break down. Blindly reaching out, she sat at the table, gripping the edge for support. Words spilled from her in a searing eruption of molten passion.

"Although we failed to set a timetable for success or failure of the hydroponics experiment, I think the time has come to make an assessment. I've fed the plants for seven days with the nutritional tablets as agreed. While it may be too soon to reasonably expect a response, I will report to you now there is none."

"Report accepted. We will wait another week. And if two weeks isn't long enough, we'll wait three weeks."

"Very well. I presumed that would be your reply. I acknowledge the wisdom of your conviction. However, I respectfully request to be released from my service in hydroponics."

"Why is that?"

Unexpectedly, Helen broke down before his eyes.

"Joshua, I'm not a soldier. I don't have a military mind. I can't turn my emotions off at will, even though logic might dictate I'm being unreasonable. Although my avocation is a technical one, I approach it on a very primal level. The need to communicate – to make our needs known – begins immediately after birth. Hunger, fear, loneliness, being hot or cold or uncomfortable: an infant must convey each, in turn, or it won't survive."

Sliding the chair back, her action forced him to retreat a step or have the backrest touch him.

"A child's first cognizant word is a milestone in its development. Learning to read separates it from the lower order of animals. A dialogue between two people, between nations, between planets is the foundation for peace."

Swiveling in the seat, she scanned his eyes as she might a computer bank, attempting to download data through the points of his irises.

"You make decisions rapidly and stand behind them with the determination of a seasoned command officer. You must judge for the whole, rather than the parts. I generally find myself arguing for the weak rather than the strong. Although, in this case I'm not certain there's a difference."

"Mark this," she continued, tilting her head back to convey a generality with specific undertones. "In English, the word 'love' is used to signify tender emotion, or an act of intercourse. A person may be 'in love,' or they may 'make love.' Two entirely different concepts, you would agree?"

"They can be," he remarked, unsure where she was taking the argument.

"On the planet Azar, their word for 'love' is used concurrently with the word 'hate.' Therefore, if I were to say to you, in the Azarian tongue, 'Joshua, I love you,' my precise intent – whether I was conveying a positive or negative emotion – would have to be inferred through inflection and the words surrounding such a statement."

"It sounds complicated," he granted, running his hands though his hair, then absently tugging on his earlobe.

"On Belias Balfour, there is no word for 'God.' Our common expression, 'God bless you,' conveys no meaning to them. In fact, I have actually seen it taken as an insult. In developing a common ground between two diverse cultures, each side has to give and take. They have to learn to distinguish between love and hate, blessings and curses."

Pausing for breath, Helen then continued over the profound silence, trusting that as his permission to carry her point.

"I do not see 'duty' the same way you do. You made a decision concerning the rationing of the nutritional tablets. I report to you the effort has been unsuccessful, but you see it was your duty to carry through with the agreed-upon course of action. That is the military way. I respect you for it."

"And how do you define 'duty'?" he inquired, evenly and without condemnation. "As pertains to yourself?"

The computer monitor flickered, casting uneven shadows across the room. From overhead came the doleful tolling of the ship's communication bell, indicating the end of a shift. Once, that, too, had defined duty.

"I see my responsibility as holding out for hope."

He paused until the last strains of extraneous sound had died before reaching past her to lower the intercom so they would not again be disturbed.

"Even if that means going back on your word?"

The answer was unequivocal.

"Yes." With his hand already in front of her face, he waved permission to continue. "You are the captain; I am the arbitrator, the conciliator. If ordered to go against your code of conduct, or your better judgment, you must obey. That is the way your life is structured. It is how the soldier functions, or there can be no discipline."

Helen touched his hand, which had lingered by the screen. "I'm not saying there aren't extreme circumstances where you, or any other officer, doesn't make value judgments. There comes a point when even a career soldier must follow the dictates of his own conscience, although it may jeopardize both career and life. You proved that with Miranda. When ordered to get rid of the cat, you did so. But fear for her safety drove you to ultimately disregard that command and seek her out."

"Then we're the same and our concept of duty is not at odds."

She released his hand and withdrew her own, so that they were out of sight.

"In your situation, I wouldn't have abandoned her in the first place." Rocking slowly in the chair, Helen's attention returned to the viewscreen. "Just as I cannot now disregard my expectations that we will be helped."

Joshua stomped his foot, then tugged urgently at his uniform sleeve.

"Then I'm like those on Belias Balfour. I have no God." It was a damning assertion, yet one she had unwittingly set him up for.

"We must both follow the guidance of our own soul. You will defend the crew as one single entity; I will continue to view them as individuals. 'First, do no harm,' Joshua. That's my concept of the universe and my place in it."

Lightly touching the controls on the key pad, Helen increased the magnification, effectively drawing the unknown closer around them.

"By contacting me, whatever alien life forms exist out there altered my personal sense of duty. In a very real way, I believe their lives are in my hands, just as mine – and possibly all of ours – are in theirs. It has... divided my loyalties." Her face remained implacable but he sensed the hurt and confusion her words had elicited. "I fight the battle now on two fronts. If you can't accept such an admission of guilt, I offer again: relieve me of duty."

Her choice was an onerous one, and he did not make it without deep introspection.

"I believe in you. For as long as I sustain that faith, I see no reason to... disqualify you from work. It's the same answer," he added, rolling back on the balls of his feet, "as I would give Brian."

"Or to Paula?" Helen challenged, subconsciously holding her breath for the answer. As he promptly replied with a negation, he was responding as a commanding officer and not on a personal level.

"No. Were Commander Burbone to abandon her duty, or speak to me of divided loyalties, I would relieve her immediately."

Helen withdrew from the vehemence of his assertion, planting her feet on the floor as a means of stabilizing her foundation.

"What's the difference between us?"

She hoped to hear him say, *I love you. Paula I barely know,* but his mind was still on "duty."

"The very differences to which you alluded: you're a civilian, pressed into service. She's a career officer."

"Paula would have sent the cat 'packing.' Without a second thought," Helen pressed, craning her neck to see how his expression would change. For the second time in as many minutes, she was disappointed.

"If she did, I couldn't condemn her for it."

I can, Dr. Fitzgerald decided. *But then, I'm not a 'career officer,' so that's my privilege.*

"Thank you," she spoke, instead. "I wanted to know."

Joshua clapped his hands together, not as applause, but as a means of ending the discussion. The action, she easily deduced, was from a long-ago class in command training.

Don't be a martinet! she wanted to shout at him. *Think for yourself. Open your mind. Be a human being. Allow yourself to feel. Grieve for those crewmen who may not survive on limited rations. For God's sake, cry on my shoulder, while I weep on yours. Let's mourn their sacrifice, as we would want them to revere ours.*

There were no tears in his eyes, however, and she doubted she could draw them out. When he mourned, it would be alone, on a sleepless night, when his footsteps would finally bring him, too, to the Observatory.

Will you hear my alien, then? she wondered. *Wrapped in the throes of guilt, will you open your heart enough to hear those musical poems?*

She did not have the answer. All she had were his words.

I believe in you. For as long as I sustain that faith, I will love you.

Only the ending was paraphrased.

CHAPTER 9

Joshua waited a long moment to speak.

"I'll see for myself the condition of the hybrids. Will you go with me?"

One final peace offering. The last time he had made a request of such magnitude, it had been to ask her to marry him.

This time, her answer must be different.

"No."

"Then I'll go alone. I must, for to do otherwise would be to deny… not your visitation, but hope as I see it," he suddenly changed. "You call it my duty, but we were actually speaking of faith in the future. I ask you to consider: our positions aren't mutually exclusive. The only thing between us is the factor of time. You're asking me to wait for your aliens to come. Since you already stated you have no idea when that will occur, you demand we give ourselves the longest possible window. I'm not disregarding your expectation. Rather, I'm merely setting a different watch and by so doing, I'm seeking a way to extend it."

"I don't understand what you're saying."

"Yes. You do. It's why you've made it a contest between us I don't understand. Is it a test of my affection for you? If it is, you're wrong. I'm not denying what you believe. In fact, no one would be more gratified than I to have help arrive. Communicate with the aliens; welcome them aboard. Say to them, 'I love you,' in a manner they'll understand. You have that power. But, don't condemn me if I want it both ways. Yes, I've shortened the time we have for them to come to us, but if I happen to be right; if the plants eventually thrive, then what I've done is prolonged the time they have to reach us. Don't you see that?" He waited for an answer while she struggled to assimilate his words. "That's humanity as I must view it. If it isn't yours, we have nothing more to say. I dismiss you from your medical and communicational duties."

Walking on tiptoe toward the door, he stopped just short of the electric eye.

"What I won't do is relieve you of your agrarian duties. No one who believes in hope as staunchly as you could serve elsewhere with better purpose."

"Joshua."

Not a question, but a simple, tender enunciation of his name; a statement not only of his private identity, but of her place in his life.

"Yes?"

"I'll go with you."

He swayed from the depth of her sacrifice, putting a hand out to steady himself against the bulkhead. What he encountered, instead, was her body. What she encountered was a man who had redefined her humanity.

"When the stars come calling, Joshua, then you'll be proven right. They will save those of us left to benefit from their gifts. Neither you, nor I, nor they set the timetable. Let it be."

He trembled in her arms and she held steady.

Steady as she goes.

Brian Hardy was waiting for them as they emerged from Helen's quarters. Perhaps not expecting them to be together, he backed away.

"I'm sorry. I didn't mean to intrude."

"We're going on an inspection of hydroponics," Terry announced without an inflection of emotion. "Would you care to join us?"

"No."

This time, softer, "Why not, old friend?"

The play for sympathy struck Hardy forcefully, compelling him to lean away from the pair.

"Because I'm not feeling kindly disposed to those plants at the moment. I'm afraid I'll go berserk and destroy the tanks."

Staring at him in stark amazement, Terry pressed nearer, so that their faces almost touched.

"It's not the plant's fault. If anything, they're as much victims as we are. We're trying to save them – to give them life, so that, as they thrive, we may also. It's a symbiotic relationship our kind has had with vegetation since the beginning of time."

"I understand that. And I'm aware it's only been seven days, but the reduction in rations has already to take its toll on me. I feel weak and light-headed and I'm so God-damned hungry, I don't know how much I care."

The sentiment, riveted with the blasphemy, propelled Terry away from the older man. Unable to come to grips with conflicting emotions of disgust, pity, anger and solicitude, he motioned Brian away. Bowing to the master, who would see the task through to fruition, the minister departed, shamed by his tacit mutiny, crushed by his weakness.

In spite of the fact he couldn't see Brian's face, Joshua understood the cleric was debating his own sentiment that God was priming them for some great and wondrous trial to come.

"Wondrous," in this case, being an open-ended word like "love," signifying either good or evil.

A task bordering on the impossible.

Paula was waiting for the captain in Hydroponics. Not expecting him to be accompanied by Helen Fitzgerald, she adopted a more formal response, saluting him as he entered. For once, Terry did not acknowledge the gesture.

In contrast to its size as the largest open area on Level Two, the room felt small and close. Adjusting the collar at his neck, which failed to facilitate his breathing, Joshua directed a quizzical glance at his officer which did not match his question.

"Where is Carson?"

The directness of the interrogative took Paula by surprise. It was only after reassuring herself it was inner, rather than outer torment which plagued him, did she reply. Taking her cue from his failure to demonstrate proper military protocol, she abandoned her usual and more formal attitude.

"Since we didn't take her into our confidence, and as I was unaware of your intentions, I decided to err on the side of caution and relieved her."

Realizing the predicament into which he had inadvertently placed Burbone, Joshua immediately signaled his approval.

"You did right. But I've decided she must be briefed. Someone with more knowledge than either of us must be made aware of what we're attempting."

"But not, sir, of the choice we've made?"

It was not meant to be an accusation, but served as one. For a moment, his spirits waned before recovering his aplomb.

"There's no need for that."

With her own feelings in flux, Paula stepped closer, trying to decide whether to pursue the matter. Were she still an ensign and he a commander, the separation between them would have been un-breachable. As his second in command, however, their present relationship needed, if not required, familiarity.

"Has Officer Fitzgerald made a report?"

"I have," she answered for herself. "I informed the captain there had been no progress. He's here to see for himself."

Paula sucked air in between her front teeth, then cradled the stump of her right arm in the moist palm of her left as she addressed Terry.

"I've never been in battle, sir. I have *done* battle – with a lifeless, unfeeling ribbon of black matter – and lost. I've fought mutineers, and now, in a peripheral sense, I've participated in a struggle time. For once, I'd like to achieve a victory."

Releasing her arm, she drew back the cloth covering the liquefied nutritional tablets.

"It's my honor – and if I may say, without lowering whatever esteem I have achieved in your eyes – my requisite duty – to assist you in the task of feeding the plants."

Her words grappled with his own disquietude, serving as a reminder of their absolute need for positive reward. In her youth and inexperience, Paula had inadvertently expressed a desire he had felt, but been unable to grasp. Their triumphs, such as they were, had all been predicated on how much worse the outcomes might have been.

None of the crew might have survived Encounter; the two Skip pilots could easily have escaped; without the courage to locate and pass through the eye of the black matter they might have been destroyed in a moment. Jingles and his engineers had come within an inch of losing their lives. While each event, viewed from the opposite perspective, had favorable outcomes, none came without cost.

By running the connotations over, Joshua realized just how young and untested the woman before him was. No longer a child, yet far from an adult, it was she who finally dared ask for optimism.

"Yes, Commander," he decided, daring to smile, so that she matched his expression with one of his own. "That's precisely what you shall do. Feed the plants. You and Carson."

"And Dr. Fitzgerald, sir? I presumed that's why you brought her."

"It was not," he explained, distancing himself from she whose hands were untainted. "You see to it."

It was as much of a gift as he had to offer.

When Burbone reported to the bridge at the change of shift, Joshua gave her report then left, ill-at-ease and searching for something he couldn't put his finger on. Checking in at the Command Center on Level Two, he found it deserted. Without knowing why, he deduced Brian had gone off to sulk and that Helen had abandoned the level altogether.

His speculations were half right.

Before leaving the deserted room, he noted the four-hour glass which they used to tell time had run out. Eschewing the obvious symbolism, he gritted his teeth and turned it before stepping back into the hall. In so doing, he nearly collided into Brian. The cleric was clutching a blanket and a pail of water. He responded immediately to Joshua's stare of puzzlement. Holding out his arms, he grinned and explained, "I'm going to deliver a baby."

If news of the wilted plants had come as a shock, this news registered on the old-fashioned Richter scale as a major earthquake. Damning himself for not having been more observant and already calculating what this event meant to the rest of the survivors, their dietary cards and workloads, Hardy put him at ease.

"Not actually a baby. A pretend one."

Brian would not have appreciated knowing how the captain filled in that image.

"A what?" he finally demanded.

"For the theatrics."

"Of making or delivering an imaginary child? And whose is it? Yours? Is this your way of getting out of being celibate?"

"I never said that restriction was part of my vows. Nor, even implied it. You made that up. We could have used you."

"As what?"

"A writer. You have a vivid sense of the dramatic."

"I've been informed otherwise." Finally tired of the repartee, he probed further. "Explain yourself in words an un-initiated can understand."

"I wasn't trying to be obtuse. The crew – which includes me, although I often feel outside their group – in staging a play. We thought it might prove entertaining. A change out of the ordinary. Of course," he hesitated before continuing, "we've been working on it for some while. Before the revelation about the tablets. Losing our supply, that is. Which, of course, they know nothing about. There was some talk of cancelling in light of the reduced rations – they suspect something's afoot – but I encouraged them to go on with it. Why not?"

"Why not, indeed."

"You're invited, by the way. And so is Paula. I was hoping you'd both attend. The bridge can be left unattended for an hour or so. Don't you think?"

Terry didn't bother offering an opinion.

"When is it to be held?"

"Today. Now. Well, almost now. In an hour. We were planning on delivering you a personal invitation."

Terry indicated the pail.

"What's the water for?"

"To drown ourselves if we get bad reviews."

Joshua wondered where Hardy's good humor had come from. He wouldn't have guessed he'd see a smile on the mystic's face until... but his mind failed to fill in the blank.

"An hour. All right. I'll see."

"Please," Brian tried to appease the moody officer. "Put away your scowl. Try and enjoy yourself. If just for the night."

"It's still evening. You forgot to turn the hourglass."

Brian attempted to turn the omission to his advantage.

"Good. That gives another hour to rehearse. Amazing how time is fluid like that. Almost as easy as going through a black hole. We might have ended up back in the 1800s. I've always wanted to meet Parson Weems."

"Who is the galaxy is that?"

"The man who invented the story about George Washington and the cherry tree."

"Because he created a lie that outlived him by centuries, or from the fact he's a cleric? Like you. And you have so much in common."

"Neither. Because I've always wondered why he chose a cherry tree. Why not an apple tree? Or, a peach tree? Or, a mighty oak, for that matter."

"No one knows what a tree is, anymore."

He left before Brian could come up with a rebuttal. Somewhat disoriented by the direction the conversation had taken and vexed he hadn't been informed of a play in the works, Terry walked the opposite direction from Hardy. Although he should have pleased the crew had used their off-hours constructively, he couldn't shake the feeling it bode ill. Lacking anything substantial to back that idea, he found himself at the roundabout. The door opened and he accepted the invitation.

"Level Four."

The lift responded, which should have gratified him, for most of the transports failed to identify his voice imprint and often failed to respond.

Or, if they did, only hesitatingly, but not this time. Because he actually had no specific destination in mind, he was taken their without trouble, further increasing his ire.

Avoiding Engineering and the Skip hanger, he wandered in the opposite direction, thinking, perhaps, to go through the cargo stowed in the brig yet again. Readily acknowledging the fact that to repeat the same action over again and expect a different result was the definition of insanity, he bypassed the confinement area and found himself at the Observatory.

He found her there, where he knew she would be. Her back was to him, and she did not turn as he entered. Feeling awkward and deflated after his conversation with Hardy, the words of conciliation he had absently composed evaporated, forcing him to speak without preparation. He issued them as he crossed to Helen, bracing himself as she finally averted her eyes from the open screen displaying the distant stars.

"The crew is preparing a little play, or something," he said, breaking into her thoughts. "As part of our 'back to normal' plan. They seem rather excited about the prospect. May I escort you to it?"

Although she had expected the invitation, it had not come in the place or the time of her choosing. Before she could think through her thoughts, words slipped through her lips.

"Is that an order?"

She succeeded in making him react. His eyebrows furrowed as he shook his head.

"Of course not. It was... merely an invitation." Waving his hand in front of himself, he erased the question. "Forget I asked."

A test. She had wanted to see how much fight was left inside him. And which direction it would take him.

"Wait a minute." Her hand shot out, preventing him from leaving. He pulled it away.

"I have work to do."

"You're pouting." She wanted him to smile. Her jest had the opposite effect.

"I won't come down here anymore. Not when you're here."

They had drawn their line in the sand and now both regretted it.

"Joshua... I was only kidding. Of course I'll go with you. I'd like to." This time, she meant it. When he gave no indication of belief, she stood, trying on a smile that did not seem to fit. His gaze was not on her, however, but was trained on the screen. His words shook her to her foundations.

"When your alien comes, I'll be proven wrong. Just like all the others. Forced into a decision which killed my people, only to find help was on the way. I will be condemned and my command compromised."

"Does it mean that much to you?"

"Yes."

She realized, too late, his one-word answer did not distinguish between feeling for the unnecessary deaths and maintaining his record as captain.

Responding to an inwardly directed anger, Helen reached out and disengaged the computer. The screen went blank. With it went her mind.

"There's nothing out there. And if there were, it's already too late. Whatever it is, its purpose is not to save us. Not in the way I envisioned."

"How, then?"

Face flushed, Helen grabbed him by his uniform, digging her fingernails deep into the fabric. Were it within her power, she would have ripped it off his body and torn it to shreds.

"I don't know. Why are you asking me these questions? Do I look like a seer? I had an impression – one brief flash of insight. It was nothing. A dream. Wistful thinking. What do I know? I don't have second sight. The stars are your love, not mine. You sit here all alone and let your mind wander. Then, you'll know, too. I want to get out of here!"

Tearing herself away from him, Helen stormed away, not toward the door, but into the darkest recesses of the room. The gloom was not deep enough to hide her contours, and he could clearly see her as she put hands to face.

His own bitterness seeping away like air escaping from a spacesuit, Joshua approached, finally daring to put his arms around her.

"Dangerous thing, isn't it?" he whispered into her ear, the softness of his breath radiating through her frame. "To know the future."

"I don't, Josh," Helen cried, relaxing her muscles so that her body melted into his. "I wish I did. I'm so confused. I don't know why I keep coming back here. I tried... I begged. I willed the... thing... to come. To save those plants. To create manna out of thin air. I'm making it up, aren't I? Like a child, wishing on a star. I should never have said anything, and yet, it was so... alluring. And when we saved Jingles and the others, it seemed like a promise. As thought I were chosen. Not because of any religious connotation, but because I'm a communicator. I know how to listen. I wish I'd kept it to myself. Never said anything."

"Don't say that. Even if it comes to nothing, your flash of insight gave you comfort. That's something we've had precious little of. Keep it; hold it; treasure it. And if I were you, I'd let it go."

"What do you mean? You just said –"

"You're trying too hard. Pressing for an explanation. It just might be that's what's keeping it at bay. Either you're inadvertently pushing contact away by forcing your thoughts back on it, or you're frightening it off. Sometimes, the best form of communication is silence. That's what I meant by letting it go."

She gasped as though a wave of water had cleansed the air.

"I've been so desperate to hurry things along I never stopped to reason it out. I presumed it… they, wanted a reply. Expected one. Perhaps all along they were only looking for a receptive mind."

"That's one way of looking at it."

Her doubts vanished and a new sense of calm descended over her being.

"The exactly right way. And it took you to understand it."

"I've been doing a lot of pushing, myself," he guardedly admitted. "I think we both need to stand back and let things happen, rather than being overly aggressive."

She tried a smile.

"That's not our natures, is it?"

"No. But, we might give it a try. And see what happens."

Helen offered Joshua her arm and he slipped his through the opening.

"How about going out on a date? I hear they're playing a live 3-D at the Orpheus this evening."

"I'd love to."

She was going to add, "Even if I already know the ending?" but decided to let it ride. Her decision had something to do with letting things go.

The theatricals started promptly at the beginning of the evening shift. A curtain had been constructed from some sort of sheer, glossy material, the original origin and purpose of which the captain had no idea. Everyone, including Commander Burbone, was in attendance and a thrill of excitement stimulated Joshua's senses as he escorted Helen inside the converted room. Chairs for the audience, separated by a central row, were set up beyond the raised platform serving as a stage. "That," the crewman handing out pretend tickets at the "gate" had summarily informed, "is to satisfy fire regulations."

An usher, attired in a loose-fitting tunic, escorted them to their seats in front. Their appearance apparently marked the opening of the play, for as they sat, the curtain carefully made its way upward. After a dramatic pause, Brian emerged. Behind him, devoid of illumination, the stage was dark.

The host was all smiles. A black cape, affixed at the neck with a silver bauble, reached past his knees. Emblazoned on the cloth was a yellow half-moon, a plethora of sparkling stars and a purple cat. Digging an elbow into Helen, Joshua winked.

"Don't tell me he's a cat fancier, too."

Shaking her head in the negative, she whispered back, "I assume he's using the cat image as a familiar."

"Yes, well, in the mood I'm in, he'd better not get too 'familiar.'" She grasped his hand, implying by added pressure she understood there was only one Meow.

"Friends, Romans, countrymen," Brian was articulating in what would never have passed for great Shakespearian acting. "I am Dr. Strangeglow and I invite you to uncover the mysteries of the past with me."

From overhead, the sound of thunder, then holographic bolts of lightning sparkled across the ceiling. A muted round of applause for the natural effect rippled through the crowd. The actor took their approval as his cue to step up the presentation.

"Tonight, we present a comedy written, acted, directed and staged by the Starlight Thespians."

The applause this time was loud and appreciative. As the host bowed, back-lighting lit the stage, revealing a small, round table and four chairs. On the walls of the seer's apartment were images of Tarot cards, ancient deities and various three-dimensional depictions of intergalactic moons.

A loud knock on the "door" began the production.

"Come in," Dr. Strangeglow beckoned. Four "seekers of the supernatural," dressed in various costumes of surrealistic design, entered. An excited intake of breath announced to the players their audience was receptive.

"Amazing, isn't it?" Helen observed, her own eyes bright with wonder. "How different people look when they're dressed in civilian clothing. We've all been wearing our uniforms so long, I've forgotten what we look like as people."

Nodding in agreement, Joshua leaned forward, elbows resting on his knees as they supported his head. Eerie flute music, filtered in over the intercom, suddenly sprung up out of nowhere. From the shadows of stage left, he could just make out the form of Jingles Gingleheimer playing the instrument. Joshua's mouth went dry, for he had never realized the engineer had such a musical talent. Perhaps with the same thought, the acting petitioners jumped, each staring ludicrously around the room.

"What's that?" thespian Winston Rey inquired with fearful expectation.

"The sound of the angels, Mr. Astro Logical." Waving his arms over his head, Brian grinned. "The spirits are present. And speaking of which...." Drawing Mr. Astro Logical aside, the mystic rubbed thumb and forefinger together. "A little something to keep the home fires burning, sir?"

Reaching into a pretend pocket, Winston withdrew invisible money which the mystic promptly accepted. "Fifty credit markers," the petitioner screamed. Brain reacted sharply, hushing him with a finger to his lips.

"Not so loud! It's gauche to mention such things." Overhead, the music turned sour. "The natives are restless. And make it seventy-five next time. My expenses are killing me."

Astro Logical sat at the table while Strangeglow extracted fees from the others. When all had "paid the piper," he swished his cloak around him for dramatic effect, then joined them, gleefully rubbing his hands together. "Who goes first?"

"I do!" yelled the second man, surreptitiously tugging on a white wig to readjust it. An intake of breath indicated the audience recognized the actor.

"My God," Helen whispered. "Is that Lamar Porteous?"

"It is," Joshua acknowledged.

"I would never have believed it. I took him for a... stuffed shirt."

"He asked to participate," a crewman at their side whispered. The continuation of the play relieved the pair of the obligation of upstaging Brian, the acting seer.

"To whom do you wish to communicate?"

"My late, unlamented business partner. He died –" The sound of thunder immediately burst upon the players. Staring up fearfully, Porteous amended his statement. "My late, *lamented* partner." The rumbling ceased. "Before he passed on, he managed to remove a considerable cache of precious gems from our safe. We were holding them as security for a client, who has now completed his back payments of two million 'parsecs.' I wish to... return them."

"Ah. Either that, or be accused of the crime yourself and sent to Zertan," Strangeglow commiserated, staring out into the audience. "A terrible fate. There, you would be forced to keep company with the likes of stray cats, unruly officers on planet duty, and female researchers."

The audience laughed, staring across at the captain and the "female researcher." Joshua hung his head in embarrassment, but Helen waved in acknowledgment.

"Horrible, indeed," she agreed. "Pity the poor researcher. Being stuck with someone whose vocabulary is limited by the shoulder boards he wears in his mouth."

For her *ad lib,* she was rewarded by loud clapping. Joshua sunk further into his seat. Brian gave him a moment to suffer, then continued.

"I shall inquire of my otherworldly contact." Reaching under the table, he produced a photograph of a cat. Setting it out, he petted it fondly as the audience stamped their feet in approval.

> "Boil, boil, toil and foil,
> Do as bidden
> Mighty spirit of feline soil,
> Where are the gems hidden?"

Tucking his hand behind the picture, Brian tapped it with his fingers, adding "movement." Cat meows filled the small theatre. "Ah. This is interesting. Very interesting."

"Tell me. Quickly," the character within a character pleaded. "I have a shuttle to catch."

Communing with the cat, Brian writhed, rolled his eyes and frothed at the mouth before divining the answer. As the noise subsided, he smiled benignly.

"Your partner traded in the gems for credits. He spent them all on an illicit tryst."

"With whom?"

"Your wife."

Shrieking in indignation, the questioner jumped up and ran off the stage. He was roundly cheered for his performance. Brian turned to Katherine Bacce, attired in a scanty costume which, in itself, was worth the price of admission.

"And you, my dear? What forbidden knowledge do you seek from the stars?"

"Before he died, Admiral Halsey promised me a promotion for services above and beyond the call of duty," she began, giving a credible performance in a Sertanian dialect. "He forgot to inform Space Command. I earned it," she continued, winking at the audience. "And I want it."

"Ah. Yes. For the retirement benefits," the seer deduced, to the delight of the onlookers.

"Rank has its privileges," she agreed. "Being a four-star officer in the Fleet gives me the right to order anyone around. I have a full supply of tooth care products I wish to dispense."

The reference to a story Terry had told of a discipline he may, or may not have been caused to suffer, brought another round of cheering and catcalls.

"An 'admirable' sentiment. Let me see if I can manipulate the Powers that Be, and promote you." Brian waved his hands over the table. Smoke issued forth in tiny swirls, curling around his fingers. "Lovely. Lovely. There!" A huge puff of reddish smoke emerged. "It is done. Your service record has been amended. You are now an officer."

Jumping up, Katherine did a dance around the table to the accompaniment of different, but equally ethereal flute music. "Never let it be said," she remarked, directing her comments to the audience, "that promotions in the Star Service are not based on merit!"

With a melodramatic swirl, she exited stage left. From behind him, Paula Burbone kicked the captain's chair. Craning his neck, Joshua caught her eye and grinned.

"Well, *you* did have a meteoric rise in position," he whispered, raising his eyebrow suggestively.

"And wait until you see what I do with my new authority," she warned, causing him to turn back quickly. The crew clapped, fully aware of the exchange. Several stood, catcalling and taking advantage of their relaxed status to unwind and finally have a laugh at another's expense.

What they didn't know, was that the joke was on them.

Waving the audience be seated, the captain succeed with all but one. Refusing to heed the friendly order, Leonard Broderick stepped out into the center aisle, eyes red-rimmed. No one in the theatre attributed the cause to excess mirth.

"Brother Brian," the crewman began, voice wavering between pathos and anger. "I want to be next."

More surprised than he should have been, were his mind anywhere but on his lines, Hardy tried to shake him off. "Let us finish the play," he tried, but the super particle analyst was not to be put off. Stepping forward, he extended his arms. Had he not reversed his hands so the palms were upward, his action might have been construed as violent.

"I want you to look into that crystal ball of yours," he cried, tone growing sharper and more demanding. "I want to know what's happening back on Earth. I have a wife there; and a child. What have they been told about our disappearance?"

"We haven't *disappeared,*" Terry responded, getting to his feet, then gliding over to Broderick's side. Motioning others back who would have assisted, he faced the jittery man alone. "We're still here. Remember?"

"We're not 'here.' We're not anywhere. And we're not going anywhere!" the scientist cried, sweat staining his uniform in an irregularly shaped line from collarbone to navel. "I want to know what they're doing about our situation."

They are not doing anything would have been the truthful reply, but the captain eschewed it for a more tactful, albeit slightly less honest answer.

"Once they determine we haven't made our routine communication, they'll address the problem."

"When will that be? When are they coming for us?" Broderick pulled away from Terry, making his way toward the stage. "My wife... my daughter. I want them to know I'm all right. You tell them!" he continued, pointing at the mystic. "Sit down now and contact them!"

Brian nodded agreeably, moving back toward the table. He did not sit, however and the rest of his thespians shuffled away, leaving him alone on stage.

"As you can see, I don't have my real crystal ball with me. It's in my quarters. Why don't you come with me and we'll get it?"

"No. Do it here. Now. You can't put me off. Use telepathy; send a prayer, Father. Anything. But do it now. I've waited too long."

Gesturing behind the man's back for Brian to cooperate, Terry crept closer. When he saw the minister had Broderick's full attention, he skillfully chopped him, striking at the base of the neck. Broderick gave a faint cry, then toppled forward.

When he was sure the man was out and secure, Joshua briefly addressed the crowd.

"That's all, ladies and gentlemen. We'll ask our actors to finish the production another time."

Amidst the grumbling and disquietude of the crew, he made his way to the stage. With Brian's help, they dragged Broderick into the wings. Helen was already there with a stretcher.

"I'll take him," she offered.

"Not to his quarters; to Sick Bay II," he ordered, placing the emphasis on the word "two." Or, to one of the offices. Isolate him until we're sure he's under control."

"Yes, sir."

As the language expert, doing business as Chief Medical Officer, prepared Broderick for removal, Brian sagged into a chair, head drooping. Guilt reeked from his pores.

"I'm sorry, Josh. It's my fault."

"It's nobody's fault –"

"I should have anticipated something like this. The subject matter of our play – it was ill-advised. I just wanted to make people laugh... forget about our situation. Instead, I brought it to the fore."

He was right. There was little the captain could offer in consolation, either to the cleric-turned-actor-turned-failed playwright, or to his crew. Leonard Broderick wanted no more than the rest of them. The only difference was, he had broken the code of silence to ask for it.

"I'm sick to death of being hungry." The comment was made by Chief Engineer Gingleheimer, although it might have come from any assembled in the crew's mess. The effects of the aborted theatricals had left them all testy and restless. Shoving aside his glass of water, he stared angrily at Burbone. "Why aren't you eating? What did you have that's better than this?"

"Nothing," she replied, tensing her muscles. "I'm not hungry."

"That's a damned lie. We're all hungry. We're starving. We can't subsist on this. Even since they cut the rations from three to two tablets, we've been hungry. Drinking all the water in the galaxy only adds to bloating. No one believes that story the Captain told of not needing the full measure. We've been lied to. What happened? We were supposed to have enough nutritional tablets to last sixteen years."

"Nothing's changed," she tried, but he was not to be put off.

"We were willing to go along with the lie, but that was before we realized what a difference it would make. Now, it's time we were told the truth."

His complaint found sympathetic ears. Pushing back their trays, several of the assembled assumed positions of hostility, arms crossed over their chests, or dallying close to the unnecessary eating utensils, which could, in a moment, be easily converted into weapons.

As the ranking officer present, Burbone became their target of inquiry. Biding for time in the hope their anger would burn itself out, she made a point of relaxing in her chair, her stump draped conspicuously over her knees.

Ruing her own words that the crew need not be informed of command decisions, she assumed an air of casual concern she didn't feel.

"This ship is being run according to regulations. You are an officer, Mr. Gingleheimer. No one need remind you of your responsibility."

"Well, I'm not an officer," Hernando Diaz objected, getting to his feet. "I'm a hungry engineer." Rather than confront Burbone face-to-face, he kept his distance, separated by the table. His position was more emotional than physical, yet one wrong move on her part could prompt him to reach over to grab her.

"What's happening in Hydroponics? I thought there was some discussion we were to be allowed inside. To get a sense of growing things. Breathe a different type of oxygenated air. Absorb the colors. Green," he whispered, almost as a prayer. "Now, all of a sudden we're not allowed there. Carson can't – or won't – say. What's gone wrong?" She hesitated too long. "It's not as though we *need* those plants. Is it?" he suddenly demanded.

"There wouldn't be any reason for that? Would there be?" Paula challenged, responding with quiet dignity to the first real threat of her authority since assuming the rank of commander. She was not without emotion, however, and the fingers on her intact left hand tightened as her self-control wavered.

"The seeds. They're not growing?" he demanded, getting around the question. "We all agreed that instead of eating what we found, we'd sacrifice them for the chance to establish a hydroponics lab. We were promised all sorts of variety. To break the monotony of the tablets. Now, we don't even have them."

"We all saw what happened to Broderick," Jingles charged.

"That had nothing to do with nutrition."

"Yes. It did. When a man's hungry, everything starts preying on his mind. None of us are exempt. Not even you," he dared charge.

"You're right," she surprised him by agreeing. "I'm hungry, like the rest of you. Like Captain Terry and Officers Fitzgerald and Hardy. That's because our bodies adjusted to the over-supply of nutrients before we made the change. We have to give them time to readjust to the proper quantity. I don't like it. They don't like it. None of you do. But, too much of anything is as bad as too little. The liver and the kidneys become affected because they can't store what's being ingested. Then, we're in real trouble because we don't have a physician here to advise us."

She stood, becoming more agitated as her brain worked furiously on the lie she was concocting that had become all too real to deny. "Brian Hardy complained about pains in his stomach. That's how we first realized something was wrong because as soon as he aired his problems, we all started feeling it. All right," she agreed, holding up her hands. "We may be wrong. We talked about it. None of us are physicians. To be honest, the discussion came down to two against two. Drs. Fitzgerald and Hardy argued against cutting the ration," she hurried on, finding the ability to weave some truth into the explanation made it easier. "They didn't want to cut the rations. They were afraid exactly something like this would happen."

Moving out from behind the table, the others instinctively backed away from her as though her sudden outburst was caused by madness rather than desperation.

"Captain Terry and I opted to go against them. It was a command decision. If you've noticed the tension between us, that's why. I'll go further, since you're insistent on knowing the truth. We decided to take the extra tablets, dissolve them in water and feed them to the plants. Not the sprouts; the hybrid seeds we started to grow. The ones which offer us real subsistence. Breads. Cereals. Protein. Food we can chew and taste." She picked up one of the useless forks they set out from habit rather than necessity. "We all crave that so badly. They require a great deal of supplemental nutrition to produce what we need. That will necessarily cut down on our supply of tablets. We thought it was worth the gamble."

Those gathered around her reacted with wonder. They wanted to believe.

"How… is it going?" Jingles asked in a hushed voice.

"Not as well as we anticipated. But, it may be too soon to tell. We're trying everything we can. You're right about hating the tablets. I think that, more than the reduced ration is what's driving us over the edge. I realize many civilizations rely on them exclusively; but, that's because they were weaned on that form of nutrition. We haven't been. Most of us seem to… lack that adaptability. We want to *eat*."

"No argument there."

"That's why you haven't been admitted to Hydroponics. That was the plan – you're correct. To step inside and get a sense of growing plants. To see, smell, *feel* the generation of new life. Crops that will thrive and develop and propagate for years to come. Even be transplanted onto the soil of a new planet we eventually discover. That hasn't happened, yet. But, it will. I believe that and Captain Terry believes it. We have a goal. If we made a mistake in not explaining this to you, I apologize. We didn't want to raise expectations because it may take time. We didn't know how long. Rather than disappoint, we opted to keep the plan to ourselves. Now, you know."

Maurice Kincaid spoke for the rest.

"Thank you, sir. We asked for the truth and you gave it to us. It makes sense and we appreciate the honesty."

Paula waited until she was sure they had actually settled down, finally seeking confirmation by asking Jingles, "Are you all right. Have I explained it to your satisfaction?"

"Yes. You've explained it."

"Then, I'll leave you. I… appreciate everything you do," she added from the heart. "I know it's hard. We'll get through this."

Jingles raised a hand as she left, giving her an uneasy feeling of camaraderie. Had she known he had kept one of the original tablet bottles and memorized the simple instructions to take *three* tablets, one of each color, with a full glass of water, she might have felt differently.

Then again, she might not have.

CHAPTER 10

On the bridge, she found Captain Terry standing by the viewscreens studying the configurations displayed before his eyes. At the moment he was the only one present. Cautiously approaching, Paula waited until he acknowledged her.

"Good evening."

"I'm not sure that it is, sir."

Turning away from the star-studded vista he returned to the captain's chair and sat. She followed him, positioning herself slightly to his left before speaking.

"I've made a grave mistake, sir."

"I'll be the judge of that."

"I just came from a confrontation with the crew. In the mess hall."

"All right."

"We were eating together. Which is to say, we were drinking water together while washing down our ration of two nutritional tablets."

"Must not have taken long."

"They were upset about the theatrics and Leonard Broderick. I thought by sitting with them I might ease their tension somewhat. By showing solidarity."

"I approve."

"Chief Jingles complained about being hungry and the discussion turned to the reduction in rations. They believed that was one reason Broderick fell apart. I felt it incumbent on me to try and explain. They didn't want to be lied to. They wanted the truth."

"And so you told it to them?"

"No, sir. I offered them a more complicated falsehood. I told them it was true the rations were cut because we had all been receiving too much nutrition. I explained how the additional protein and vitamins would damage the kidneys and liver. But, I couldn't stop there because that wasn't enough. So, I told them the extra tablets – one-third of our rations we didn't need for ourselves – were going to feed the plants. I explained on how we counted on the hybrids to eventually sustain us by providing all the dietary nutrients our bodies required, with the added benefit of having bulk. That they would provide us something to chew, taste and enjoy. Breads.

Cereals. Whatever else we could think of. What a relief it would be to have real food, again."

He waited, aware there was more to the story.

"When they asked why they weren't allowed in Hydroponics, I explained that the plants weren't thriving. That, in fact, they were languishing. I said we didn't them – the crew – to become discouraged, so we placed the area off-bounds."

"How did they react?"

"They believed me, sir. They… thanked me for being honest with them. I wasn't, of course."

"How did that make you feel?"

"Not how I expected."

"And, how was that?"

"Initially, proud of myself for facing a crisis. Of thinking fast and restoring order."

"And instead, you feel as though you betrayed them."

"Yes, sir."

"Welcome to the secret world of command, Officer Burbone."

"It's not what I thought it would be, Captain."

"It's not what any of us thought; those who've been tested by fire. We're taught and we tend to believe that being a commander means battle decisions. Strategy. Heroic actions. Personal bravery. Split-second decisions with a positive but not always perfect outcome. What we fail to realize is those outcomes are not only rare and far between, but they turn out to be the easiest part of the job. It's the day-to-day personnel decisions we make; the judgments between what to reveal and what to hold confidential. How to handle situations of trust, that really proves the leader. I think you not only handled it properly, you displayed great insight and courage."

"They asked for me to be honest with them and I wasn't."

"You were far more honest than they had a reason to expect. If a lie is told, they have to believe I, or you, or anyone else, will adhere to that lie. You didn't. You expanded it by giving them half a truth. We are using the extra tablets to feed the plants. We do expect them to thrive and become the staple of our diet. We did block ingress to Hydroponics to save them from seeing how far away we are from that point. What you told them was concise, reasonable and verifiable. It also saves us from worrying that Carson may inadvertently – or purposely – revealing our secret, thus solidifying one half of our story."

He indicated she sit in the command chair and she did so, turning it to face him.

"By doing that, you preserved the more important truth: that we're running out of food. To have given them the entire truth would have left them angry and frightened. At the moment, we can't handle that. We're playing for time. We need everyone being supportive so we can deal with the next crisis."

"The failure of the plants?"

"The unexpected-expected arrival of some unknown, sentient life forms that will either help us, ignore us or destroy us."

The manner in which he expressed the sentiment caught her off-guard.

"How would Dr. Fitzgerald react to your description of 'her' aliens?"

"She'd say questioning their motives was better than outright denial."

Paula readjusted her position, turning slightly away from him.

"May I ask you a question?"

"You may."

"If Dr. Fitzgerald hadn't had her... vision. If we didn't have the option of considering outside intervention, how would you have handled the situation after you discovered the cargo was mislabeled and we were critically short on food?"

"The same thing. Except that I would have selected a planet that held the optimal chance of being habitual, set the coordinates toward it and went in that direction at full speed."

"That was what Brother Brian suggested."

"I didn't say he was wrong."

"Thank you, sir. You've made me feel better. I was afraid I'd ruined everything."

"There's no going back to the Academy for you."

Startled, she asked, "Sir?"

"Isn't that what you've thought? That if we're somehow rescued and returned to Earth, you'd be sent back to complete your education?"

"Yes. But, how could you have guessed that?"

"Because I've already considered it. Months ago. We were both wrong. The requirement you complete your degree is no longer valid. You've proven yourself. The Academy diploma is already hanging on your wall. Your next assignment would be on another star cruiser as a senior officer."

"I'll only accept it if you're the captain, sir."

She didn't expect him to answer, but he did.

"We make a good team, don't we?"

"Yes, sir."

"Shall we take the rest with us?"

"All of them. Even Jingles."

For a moment she thought he would smile. She was correct, but slightly off target.

"Then, Commander, we might as well stay where we are. Because we've already got all that."

Which put a period on their discussion.

As a point of punctuation, language expert Helen Fitzgerald would have to agree.

He was dreaming. Before Encounter, he never remembered any of his nighttime wanderings. He might even have argued he never dreamt. Since that time, however, nightmares were his constant companion. He need not have wondered why. Stress, combined with a perverted form of insomnia were a poor mix. Yet, there was no question but that his mind was warped by the convolutions of sleep. That awareness brought no comfort.

"Red Alert! Red Alert!" Joshua Terry was shouting, although there was no need. The sirens were blasting from the walls, nearly shattering his ear drums with their high-pitched noise. No words, issued from mortal lips, could possibly have been heard over the destructive din. In this case, knowledge was powerless to seek redress.

Not surprisingly, *Target* was in the throes of self-destruction. Parts of the bridge were coming unhinged. He ducked, but the missile, hurtling from some dark corner, struck him squarely on the head. Shrieking in pain, he watched as his nostrils burst forth crimson fluid. Raising a hand to staunch the flow, he realized with unutterable horror, both hands had been severed at the wrists.

"No! This is a nightmare! I'm transposing images!"

Reality was impotent.

"I won't live through Encounter again!"

The alternative, clearly, was that he would die through it.

"There has to be another answer!"

Before his eyes floated the image of Brian Hardy. Joshua did not question the incongruity. Brian had not been on the bridge when the ship touched the ribbon of dark matter.

"Brian! Help me. Tell me what to do!"

The good brother beneficently smiled. Bowing his head, he uttered a one word suggestion.

Pray. His mouth did not move. He communicated telepathically. *The Lord helps those who help themselves.*

"Tell that to Captain Nguyen!" Terry screamed, pointing an arm toward the prone body sprawled at the base of the command chair. Not even in his dream could he resurrect the dead.

A crack of thunder-like intensity, then the ceiling caved in, drowning him in a sea of pincer-hot sparks. Terry fell to his knees. As the deck rolled, he plunged headfirst onto the floor, driving his lower teeth into the soft palate of the upper. Without a doubt, his jaw was broken, permanently disfiguring him.

Frankenstein's Monster flashed through his dimming subconscious.

"It isn't real! This can't be happening again!"

Another jolt, then a horrific tearing sound of tortured infrastructure, as a portion of the ship was blown away. Hurled across the debris-strewn floor, he came in sharp contact with a disembodied hand. He gagged, then imitated the action of a malfunctioning shuttle by skirting sideways, so that he was in position to kick it away. Despite his best attempts, the hand would not dislodge.

He cursed, not caring that a moment before it had been attached to a living, breathing crewman. One of his own arms, perhaps.

Another sound took precedence over Red Alert. The ship's bell. He froze, counting the chimes. One. Two. Three. Four. Five. It was five bells: two-thirty o'clock. His rapid translation irritated, rather than soothed his nerves. Craning his neck in an anatomically impossible one-hundred and eighty degree turn, he waved a mysteriously reappeared fist at Nguyen.

"This is all your fault! No one else in the fleet uses that damned antiquated system of keeping time. It's an embarrassment."

Without doubt, the dark matter had been placed exactly where it would strike *Target* to eradicate that arcane method of marking the passage of hours. "Bells" were for sailing vessels, not space craft. The gods of deep space had been offended.

"Deep space," he growled, glancing upward in time to see a light fixture come crashing down, "is redundant. You can't have blacker than black. You can't be deader than dead. There is no such thing as 'shallow space.'"

More repetition from a damaged psyche.

Fire spurted from the severed veins and arteries of the inhuman illuminators, spreading across the deck with malignant force. Before he could scramble away, the cuffs of his trousers ignited. The fire-retardant material dissolved as though it were actually made of paper or wax. The pain from seared flesh had a stimulating effect, arousing him to a frenzy of passion. He threw back his head and howled.

There was no one to hear, no one to help. The burnished gold of his uniform shirt turned black, then wafted off his arms like bits of tossed confetti. He sneezed and felt a lung burst.

"Get out! Run for it!"

No possible way of executing that command. His legs would not support him. Joshua Terry crawled on hands and knees, reaching the roundabout after an hour, two hours. That made it seven bells. He cursed again.

"Hell's bells!"

The cadence of the rhyme made him smile, and he was laughing hysterically as the lift doors closed behind him. Choking on his mirth, he directed his gaze upward at the controls, as though they were a long-lost friend.

"Level Four," he directed.

"Level Four," the mechanical voice, strikingly real and femininely alluring, repeated. "Fasten your seat belt."

The device was not programmed to respond in that manner. He stared around himself, madly trying to ascertain whether or not he were alone.

"Who's here?" No answer. Smoke poured in from gaping holes, causing him to cough, then choke. His heartbeat accelerated, racing beyond the speed of light.

"That's impossible," Helen reassured him. She had not been there a second ago. "I've checked the Med Doc computer. A heart cannot beat that fast." Reaching out a hand, she attempted to take his pulse. Her fingers were cold. Ice cold. Corpse cold.

"Get away from me!"

The doors parted and he plunged into the swirling darkness of Engineering. Tendrils of even blacker fog wrapped themselves around him, yanking him down. Those he could not shake off weighed him down.

"Move. Keep moving."

To his left he glimpsed Jingles. The engineer was playing his flute. Seeing the captain, he lifted a hand in friendly greeting. Unaccountably, removing his fingers from the instrument did not affect his performance. Terry's mind filled with music. The incongruity of the scene maddened him.

"The ship has been struck! We're going down!"

The engineer professed not to hear. He resumed his playing.

"Stay behind, if that's what you want. I'm getting out of here."

Shaking off the leaden restraints around his ankles, Joshua groped ahead, making it to the Skip hanger. An overwhelming sense of freedom, couched in the guise of vertigo, assailed him.

"Get out. I've got to get out."

A crew-woman stood by the entrance portal, blocking his way. Her face wore an accusatory expression.

"You know the way out. Take me with you," she begged.

Recognition came slowly. Finally putting a name to the face, Terry's eyes flew open in dread.

"Annie Devine."

He might as easily cried, "Oh, dear God!"

Attempting to retreat, he found a wall of impenetrable smoke blocking his path. Overhead, just within earshot came the filtered notes of Jingles' flute. Terry irrationally decided the big man controlled the viscosity of the smoke by the tempo of his music. At the moment, he was playing the climax to the "William Tell Overture."

Compelled to deal with a ghost from his recent past, Joshua extended his arms as a gesture of conciliation and a more latent act, he hoped, of preventing her from coming any nearer.

"Please," he began, attempting to articulate slowly, although his impulse was to scream. "You're dead. You don't need me to show you the way out."

"Take me with you. Don't leave me, again." Her eyes were sunken, glossed over by the film of death. He could see clearly she was not breathing. He decided it had been her voice in the elevator.

"I'll send someone back for you." He had said those words before, with equal truthfulness. This time, however, Annie was armed with hindsight.

"Dr. Young is coming," she jeered, revealing chipped and blackened teeth. He cringed at her reference. Too many times had the survivors evoked the name of Dr. Lee Young, expecting the chief medical officer to appear and save the wounded. In every instance they had been rebuffed.

Realizing he was in a nightmare did not lessen the blood-curdling terror of hearing that promise from the lips of the unsaved.

"If you know where Dr. Young is, go to him. He can show you the way; reunite you with the others. So you won't be alone."

His voice choked at the misery of his suggestion. He had never meant to lie to her and Annie's unrest now affected him deeply, in levels of his subconscious he seldom reached.

From behind, the music reached a crescendo. As the discharge of cannons roared, the mutable wall spasmed inward, propelling him forward.

Losing his balance, the captain stumbled, his corporeal body passing through the goblin shape of the technology specialist. When he recovered his footing, he was past her.

Annie seemed not to have noticed. She was speaking again, but this time, to a figure beyond the wall. Not wanting to see the distorted body of Lee Young, Terry raised an arm over his eyes and plunged ahead. Before him was a Skip. The entrance portal was open. Sobbing like a child, he raced inside, quickly reaching the cockpit. Strapping himself in, he discovered the power pods would not engage. The reserve energy had been drained. The two mutineers, Marr and Radcliff, had been there before him and sabotaged the ship. He had forgotten.

Struggling wildly to extricate himself from the "X" shaped safety straps, he emerged from the shuttle, breath coming in ragged, irregular gasps.

Smoke was creeping into the hanger. Beyond the grey, swirling cloud he could just see a form take shape. For the first time in his life, he prayed, *Dr. Young is not coming.*

With a wail of furious despair, Terry wildly scanned the suddenly crowded hanger. There was no point trying to escape on any of the other shuttles. They had all been eviscerated for scrap parts.

Never underestimate the cunning of evil minds.

A bulkhead blew, sucking the Skips out into deep space. Unsecured equipment hurtled past his head. From peripheral vision he noted the flashing red warning signal: *Atmosphere has been compromised.*

He held his breath. Stopped breathing. His lungs – whether he had one or two functioning organs – burst, forcing him to gulp air.

"Must get out!"

Without questioning how he could breathe, or why he had not been swept away like so many others after Encounter, he continued running, this time without direction.

"Keep looking."

Blue-filtered light, made hazy by myriad particles of dust, lit his way. The effect simulated moonlight. Were it not for the maniacal pounding in his head, he might have felt romantic.

I'm perverted, he thought.

"Escape."

Where to go?

The holding bays. He had forgotten all about them. There just might be a Skip there. Nonsense. *The holding bays have been blown away. The outer walls disintegrated.* He had seen that from his initial inspection on the bridge after the original disaster. Or had he? Which time? After Encounter, or in one of his too frequent nightmares? He no longer possessed the ability to distinguish fact from fantasy.

What did it matter?

"Keep going."

His progress slowed to a crawl. Glancing down, he realized his feet were stuck in a morass of congealed blood. He slipped, righted himself, inched forward. He tripped over a severed leg and went down. Bile filled his mouth.

"Spit it out!"

He tried but found he could not expel the sticky matter. He swallowed, choked, then remembered he was ravenously hungry. Scooping his hand into the knee-high conglomeration, he made a ball of the putrid mass, then crammed it past his teeth. He found he could not chew it, so gulped it whole. Rather than vomit over the flavor, he found it delicious.

Sick bastard.

Cannibal.

"Get out."

Eating his way through, he made a path. Why hadn't he thought of this before?

Good question.

Only in dreams.

"I'm not dreaming."

The door to the cargo bay was sealed. "Open sesame." He waved his hand before the electric eye. Showmanship. Memories of childhood rhymes, like Helen's poems from space. Conveniently, the door parted. He took a step, then retracted his forward movement, realizing almost too late there was no floor. It had been torn away. Just beyond his grasp was a Skip, suspended in midair. Hovering, like a monster, the emissions from its engines flaring in fair imitation of dragon's breath.

Launching himself into the air, which was not air at all, but the vacuum of space, he floated toward the small spacecraft. If only he could get inside, he would be safe.

Safe. Wall safe. Safe and sorry. *All-ee, all-ee in free.*

Stretching his fingers, he groped, grasped, pried with his fingernails, pounded on the door. No response.

"Let me in!"

He struck too hard. The ship floated away, tantalizingly out of reach. Balancing on the balls of his feet, he tried to hold it back. Too short. Just missed. He tried again, curling his toes around thin air, straining, stretching, willing his arms to extend beyond their limits.

"Come back."

Too far. His "toehold" gave way. Wildly gesticulating, he spun off into the absence of light, floating, a punctured balloon. Swimming in nothingness. Dream reality faded.

"Wake up," he ordered himself. As a dutiful officer, be obeyed.

Joshua's eyelids fluttered open. He was drenched in perspiration, tangled in his blanket. His nerves were jangled, causing his limbs to jerk and twitch. All around him was blackness. His brain was screaming. Breathing was impossible.

"Hell!" he gasped.

A good approximation.

"Nightmare."

He had been closer the first time.

Cargo Bay.

The perspiration on his body turned cold. He shivered. Wrapping his arms around himself, Terry stood, flexed his muscles then did a dozen deep knee bends before allowing his mind to return to the netherworld it had barely escaped.

Most of what he dreamed was easily understandable. The images were all lifted from reality. While each in their own way were chilling, he did not require the professional services of an analyst to interpret them. Some he had juxtaposed; others were augmented, or abbreviated.

Except for the two cargo bays. While it was accurate to say he had scanned the outside of the ship, determining the two auxiliary bays had been destroyed, one had proven serviceable enough to store the ice they had extracted from a meteor. The condition of the other, although appearing grossly deteriorated, had never actually been explored. Up until this point, there had been no need. The fact he had gone to it in his dream made him wonder if parts of it had survived Encounter.

And if it had, what was the significance?

During routine assignments, cargo bays were utilized only when bulky consignments were to be delivered to distant waystations, and then, merely as supplemental storage space. With heavy traffic coming and going, cargo Skips occasionally docked outside, were unloaded and sent back. To his knowledge, they had not been utilized for that purpose in over two years. Whatever had come through those portals was long dispersed.

But then, his knowledge was not absolute.

"This is nonsense," he argued, pulling his uniform tunic, the color of muted gold, over his head. "It was just a dream. I was looking for an avenue of escape; trying to distance myself from the dirty work Marr and Radcliff did to the Skips."

The argument was valid. No one in their right mind acted on the images of nighttime wanderings.

Terry would have been the last to protest he was in his right mind.

He was half way down the corridor before he stopped. Remembrances of another dream and a solitary trip assailed his mind. By disregarding his own rules that no crewmember ever wander the corridors alone, he had nearly lost his life.

Fool me once, shame on you. Fool me twice, shame on me.

Running his third eye over the duty roster, the captain dismissed those awake and available. Not because he lacked trust in their discretion. Rather, he did not care to look the fool in their eyes. Dragging a crew member to the bowels of the ship on an errant mission would make them question his judgment. That left him with three choices for a companion: Brian, Helen or Paula. Of all aboard, only they could be expected to keep their opinions of his illogical behavior to themselves

Helen was his first choice. Tiptoeing silently to her quarters, he whispered an announcement of his presence and received no reply. Daring to manually open the door, an act he was loath to perform without permission, he discovered her missing. That meant she was on Level Four, in the Observatory. He would not enter there for the world.

Not when she was communing with the stars.

Hardy was his second option. There was no personal risk of re-entering their shared sleeping apartment unannounced and he did so without a second thought. Brian was curled onto his makeshift bunk, fast asleep. A gentle nudge of his shoulder failed to rouse him.

"Sleep tight, old friend," he whispered and retreated. If Brian were that tired, it would be cruel to wake him. They were all functioning without adequate repose. If the minister had finally fallen into a deep slumber, then he needed his rest. And the chance to dream.

Better ones than the captain experienced, he hoped.

Waking Paula was the least attractive of his options. Although she slept alone in a converted office, he had made the mistake once of rousing her for a late night conference. To commit the same act again was tantamount to insanity. His relationship with Helen was already strained. Having to explain why he summoned Paula instead of her would exacerbate her suspicions. Once too often.

He had almost made up his mind to go alone and take his chances when he remembered the communicators. He could try waking her with one of those. That way, if Paula rose and left the apartment, it could not be assumed she was on a mission to join him.

Activating the small, hand-held device, he punched in the code for her unit. Rather than speak a verbal message, he tapped in a short series of numbers. They would not mean anything. If he succeeded in rousing her, however, she would undoubtedly try to locate whoever had summoned her.

The rouse worked. Within minutes, his second in command was beside him. This time, she was fully dressed, indicating she either slept in her clothes, or did not want to make it appear she was dressing.

"What's up?" she whispered.

"Want to come on an adventure? One that probably won't lead anywhere?"

By couching his request in such a way, he hoped to mitigate expectations.

"You know I do. Where to?"

"Level Four. The holding bays."

He did not have to see her expression to read puzzlement.

"You're looking for something trapped in the ice?"

"No. The one beyond it."

"I believed it to be demolished. We've seen the cavity in the side of the ship."

"That's true. But, we've never really taken a closer look. That requires inspection with a Skip, which, until recently, we didn't have. Or, manual exploration in spacesuits. I've been down there before to help remove ice chips but I've never gone beyond it into the second bay. It didn't seem worth the risk."

"Yes, sir," she agreed, falling into step beside him. "Eventually, we'll have to make a thorough inspection. As much as life for us has crawled along, it's actually flown by. In half a year we've only started to see improvements in our living conditions. What made you think of the holding bays now?"

"A dream," he confessed, feeling foolish. "A nightmare, actually. I was trying to escape –"

"No surprise," her voice overlapped.

"– and found myself down there. There wasn't anything, really... no floor, no ceiling. Just a Skip, floating in space. I don't expect to find a shuttle," he added in case reassurance was necessary. "Just – something. Who knows? I'm not that familiar with Level Four. Captain Nguyen might have ordered supplies stored there," he listlessly added.

"No need to explain. Calling it an 'adventure' is good enough for me."

She meant it and he believed her. Paula did not ask why she had been chosen to accompany him and he did not volunteer the information. Stepping inside the lift, they maintained an adequate distance between them before disembarking at Engineering. He made an obvious point of not looking toward the left, in the direction of the Observatory. Paula pretended not to notice.

"Who's on duty down here?" she inquired when they were safely past.

"Bacce," he informed her, putting a finger to his lips.

"Going to alert her we're poking around?" she responded, copying his example as a means of agreeing with the denial she anticipated.

"Wasn't planning to."

The decision was left standing. Weaving their way down the corridor, the two officers bypassed the Security office. Without seeing the technician, both felt her presence. It was reassuring without offering familiarity.

"We'll have to don protective suits. If I'm wrong – and I presume I will be – we'll be opening a door onto nothingness."

"So, we secure ourselves in order not to be swept away. That shouldn't be any problem. If we don't discover anything, we can simply add it to our report in the morning. It will save us that much effort later."

This journey to the cargo bay was far more pleasant than the one accomplished in a dream state. Finding the corridors empty, the walls solid and their conversation the only noise to break the stillness was reassuring.

Crossing the hanger and moving into the secure connecting space between it and the first cargo chamber, Joshua indicated a row of spacesuits hung along the back wall. Arms and legs of each unit were positioned at thirty degree angles, so that they resembled headless stick figures. Each were gently rippled by a low pressure blower positioned above, maintaining an artificial circulation to keep the complex interior fabric viable.

"It looks like they're breathing," Paula whispered. Joshua agreed with a half grin, remembering the first time he had been exposed to the phenomenon.

"When I was a cadet, it used to be said space gremlins occupied them. We blamed the gremlins any time one of us messed up."

Paula clucked her tongue, then mitigated the less-than-flattering noise by adding, "We said the same thing when I was in training."

The cherry-red suits all bore the emblems of the UPE on the right arm, while below the left collarbone the word "TARGET" was emblazoned over a miniature depiction of the ship. Surnames, in a phosphorescent silver were situated directly across, on the right side.

Bypassing the first, identified as "Nguyen," Joshua picked out his own suit. With Paula's assistance, he slipped easily into the protective womb. Encased inside, he wiggled his arms for inspection.

"Too big. We've all lost weight." Waiting a moment, the interior mechanism of the suit spontaneously worked to conform itself to the new body contours. Running his gaze down the closet, he indicated a suit with the name Vanessa Tolbray on the front.

"Try that one on. If I remember correctly, you and Tolbray are about the same size."

When it became apparent Paula could not dress herself one-handed, Terry offered his help, securing the fastenings so that the suit fit snugly.

"Who was Vanessa Tolbray?" she asked, subconsciously employing the correct verb while reaching overhead to the upper shelf where the helmets were stored.

"A Skip pilot."

"Did you know her well?"

"I didn't know any of them as well as I thought," he admitted. "Do you mind?"

"Wearing a Skip pilot's suit? Not at all. I don't condemn all for the transgressions of the few." When he made no comment, Paula glanced sharply at him. "Do you?"

"I don't know," he cautiously replied, balancing the weight of his own helmet in his hands. "I think perhaps I do."

"Shall I take another? I wish I had one of my own," she continued without pause. "But ensigns on training missions aren't issued private suits."

"No," he agreed, affixing the helmet over her ears. "I remember when I got my first one – with my name on it," he added, gently brushing his hand over the letters "Terry." "I had finally come into my own in the Fleet."

"Considering the value, it's no wonder. I heard one of these costs thousands of credit marks."

It took him a moment before he realized she was joking. Working a smile up, Joshua tapped her lightly on the head.

"And I suppose you wouldn't have been excited?"

Paula matched his expression while flexing the fingers of her left hand beneath the attached glove.

"I'm excited enough now to change my name to Tolbray."

"Yes, well, reign in your enthusiasm. Come on. Let's make this brief. A quick look around ought to be enough."

When they had tested interior environment and communications, Terry indicated he would depressurize the chamber. Waiting until he received a thumbs-up, he performed the simple operation. As the green light turned to red, they made their way forward, floating easily across the threshold to the second door.

"I feel like a little kid investigating a haunted house," Paula analyzed, her youth and eagerness getting the better of her normally staid demeanor.

"Let's hope we don't find any ghosts," was the best he could muster in return, for Terry was not only older, he had the disadvantage of a nightmare to cloud his enjoyment. "All right," he cautioned, depressing the touch pad to open the door. "Stand ready." Signifying she understood by a quick salute, Paula attempted to calm herself, then as the massive, rolling wall responded, she boldly walked through. He followed, making certain the opening remained stable before going further.

The overwhelming darkness was too deep to penetrate with their eyes. Not until they had activated the lights designed into the arms of their suits could they make out anything of what lay beyond. What they beheld was a massive mountain of ice. Bits of crystal caught the illumination, sparkling like a million distant stars and giving them both pause as they absorbed the majesty of the spectacle. The only mar in the wondrous panorama were small indentations on the side nearest them, where crewmen had extracted small chunks to be used as drinking water.

"It looks as though we've created our own little world here, Captain. A world within a world, within a galaxy. It's breathtaking."

Taking in the sights with new eyes, he nodded, before motioning to the right.

"We'll have to try and go around. I'm not even sure we can."

Guided by their lights, the pair worked their way to the back and then across, occasionally climbing over shelves of irregularly-shaped ice to make it to the rear. Taking a moment to catch their breath, the captain indicated the wall separating the cargo bays. Once straight and firm, a slight buckling indicated the damage sustained by the tremendous force which had ripped *Target* apart.

Motioning they affix guide wires to their suits, he operated the controls in an attempt to slide back the door. It failed to respond. Undeterred, Paula attempted to calm herself, then kicked a leg out. The wall remained intact. He tried again, this time eliciting a slight movement from the massive, rolling bulkhead. A third time provided them with a three-foot ingress.

"Just wide enough," she declared, stepping forward.

What they beheld was a scene of wanton destruction. What had once housed a vast empty storage space was now merely a hole. Jagged edges outlined the areas where the structure had been torn from its foundations.

"Takes your breath away," he remarked, overwhelmed by the force which had so powerfully destroyed that portion of the ship. "Nothing. All gone. I was wrong."

"Not 'nothing,' sir," she advised, shining her torch along the line of the ship. "That wall is still holding. There may be something beyond. I can't be sure, but it looks as though it's intact."

Nodding agreement, Terry made certain their fastenings were secure before proceeding. With a slight shove off the lip of the remaining floor he had seen so clearly in his dream, he floated ahead.

The journey across the open expanse was tedious. Not physically, but mentally, for his concentration was directed between the task at hand and the almost physical shattering of his psyche at the wounds inflicted upon what had become his first command. Without the ability to absorb the wonder, he missed what had, to Paula, become the larger issue. When she cried aloud, his first thought was that his companion had injured herself. The illogic of his reasoning did not lessen the fear.

"Look at me! I'm flying." And indeed, she was, floating meters above him, arms soaring over her head.

Terry could not properly react until he had swallowed the lump in his throat.

"What the hell are you doing?"

While spoken with privileged irritation, she was not fooled. Or if she were, the twenty-four year old ensign-turned-commander did not let on.

"Are you deaf?" she called, her voice sounding terribly young over the spacesuit transmission. Had she actually said, *Peter, Peter, pumpkin eater, Had a wife and couldn't keep her,* he could not have been more shocked. Insubordination was the last thing he had ever expected from her.

He corrected himself with an addendum: *insubordination with humor.*

"You're 'flying'," he correctly identified.

"Good for you, sir. It's been so long since I've been 'outside.' And never when it mattered. I'd forgotten how much fun it is!"

Waving her arms in wild abandon, Paula completed a somersault, then reversed herself, going head over heels. It was too dark to see his expression. The one she supplied in her mind was adequate for her needs, if not reality.

"Come on, Joshua Terry. Let's play!"

"Play?" He might have been an alien, trying a foreign word on his tongue. Apparently he did not succeed in copying her enunciation, for she repeated it.

"Play!"

He did not make a second attempt. It was beyond his power.

CHAPTER 11

"Come back here, immediately."

"No, sir."

Her denial was tauntingly petulant.

"We have work to perform," Joshua argued, pointing toward what remained of the second Holding Bay.

"Of course we do," Paula agreed, hovering tantalizingly beyond his grasp. "But it can wait. Five minutes. Ten. What difference does it make? Whatever's in the Holding Bay isn't going anywhere."

"We'll be missed."

It was a weak try at best. And inadvertently, he set her up for the comeback.

"You know damned well Katherine Bacce is monitoring us. We may have snuck past her, but the moment we left the ship, she had us on sensors. Want to bet she's wishing we had invited her out for a spin?"

To augment her use of the word, Paula began twirling in space. She floated past him, almost close enough to grab. Almost, but not quite. His hand sailed past her.

"You're oxygen deprived," he groused. "Try taking a few deep breaths. It will clear your head wonderfully."

"I'm not. I'm in perfect control."

Which was precisely true. The moment her feet had left the stability of the ship, Paula had experienced the absolute joy of being freed from all constraint. She also realized, where her stoical captain did not, the necessity to lighten the mood. Protestations to the contrary, he had placed too much stock on finding something in the cargo bay. She had no idea whether anything was there or not, but she did realize if they didn't make a game out of something, they would all go mad.

"Catch me," she continued, taunting him. "If you can. Or are you too old to try?"

That turned out to be the magic question. Gritting his teeth in annoyance, Terry maneuvered after her, using his arms and legs, as she had done, to propel himself forward.

"I have boosters in this suit," he warned. "If I activate them, I can catch you in a second. And haul you off to the brig, where you belong."

"I know all about your penchant for locking people up. Brother Brian filled me in on the details. He said you were a stickler for regulations. And he escaped."

"He hypnotized the guards. Or used drugs. It wasn't a fair contest."

"This one isn't either. My suit has projectiles, too. See how far you'll chase me."

Before he could object, Paula activated the device, sailing bravely off into the depths. He had no choice but to follow.

If Brian's multiple escapes from the brig were not a fair contest, neither was this. With her head filled with pure joy, Paula evaded him, dancing tantalizingly just outside his grasp. When she saw she held the advantage, she somersaulted again, this time positioning a well-placed kick toward his face shield. Reacting too slowly, the captain was struck and went tumbling backwards.

"Don't tell me you failed Space Walk 101," she cried. "However did you get your pilot's credentials?"

"I-did-not-fail," he hissed, making a second stab at her. Her body was tensed for the assault, however, and she eluded his grasp.

Swimming merrily away, Paula continued her aerobatics, laughing at his inability to stop her.

"I'm going to assign myself to do this more often." It was a brag and a dare. "I'll think of some excuse —inspecting the exterior of the ship. I'll amend the duty roster while you're recovering."

"From what?"

"A bad case of stuffiness."

This time he managed to get his hands around her wrist. Jerking it upward, he lost his balance, causing them both to tumble. Refusing to abandon that which was so hard won, he maintained his grasp, going over and over, until their two bodies were entangled, arms and legs pointing in opposing directions.

"Damn you, you're acting like a space cadet." Behind the insult, however, she finally heard happiness.

They romped in that manner for what a chronometer would have registered as fifteen minutes, or "half a bell," but which, to the clock in their brains, was an infinity of time. Only when they were out of breath and puffing rapidly, did the commander direct her movement toward their ultimate destination.

"Come on, Captain. Enough of this foolishness. We have work to do. Or have you forgotten?"

"Forgotten, hell. Leave it for another time. It was only a dream." His mood fading, he had begun a slow retreat when Paula called him back.

"We haven't done enough dreaming, lately, Joshua Terry. It doesn't matter what we find – or don't find. We're no worse off if the remnant of the bay is empty, and a lot ahead."

Drawing to a standstill, he waited a long beat, arms floating loosely at his side, before speaking,

"How do you figure?"

"It got us out here, didn't it?"

Because he was behind her, she did not see him nod. She did not have to. Her point had been made. Now, whatever they discovered could not be a disappointment.

As their breathing regulated, the two space children made their way toward the outer rim of *Target*. Manipulating their lights, they easily discovered the manual controls.

"Think they work?"

"Only one way to find out."

Hitting the button with her gloved hand, Paula activated the switch. Amazingly, the door slid open.

Like his vision, much of Holding Bay had been torn away. There was no Skip hoovering in empty space, but what they saw in the small, sealed compartment was even better. Row upon row of crates, carefully fastened against the rear wall, presented themselves to the eager explorers.

"What do you think they contain?" she whispered, suddenly awed by the unexpected revelation of so great a treasure.

"Coffee," he decided.

"And I think there's tea over there. From the East India Trading Company. I recognize their logo."

"You're not British," he demurred, shaking his helmet. The small beam atop the encasement splayed light across the area in drunken abandon.

"No. But I've been to Massachusetts. Want to dump some overboard? 'No taxation without representation.'"

"I'll pay the tax," he reverently avowed. "Besides, Brian would never forgive us. Without tea, he can hardly be expected to read tea leaves."

Moving ahead, Paula touched one of the supply crates. "What do you think is really in here?"

"More than we had before," he rephrased. "Can you believe it?"

It was the right thing to say and the proper moment.

"Yes. I can." Turning her body so she could see through his face shield, Paula reached out, touching him lightly on the helmet. "You knew."

"I wanted to know. There's a difference."

"You're a mystic, sir."

"Joshua," he corrected, remembering Helen's admonition that George Nguyen had failed to familiarize himself with the crew. As her face contorted, he placed his arm on hers. "Paula."

Suddenly embarrassed, the former ensign shut her eyelids. He allowed her a moment for her thoughts to solidify before shoving away.

"Come on, fellow pirate. We have booty to retrieve."

Privately extolling the fact they would not be disappointed if it turned out the cargo contained nothing of value; or worse, if the contents had been ruined by exposure to Encounter, they began excavating. After twenty minutes of hard work, their expectations fell somewhere in the middle.

Nearly half of the containers stored in the adjunct holding bay were destroyed, either by exposure to space or as a result of contact with the dark matter. All that remained of them were empty shells, which, from a distance, had given the illusion of completeness. What lay behind them in the second tier, however, appeared to be intact.

"If you see anything marked 'snack food,' it's mine," Paula joked, carefully prying away a destroyed portion of wall. "I remember ordering a consignment before we left Alturian."

"I know," Joshua agreed. "You were going to set up an illegal concession stand. Space Fleet knew all about it. You were under surveillance. Augmenting one's salary is illegal. Be careful," Joshua warned suddenly, observing her try to remove another protruding obstruction. "We'll have to come back with the proper equipment and burn some of this away. And the edges are sharp. Don't compromise your suit or your gloves."

"I won't." Hefting the large container she retrieved, Paula wrapped her hands around it as though it were a birthday present. "This is all I can handle."

Taking another of equal bulk, Terry indicated they return.

"The rest is secure. Let's see what we have. But don't get your hopes up. Whatever's in here has been exposed to zero gravity and space temperatures for half a year. It's probably ruined."

"Deep frozen, at any rate. I'm ready."

Maneuvering the bulky storage crates was difficult but not impossible in the weightless conditions. Returning to the ship, they managed to part the outside door to full width, carefully bringing the cargo inside. After securing it with cord so the crates would not crash to the floor when exposed to gravity, Terry compressed the chamber with life support.

"I wonder where Bacce is? I thought she would have had a welcoming committee here to greet us."

"Let's be glad she didn't. Not until we see what we've got."

Once the room was warm and the air breathable, the space explorers removed their protective clothing, taking care to stow them before continuing.

"Any markings on the box?"

"No. Just the point of origin – Alturian – and destination; *Target.*"

"Well, at least we know we haven't discovered contraband."

"I was almost hoping we had."

With a snicker which might have been agreement, Terry gasped as he pried away the top covering.

"What is it?" Paula inquired, maneuvering herself awkwardly toward him. With the return of gravity, her muscles had not yet recovered their full flexibility.

If the captain had been a religious man, he might have crossed himself.

"Hydroponics equipment. At least, that's what it looks like."

Peering into the treasure trove, Paula's breath caught.

"Damned right. Official, too. Once we get this set up, we can replace the jury-rigged set-up we have and double or triple what we've already got growing."

Left unsaid was whether they would have any need.

"Let's see what you have."

Abandoning his prize for the moment, the two officers dug into the second crate. Removing the protective packaging, they stared at the unfamiliar machinery.

"I know I should recognize it, but my mind won't place it," he finally admitted.

"Ride a comet's tail!" she exclaimed, drawing back in wonder. "I may be wrong, but I think what we've got is a food processor."

Waves of excitement, the like of which he had not experienced in a very long time washed over Terry's body. Pausing a moment, he stared down in awe.

"If it still functions, this is wonderful news." He hesitated a beat before adding, "Once we harvest the crops we can make bread. Or, at least, turn the green sprouts we do have into wafers or mixed salads."

"Well, I guess you've separated the wheat from the chaff," she decided, rubbing her hands together in satisfaction. He groaned at her joke, but deeply appreciated the sentiment which was more upbeat than his.

"Let's go back for the rest of it."

"No. Wait a minute." She gave him a quizzical look, but he was adamant. "Now is the time to alert the crew."

"They can't help us; none of them have training in the suits."

"That's not what I mean."

She caught his implication and let out a deep exhalation.

"You're right. Sorry. I forgot. With a discovery this important, everyone ought to be in on it."

Indicating she follow him, he walked carefully toward the exit.

"Come on. We'll make an announcement."

"Tell us again, Captain," Lamar Porteous pleaded, arms extended. "You said it was a dream? You had a vision there were supplies stowed away in Holding Area Two? And there was? And these are what you brought back?" he demanded, a quiver to his voice. "From an area that was destroyed?"

"The second holding area was destroyed. These crates were found sealed in a preservation unit. From our initial assessment of the exterior, it appeared everything was gone. That was incorrect. But, it wasn't a vision in the manner you think," Terry protested. Yet, he was preaching to the unconverted. Unlike the typical scenario where the holy man lectured the believers, he acted the skeptic while his parishioners made up the faithful.

"This is the second time, sir," Janice Miles added, raising her hand from the back. She need not have, but at this moment of revelation, politeness was the order of the day. "You dreamed about the meteor with the ice volcanoes, too."

"No, no, that's –" He turned to Brian, seeking help from the ordained minister. "You explain it to them. They've taken something ordinary and make it… mystical."

"I can't say that they're wrong," Mister Hardy, Doctor of Divinity, demurred. "The gift of second sight has acknowledged roots as far back as the beginnings of recorded history. Probably further."

"I don't have psychic power – I don't pour over palms or read tea leaves. That's your domain," he accused the cleric.

Reading the look of anguish behind the words, Brian finally shrugged, then rolled his eyes.

"Just what I need – competition." Altering his voice into what charitably could be called a Western dialect, he intoned, "This ship ain't big enough fer the both of us, cowboy. Only one water witch to a town. Now put up, or prepare to use yer six-shooter."

"I'll shut up!" Joshua quickly acquiesced.

"That's because he wants to play the peacekeeper," Jingles observed, making his way to the front. Elbowing aside the crewmen who had crowded around the treasure, he poked a finger toward the crates. "It was well enough watching you and the Commander fetch this haul back, but I say let's get on with the real business at hand. Opening the rest of this cache." Motioning forward his two engineering technicians, those loyal to his personal authority, the chief engineer snapped his fingers. "Git to it."

"Yes, sir," Diaz agreed. Utilizing a small laser tool, he rapidly broke the seals. Before he could dig eager hands into the packing material, Helen took command.

"My turn. You gentleman have done the dirty work. Now it's up to the ladies."

Pretending more animosity than he felt, Hernando backed away, inadvertently bumping into his superior. With a grunt, Jingles wrapped his arms around the offender and physically set him to the side. ·

"Don't stand in my way," he warned. "We may have a lawman, a preacher and a female –"

He cleared his throat but Helen was quick to fill in the void he purposely left hanging.

"Mayor."

"Mayor," he repeated to everyone's pleasure. "But I'm the blacksmith in this here town."

"Aptly called 'Target,'" Paula supplied, readily accepting the Old West analogy. Applause went around the room, as the "citizens" approved the name.

"Target. And without a smithy to shoe the 'horses,' none of you are goin' anywhere. So mind yer manners and let me see what we all got."

Without remanding her authority, Helen and Jingles peered into the box. As their eyes widened in surprise, both dove into it.

"If it ain't Santa Claus come early!" Jingles observed. There was no mistaking the piety in his voice.

"What did we get?"

"What's in there?"

"Take it out and show us!"

"Move aside so the rest of us can see!"

"Packages from 'Back East,'" Helen announced. "I'd say our tinker came well prepared to make a 'good sales commission' in *Target.*"

Removing a large package, clearly marked "Logistics Officer," she hastily removed the top covering. "Oh, my God. Your wish came true, Sheriff Terry. Crackers; honey; nuts. Dehydrated soup." Bending down, she made a rapid determination. "There are three more, labeled the same."

"Fruit juice; syrup," Jingles read. "I'm commandeering those for Engineering."

Holding a large package to his chest, he attempted to make a rapid exit, but was blocked by Janice Miles. "Nothing doing, pard." Grinning more amicably than anyone could remember, the "blacksmith" handed her the box. To everyone's delight, the Technology Specialist staggered under the weight. She laughed. "I guess in our fantasy town, I'm the newspaper publisher. Can't expect me to be as musclebound as those who live by their hands."

Placing it carefully on the floor, she indicated they remove the other packages.

"Let's see what else is in there."

One word said it all. And it was said by all.

"Candy."

Life on *Target* had risen one notch on the endurance level.

As the crew rushed in, decorum forgotten, Captain Terry held up his hands. Not a few of them inadvertently shoved him as they retreated.

"All right. I know you're all eager to share in the spoils. So am I. But we can't rush this. What we have here is going to have to last us... a very long time."

"There are other crates," Winston Rey protested, a sudden edge to his voice. Responding before the others, Brian interceded. Smiling amicably, he held up his hands, palms outward, pleading his case of *I'm one of you* successfully enough that the sudden anger dissipated.

"The captain and commander have inspected those containers. None were marked 'Perishable.' We must assume, therefore, the others contain equipment or technical supplies."

"If one of them contains computer chips," Lieutenant Miles complained with melodramatic effect, "I'm going to walk out an airlock. There are four hundred and fifty-nine thousand, thirty-one non-functional chips for every man and woman aboard ship. Any more and I say we start using them to construct walls."

"A lot of good that will do you if you're taking a spacewalk without a suit," Maurice Kincaid opted. The rest nodded and retreated back, ashamed at their sudden and compelling negative emotions of the moment before.

"O.K. We're sorry." The apology could have come from any one of the assembled. "What do you suggest, Captain?"

The word "suggest" was tantamount to his less than absolute control of the situation. Terry let it slide. Language, he decided, was Helen's domain. Not his. In their place, he might have used the same word.

Might have, but would not have.

The times, they were a changin'.

Emptying the contents before the eager eyes of the crew held the advantage of fairness, which had been his original intent. If everyone knew exactly what they had found, there could be no suggestion of collusion. On the other hand, a point he had not considered when ordering the crew assembled, it would enable them to take stock, making an ongoing accounting inevitable. He had managed to avoid that with the food scavenged from the "vending machines." He was not so fortunate a second time.

Purposely avoiding Brian's piercing stare, he made his decision, knowing it was not going to please everyone. But in this instance, the majority ruled.

"I say we make an inventory. Then we all get to pick something from the 'pot.' The rest will be issued by Dr. Fitzgerald as part of our rations. Fair enough?"

"More than fair," Brian decided, without bothering to wait for the democratic process. For the time being, his reluctant stamp of approval carried the motion.

"All right." It was Helen who took over. "Captain Terry, since it was you who found the cache, I suggest you be the one to play Kris Cringle."

The suggestion was appealing, for it held within it the chance to solidify his position. But there were other, more pressing issues.

"I appreciate that, but I want Mr. Gingleheimer to handle the honor."

Surprised and flattered, the engineer started to demure, then gave in to his excitement.

"Thank you, sir. I'd like to. Besides, I'm more 'fit' for the job."

Indicating his girth, then interlacing his fingers, he bent them back until his knuckles cracked, Jingles stepped forward. With the enthusiasm of a ten-year old, he dipped into the container, removing a jar, the size of a personal monitor. Prying back the lid, he gasped, then sighed in contentment.

"Sour balls. Two gross," he rapidly calculated.

"Sixteen-point-nine for each of us," one of the computer wizards quickly calculated.

"We'll round that out to sixteen and save the extras for a spot drawing," Terry decided before they lost themselves arguing over a trivial point. "What else is in there?"

Before disappointment could settle in, the engineer removed the second box.

"Chocolate bars."

A ripple of excitement spread like plague.

"How many?"

"Two dozen," he replied. "The tag on it says 'Captain Nguyen.'"

Before a wave of distress could settle in, with ownership clearly transferred to the new captain, Joshua spoke.

"I'm sure George would appreciate having his personal supplies distributed to the crew. We'll call it his last official act."

"I'll make a note in the record," Paula offered. The motion was unanimously carried. "What's next?"

"Jelly beans," Jingles promptly reported.

"We can use them for the booby prize."

Calls for "I'll take it," played down that suggestion.

"Look at this!" Holding up a packet, Jingles displayed it to the crowd. "Computer chips." Janice Miles groaned, but he spoke over her feigned protest. "Not really. Lounge wear. "Turning to the captain, he grinned. "Looks like this consignment was for the 'Dispensary,'" he concluded. "The R&R shop."

"So it does," Terry agreed. Like the crew's quarters and the physical fitness areas, the Rest & Recreation shop, where non-regulation items could be purchased, had been lost on the starboard section. In fact, he had forgotten about it until this moment. "It must have been stored away until needed. What good fortune for us."

"I'll say," Helen agreed, pointing to the crewman nearest her. "Our uniforms are deteriorating to the point of indecency. This loungewear is going to be assigned on a next-to-naked need."

They laughed and could hardly disagree with the assessment.

"But how can we pay for the items, now? We don't have any credit; all those records were lost."

"We're not even drawing a salary. Or are we?" Lamar asked.

"I suppose we are. But that's an issue for the Space Force to settle with us. These items are not for sale. Unless," Joshua continued, the idea striking him. "We all pool whatever personal things we have and make a new R&R shop. We can trade or barter with each other. I don't see why we couldn't include some of these items into that store."

The idea was immediately taken up and agreed to.

"Janice, you operate it."

"All right," she said, warming to the idea. "I think something like that would be a great idea."

"But that's unfair to those of us who don't have anything," Winston Rey objected. "We'll be done out."

"We'll include personal service. You're an historian. Maybe someone would like their personal history set down for posterity. We all have skills. Let's put together a bulletin board, offering what we have, or offering to trade any special talents. That way, each of us can be involved."

"That's a good idea, Helen. See to it, Janice."

"Yes, sir."

The remainder of the goods were examined, then each crewmember was allowed one selection before the remainder was set aside. Afterward, the crew was dismissed, happier and more content than they had been a day previous.

"You did a good thing, finding those stores," Brian decided when he, Helen and Joshua were finally alone. "And you handled it very well."

"Praise from Caesar. What we have left?"

"I'll have to see. The food we can dispense, as you suggested; as a supplement to our meals. Depending on how much there is – and its condition," she underscored, "that gives us some breathing space."

"For the plants to grow, you mean."

"That, certainly. What we've found isn't a life saver, but it's a reprieve. Added calories and real food to chew and taste," she determined, having already given the matter consideration. "Some of it may possibly be issued as a reward for extraordinary services rendered. Or, as a break from the doldrums. We've already seen how well that works," she added, remembering his handling of the engineer.

"It was your idea. Thank you."

"You're welcome. And now, what do you say to getting some rest? You were up all night."

"Yes. I'm tired; bone weary. Want to come with me?" he shyly added.

The request was not as innocent as it sounded. She was tempted, but afraid of the timing.

"I'd like to. But you need sleep more than anything else."

"Do I?"

"You've had your treat," she said slowly, referring to the piece of hard candy he had taken as his share. "Anything else might go to your head."

Pouting in real disappointment, Joshua nodded. "I just thought –"

"What she means," Brian added in the uncomfortable pause, "is that we all want you to have a chance to dream. God only knows what else will come to you from the Land of Nod."

Which was not what she had meant at all, but it was an excuse to end the conversation.

"Good night."

Hanging his head, the captain made his good-byes and left, leaving the score at one great discovery and one disappointment of greater or equal value.

CHAPTER 12

With the parting of the lift doors, both Paula Burbone and Anna Bates glanced up from their work. Bates had already put in two hours of her four-hour shift. She would be relieved at eight bells by Casey Hanson, an astrophysicist by trade. Both were in training to assume the responsibilities of bridge personnel; Bates at navigation, Hanson at data processing. The remainder of their duty was spent on Level Two, where they studied star charts and performed astrological research on the open, undiscovered space encompassing *Target's* immediate future.

The process of teaching civilian specialists new lines of work was a slow, laborious one, yet absolutely necessary for the survival of the ship. As long as the crew was abandoned in unchartered space, the bridge and ancillary services would have to be manned. In the absence of professionally trained officers, they were the ones who would allow *Target* to function, albeit on a subsistence level.

Saluting the commanding officer, Paula rose from her station at command stepped aside. Beside the captain, she was the last of the original bridge contingent. Maintaining military form was not only her training, but her pride.

"Good morning, sir," she greeted. "All quiet. Steady as she goes."

"Very good," Terry acknowledged.

An exchange of words as old as clipper ships and steamboats. The only thing missing was the pair of white gloves they would be wearing as part of their uniform when assuming the responsibility of the great wooden wheel.

Beginning at navigation, the captain made the circuit, crossing communications, astronomy, data processing, engineering and the helm chairs before positioning himself in the middle of the nearly circular bridge. There, from a standing posture, he surveyed the massive viewscreen. On it was depicted the vast array of distant stars immediately ahead of them. To his left and right were smaller monitors displaying port and starboard.

Hope, Brian was apt to say, *is in the eye of the beholder.*

With a disquietude he could not explain, Terry shifted his attention to the hand-held computer Burbone offered. On the graphs were *Target's* location, speed and flight data from the previous day. At his desire, he could review past history or calculate speculations of future progress. At the moment, the lines and numbers blurred before his eyes.

They did not tell him what he needed to know for they lacked insight into the fourth dimension.

Observing his expression, Paula squinted in question, then withdrew a step.

"Sir?" She received no answer. "Sir? Is everything all right?"

Which was the command interpretation of *Is anything wrong?*

Handing her back the clipboard computer, he shook his head.

"What's out there?"

Nothing was the inappropriate and thus un-verbalized response. Adjusting herself so that she stood, shoulder to shoulder, with him, Paula scrutinized the screen.

"Computers report nothing out of the ordinary."

"Then it's something the sensors can't detect." His words were chipped, official and contemptuous. Nodding his head up and down as though to confirm his suspicions for himself, he drew a rapid, totally unscientific conclusion.

"Call Dr. Fitzgerald. Get her up here."

He could as easily have done it himself, but the thought did not occur to him. He did not want to be diverted from his concentration. For good or evil, their space had been penetrated by the unknown.

"Dr. Fitzgerald to the bridge. Dr. Helen Fitzgerald. To the bridge, please."

She was in her office, just beginning an inventory of the cargo they had rescued from Holding Area Two when the summons came. Her first reaction was one of surprise. There was no reason why her presence should be required on the bridge.

The second took her breath away.

Spontaneously reaching out a hand, she activated the newly renovated intraship communications. Repeating her name seemed superfluous but under the circumstances, she felt a need for formality.

"Dr. Fitzgerald here. I'm coming."

After disengaging the unit, she felt foolish. Technically, her obedience was assumed without acknowledgment. Allowing a flush of embarrassment to grow up her cheeks, Helen stood, then steadied herself by placing her hands flat against the desk. Had she suddenly been caught in a gale, her reaction would have been the same.

Summoned topside. That's how Joshua would phrase it. He would use the nautical expression with a grin and then doff his hand to her by way of salute. *Duty calls,* his gesture would imply. *Gotta go. We'll take up where we left off when I return.*

Helen Fitzgerald seriously doubted there would be any resumption of normalcy by the time she got back to her office.

It was coming.

By the time she entered the bridge, Joshua was sitting in the captain's chair, hands splayed across the arm rests. While his demeanor was calm, the potential energy in the enclosed space snapped like sparklers. His eyes were riveted to the main viewscreen.

Ignoring the impulse to join him, Helen crossed in front, placing herself between him and the monitor. Unaccustomed to looking at the screen, it took her a moment to orient her spatial senses.

"Yes," she said, running the word over in her mind before articulating it. From this moment on, every thought, each sentence would have to be terse, precise and accurate. "I sense it."

"Is it what you were looking for? What you expected?"

His voice, although coming from behind, rang in her ears from all points of the compass.

"Yes."

"What is it?"

"I don't know."

"Corporeal or mechanical?"

"Both." And then, for she fully comprehended his larger meaning, "A life form aboard the approaching vessel."

"One, or more than one?"

The reply was slower in coming. "I'm not sure." Her failure weighed heavily.

"Friend or foe?"

He could have as easily phrased the question, "Foe or friend?" She appreciated his willful choice, while acknowledging to herself that common usage of the expression was always the former.

"I wish I knew."

"Thank you."

That was a dismissal. Anger welled inside. Whatever was coming, *foe or friend,* belonged to her. She had sensed it, felt it, nearly touched it in her mind. She would not be discharged that easily. Making a one-hundred and eighty degree turn, she met his gaze.

"I will stay."

"I think not." Helen's fists clenched at her sides. "Kindly return to duty," he ordered.

Eyes slanted at his summary discharge, Helen saluted, then spun around, walking toward the elevator. She fully expected him to call her back. He did speak, but what he said was not what she hoped to hear.

"Send Brian to the bridge."

All prior thoughts of discipline dissipated as the idea of slapping his face nearly overcame her. He was pulling rank. When he had determined all she knew, her usefulness had evaporated, making her superfluous. Because she could not strike him, Helen used the one tool always at her disposal. Language.

"Dr. Hardy will not be able to help you."

Terry's head drew back as his eyes scanned the back of her head.

"He's less emotionally involved that you."

"And you aren't?"

It was Paula Burbone who stiffened at her question.

"I will call him, sir."

"No need. Dr. Fitzgerald will notify him." *Won't you, Helen?*

"Yes. I'll be in my office if you need me."

Not the dispersal of information, nor an agreement that she would return to duty, her statement was a warning.

You will need me.

Nor, did she respond to Burbone's quiet statement, spoken to those chosen to remain on the bridge.

"Sensors indicate a disturbance, sir. Incoming data indicate it is a ship."

The words she had been longing to hear did not relieve her tension. The ability to relax had *passed away,* in the ancient yet ever-present meaning of the words. *Died.* The concept of "a relief from pressure" had been struck from her extensive vocabulary. *It was coming.* Life, death and everything in between hung in the balance. While a cleric might attempt to rationalize the unknown into metaphysical terms, only she could identify the incoming presence for what it was.

If Captain Terry choose not to arm himself with all the facts, that was his weakness and not hers.

After informing Hardy his services were required on the bridge, she went back to her office, as promised. Her tour of duty was four hours. After that expired, she was on her own. He would know where to locate her.

In the Observatory on Level Four.

Helen Fitzgerald was conspicuously absent. Gathered in the Command Center on Level Two were Brian Hardy and Captain Terry's second in command, Paula Burbone.

Two four-hour shifts had passed before the conference was called. It might as easily have been conducted on the bridge, but there, a sense of being overheard by an entity or entities unknown made communication awkward. While it was unlikely they were any more secure on Level Two, the semblance of having taken all precautions somewhat eased their wariness.

There were larger issues which would more than compensate for that respite.

Terry was the first to speak.

"Report."

His nod toward Burbone was her license to begin.

"Sensors on the bridge indicate –"

He cut her off with a curt gesture toward the computer which hummed to her left. Divining his meaning they would get to that once routine matters were set aside, she responded with alacrity.

"Carson's daily assessment from Hydroponics, sir. The plants – those grown from seeds from the vending machines – continue to prosper. Her charts on the hybrids show nearly flat growth lines. They are alive but have failed to thrive."

"How can that be?" Brian grumbled, disguising his disappointment with sullenness. "We've given them all that additional nutrition. According to the researcher's notes, those infusions should have been enough to spurt renewed activity."

His statement spoke for itself and was not, therefore, addressed.

"Commissary report?"

That was Helen's domain. In her absence, Paula consulted the computer for her latest entries. Her sigh, although inaudible, was patently obvious.

"None of the sustenance retrieved from the Holding Bay have been catalogued. Measured rations in the form of nutritional tablets continue to be dispensed. That is Dr. Fitzgerald's report, sir."

"A more thorough accounting is required," Terry began, running his hand across the computer before abruptly addressing Hardy. "She should be at our next meeting to report in person. I want hard data –"

Puzzled, the cleric glanced at Paula, who offered him a noncommittal stare.

"On the quantity of food left?" he hesitated. "Or, the accounting of what we recovered?"

"Carson. She's in charge of Hydroponics. It's her responsibility to come up with answers. There has to be something in the research to explain our lack of success. I want it found and put into a formal presentation. Is that clear?"

"Yes. Of course. I'll see she's at the next briefing," came the promise.

"Stagnation of the hybrids is unacceptable. If she can't find an explanation for their inability to grow, have her alter the ratio of nutrition: a different combination of the tablets. What we're using now isn't working."

Leaning back, he made a point of meeting their stares.

"We've already let too much time elapse. The stores Paula and I recovered have given us breathing room in the sense of relief from the mundane rather than time. Especially not when the bulk of them are... snacks, rather than sustainable nutrition."

"Understood."

Retreating from the subject brought him around to the pressing issue which had occasioned the meeting. Crossing his hands, he prepared for a siege; a non-physical battle of another sort.

"Data indicate a ship has penetrated the outer regions of this sector. Without long-range capacity, we are virtually blind. Commander?"

"The area of space we occupy is totally unexplored. Whatever mapping records made by *Target* before Encounter were rendered useless after we passed through the eye of the ribbon. I therefore cannot determine whether this ship of unknown origin originated from a planet in this sector, or is far away from its home base as we are."

Reactivating her computer screen, Paula consulted her report. Brian's foot shook nervously as they waited.

"Without fixed points, I lack the ability to triangulate its exact speed, but it appears to be moving through space with incredible velocity. Much faster than our capacity, even at maximum."

"On a course to intercept?"

"Indications would indicate so, sir. But again, at this distance, that is only speculation."

"What we may assume," Joshua began carefully, aware of their attentive postures, "is a technology greater to or equal to our own."

"Why?" Brian blurted, aware of his own shortcomings, yet in need of full comprehension.

"The fact they're out there, to begin with."

The observation was so obvious Brian snorted, then grinned sheepishly before biding Joshua continue.

"Add to that their velocity; propulsion."

"All right." The point was carried. "What does it mean to us?"

Over Paula's abrupt stare at Hardy, Terry continued.

"Whoever is aboard that ship is aware of our presence. And likely a great deal more informed of our capacities than we are of theirs."

The captain leaned back, surveying his crew with the same critical eye he would access an unknown entity.

"They also possess the power of navigation; something we're deficient in. If they want to avoid making contact, they will. If they wish to engage us.... there's nothing to stop them."

"Is that a concern?" Brian pursued.

Rising from his chair, the captain stood, looked around the cramped room, then opted to reseat himself at the makeshift desk. With hands interlaced, he bade them wait before offering his thoughts.

"It's against my nature to assume any alien contact is dangerous until they prove otherwise. On the other hand, they cannot fail to have ascertained the fact *Target* is crippled. Therefore, while I fully intend to arm the main lasers, I will not be the aggressor. Disagreements?"

"None, toward your point of non-aggression," Brian promptly retorted, catching Paula's eye the moment before he spoke for her. "It might help, however, if we were able to communicate before you're required to make that judgment. That's Helen's forte." Terry pursed his lip, nodding deliberately, as though his head were too heavy to move with more authority.

"Yes," he agreed. "It is."

Brian picked on an eyebrow, critically observing the eyelash removed before pursuing the sensitive issue.

"Why isn't she here?"

Terry's head rose sharply, until his chin was in a vertical line with the floor.

"Because she's a civilian and not a military officer."

Brian's hand went back to his eyebrows, as though personal grooming marked his own delineation between civilian and military.

"If I may take the liberty of speaking for her," he began carefully, meticulously choosing his words. "Neither she nor I have ever been present at a council of war."

"No one used those words," Terry irritably interrupted, shaking his head in denial. Brian waved him down, but not without first judging the consequences of his own position. While hardly acceptable, he assumed the risk for Helen's sake.

"That is true: but when you speak of arming our weaponry, you acknowledge the possibility of conflict."

"I do."

"And possibly you can do no less," came the guarded agreement. "Dr. Fitzgerald is a communicator. Her avocation is to negotiate peace. As an ordained minister, I have had considerable dealings with civilizations vastly different than our own. More so than either of you," he added, then physically withdrew, wondering if he had gone too far.

"Your presence here is not in question, Dr. Hardy. Helen chose to absent herself."

Affixing his gaze on his hand, Brian clenched and unclenched his fingers before setting them on the table like a deck of cards.

"No, sir. You discharged her from the bridge when she was attempting to give her interpretation of incoming data. When she was trying to perform her *duty,* Captain," came the harsher accusation. "By summarily dismissing her, your aggressive reaction meant war: to her and toward that alien ship. And thus you see why I called this a council of war, and why I cannot accept your excuse for her absence."

Stung by his attack, Joshua stood, approached the conference table, then began a slow revolution around it. Paula would have joined him, but he motioned her down.

"I agree that I over-reacted on the bridge. My attitude was predicated on my own inability to receive and interpret conventional data. Relying on speculation and... telepathy runs counter to my training. That was my mistake."

"Then tell her that."

"Or, I will," Burbone abruptly volunteered, finally moving from her position to stand before Terry. "She might respond better to a woman."

The idea was tempting, but he could not send Paula.

"No."

"No." Brian's denial perfectly overlapped Joshua's. Feeling small by being the only one seated, he rose, hoping the added height would give him an advantage, if not equality.

"Your mistake, Captain. You said it – and you explained why. Now, tell her yourself. She's our link to whatever's out there. All the sensors and triangulations in the universe won't do us any good if we can't understand one another. She's our spokesperson: *Target's* and mine and yours. Make her believe this is no longer a council of war but the first step toward peace."

He had his say and was oddly exhausted by the effort. Leaning against the table, Brian breathed heavily. As though the air had actually gotten thinner, Terry's chest also heaved with exertion. To speak proved difficult.

Clearing his throat, then briefly touching the command insignia on his uniform, he shook his head.

"I cannot do that."

Brian was clearly surprised. Pulling himself together by tugging at the hem of his tunic-shirt, he stared at amazement at the captain.

"Why not?"

No officer of the line would have dared question him in that manner. It was not their prerogative. While they might not fully comprehend the reasons behind an assignment, to blatantly demand an accounting was insubordination.

If Brian read those thoughts in Terry's eyes, he did not let them bend him from his purpose.

Sensing an impasse between the two men, Paula stepped between them. In her limited experience, she had never encountered a physical confrontation in any briefing to which she had been privy, but that did not preclude the possibility of one here. *Things,* she remembered, *were not as they were.*

"I repeat my offer, sir." Although she spoke to the captain, her eyes remained on Hardy. "To speak to Dr. Fitzgerald."

"I would prefer you to do that," Terry addressed Brian, inclining his head to look around Paula. The minister remained obstinate.

"Not until you tell me why you won't deliver your own message."

Convince me, he mentally begged. *You know I'm right. So why won't you face Helen?*

The stand-off was protracted an uncomfortable. All three parties shifted weight. The muted ringing of the ship's "bell" told them the hour.

When enough time had elapsed for Terry's thoughts to congeal, he placed a hand on Paula, gently moving her aside. There were already too many barriers between him and Brian. The removal of one was as much as he would concede.

"Your very words, Father. You wish me to convince Helen we're taking the first steps toward peace. As far as it goes, that's true. But peace may, or may not be the end point we achieve. I dare not misrepresent myself again."

As he inched forward, Paula backed further away, positioning herself to stand shoulder-to-shoulder with the captain. Her proximity did not relieve the strain he was under.

"Helen sees me as one man, integrating both my military and non-military sides to make a whole. I have been taught to separate the two. Right or wrong, I must stand by my own consciousness of self. I am officer first and fiancee second."

Pointing upward before Terry continued, Brian and Paula's heads tilted back to see, in their mind's eyes, the approaching space craft.

"I disagreed with your definition that this briefing was a council of war because to me, that predisposed us toward aggression. The potential for violence is predicated on unknown factors. She stands between us and what's out there. It may very well be in her powers of arbitration to avert bloodshed. Coming from me," Terry continued, tapping his chest, "she may read treachery. I charge you to present my case in such a way as the positive outweighs the negative."

Brian backed away, his eyes still piercing through the ceiling toward the unknown.

"May I have the liberty of expressing your... regret... at dismissing her from the bridge?"

It was a hard question to answer. One he was unequal to.

"Use your own discretion."

"Where is she?"

"In the Observatory on Level Four."

Brian got to his feet, saluted as though to belie the captain's faith in his dual capacity, then departed, leaving the two career officers to ponder what the next days would deliver onto them. And which of the crew they could trust. Which was nearly as sobering as the vessel bearing down upon them.

"All for one and one for all" had become a cruel disillusionment.

CHAPTER 13

Joshua Terry was wrong. While he would never know it, one of his assumptions imparted to Brian Hardy was in grave error.

Helen Fitzgerald was not in the Observatory. By itself, the fact was trivial, of no consequence. It cost the cleric no more than a furtive trip to Level Four to ascertain the fact. Yet the captain's mistake loomed large. It was one more mistake, added to others, so that the sum of the parts grew disproportionately large.

Brian needed faith; his entire being was constructed around that concept. His belief in God was no less strong than his adherence to the principal that trust was paramount to life. Without one, the other faltered. Because Joshua erred, Brian's belief wavered. In weakness came a nearly overwhelming sensation of betrayal. The expression, "council of war," weighed heavily upon him as he retraced his path to Level Two.

Helen's office was empty, devoid of life. While that fact narrowed his search, it did not cheer his demeanor. *Separate,* he rued, *was never equal.*

If he had not seen Ensign Carson emerge from Hydroponics, his destination would have been the bridge. There was no logical reason to think she had gone there, but logic, by itself, was suddenly open to interpretation.

Two plus two might equal four in the space he occupied, but there was no guarantee that equation held true where he was going.

Making a point of taking well-measured steps, by placing one foot equidistant to the other, he inadvertently walked like a man trying to prove his sobriety to a skeptical observer.

The door parted before him and he figuratively crossed the Red Sea.

Helen stood across from him, her back facing his front. While she gave no indication of having heard him enter, he sensed her level of alertness sharpen.

Without need of ascertaining the identity of the intruder, the doctor of languages moved away, knowing he would follow. When they were out of sight from any who might enter, she finally faced him and broke the silence.

"What does Captain Terry want to know now, that he didn't before?"

The directness of her question surprised him, although it should not have.

Leaning against one of the tanks, Brian affected a professional but not condescending grin.

"Oh, he wanted to know before. He just didn't know how to ask."

Breathing out through her nose, which was more for her benefit than his, Helen clasped her hands together, then pulled them upward, toward her face. She was about to speak when the sight of a leaf dropping off one of the hybrids diverted their attention. Both shivered, but for different reasons.

"Not here, Brian. I can't concentrate. Out there," she indicated, nodding beyond the room, "is life. Call it benevolent or evil; anticipate it or fear it, but don't make me contemplate 'my alien' here in this place of... stagnation. Too much has disappointed within these four walls." Angrily touching the bulkhead, her fist clenched. "You come to speak of tangibles. Life is tangible; the mechanics of death are real. We watch a heart stop beating; we listen for breath which comes no more. We wait for the moment of the soul to pass, and yet we do not see it. That is intangible. Whatever you have to say is inappropriate for this area of hopelessness."

"To your office?"

"To the Observatory. Where I first found hope."

There was an irony to her suggestion with which he could not argue. Bowing gracefully, he allowed her to proceed him. As they passed row after row of wilted plants, his heart strangely went out to them, understanding on a subliminal level they were trying their hardest to live, and yet could not explain why.

He knew the feeling.

Janice Miles waved to them as they passed her in the corridor. Neither returned the friendly salutation. Their snub caused hurt, for she was lonely and in need of reassurance. A smile would have served her purpose. But smiles were like hen's teeth; hard to come by and either miraculous or false.

Hernando Diaz was getting out of the lift as they moved forward to enter. He gave no greeting, replacing a gesture of civility was a frown. He, too, was lonely, but the companionship he sought was far away. Unlike hope, it was definable. Like positive expectations, it was unattainable.

"Level Four."

The roundabout shimmied the way a cat on the prowl stalked pray. When it reached its destination and the passengers departed its confines, the mindless, soulless machine worked its way upward.

Another hand had called.

Had Brian been thinking along religious tracks, he might have observed, "Let those with ears hear."

The Observatory was dark and uninviting. Instead of activating the overhead lights, Helen crossed unerringly toward the monitor. Without visible instruction, the screen snapped to life. That was her impetus to speak.

"I already told Joshua everything that's in my mind. There's a ship out there. It's manned. I get no impression of hostility, but rather a sense of wariness. Has that changed from my initial reaction? Yes," she answered her own question, hurrying on as though in a race to speak before lapsing into permanent silence.

"At first you might say I was eavesdropping – listening in to some entity singing alone for its own pleasure. After that, I felt an almost a tentative seeking: *are you out there? I know who I am, but who are you?* Not that, specifically, of course," Helen continued, reaching out to engulf Brian's hands in her own. A flush of excitement reddened her cheeks. "In fact, that's the first time I've ever been able to express it in words." Finishing with a rush, Helen's eyes closed as she envisioned the mystery, drawing ever nearer. "I've said a lot, haven't I?"

"Yes."

"More than I supposed I knew."

He returned the squeeze on her hands, then extracted one of his own to touch her gently on the arm. His own orbs were glistening with emotion.

"Perhaps you're still analyzing the data – running the possibilities over in your mind – trying out different words and phrases until they come out the right way."

"You make me sound like a computer," she complained, but without condemnation. "I still haven't divined anything tangible. It's all speculation."

"That's what command conferences are for," he dared point out. "That's what Joshua and Paula and I were trying to determine – without your help." She shrugged and he increased pressure on her arm. "You should have been there."

Scrunching up her face, Helen bit her lip as she swallowed bravely.

"He dismissed me from the bridge as though any further contributions on my part were not only unnecessary, but unwanted."

"And by avoiding the meeting, you missed having received Joshua and Paula's apologies in person. Now, you'll have to take them from me, and I'm a poor substitute."

Softening considerably, Helen ruffled his gently receding hair, then tugged on his long locks at the back, eliciting a sad smile.

"No, you're not. You're not a poor substitute for anyone." Spontaneously, Helen reached out and threw her arms around him. Hugging Brian tightly, she kissed the old man on both cheeks before reluctantly releasing him. "Brian, I do love you so."

Responding to her warmth, he reciprocated the gesture by pressing his lips to her forehead and holding them there for a long beat before reluctantly withdrawing.

"We're all scared," he began, after both went through the motions of controlling themselves, Helen by brushing back her own hair and Brian by wiping his eyes. "Joshua, no less than the rest of us. There's a lot of responsibility riding on his shoulders. He's used to having high tech instrumentation take the guesswork out of such a potentially dangerous situation. And for that matter," he added, glancing upward and to his right where the bridge lay, "what he's actually used to is having his input taken into consideration, *not* rendering a final verdict on anything."

"He was a commander," Helen protested, but Brian shook her off, pointing figuratively through three levels.

"Captain Nguyen was an officer who believed in the delegation of all duties except command decisions. Those he jealously guarded for himself. Had he survived and not Terry, neither you nor I would have to worry about the line between civilian and military duty. There wouldn't be one. We would both be excluded from any meetings."

"Then he'd find himself sitting on the bridge alone with Paula," she observed, watching him with a cat glare as she drew his conclusion to its logical termination.

"Not even that, I shouldn't wonder," he pursued, dissecting the ceiling with a piercing stare of his own. "At Encounter, she was an ensign. You may well believe that's the rank she would have maintained – an officer in training, not yet a fully qualified crewmember, ready to advance."

"But Joshua promoted her for that very reason – because she had proved herself worthy."

"And," he added, waving a pointed finger through the air in a curling motion, "to provide for a line of succession, should something happen to him. Captain Nguyen would not have been so generous."

"Why not?" Helen whispered, a sense of camaraderie for her own two ranking officers washing over her.

"George Nguyen viewed people as months and years of service, rather than judging their potential. George had put in his time: he earned his rank. No one could question that. He was a king, commanding, if not by divine right, then by service 'to his country.' That's the 'black and white' he lived by."

Walking to the small table upon which were placed a dozen chess games and items of recreation, Brian rearranged the pieces with a purpose, understood only to himself.

"Joshua immediately grasped our true situation that Technology Specialists had to be moved into ancillary departments – Carson to hydroponics, Bates and Hanson to the bridge and Janice Miles to command. I can't see George doing that; at least not by the volunteer method. He would have searched the personnel records, making job assignments on calculated, recognized formulae." Looking up, he caught her eyes. "If your personality profile indicated you were better suited to engineering, that's where you'd go – without argument."

Lining up the pieces in two equal rows, he carefully dispatched them to various sections of the multi-level game board.

"I seriously doubt we would have had a mutiny from Marr and Radcliff because Nguyen would have accorded them their superior status as Skip pilots. They would have been required to do no more than what their pre-Encounter assignments dictated."

"But that's..." Helen faltered for the words, then shot her hand out, removing a king from Brian's line-up. "That wouldn't have been just."

"No," he agreed, reaching back for his king and reinstating it in its original position. "But it would have been proper military protocol."

Irritated at his insistence, Helen purposely realigned the game, destroying his well-placed symmetry.

"But if they had mutinied," she pressed, the fingers of her right hand clutching the knights as figurative pilots, "would he have gone after them? Knowing, as we did, they had stolen our food?"

Licking his lips, Brian picked up the bishop, turned it over until it made a complete revolution, then thrust it between his fingers.

"Well," he decided, blowing a gush of air out between his cheeks, "He probably would have joined them."

Withdrawing with a cold shudder, Helen dropped the knights, then wiped her hands on opposing sleeves.

"You can't mean that."

"Look at it logically," Brian demurred, retrieving the object, then "flying" it through space. *"Target* is crippled – beyond repair. For all practical purposes, we're not going anywhere. The odds of all of us surviving were virtually nil." She attempted to rebut his argument, but he continued over her objections.

"Nine were injured; it's not worth expending resources to save them. Of the thirty-four original survivors able to function, thirteen were untrained civilians. They couldn't operate the ship, and were, therefore, consuming valuable resources, better used by those who could."

"You mean the captain, Marr and Radcliff and Joshua were the only ones –"

"That's exactly what I mean," he dismissed, carelessly knocking down a piece on his game board.

"So you're saying –"

"If Marr and Radcliff went to Nguyen with their plan to steal our food and water and escape this hulk on a shuttle, he would have seen their logic. Better to save four than lose everyone. The idea of the captain going down with the ship is an antiquated one, fit only for poetry and recitations of history."

"That's murder."

"That's military."

"Then Joshua –"

"Captain Terry, whether he truly comprehends it or not, is walking a thin line between both worlds. He was bred in one and educated in the other."

"And yet, Joshua told me himself he respected Captain Nguyen. He felt he was the best line officer he ever knew. How does that fit into what you're saying?"

The game pieces went crashing to the floor with one sweep of Brian's arm.

"Possibly, because he never witnessed him under stress. Or, more likely, he's a better human being."

The pronouncement was startling. Gasping its implications, Helen mechanically stooped to retrieve the scattered "crewmembers."

"I made it more difficult for him, didn't I?" she intoned in a low voice, hiding her head so he was forced to stare at her back.

"It isn't over by a long shot."

"No," came the humble acknowledgement. "It's just beginning."

"A second... or a third beginning," he amended, finally returning his attention to the view screen.

The darkness of the room descended upon them as though a black sun had set. The temperature was no colder, but the atmosphere was. With a nervous plea, Helen placed a hand on the monitor. When she felt nothing, she reluctantly altered the view. In a moment, the stars of future determination twinkled out at her.

Leaning forward, Brian tried to see what she saw; to open his mind and receive whatever impressions were floating on the star dust. With religious fervor, he clasped his hands, praying for inspiration. While his mind wandered, it detected nothing which might be construed as alien intervention.

In the shadowed dimness, made possible by the celestial glow, Helen observed his machinations. She did not have to be a mind reader to calculate his failure.

"Nothing," he admitted, verbalizing the obvious as a way to soften his failure. Responding to his disappointment, Helen brushed shoulders with him as a reminder that he was not alone.

"May I view it from the bridge – this ship that's bearing down on us?" she tried, to break the silence. "Is it big enough to detect with the naked eye?"

"Not yet."

"How long before it arrives?"

"We can't 'triangulate' that data."

Making a low noise half way between humor and deprecation, Helen moved back, considered the objects she had replaced on the low table, then straightened them back into parallel lines.

"Tell me, Brian: are you excited or frightened?"

"By the possibility of encountering new life forms?" She nodded, watching as he set the game pieces into some order that suited him. "Joshua told me once they use this game at the command academy. He said cadets were encouraged to use any means possible to beat the computer. Each cadet was given three tries. Those who lost one or more games were relegated to the bottom of the class. The trick, he said, without being explained by their professor, was to cheat. To move a piece counter to the rules. The computer was programmed to continue play as though the move was legal and was thus forced to change its strategy. If you did it enough times, in theory, a skilled tactician should win. Not just once, but every time."

"What was his outcome?"

"He never lost a single game."

"He cheated."

"He didn't play. By not playing, he never lost. Losing, you recall, was the criteria by how you were judged."

"That would never have occurred to me."

"I found that fascinating. Personally, I would have cheated. I like an advantage and I hate to lose. You wouldn't think that of me, I presume, but I'm hard-headed and stubborn, although I like to think I'm open to new ideas and beliefs. But, I'm not without my fears. Maybe, as you get older you want things to be predictable and clear."

He picked up a piece and then "captured" it with a piece of the opposite color. "I guess what I'm getting at is that I want these approaching alien life forms to be like us. I want them to think, feel and have emotions. I want to be able to deal with them on an equal basis. That excites me. If they're not like us – if they're cold and mechanical and incapable of some exchange of give and take, then I'm frightened."

"We might not know that until it's too late."

"That tips the scales toward being frightened. What about you?" he prodded, playing a black piece although it was the white's turn.

"I'm not worried about myself. It's the others I'm frightened for."

"Why?" he asked, continuing his one-sided play. Her answer was terse and cutting.

"Because, like you, they don't like to lose. In all fairness, they can't afford to. But their perception of winning – and the manner in which they cheat to attain victory – eludes me."

"You don't mind being beaten?"

"That depends entirely on how I view the circumstances, doesn't it? What does cheating a computer prove? You're more clever because you can divert its programming? Go beyond the rules of fair play? Then what's the point in playing in the first place?"

"To feel good about winning," he suggested, watching as Helen took his turn with the white queen.

"Only if you view life as a game. I think you do yourself a disservice, Brother Brian."

He refused to give up the point.

"There's winning for the sake of winning; bloating your ego in an unfair contest. You can point to your score and say, 'See what I did. Look how smart I am. It doesn't hurt the computer's feelings any."

"Do any of us really know that?" Helen questioned, watching the game she had joined in progress. When her turn arrived again, she purposely placed her knight in jeopardy. She waited for Brian to capture it before continuing. "It doesn't offend your morality to use computer aides and suggestions to beat it, because your opponent is different than you are – a life form on another plane, shall we say, so you see no wrong. And perhaps there is no moral consideration. The point of competition is to triumph. That," she stressed, "is the military way of playing."

"And your way?" he pursued, purposely avoiding using the phrase she had set him up for: *And the civilian way?*

"My way is not to view it as a contest at all. My definition of 'game' is to enjoy the challenge, rather than the outcome. Especially when only one side has the ability to manipulate the rules to his own advantage."

"Agreed," Brian sighed, holding out the black king. "You're afraid Joshua and I and the rest of us will set one standard for your aliens and then baffle them by ignoring our own code of ethics, just for the sake of triumph," he added, returning the king to the board.

"No," she demurred, moving her king into checkmate. "What I'm afraid of is that 'my aliens' will still be playing an innocent game when the rest of you make the playing field a real contest of life and death."

Although the game was technically over, Brian continued playing.

"That's a harsh accusation."

"Yes," she admitted. "Because none of you were – or are – actually playing a game. Your defense is no more than veiled offense."

"Then it behooves you to be the moderator."

Helen finally smiled.

"And to think," she remarked slowly, standing up and walking toward the door, "I was beginning to wonder if I had lost my powers of communication."

She thought she heard him chuckle but the impression was a fleeting one.

"Helen."

"Yes?"

"Standing between two combatants is the most dangerous position of all."

"Correct. You might *both* cheat on me."

Crossing the threshold, she left him with an unfinished game. Which was precisely where Joshua and the aliens and Brian's God had meant her to do.

Know it or not, the playing field had leveled.

CHAPTER 14

Captain Terry sat in the command chair, eyes riveted on the screen. Flashing green lights, interspersed across the arc of the bridge gave the star cruiser the equivalent of a sentry singing "All's well." To the left, a large panel displayed environmental data; green numbers on a black background, all correctly within the yellow bars indicating tolerance levels.

To the officer's right, had he looked that way, he would have assimilated the image of *Target,* outlined in orange. All decks were color coded: green for the bridge, silver for the computer labs beneath. Sick Bay and the research facilities on Level Three, as well as the starboard side of the ship that had once existed and did no longer were blacked out, indicating no power or environment. Engineering, security and the cargo bays on Level Four were brown, interspersed, as was Level Two, with large black areas, creating the impression of a giant spider web slowly taking over their living space. Set on a black background, the three-dimensional hologram changed at pre-arranged times, displaying, in intricate detail, the status of the entire ship.

In a pessimistic frame of mind, it might be construed that the spider's web was widening to entrap them all. What expectation survived aboard ship was couched in the intangibles of a miniscule dot, representing life of a different sort.

Commander Burbone "manned" the navigation console. With limited ability to maneuver, her position was one of observer, rather than director. Like the captain, her attention was fixated on the screen. To her far right, in a nearly parallel line between her post and the command chair in the middle, data processing, astronomy and communications were conspicuously vacant.

Shattering the false tranquility of the bridge, the lift doors parted, admitting Helen Fitzgerald into the private sanctity. While neither altered their position, both pair of eyes snaked toward the newcomer.

The communicator's attitude spoke for itself. Helen had received her briefing from Brian Hardy. The success or failure of his mission was to be delivered in person.

"Thank you for coming," Joshua began, having hoped Helen would be the first to speak.

"Thank you for inviting me."

"Will you sit at communications?"

Crossing the open area, Helen debated whether to move in front of the captain's position, or walk behind it. Before she had quite decided, a blip on the giant monitor caught her eye and she froze, arm pointing outward.

"Is that it? The ship?"

"Yes." Rising from his chair, he joined her. "We're just able to enhance the image enough to get a glimpse. There isn't much to see," he apologized, as though the destroyed technology were a direct reflection of his personal failure. "It's still too far away. But it's something," he concluded in a whisper.

"Something," she agreed, finding herself transfixed by the tiny blur of light what was neither star nor comet, friend or foe. It was what it was: an unknown. A potential.

A host of possibilities.

Possibly even a game with an entirely new set of rules.

"It's so difficult to absorb," Helen confessed finally as he guided her toward the communications post. "I've never been... how would you express it? In the front lines before. My skills have never been called upon to open channels." Shaking her head ruefully, Helen sat before the tiered panel, trying to make sense of the controls. "But rather to repair them," she concluded, easing naturally into her next thought. "I'm afraid I don't know how to operate this."

The grace with which she spoke glossed over what might have been the professional interpreter's condemnation of those who attempted to conquer new frontiers without the fundamentals of common language. If the officer took her comment as a reprimand, it was one to which he either agreed, accepting responsibility for the past mistakes of his kind, or let slide as irrelevant to the present situation.

"Let me show you."

Daring to take her hand in his, Joshua guided it through the complex series of maneuvers, until a light at the top of the panel flashed green.

"What frequency are we transmitting on?"

He pointed out the code, which he expected her to read.

"The universal cycle of alternating currency, traveling at the speed of light. We were fortunate the back-up system was repairable. Otherwise, we'd be deaf and dumb."

Nodding her acceptance, Helen devoted herself to the task, completing a circuit with a satisfied "Ah!" Digesting the results, her hands flew over the touch pads. "Now I see. Your set-up isn't that different than what I'm used to – only less conveniently arranged. And without," she added quickly, running a search through the software, "my more advanced programs. With your permission, I'd like to ask Janice Miles to install them for me."

"Please do," Terry readily agreed, noting her use of the technology specialist's name in place of her rank.

"Of course, I don't have Fleet Command's authority to use it," Helen continued, "but I assure you, its data banks and ability to convert our language accurately into thousands of different spectrums via audio, light and visual mediums gives us a far greater chance of being understood – and of understanding – hitherto uninterrupted methods of communication."

"Excellent. The sooner you do that, the better. I'll send a communique to Command," he lightly added. "Informing them of my decision to utilize non-regulation, experimental software aboard ship."

For the first time Helen heard pride in his voice and felt herself equal to reaching out and tangibly touching "her" aliens.

"What about mental frequency," Terry interrupted. "Is it possible to augment your personal brain waves, or in some manner increase your own powers of perception? That is, after all, how they first reached you."

"I don't know," Helen admitted. "It's an interesting concept, but I haven't the technical competence to go about it. What I can do is encapsulate my identity – my name and position – along with more conventional data – the name of our ship, planet of origin and peaceful intentions. That way, if indeed the vessel contains the life form which contacted me – they may be able to respond in like manner. One we can all understand."

"Do it," he ordered, withdrawing his presence as being superfluous. Before he had backed away too far for her to reach him, Helen responded by unexpectedly grabbing his arm. Allowing himself to be pulled forward, Joshua lowered his ear so that what she had to say would be between them, alone.

"Promise me I'm not lying to them, Josh." His puzzlement appeared sincere, but she was learning not only how to communicate on different levels, but how to interpret the command demeanor of her species. "About our peaceful intentions."

She did not let his stoical expression deviate her from the desire for a direct answer. Raising his voice, he looked around the bridge before speaking.

"I promise you our intentions are honorable."

Accepting his words for what they were – a declaration of the moment – Helen released him. He withdrew from her grasp as though fighting a force of vastly superior strength, taking several steps back before regaining his equilibrium.

Returning her salute out of respect, Terry returned to his own position. Commander Burbone made the same gesture as a pledge to follow the dictates of her superior in whatever course he eventually navigated.

Not for the first time, but with acute awareness, Helen Fitzgerald fully comprehended that she was alone.

With an alienation and a resolve she would not have thought possible six months ago, she returned to her job.

"I have received no reply. Shall I keep trying?"

"Until they answer. Thank you. Yes."

Three words, two words, one word. She performed a countdown in her mind. The next sequence would be silence.

In that, she was not disappointed.

To mitigate the awkwardness of his position, Joshua trained his eyes on the panel, as if by force of will he could pull in a wayward signal. In that, he was disappointed.

After allowing him a grace period, Helen tried again, this time making seven separate attempts, widening the scope and magnitude of her signal. No reply was forthcoming.

"All right," the captain abruptly declared. After clearing his throat and shifting his weight he crossed to the astronomy section. Viewing the "blip" from several different angles, he came to a decision.

"Until we hear from them – until we know for certain they won't attempt to communicate, I'm asking you to alter your duties. Stay at communications. Keep repeating our signal."

"I can do that by putting it on a loop."

"Yes," he acknowledged, failing to catch her gaze. "But a signal, issued at regular intervals, sounds like exactly what it is – automation. It lacks the human touch... the sense of vibrancy and response. Do you agree?"

"Implicitly," she responded.

"Helen, it's in your hands. You're the communications expert." He left it unsaid whether he meant the telepathic sort, or that which transmitted via more tangible methods. "I want you on the bridge."

With me or against me? she wondered, but replied, "Of course."

"When you leave, make sure the officer in charge is aware how to contact you. When you return, report in, just as any other officer. I want a constancy – an awareness that when they're ready to open a dialogue, it is to you they will speak."

"But I won't be speaking just for myself," Helen objected. "Not the way it is in my mind. When I'm here, I'm your spokesperson."

He frowned, shaking his head slightly while running his hand a centimeter above the console.

"Are you saying you'd rather not stay on the bridge? Or that attempting to make contact with your mind is the only way you feel sure of success?"

"Neither," she corrected, rechecking her panel, then making an adjustment. While the distant ship did not appear closer to her unassisted eyes, it felt so to her other senses. "If those aboard the approaching craft harbor the one to whom I am listening, then I think it only fair they understand that circumstances have altered. What I transmit to them may, or may not be, my own words."

Without being physically confronted, Joshua responded by jerking away his face. As his hand went up to rub his jaw, he sighed audibly.

Were he being judged in a training exercise, that would have been scored against him.

What came next would have prompted his judges to fail him.

"Helen, I will not ask you, nor order you, or in any way coerce you into lying, putting forth falsehoods or betraying confidences." And then, more softly, "What kind of barbarian do you take me for?"

Her answer was direct and aimed at a point directly above his nose.

"One who places his duty to ship and crew over moral considerations."

Paula flinched and made a move to stand, but the captain motioned her down. This was between him and Helen.

"I'm not sure the two are distinguishable as separate entities," he retorted in clipped, carefully enunciated words.

"I'm not either," she readily supplied, attempting to defuse the bomb she had ignited. Her reply left him more confused than before.

"Then, what is your point?"

"I will do everything in my power to provide you with a medium through which you can talk to the aliens. Once that is achieved, I expect *you* to speak for the ship."

"Once I no longer need an intermediary."

"That is correct."

An expression of sadness crossed his features, bringing down the points of his mouth. His shoulders sagged and his hands went limp. Before him was a stranger. One he should have gotten to know a long time ago. The pain of his omission was acute, bringing back other betrayals. When he spoke again, it was for her ears alone.

"I went after her, Helen. Miranda. The cat. It wasn't too late. I grieved for my mistake and I did everything I could to make it better. I thought... you had forgiven me."

"I thought so, too. I was wrong."

"What will it take?" Finding the power of locomotion, he crept slowly toward her, not stopping until he was no more than a meter from her chair. "Must I sacrifice *Target* to prove my good intentions?"

"My love is not selfish, Joshua. On the contrary, I think it is all-encompassing. I loved that cat the way I love that alien." Pointing toward the central viewscreen, her action compelled him to turn so he could see both the woman and the small dot, representing the distant ship. "In their own way, both reached out to me. Miranda sought shelter for her soon-to-be-born kittens. I don't know what that alien wants. But I do know I don't have it in me to turn it away."

"Even if they prove hostile?"

Inhaling cautiously, she nodded.

"A cat may scratch to defend its young, or it may inadvertently draw blood while playing with an unprotected hand."

"Or, it may attack from some deviate reason of its own."

"Until I know with absolute certainty – until I fully comprehend its motives of innocence or intent – I will take its side."

"Even against your own kind?"

"Yes, Captain Terry. If I have to."

It was time to distance himself; time to revert to his training and his avocation. Time to set the lover aside, for he could not betray that which made him what he was: his ship. If she were looking for Joshua Terry, she would find him there.

"Very well. I accept your terms. You make it possible for me to communicate with those aliens and I shall ask no more of you. I grant you leave to speak for no one else but Helen Fitzgerald."

It was what she had demanded, but the toll had been great. Bowing her head in humble appreciation, Helen whispered, "Thank you, sir." And then, to herself, or to those powers beyond human comprehension, she prayed for avoidance of any further confrontations which would pit her against the man she truly did love.

At the end of her shift, Helen informed the captain she would complete some of her personal work at communications. He thanked her and offered to bring her something to eat. She declined.

He left at two bells, retiring to his quarters. Exchanging his shirt top for a casual pullover the crew had designed for him to replace, in times of leisure, his fraying uniform, he lay down, forcing his eyes to shut. With his thoughts racing and his body too restless to go through his sequence of relaxation techniques, he finally arose in resignation. After working nearly an hour on stretching and isometric exercises, he abandoned any idea of sleep.

Stepping out into the deserted corridor, he sought inspiration.

None was forthcoming, which did not surprise him.

Telling himself he was not lonely, he nevertheless went in search of Brother Brian. He found him in Hydroponics. He was tinkering with the newly retrieved food processing unit, the tufts of his long hair standing nearly on end, so that a child with a wistful imagination might suppose he had run the current backwards several times while trying to operate the "infernal machine."

Bouncing on the balls of his feet, Joshua hopefully inquired, "How's it going?"

Without looking up, Brian shook his head.

"It didn't come with instructions."

With an unanticipated irritation he could not have disguised if he tried, the captain poked his finger at the equipment.

"How complicated can it be?"

"If you think it's so easy, you operate it."

Moving aside, he swept his hand across the area, giving the captain free reign. Divining Brian's mood was even lower than his own, Joshua stared at the mechanism, pursed his lips, then made low, confirmatory remarks under his breath.

"What's the problem? You make a selection, press this button and whatever you want pops out here."

The muscles of Brian's jaw slacked and he was on the verge of a tart rejoinder when he "got" the joke.

"Yes, well, very good, sir. You're exactly right. Even I figured that out. It's what you put into it and how you set the controls to prepare the food that complicates matters."

Pretending to be surprised, Terry lifted the top and peered inside.

"Little more complicated than a 'vending machine, is it?" he admitted.

"Just a tad."

"I don't suppose there's an instruction manual in the computer?"

"I don't suppose."

"Did you look?"

If the statement were meant to be humorous, the minister did not smile.

"Yes."

"What about the tried-and-true approach of 'trial and error'?"

"We don't have enough food to waste if I make a mistake."

"What about asking Jingles?"

"I did. He refused." The answer was not what Joshua expected.

"Well, keep at it."

Having discovered he was not as desperate for company as he thought, the captain paced the rows of water tanks, observing them with a critical eye. Rising from her desk where she had been preparing a report, LaTanya joined him. Unlike Hardy, her mood was meant to convey optimism.

"Look at these, Captain. We're going to harvest our first crop of radishes soon."

Ordinarily, the news would have pleased him, for although radishes were not a food staple, they offered a change from what they had been eating. At the moment, however, the fact seemed ludicrous. With a ship of unknown origin bearing down on them and his own crew hungry and jittery, the harvesting of a delicacy seemed small recompense for their problems.

Running his hands through his hair bought himself some time. Civilians were not military personnel, he bitterly reminded himself. Brian's bad humor had reminded him that the ebb and flow of emotions was standard procedure for those who had never been instructed in the strict adherence to discipline.

Responding positively or negatively to the moment, his Technology Specialists, language professional and cleric needed his guidance. His mood was an infectious as a virus. Turned black and virulent, it could poison those aboard in a matter of minutes.

Taking in a deep breath, he swallowed, then tried what he hoped was a pleasant expression.

"I've been on the bridge all day; we canceled morning conference. I would like to have an update on the hybrid plants." Lowering his voice from habit, rather than necessity, he added, "Have they responded to the aqueous feedings?"

Had he realized how far short he accorded Carson's understanding, he would have been ashamed.

"They look better, sir. The graphs are beginning to show an upward trend."

Reacting quickly, he crisscrossed the rows, but nonetheless arrived after the technician, who was more familiar with the layout. Positioning herself like a sentinel before her post, LaTanya set herself at attention. One glance informed him "better" had been a euphemism for "slim."

His expectations cruelly dashed, Terry's face reverted to stoicism. She hopefully responded to that expression.

"They're alive, sir. Which they wouldn't have been without the nutrients."

"Is that what you meant by 'better'?"

"Alive is a damned sight better than the alternative. Sir," she supplied, knocking him down a notch with her carefully chosen sentence. While her reply was non-regulation, it did serve the purpose of putting him on the defensive. Not even an admiral's offense could counter "wilted" to "alive."

In her own way, she was waging a war with him. That, the captain could not argue, was non-military.

"Look at the graphs," she boldly continued, resuming her attack. "They show a definite upward trend."

His eyes could not confirm her statement, forcing him to rely on the miniscule upward numbers depicted by colored numerals. LaTanya astutely noted his shifting gaze, giving him a moment to compute the results before striking a third time.

"You are not, perhaps, used to reading complex computer generations, sir. That is my specialty. But the numbers speak for themselves."

Finding himself in a face off, he was compelled to concede.

"Explain them to me. If you will," he continued, unconsciously exchanging positions with her.

"Certainly, Captain."

Sidestepping his lanky body, she deftly worked the controls designed into the overhead monitor. Immediately an entirely different series of equations and graphs appeared.

"Taking what little data I was able to garner from the developer and botanists, I extrapolated the data pertinent to our present situation. Viz: chronic malnutrition and unfavorable growing conditions. While their hypothesis were based on planet-grown specimens and never confirmed by actual testing, I was able to compare a reasonable case-by-case scenario."

"Go on," he ordered, responding to the authority in her voice.

"In laymen's terms, what we have here is a guarded success. The plants, extremely vulnerable in the early stages of growth, have passed the critical phase. Their progress has been set back but not eliminated. According to plan, the next stage will be stabilization, followed by gradual regeneration and eventual harvest.

"Presuming," she brusquely hurried on, as though reporting on lab results which had no wider application than the triumph or failure of an experiment, "we continue the regimen. And, assuming our original information to be correct."

"The prognosis, then, is favorable."

"At this point."

Pacified by the news, as well as her delivery, Terry directed his attention toward the plants themselves. For all her glowing reports, they appeared turgorless and languishing.

"How long before the possibility of a major harvest?"

As behooved a well-trained subordinate, LaTanya rapid-fired her answer.

"Six months."

If she had said "six years" the statement could not have been more terminal.

"We don't have six months."

Although she had not been privy to that information, her face reflected no emotion.

"That, sir, is the extent of my report."

Expertly, the technician brought back the original screen, adjusting it into conformity with the others in the lab. The captain nodded, appreciating her penchant for technique. That, he could identify with.

"Thank you."

"You're welcome."

"Carry on."

LaTanya Carson returned to her duties, leaving him alone. When he retired through the hydroponics chamber, he noted Brian Hardy had abandoned his post.

There was no comfort in the realization he had won one battle and lost another.

CHAPTER 15

There was no place to go but back to the bridge. Helen and Janice Miles were holding the com. Neither attempted to catch his eye as he moved to the command position.

"It's much closer, sir," Miles reported. "Almost within scanning range."

"I see that. Still no communication?"

"No, sir," Helen reported.

"No other... contact?"

"Telepathy, you mean?" He nodded. "Nothing's come to me. But then, I haven't tried."

Swiveling in his chair, he forced himself to look at her.

"Maybe if you went to Level Four. Opened your mind."

She sucked in her lower lip, then shook her head.

"I don't think so. I don't feel anything. Whatever I was getting... or thought I was getting has stopped." Her voice broke as she continued. "Purposely."

Tapping the arm of his chair, Joshua digested her comment. On the surface, the loss seemed innocent enough, but upon reflection, the sudden silence appeared ominous. Once they had begun the transmission of an actual signal, those aboard the ship bearing down on *Target* had grown quiet.

Why? Because it was only Helen to whom they wished to speak? Not to the captain? Was he somehow perceived as a threat? If so, why was she safe?

The most obvious answer reflected on his face. She was quick to read it and equally fast to respond.

"No, Josh." He would not accord her the right to read his mind. Arching his eyebrows, he demanded a more elucidative statement. "Not because I am a woman and you are a man."

"You have to admit it's a possibility."

Withdrawing from her station, Helen swirled to address the entire bridge, although there was only one additional person present.

"Your supposition assumes whatever is out there can read all our minds."

"I can't exclude that possibility."

"Then consider this: aside from you, Paula and Janice are the only ones who have been on the bridge."

"And Brian," he scowled.

"Women still outnumber men three to two." Checking the chronometer on the console, Helen made a rapid calculation. "Janice and I have been alone here for two hours and twelve minutes. More than enough time for the... aliens... to determine your absence – if, in fact, they can read minds that clearly, which I by no means concede – and send a transmission."

"All right. Then what's the answer?"

Shaking her head, Helen resent a series of encoded messages, but waited only a second before continuing.

"I don't know. Either I haven't used the correct translations, or they don't have the capacity to reply. Not every ship in the universe is equipped with a 'frequency transmitter,' you know."

"No, but under present circumstances, it defies reason. And it doesn't explain why you haven't received any other telepathic messages."

"They don't come on a regular schedule," she cried, wringing her hands in frustration. "All I know is that I feel the loss acutely."

"You are the least likely to initiate aggressive action," Terry pointed out as his muscles stiffened, prefatory to action. "Now that they have categorical proof you've told others of their existence, and that – presumably – you've been ordered to employ conventional means of communication – one others share – they chose silence over a friendly greeting."

"You make everything sound so hostile. There may be dozens of reasons why they haven't spoken."

"And of those dozens, the majority point to stealth. I have to presume they want to keep us in ignorance; keep us guessing, off-guard. To me, that represents an unfriendly act."

"Or fear," she blurted, straining forward, attempting to convince through body language where words had failed.

"Fear?" He was incredulous. "That, I cannot accept."

"You're frightened," Helen accused, pointing a finger at him. Terry resented the accusation and turned defensively so that his profile faced her, rather than his full body.

"I'm commanding a crippled ship, without any appreciable chance of outrunning or outmaneuvering that approaching vessel. Their weapon capacity is unknown, but I must assume it to be greater, or at least equal to our own. Furthermore," he continued, standing behind his chair, "I have every reason to assume that where there is one ship, there are two or three more lurking in the distance. What then?"

Before she could counter with a hypothetical argument, the captain strode toward Janice Miles, speaking to Helen as he walked.

"Cease what you're doing. Stop all transmissions. Immediately."

"Why?" Helen whispered, loath to obey.

"They're close enough now to have received our messages. Repeating it over and over won't compel them to answer. We've told them we're peaceful. They have told us nothing."

Janice stood, permitting the captain to take her place. His fingers flew over the controls.

"What are you doing?" the erstwhile communications officer asked.

"Activating the protective screens. Until I ascertain their true intent, I don't want to be caught unprepared."

"They may take that as an act of aggression," she tried, watching his movements with an impending sense of doom.

"Just as I interpret their silence as potentially dangerous."

Setting the security device in place, a series of colored lights flashed over the panel. Across the main viewscreen a phosphorescent blue outline appeared, accompanied by a low, underlying hum. A moment later, three red alert lights burst into activation: *Lasers Armed. Stand-by. Red Alert.*

With resignation came horror and more slowly, a numbness of acceptance. Helen Fitzgerald eased back in her position, stretching her back before deactivating her communications equipment. As the console went dark, it took with her the impetus to fight. She listened to his next words as though from an incalculable distance.

"According to present calculations, that ship should be upon us in twelve hours."

"Within laser range," she clarified, more for the sake of hearing herself speak than actual need.

"If you wish," he agreed, subconsciously imitating her action by tightening, then loosening his own tense muscles. "When that time comes, I want you and Brian and Commander Burbone with me on the bridge. You'll need some rest before then. I don't want any of us making a mistake because we're tired."

Helen disengaged herself from communications, then walked toward him, hand extended. If they were only to have twelve hours, she wished them spent in peace.

"Then take your own advice. Come with me. We can... have something to eat. Together."

The invitation caught him off guard. Recovering quickly, Joshua took her hand, squeezing it with unaccustomed warmth.

"I will come. Lieutenant Miles, I'll send Hanson up. I don't want you here alone."

"Very good, sir," Janice responded, nodding respectfully.

Attached at the fingers, the first couple of *Target* moved toward the lift. It was slow in responding but neither noticed. They stepped in together.

"Level Two," Terry announced. The doors closed and the downward progression began. Simultaneously, they sagged against the rear wall, as though drawn by magnetic force. He grinned, tacitly accepting her overture of camaraderie.

"Nothing like learning on the job." He did not specify whether he meant Miles and Hanson or himself and his companion. Helen decided it was applicable to all four.

"I'm hungry," she tried, running a hand over her stomach. "I wonder what's for dinner."

"Radishes," he supplied, forcing her to do a double-take.

"Really?"

"Tomorrow, or the next day, anyway. LaTanya told me they were almost ready to pick."

"Yum. What about that dehydrated soup we found? And the fruit juice? I don't see any point in depriving ourselves, now, do you?"

If he tried hard enough, he could just make out the reflection of her face on the opposite wall. Too vague to allow him to read her expression, there was no mistaking the smile which flashed as she caught his eye in the metal.

"No. My God, that sounds wonderful. If only we had found some coffee, too."

"Don't get greedy," she advised as they emerged together, then walked down the hall. In their wake, they left happy expressions from those crew in the corridor. For the moment, at least, life had resumed a sense of normalcy.

Brian was waiting for them in the Command Center when they arrived. Upon seeing them, he rubbed his hands in anticipation.

"I've been expecting you," he explained to their upturned eyebrows. "Dinner is prepared."

"Don't tell me you've developed second sight," Terry complained. Behind the acting, however, was a tautness not to be ignored. Brian was quick to reassure him.

"Not a bit. Paula called from the bridge, saying she threw you out for 'loud grumbling of the stomach,' or something like that."

He had pulled it off until the inadvertent mistake with the name. Paula had not been on the bridge, although it was a logical conclusion.

"No," Helen began, hoping to gloss over the error before Joshua caught it, but they had both made the connection at the same moment. Appreciating her concern, he gave her a wink before stamping his foot in exaggerated pique.

"Not that," Joshua dismissed, waving his hand over the paltry repast the cleric had prepared. "Soup and juice is on the menu tonight."

"Plus three glasses of refreshing water," Helen supplemented, settling herself down at the table, sighing audibly that one crisis, however, slight, had been averted. Brian looked from one to the other, debated his options, then plopped himself beside Helen.

"Great! I'm starving. What's the occasion?"

Lifting him up by the armpits, Terry assumed Brian's vacant seat.

"For whom the bell tolls." No further elucidation was necessary. "I want the same fare issued to the crew."

Simultaneously shaking his head to countermand his own order, he crossed to the door, regally waving his hand over the electric eye. Like the ancient oceans of yore, it parted before him.

"You!" he exclaimed, pointing a finger at Maurice Kincaid who happened to be walking down the corridor toward the crew's mess. "I have a matter of some urgency to discuss with Chief Engineer Jingles. Will you ask him to present himself to me at his earliest convenience?"

Earliest convenience was Fleet jargon for *right now, exclamation mark.* Kincaid paled, swallowed nervously, then saluted. Spinning on his heels, he raced back the way he had come. The captain watched him until he was out of sight, then stepped back inside.

"Remember," he advised Helen with an exaggerated scowl. "If this doesn't work, the whole thing was your idea." Before she could assimilate the warning, jest having been low on her list of expectations, Terry turned on Hardy. "And you –"

"Yes, sir?" he gulped, less innocently than pretended.

"Draw the rations for the crew. Put them..." Sizing up his options, he opted for the chair he had so recently vacated. "Here."

"I'll help," Helen volunteered, springing to the cleric's aid. While they gathered the requisite supplies, Terry waited by the door, a cat ready to pounce. Simultaneously with the pronouncement, "We've assembled the food," came the polite "Chief Engineer Jingles, sir" through the intercom at the entrance.

"Enter," he was bade.

The Woolly Mammoth Man entered, face flushed with exertion, inhalations coming deep and rapid. He saluted, then stiffened.

"At ease."

The order had little effect, for the man's expression clearly indicated the worst.

"Is it the alien ship, sir? Has he shown aggression?"

What Captain Terry implicitly comprehended was that Jingles spoke for the crew. Whatever passed between them would duly be reported to the remaining fourteen, unless measures were taken to assure absolute secrecy. That ran contrary to his present mood.

Of all the methods at his disposal for informing the men and women of his command about the exact implication of the Red Alert, the one they would accept most readily would come from their officer-designate. No matter how peculiar he found their choice, Jingles had become the conduit between himself and the crew.

"Negative. We have had no communication from them; neither have they exhibited any threatening action. The only thing we can presume with certainty is that they will soon enter our sphere. That is not the nature of the crisis."

"Tell me, sir."

Straightening himself, arms positioned at his sides, Terry indicated the cache.

"My technical experts advise me that a portion of the store of supplies rescued from the Holding Area must be consumed within the next twenty-four hours. You are to see to it none of it is wasted."

Recognition was slow in coming. When it did, Jingle's face revealed both faith and disbelief. Terry bade him pursue the latter with a curt nod.

"Our last meal, sir?"

Relieved that he had extracted an honest and forthright question, which had been his desire, the commanding officer demurred. While his reply in this situation was critical, he felt more equal to the occasion than he had since Encounter.

"A celebration."

"Explain, sir," Jingles requested, flinching backward before righting his weight evenly to inch has massive body forward.

"The mission of this ship is to explore uncharted space. Part of that assignment is to reach out and contact the unknown. Rather than address our current situation with trepidation, it is my opinion we face it with anticipation."

"But we're hardly able to defend ourselves."

"I would match your wiles with that of any alien," Joshua rewarded him. "Not, however, on an empty stomach. The same could be said for the rest of us," he graciously and truthfully added. "Therefore, we are all going to partake of one decent meal before we encounter the visitors."

Gingleheimer considered carefully before accepting the proposal at face value.

"You've something else on your mind."

"Correct. But this has a more personal application. To you."

Placing his hands on the back of the "supply chair," Jingles set his jaw into at attitude of sharp attention.

"I am listening, Captain Terry."

"What I am about to reveal I leave to your discretion whether or not to disseminate." The engineer's knuckles whitened as he increased pressure on the chair. "We have registered positive growth response from those plants removed from the research labs. As you are aware, we are depending on those specimens to eventually supply the bulk of our subsistence."

"Aye, sir."

"Because they are experimental hybrids, it is impossible to accurately predict a date of harvest. However, when that time comes, we must have the food processor ready."

Moving around the chair, Terry came face-to-face with the engineer, with a latent hint in his demeanor that this request bore more significance to him than the impending crisis of the vessel bearing down on them.

"That, sir," he continued, "I must ask you to undertake."

Jingles' eyes narrowed into slits as he faced the proposal he had rejected once before. There was no thought of denial, but rather the challenge of saving face before his superior officer. Terry's softening expression allowed him that grace.

"Engineering is in bad shape, Captain. There's a lot to be accomplished down there before I can think of non-regulation duties. But," he tried, experimenting with an uneven grin, "I ought to be able to work on it in my off-hours. As a hobby, you might say." He had almost let Joshua off the hook, but his orbs suddenly flashed with confrontation. "How long have I got to complete the project?"

What he was asking was patently clear. It also bordered on disrespect, for the non-answer to his question had already been supplied.

This time, however, Joshua actually smiled, the white of his teeth dominating his face.

"That depends on whether you wish to eat raw soy beans in your radish salad, or supplement it with bread and cereal."

The statement was exactly right. Jingles chuckled, the sound rumbling from deep within his chest.

"I shall have the 'Gingleheimer Oven' ready and tested when Officer Carson presents me with the first crop."

"That," Joshua nodded in hedonistic satisfaction, "is acceptable. Now, if you will do the honors?" he concluded, indicating the food set aside for the crew.

"I will, gladly, Captain," he agreed, rolling his body and the chair back in one graceful motion. "Thank you."

"George Nguyen is spinning in his grave," Brian exclaimed as the engineer made good his exit.

"George Nguyen," Terry retorted, returning to his place at the table, "is dead."

His statement was both an ending and a beginning. Captain Terry had thrown the command training manual out the proverbial window. They were, for all practical purposes, on their own.

"A work," Brian observed, "in progress."

All three assisted in the preparation of their food. The task was uncomplicated, and Brian whistled as his hands flew over the pleasant job. When the soup was hot and the juice hydrated, they settled down together at the makeshift repast.

"This is our first real mean since the tragedy," Helen observed as they raised their glasses in toast. "It seems so simple: three friends sitting down to eat. And yet, it is one of the most important things we have ever done together."

"That, and breathe," the captain observed somewhat dryly before replacing his untouched glass on the table. "Brian, would you say grace?"

Caught off-guard by the request, coming from such an unexpected source, the man of God happily acceded. Bowing his head and interlacing his fingers, he repeated a rhyme which had never been taught in the seminary.

"God is good, God is great, and we thank Him for our food. Amen."

"Amen," Helen repeated. "That was beautifully expressed."

"It's something parents teach their children," he confessed. "It's one of the first prayers I can remember saying. I think it brings me more comfort than nearly any other."

"Why?" Joshua inquired, swirling the spoon around in the bowl before bringing it to his mouth, prefatory to blowing on the hot liquid before sipping.

"Because it's pious simplicity reminds me not to make things overly complicated." Wiggling more comfortably in his chair, Brian ate in contemplative silence a moment before continuing. "Life is actually a confluence of perceptions, merging together to make a whole."

"I thought he was going to keep it simple," Joshua winked at Helen. Brian caught the exchange but it did not deter him.

"A man may have little in the way of worldly goods, and yet be happy. Another might have all the riches in the universe, and be miserable."

Terry rolled his eyes, but they were gleaming with emotion.

"The good man is preparing his Sunday sermon and we're his unwitting victims." Squirming in his seat, he pursued the easy thread. "Isn't there some sort of listener's fee we're entitled to?"

"Only if you offer suggestions, which I haven't heard, yet."

Shaking his head, then sampling the fruit juice, Joshua rolled the sweet flavor over his tongue, the way ideas jumped across synaptic connections.

"Go on. I'm ready to listen. With your permission," he added, staring pointedly at Helen.

"By all means."

Her agreement was both an acknowledgment that she would approve Brian's sentiments and a tacit thank-you to Joshua for permitting him to elucidate. Without purposely calling a command conference, they were breaking symbolic bread over what might prove to be the most far-reaching meeting ever held aboard *Target*.

"You know," Reverend Hardy began, modulating his voice to imply familiarity, "we're really on a great adventure. This alien ship − not knowing anything about it − is exciting." He paused, waiting for an objection. When none was forthcoming, he resumed. "It's why we're here, isn't it? You stated it eloquently to Jingles. "*Target*. is an exploratory ship. Her mission is to chart the unknown − from black holes to exploding stars, to warps in space and hitherto incomprehensible life forms. Whatever is on that approaching ship I find invigorating."

It was a prompt for the captain to retract his former sentiments, or to qualify. Set up as the debating opponent, he chose his rebuttal carefully.

"I'd be a little more thrilled if *Target* had the capacity to maneuver; of flight," Joshua declared. His tone was not hostile, but reflective.

"That's your military training. But you're really an explorer, not a conqueror. I think we're looking at this all wrong."

"Tell us more," Helen encouraged, pulling a cloth from the shelf and wrapping it around her shoulders. "I like what you're saying."

"It's nothing more than you know yourselves. We don't need protective shields and lasers to feel confident in facing the unknown. What we need is an inquisitive mind, the capacity to accept that which is foreign to us, and – some caution."

"I'm glad you added that last, Father Hardy. Danger is more than a perception of comfort or discomfort. Like instinct, it serves as a warning that things may not be as they seem."

"But we must be equally ready to face good as we are to confront evil."

Joshua dropped his gaze, staring absently at the floor, uncomfortable, not with the concept, but with the consequences. Neither of his companions spoke. The challenge was left in his corner.

Retrieving an empty glass, the captain hoisted it slowly to his eyes, staring through the looking glass as though it were a portal to past and future events.

"The peacemakers are not always right. Sometimes it takes aggressive action to prevent a war. A preemptive strike is sometimes better than waiting too long."

Brian folded his hands, settling them on his lap, then leaned forward, eyes bright.

"How do we know that? No one can say what might have happened. Because aggression might have had a positive outcome does not preclude the idea that humanitarian effort might not have produced a better one. Picking up the pieces and putting them back together always leaves scars. Repairing a body which remains intact may seem more difficult and may take more time, but in the end, it could be the more optimal choice.

"Isn't it better to save the innocent while exorcising the evil, instead of lumping the good and bad together, so both lose?"

"You should have been a lawyer, Father," Joshua observed as he continued to stare at him through the warped perception of the nearly translucent glass.

"I'm arguing God's case before a select tribunal. We're very adept at destroying one another. Bloodshed is easier than diplomacy. But is it the better answer?"

"Turn the other cheek?"

"Love they enemy as thyself."

"Christ was crucified, Brian," he concluded, finally removing the optical and setting it carefully on the table.

"And His example as stood for nearly three thousand years. Can that be said of an aggressor? Any military general?"

"There are always individuals who can't be reasoned with."

"That's why we have a system of law and order. It's called justice."

"Justice, they say, is blind."

Covering his face with his hands, he then separated his fingers to give him sight.

"It can be. Mistakes are made; Concessions may lead to tragedy. I'm not saying there's any one, universal, perfect solution. If there were, we wouldn't be sitting here now. All I'm trying to bring out is the fact the aliens on that ship stand an equal chance of being friendly. We don't know. We don't have any facts. Until we do, I say we err on the side of righteousness. Which is," he concluded, staring at Helen, "a subject upon which I've given considerable reflection. And not a little backtracking."

"Did you get that from your crystal ball?"

"No," Brian demurred, placing a hand on his chest. "From my heart."

Digesting his words, which were no more than his own tenets verbalized, the captain rubbed his stomach, afraid they would somehow poison him.

"Wouldn't want to read the tea leaves, would you? Maybe that's why you saved them: so we could find the means of divining the future."

Helen smiled while Brian stamped his feet to restore circulation, staring up at the floor while making his confession.

"Thought about it."

For a moment, no one said anything, then simultaneously, all three laughed.

"We may hold you to that, Father Hardy. Not exactly regulation, but it's a consideration. But now, before we consult the occult powers, I think we need some sleep. In twelve hours, we're going to need all the inspiration we can get."

"Just remember," the man who had staked much remarked as he and Terry made their way for the door, "we represent the stars."

It was a staggering reaffirmation of faith.

After spending an hour with the crew while they ate, the trio returned to the Command Center. The door slid open. With it came the awareness someone had been there before them. Holding out his arm, Terry shielded Hardy from the potential danger.

"What is it?" he whispered.

"I don't know." Listening for any untoward sound, he heard nothing, yet the feeling of having is private quarters penetrated failed to dissipate. "Hello?" he called, then, more guardedly, "Who's here?"

"Look!" Brian's shout nearly depleted the wind from his sails. "Over there."

What he saw put it back. Changing course, Joshua charged the room, crossing with over-wide strides to the "intruder." Neither a crewmember nor an invading alien, what he encountered was a prodigious, high-backed chair with generously padded arms. Its best feature, however, was wheels.

"What's this doing here?" he asked in a delighted, childlike voice, dropping down then immediately testing the maneuverability. With the captain "aboard," the chair rolled admirably across the room.

Scratching his head, not at the mystery, but at the sudden appearance, Brian casually inquired, "Don't you know?"

"No."

"I assume it's a present."

"From whom? Santa Claus? Or Saint Turyan from the Genovian Sector? No one," he pursued, spinning himself around, "ever called *him* a jolly old elf."

"From Jingles. It's his throne; or was," he added in an undertone. "Where he ruled the Kingdom of Engineering."

"How do you know this?"

"I'm permitted access to areas of this ship even you are denied," came the answer, delayed by Brian's hesitancy to admit as much.

Stopping in mid-spin, the captain stared quizzically at his friend.

"Why is that?"

"I'm a peer; you're the nobility."

"Speak more plainly."

The cleric shrugged, but that did not lessen his enjoyment of observing Joshua play in the chair.

"How would it look, having such a position of authority somewhere other than the bridge?"

Joshua's blank expression finally gave way to puzzlement.

"Why would I complain?"

"In some circles, it might be considered mutinous."

"Who could possibly misconstrue..." Getting the point, he threw up his hands before landing them with a soft thud on the padded arms. "George Nguyen."

"Quite a compliment for you, discovering it here."

"But why would Jingles make such an... overture? *Loan* me his throne?"

Brother Brian understood the clarification, making a gesture with his hand, rather than directly addressing the interrogative.

"Wait a minute. There's a note on the back."

Crossing easily to the captain, he detached the handwritten paper and handed it over without once crossing his eyes over the penmanship. Whatever it said was the captain's to share or not as the occasion warranted. His reticence was immediately rewarded as Joshua read aloud.

"'I've lost so much weight I don't fit in my chair anymore. It takes a big man to fill this seat. It's yours, now. J.G.'"

The sentiment caught them both off guard. It was a long moment before Joshua reacted. He did so by dropping his head.

The crew had not only accepted his gift of the special meal, they had sent their own message back. *We accept your leadership. We trust you to make the right decisions.*

Joshua Terry had officially become the captain of *Target*.

"Who said," he intoned in a barely audible voice, "this wasn't a democracy?"

He had said it, and had now formally, if belatedly, received his answer.

CHAPTER 16

Jingles Gingleheimer, Janice Miles, Helen Fitzgerald, Brian Hardy, Paula Burbone and Joshua Terry: six human beings "holding the com." Waiting for the unknown; the "alien invasion," as the chief engineer styled it.

No one had asked if he were jesting.

It was better not to ask.

The good brother had broken regulations by issuing Mr. Gingleheimer two pieces of hard candy in the hopes of occupying his mind and restoring whatever humor would keep his mouth shut.

He would be duly noted for a commendation in the log.

If one were ever dictated.

"Data coming in, sir," Paula sang. With a twinge, Joshua recognized the cadence as that of Ben Caldwell. Whether subconsciously or not, she was imitating their former navigator. When she did not follow it up, he was prompted to reply, "I'm listening."

Which, as Brian would say, *was the God's truth.*

"Confirm approaching object as a small ship; propulsion unknown. Origin unknown. Symbols on the ship are not registered in our computer banks."

"Conclusion?"

"A previously un-encountered civilization."

Terry's attention snapped toward Helen.

"Dr. Fitzgerald?"

"I don't recognize the language."

"Translate it."

"Yes, sir."

She was ahead of him. His request and her acknowledgement were for form. He turned back to Commander Burbone in one fluid movement.

"How small? Crew capacity?"

"Hard to say without getting into it. I don't know their body size."

"Base your estimate on human dimensions."

"Twelve if they like to be crowded; half as many ought to fit comfortably."

"Hardly a battle cruiser."

That observation from the minister.

"Indications of weaponry?"

"Nothing external. Although I wouldn't bet against it, sir."

"Neither would I."

Jingles, Janice and Brian stood together, shoulder to shoulder, at the front of the bridge. Between them they represented silent sentinels at their post; guardians of what was, administrators of what might be.

In the Captain's chair, Joshua heralded the position of present moment. Behind him sat Helen at communications. With the board activated, tiny points of light flickered off her face. From his peripheral angle, he thought she looked alien. The idea neither disconcerted nor comforted him. What rang peculiar was that he had never before witnessed such a phenomenon in any other officer manning that seat.

Paula had placed herself at navigation. Even though Terry could operate the controls from where he sat, that had become her accustomed spot. Her right arm hung by her side, but she had placed her useful left on the controls. Muscles tensed by expectation, she gave the impression that were an order to come "hard starboard," or "thirty degrees port," *Target* would respond to her touch with pre-Encounter alacrity.

Maneuvering the chair so that he had a rotating view of the entire bridge, Terry registered the sights, the low sounds of breathing and computer equipment, the scents of re-filtered air and body presence before redirecting his attention to the screen.

"Any attempt at communication?"

"Negative," Helen replied. "Nothing. Not a peep."

Without turning a second time, he addressed Burbone.

"Any chance the ship is unmanned? Set on manual? Computer or robot controlled?"

"Unknown."

"Speculation?"

She rechecked her panels, then rose and crossed to data processing. While the action consumed no more than three seconds, the wait seemed interminable. Her walk, the way she carried herself reminded him of... but the name of a former crewman eluded him and before he snatched it from memory, the moment vanished.

"There have been four course changes, sir, since we first detected it. All bringing the craft into closer proximity with *Target*. It has slowed speed considerably in the past hour."

It was not an answer. He started to wave her off, when she jumped to attention.

"Slowing again, Captain. Coming to a stop."

He snapped his fingers at Helen.

"Open a channel." She complied, signaling the console at his arm active. He addressed his comments there, while maintaining visual contact with the ship. "This is Captain Joshua Terry, of the star cruiser *Target*. We are representatives of the United Planet Earth and the M100 Consortium. Our mission is a peaceful one. Identify yourselves. Over."

He waited, as Helen had done before. The crew, if there were any aboard the alien ship, made no reply.

"Repeat: This is Captain Terry of the *Target*. We are peaceful and mean you no harm. If we have inadvertently entered your space without permission, it was done without malice. Request identification. Over."

Silence. Closing his channel, he manipulated the controls at his hand, increasing magnification of the ship. The small craft filled the viewscreen.

Unlike their Skip shuttles, designed for short runs into space, the vessel before them was clearly designed for distance. Sleek, utilitarian and silver-coated, it shone like a beacon. It was nearly round in shape, but narrow, indicating it was no more than one level in depth. Small jets or power pods were placed beneath. Writing, or cuneiform clearly identifying the ship, were displayed boldly in a circular pattern around the top. Although he could not interpret it, the markings provoked no obvious signs of hostility.

By design and construction, the craft appeared to be perfectly suited for extended space travel. Yet there was something about the picture Terry could not quite put his finger on.

"Commander – scan the exterior."

"Yes, sir." She was a long moment at her task before she reported. "Indications of prolonged exposure to deep space, Captain. Look."

Closing in on what they presumed to be the name of the vessel, he saw what she meant. Whatever had been used to affix the words to the silver protective coating was pitted and worm.

"It's been out here a long time."

"He hasn't had a good waxing in a dog's age," Jingles decided, reverting to his personal penchant for calling all space craft by the male pronoun.

"Orders?" Miles questioned.

"We wait." She looked over her shoulder for clarification. "We can't outrun her and they won't talk to us. The next move would seem to be theirs."

"I say we buzz them a little with our lasers."

"Thank you, Mr. Chief Engineer. Observation noted. We wait." Crossing his legs in the attitude of a man with great patience, Terry signaled Helen. "Anything?"

"No, sir. Not from... any form of communication I can pick up."

"Thank you."

They waited. One hour, two hours. Jingles, Janice and Brian finally seated themselves in the empty console chairs. Time grew heavy.

Joshua memorized the square meter immediately before his captain's chair. Nothing escaped his eye, including his own boots, which he occasionally consulted for inspiration. When his patience had run out, he lifted his head and stared wearily at the crew.

"Time's up."

"We attack?" Jingles responded, head jerking back in anticipation. Joshua caught Brian's attention and the later smiled. *Jingles is not a blood thirsty man,* his expression conveyed. *He's one predicated on instant gratification.*

"Negative. We have neither the military, nor the moral right, to contemplate such an action at this juncture. The crew of that ship has made no aggressive move toward us."

"They're getting on my nerves."

"'Jingling' one's nerves is hardly cause for attack," Paula tried, defusing the situation by making a pun of the man's name.

"They're threatening us by their very presence," he protested. The comment was directed at Terry.

"Even as crippled as we are, we're ten times the size of that little..." He groped for the word. When he found it, goose bumps spread over his body with the force of an exploding star. "Rover."

Rovers were one- or two-manned space craft. They were used primarily by explorers, loners who traversed the depths of space seeking eclectic knowledge useful only to themselves. Rovers were for individuals running from civilization, or those in search of answers to questions no one but God was privy to. Rarely, traders who dealt in obscure artifacts used them to planet hop. They were the modern equivalent of canoes, pack mules and sled dogs.

Swallowing the lump in his throat, the captain's heightened senses made up his mind for him. Rather than wait out the situation as he had planned, relieving the bridge contingent with a fresh crew, he knew what they must do.

"Commander, you have the com."

Burbone read his mind with the certainty of one in telepathic communication.

"Aye, sir."

"Helen, Brian, come with me. Paula," he added, rising from his chair and heading toward the lift. "I want Lamar Porteous to meet us in the Skip bay."

"Yes, sir."

"And don't worry. If we find anything interesting over there, you're the next to 'visit.'"

With an unaccustomed show of gratitude, she waved a good-bye.

"Thank you, Captain."

As the door closed behind them, they heard Jingles startled, "Where are you going?" For once, it was a relief to have someone else deal with his interrogative. *It would be,* Joshua thought, *good practice of Paula's command technique.*

Being more attuned to the captain's thinking, Brian rubbed his hands together in unmitigated glee.

"We're going over there."

"What made you decide?" Helen inquired, as pleased and excited as her companion.

"By any other name, it's a Rover, Helen. The fact no one aboard has responded to our overtures may mean the crew inside is in trouble. I'm going to play it like that until circumstances prove otherwise."

"I approve," the communications expert said, gently putting a hand to his arm. "And I appreciate you taking me along."

"I have to," he stated with what might have been a non-regulation grin. "You'd never forgive me if I didn't. Besides," he continued as they reached Level Four and walked out, "You're our best bet if we want to talk to our fellow space travelers. If anyone can reach them, you can."

"And me?" Brian probed, his own curiosity at a peek.

The captain did not break stride as he answered.

"We don't know what's going on over there. Your services as a minister may be more apropos than ours."

While his observation dampened their enthusiasm, it did not serve to lower their eagerness. *This is what they had gone into space for: to confront the unknown. Come what may, they were ready.*

Or hoped they were.

Chief security officer Porteous was waiting for them in the Skip bay. He saluted as they arrived.

"Commander Burbone alerted me, sir. The Skip is ready to go. Checked and rechecked; power levels and fuel supplies at maximum." His voice lowered. "But, you're aware, Captain, she's only been tested the one time you took her out. You didn't cover any distance and the flight was of short duration. Taking her out without a full test is risky."

"No more than waiting for the aliens to make the first move."

"How to you propose to get inside that ship?"

"It's too small to consider bringing the Skip aboard. Once we get alongside her, I'll space walk over and see if I can get inside."

"That could prove dangerous, sir."

"So could doing nothing. Stand by to operate the hanger controls."

"Yes, sir." Eying the two civilians, he frowned. "I'd rather it was me who accompanied you, sir."

Terry put his hand on the man's arm.

"If there was room, I'd take you. As it is, we're going to be crowded."

Porteous was not yet ready to give up the argument.

"If there's trouble, I'm better suited to help you."

"If there's trouble, I doubt anyone will be able to help me."

Accepting that as the last word, the security officer stepped back. The three astronauts walked across the hanger floor to where the Skip awaited them. Activating the gull-wing door, Terry led the way inside, indicating to Brian where the spacesuits were stowed.

"Are you sure you're up to this? I realize you've had minimal training in this type of excursion. I can't predict what's going to happen. If I manage to enter the craft, your presence may prove useful. I have a hunch I'm going to need multiple perspectives to analyze what I encounter. That said, what I'm asking you to do is dangerous." He turned to Helen, including her in the conversation. "If your presence is required you're going to have to cross over. While you'll be tethered to the Skip, maneuvering in the suits is tricky until you get used to them."

Realizing the warning was mean primarily for him, Brian shook his head.

"I couldn't say no if I wanted to. You know I believe everything happens for a purpose. You and I and Helen are here because we're meant to be. To deny that is to deny my faith. I'm more than willing to do whatever is required to follow your lead. Besides," he grinned, turning to Helen, "I have an expert with me. She's had flight training. I'll just close my eyes and do as she says."

"I appreciate the vote of confidence. Just don't look down and you'll be all right."

Terry helped them both don their suits, then slid into his own. When he was satisfied they were ready, he indicated a position behind the co-pilot's seat.

"That's where you'll have to squeeze into, Dr. Hardy. I'm sorry I can't do better. There's no way for you to be strapped in, so I'll try not to give you a bumpy ride."

"You won't hear me complain. At least for the first ten minutes."

Joshua and Helen waited until he had forced his way into the craft before she assumed her position in the co-pilot's seat and he slid into the command position. Once buckled in, he opened communication with the bridge.

"*Arrow* to *Target*. Do you read?"

"Loud and clear," came Burbone's voice. "You're cleared for departure. No further movement by the alien craft."

"Copy." Switching channels, he spoke to Porteous. "Confirm departure."

"Aye, aye, sir. Preparing the hanger for departure. Steady as she goes, sir. Don't push her until you're sure your vessel is stable."

Jingle's voice from the bridge over-road what else the security officer had to say.

"Remember, if the Skip malfunctions, the tractor beam here isn't functional. The most we can do is follow you and get close, but you'll have to maneuver back by yourself."

"I copy. Engage departure procedure."

The hanger depressurized and the bay door slowly opened. Riding forward on the rollers until the ship was at the entranceway, Terry engaged the power pods and the *Arrow* maneuvered slowly into space. Once away from the main ship, it increased speed and Terry worked the controls, setting them on an intercept course with the alien vessel.

Although their destination had appeared at a lengthy distance, the trip required no more than twenty minutes before they were upon it, hardly giving the two civilian members of the boarding party the opportunity to quell their mounting adrenaline before they reached their destination. Working the controls on the console, he pre-programmed the return flight before setting the auto pilot. Nodding to his companions, Terry made one final attempt to broadcast their peaceful intentions.

"Ship to ship. This is Captain Terry. Request permission to board." No answer. "I am coming over in an attempt to enter your vessel. My motive is non-hostile. Your inability to communicate indicates you may have wounded aboard. We wish only to offer assistance. Over."

At this juncture he did not expect a reply and was, therefore, grimly satisfied to be correct. With a mounting anticipation of his own he had not expected, Joshua unstrapped himself and moved to the dis-embankment chamber.

"I'll stay in contact," he advised, fitting the helmet over his head, then testing the radio. "I've programmed communications so whatever I'm saying will be transmitted back to *Target,* allowing the bridge to hear me, as well. You can watch what's happening on the viewscreen. If I manage to get inside and it appears safe, I'll summon you over."

"What if we don't hear from you?" Brian asked, fastening the helmet for him.

"Then you have to assume I'm in trouble. In that case, I don't want either of you following me. Notify *Target* and let Commander Burbone direct you. The return course is already plotted. Helen, engage the power pods and the ship will return on its own."

Pressing her lips to the bubble of his visor, Helen kissed her fiancee. "Be careful."

"God bless," Brian added, drawing her back. When they were out of the chamber, Terry decompressed the atmosphere and he slipped outside.

Brian held her hand as they watched him maneuver away from the vessel.

"He'll be all right."

"I know he will. What I'm not as sure of is what he'll find there," Helen admitted. "I wish I were going with him."

"He'll call us."

Crowding at the one window which offered a view of the exterior closest to the alien ship, they fixed their eyes on the captain as he made his way across the short distance. Approaching the ship, his voice suddenly broke into the preternatural silence of the Skip.

"I'm at the outer perimeter of the craft," came the filtered words of the space walker. "Our original data is correct: this ship has been out here a long time. Evidence of pitting and scaring on the outside. Nothing major. No outward indication of damage. She's just an old ship."

On the bridge, the small contingent watched with equally intense interest.

"Imagine the technology," Jingles reverently whispered, checking the onboard data Terry's sensors were transmitting. "He's right. That little baby's seen service for decades. Wherever he came from, they knew how to design. He's beautiful. A marvel. We could learn a lot from that ship."

"Yes," Commander Burbone agreed, her own awe increased by the view. "Let's hope there's a crew aboard willing to teach us."

While the entrance portal was nearly invisible, Terry found it without trouble, precisely where he expected it to be. Emboldened by that knowledge, he comprehended it to be a link between the two races.

The triumph was short-lived, however, as he was unable to locate any exterior controls, which was not, by itself, unexpected. Debating how best to proceed, he turned toward the Skip. Reading his body language, Helen had her answer ready.

"Knock."

Although too distant to discern individuals, Terry nevertheless repositioned his body as though searching for eye contact.

"Didn't copy. Helen, was that you?"

"Yes, Captain. Try knocking."

"You're joking."

"Where are your manners? Weren't you taught to knock before entering an occupied room?"

"Whoever is inside can't possibly hear me."

Her reiteration was adamant.

"Do as I say."

With a shrug more theatrical than sincere, he easily maneuvered himself in the weightlessness so that he was positioned by the entranceway. Raising his right hand, he balled his fingers into a fist and knocked. The hatchway slid open.

Less surprised than he should have been, Terry stared into the opening but made no move to float up into it before speaking.

"Request permission to enter," he politely called. "I will take your silence for an invitation. If this is not your intent, please state so and I will not board your vessel."

All around him was silence. Casting a glance toward where he presumed Helen to be watching, he gave her a thumbs up and hoisted himself through the portal.

There was a long pause before his voice reached the Skip.

"I'm going to leave the mic open. I'll give you the guided tour as I go."

"We appreciate that," Brian responded, straining with his eyes to penetrate the opening with his imagination.

Terry had not emerged into the pitch blackness of a small bay as expected. Shoulder-high lights, placed at regular intervals, dimly illuminated the chamber. On the walls were more esoteric symbols, which he concluded were instructions, the kind which might be placed in any such boarding/dis-embarkment area. The life support and gravity were off, requiring him to use his own suit for environment.

"So far, so good," he acknowledged to the Skip. "I don't see anyone, but there are definite signs of occupation."

Drifting toward the far wall, he discovered a control panel and a door.

"It looks like an ordinary Rover," he confessed. "It's got lights but no atmosphere. I'm going to try sealing the hatchway and activating the controls."

"We copy."

Aware that working the alien system out of sequence would compromise any life support that might fill the room, he studied the myriad color-coded buttons before depressing the black one. Immediately the hatch closed.

"One for one."

He tried a red control next and nothing happened. Before he could go to the third, a green light flashed. Assuming he was being guided to perform the operation, he put a finger to the blinking button. Pressing it down, a hissing noise filled his ears. A moment later, overhead illumination came up, fully brightening the room. Digital symbols scrolled across the screen, then the main door to the interior slipped apart.

Jumping back in surprise, he began to float away then fell heavily to his feet as gravity reasserted itself against his body. Recovering quickly, he tested the force weighing against him, determining it roughly equal to that of his own ship.

The micro scanner in his suit assessed the atmosphere.

"Breathable," he announced to his crew. "I've got gravity and oxygen. I'm going inside."

"Be careful," Brian warned.

"Say a prayer for me," Joshua grinned, knowing his friend was doing precisely that.

Stepping through the open portal, he emerged into a second small room. Like the first, this was flooded with warm light. Equipment hung along the walls, remarkably similar to that which he had aboard *Target*. The difference here was that an air of disuse clung about them, giving him the odd impression of entering the quarters of a long-dead acquaintance.

"Tools," he identified for his listeners. "No signs of life."

His curiosity piqued, but he did not have time to thoroughly investigate the chamber. That would come later, depending on what he found in the main body of the vessel.

While there was no indication the air was unfit to breathe, he did not feel comfortable removing his outer protection. Maneuvering slowly toward the next door, he went through the control sequence again. This time, the red button opened the divider.

He found himself in a corridor. To his right and left were other closed doors. Ignoring them, he began walking, taking his time so as not to give the impression of haste or aggression.

Remembering Helen's admonition on manners, he spoke as he went, attempting to alert those inside of his progress.

"Hello? I am Captain Joshua Terry. I am in what appears to be the main hall. I am walking down it. Please advise if my intrusion is unwanted and I will return to my own ship."

Still, silence reigned. With adrenaline forcing his heart to accelerate, he continued his forward progress, finally reaching the end of the walkway. What confronted him was an elevator.

"It's bigger inside that we thought," he dictated. "At least two levels. I'm going to try and get into the lift and go up."

Recognizing an electric eye, he flashed his hand over it. The door instantly parted.

"Bridge," he tried. The doors sealed. Without any detection of movement, lights on the interior flashed, then the transport opened. What he saw took his breath away.

"The bridge," he whispered, awed by the beauty of the interior. "What an incredible sight."

Unlike the huge, circular space devoted to numerous stations and a dozen personnel on *Target,* this command center was clearly designed for two. A pair of seats, positioned by a main viewscreen were placed front center. Around them, at arm's length were various control panels and smaller screens. All but the primary one were blank.

The ceiling was low, no more than six feet high, compelling him to stoop as he entered. Everything about the bridge was small, giving him the fleeting impression of a child's space ship. Logic to the contrary, it was a thought he could not shake.

As opposed to the embarkation area, the bridge had the air of expectation and function, but like the rest of the craft, was devoid of life. Lights indicated the controls were functioning, but no hand directed them.

"Hello?" he tried again. "Hello? I come in friendship. I mean you no harm."

He waited, straining his ears for any non-mechanical noise. Suddenly, he was assailed by an overwhelming dread of discovering the craft to be unoccupied. He did not want that. Before him was a well-loved bridge. With little effort, he could easily envision caring hands working the controls, voices uplifted in pleasant banter. He could feel the anticipation of discovery, the gentle passage of time as the ship maneuvered through space.

Alike, yet peculiarly different from any vessel he had ever seen, this, he concluded, was a home. A self-contained world.

"Helen. Brian. I need you over here."

"Roger. We're suited and ready."

"I'll meet you in receiving." Reacting to his own word choice, he paused to analyze the peculiar expression. One which had sprung spontaneously to his lips. *Receiving.* A visitor might be received. A baby was placed in a receiving blanket. A man received a gift from a friend.

Attempting to shake off the impressions flooding his senses, Terry returned the way he had come without a false step, making him believe he could have done so blindfolded, conveying the same sense of familiarity he experienced aboard *Target.* Already at home, whoever had lived here had made a distinct impression on his psyche.

Entering the "receiving" chamber, a screen flashed on, revealing the exterior of the ship, enabling him to watch as Brian and Helen made their way across space. Attached by connecting cords, there was no way to lose them, yet he did not breathe a sigh of relief until they were firmly aboard.

Motioning with his hands, he removed his own helmet while indicating they do the same.

"Oxygen-nitrogen. Pure textbook. Could have been set up for us."

"Maybe it was," Brian remarked with enough strangeness in his tone for Joshua to pause before answering.

"Why do you say that?"

"You didn't find anyone, did you?"

Backing away, the captain held up his hands.

"That doesn't mean we won't. I'm not sure where you're going with your thinking, but there *have* been people on this ship. People who lived here – loved here."

"You've discovered an awful lot by one quick inspection."

Using the pretext of modesty, Brian turned his back while Joshua helped Helen remove her helmet. As they worked, the cleric took advantage by inspecting the alien writing across the wall which came just at his eye level.

"Comfortable for a human being to read, assuming his height to be five-foot seven or eight," he decided.

"I'm six-foot one," came the sour retort from the captain. "If you're implying the Great Unknown Force made a new Eden for us, then He had you in mind as Helen's mate."

"Stop it!" she cried in dismay, thrusting her helmet at Joshua. He gathered it in, then hung it from a convenient hook on the wall, as she accused Brian. "You're wrong. It's nothing like that! The very idea is ingenious."

"Is it?" he asked, arching an eyebrow and finally meeting her gaze.

"Yes. I will never argue against the belief Divine Will plays a role in human destiny, but this is not our ship. It wasn't created for us. It's not ours to keep."

"Who does it belong to?" The interrogative was canny and distant. She bristled then shook her head.

"If you want to know what impressions I'm receiving, then ask. Don't play games with me. I don't appreciate it."

"I wasn't, but I'll make a note." Moving to her right, Brian began to remove his own helmet, then, apologetically, dropped his chin. "I wasn't intending to come off as clever, or devious. To be honest, I was speaking the first ideas which came to me; expressing my first impressions. I tend to look at situations from a different perspective. I'm sorry."

"No offense taken," she relented, although far from appeased. "But you're right: we should say or record our impressions. They may help us later. The more we discover, the more our original thoughts get perverted. We alter them to fit what we've learned, but that doesn't always form a correct picture.

"It's something the study of language taught me, she continued, warming to the subject as though the ship, itself, had soothed her anger of a moment before. "When you're first learning a foreign tongue, you make mistakes – in pronunciation and in use of idiomatic phrases. As you become more fluent, those early errors are overcome, but never completely erased. What you end up doing is combining the old with the new. Let's be careful. When the first lessons are incorrectly programed in our thought patterns, they have a tendency to stay with you. You end up repeating your mistakes."

"Good point. Come on." Leading the way, Terry guided them into the long corridor. "I didn't look in any of those rooms. We can do that later."

"If we're invited to do so." Helen objected.

Stopping abruptly, he waited for her to draw alongside.

"Is there someone aboard?"

"You know there is," she replied with conviction.

"Someone who knows we're here?"

"Of course."

"Someone lying in wait, or someone going to welcome us with open arms?"

Her reply was succinct and dry.

"Neither."

He tried again, drawing her beyond the point she wished to go.

"Friend or enemy?"

"I would say, Joshua Terry, the answer to that will prove to be entirely subjective."

Leaving him with his lips pursed, she pushed past, finding her own way to the bridge. He followed, suddenly not at all sure he was doing the right thing.

CHAPTER 17

Everything was as he left it, without signs of occupation. Helen had already proceeded to the dual command chairs, where her hands had settled on the backrests. For a moment he believed her to be caressing them.

"Be careful," he warned. "Don't touch anything. Not until we find out how this ship operates."

"We wouldn't want to be catapulted into deep space," Brian agreed. "At least, not without our passports."

"I have mine with me," Helen retorted before she removed her hands. Brian and Joshua exchanged glances, then stepped away from one another, each taking a small section of the ship to explore.

Without purposely meaning to, the captain gravitated toward the controls where his fiancee stood. He had no trouble keeping his eyes from her, for the instrument panel held his complete attention.

"It's a thing of beauty," he whispered, not caring whether he was overheard or not, for he was actually speaking for and to himself. "A marvel. Functional artwork."

Ignoring his own previous admonition, he settled down in the left-side seat, then reached out, holding the undersides of his hands over the panel. His fingers pantomimed activating the controls, while his face, directed toward the viewscreen, envisioned a cavalcade of stars rushing past.

"I can almost... feel the wind in my face."

The analogy was as scientifically inaccurate as it was poetic. It made no difference.

Drawing back, he stared beneath, toward his feet. There was room, just barely, for a pilot his height, to sit comfortably. Turning to his right, his mind light years away, he was startled to see Helen had positioned herself beside him. His grin was large and spontaneous.

"Do you feel it? The majesty of this ship? The... inner beauty? A man could challenge all the unknown in the universe and never fear a thing. Whoever constructed this craft was an artist; someone who understood creation. This isn't a machine; it's a living being."

Helen's expression was enigmatical. Averting his gaze because he couldn't read it, he sought Brian.

"A man could never be lonely here."

"I wonder if that's true?" the minister questioned, shaking his head slightly. Then, having found nothing to move him the way it had Terry, he crossed toward them. "Does it appear the ship was on manual control? It was obviously constructed for people to fly, but we haven't found the pilot. Or any crew. Was it programmed to direct itself toward the first vessel it encountered?"

It was a tempting question which ran contrary to Helen's assertion that the ship was occupied. One, if answered in the affirmative, might offer Joshua the opportunity of a lifetime.

Checking the instruments with an ill-disguised eagerness, he attempted to assimilate the complex controls.

"I can't tell. Not at a glance. I'll have to study it. While it appears simple, I suspect the instrumentation is very highly sophisticated."

Losing interest in his quest, or perhaps afraid of what he would find, Helen rose from the chair and crossed the bridge. Beyond it, in an open, easily accessible area, were the living quarters. If she were to discover any answers, it would be here.

Similar to the command center, she noted the room was filled with technical equipment. Some, she divined, were view screens, although not for exterior scanning. A number were placed on low tables. Numerous touch pads lined their sides, serving as keyboards. Others were mounted on walls, easily observed from the low, comfortable couches. Sources of entertainment, surely.

Moving further inside, she detected that immediately under them were rows of shelves, all protected by an opaque substance, like glass. Putting her hand to it, she discovered it to be soft and pliable. Behind it were literally thousands of discs. *Music,* she thought. *Or recorded dramas.*

Turning opposite she identified other shelves. The discs contained therein were all of different colors, a virtual rainbow of red, yellow, blue and green hues. Taking one out, she noted the same type of cuneiform imprinted on their surface. The titles of books.

Dominating the space were two cream-white couches, placed side-by-side. Crossing toward them she was tempted to sit in an over-large chair of the same material, situated in front, by one smaller computer. Beside it were six discs. They were what caused her to pause.

In appearance, the discs resembled the ones she presumed to contain entertainment. Unlike them, however, these pulsated with latent energy. Not a physical emanation but a psychic one.

Placing her hand to her head, Helen divined that whoever resided within this magnificent space ship treasured these above all others. They were the ones which evoked memories, brought solace, touched the heart strings.

As much as she wanted to handle the discs, she dared not. That would be sacrilege. Were it within her power, and she knew it was, no one would touch them. Not without permission.

A premonition she clearly understood, which would never be forthcoming.

A gentle caress touched her cheek, so slight it might have been the exhalation of warm breath. Drawing back, she expected to see Joshua leaning over her, a hushed exclamation on his lips. She was alone. He and Brian were still at the controls. With her auricles pounding, Helen lowered herself into the chair. A sense of abiding comfort nearly overwhelmed her.

Just as Terry had felt at home on the bridge, this, she knew, was her special place. But it was not hers. It belonged to another. That, she sharply warned herself, was a fact she must never forget.

When she saw it, a gasp, so low that no one listening with ears could hear, escaped her lips. Hardly daring to believe her eyes, she draped a hand over the side of the chair. Her fingers touched something soft and furry. It did not move. She probed it, then hesitated, giving the creature, if indeed it were alive, a chance to escape. It remained still.

Still, but not dead. The object under her hand had never lived. At least, not in the corporeal sense.

Gently wrapping her fingers around it, Helen drew forth the small object. It was brown, no more than a foot tall and six inches across. The little figure had two arms and legs, rounded ears, a tiny snout and a pair of luminous glass-like eyes with yellow pupils.

"A teddy bear," she intoned with sacred appreciation. "A child's toy."

No, she immediately corrected herself. *A child's companion.*

Bringing the bear to her lips, she rubbed her nose against the grain of its fur. The eyes seemed to blink and she fully comprehended that such an act was well familiar to the companion.

"What's your name?" she asked, without feeling foolish. In another, the question might have been rhetorical, the act of an adult pacifying a child, but not to her. While she did not expect a verbal answer, she somehow felt the creature would divine her good intentions.

Smiling gratefully, she continued her one-sided conversation.

"You're very pretty. I love you."

The words were spoken without thought, without consideration. They bubbled from her soul, as though the diminutive owner were a cherished friend and this teddy bear a tangible part of his essence.

Helen Fitzgerald did not hear a noise. She did not see any movement. It was the celestial humming of the stars which alerted her that her actions were being watched. Appraised. Not by the teddy bear companion but by someone with the innate ability to see through its eyes.

It was *he*. Her distant communicator. The voice she had heard from light years away.

Of that, she would have bet her immortal soul.

I am here, Helen thought to him. *I have come.*

"Finally," it thought.

I am sorry it has taken me so long. I never doubted you.

A whimper, perhaps, or a low cry.

I am with others. Two others. They mean you no harm.

Silence, then, possibly the blinking of eyelids.

My name is Helen. What's yours?

The crinkling of a nose, then withdrawal.

I am your friend. And then, more emphatically, *You know that.*

Hesitation. Confusion. The whirling of thoughts.

I am like Teddy Bear. I have come to be your companion.

Fright. Panic.

Please. Stay hidden. It's all right. I won't come looking for you unless you invite me to.

Deep puzzlement. Consideration. Conflict.

There is no hurry. Do you understand time? Take your time.

"Come to me."

Not in speech, but silent verbalization. Helen absorbed it through her pores.

Rising slowly, the little, brown furry companion clasped to her breast, she moved so that she could peer into the furthest reaches of the den. What she saw were more computers, banks of equipment. No recess to hide. Until she detected the small crawl space leading behind the towering mechanisms.

May I come closer?

"Yes. No. Maybe."

The fright of an innocent being.

One baby step, then two and three, until she was at the wall. Swallowing her own fear, not a physical dread for safety, but a trepidation of unmasking that which no one before had seen, Helen peeked around the corner.

He was there, huddled at the far end, arms drawn up, crisscross around his chest. Like his companion, his eyes were large and luminous, sparkling with emotion. A crop of tangled black hair, worn elfin-style, in bangs, decorated his beautiful, symmetrical face. His cheeks were clean-shaven, though he was not a child, but an adult. Or perhaps more accurately, a youth, for the guiltlessness of age was stamped upon his countenance with unmistakable simplicity.

He was dressed in a yellow-tan, long-flowing tunic, reaching half way to his knees. Beneath, he wore dark trousers. On his feet were simple shoes, more like slippers. Around his waist was an undecorated sash of softly flowing silken material.

"I have found you." She spoke in hushed tones, for she intuitively felt he was unaccustomed to loud noise. "I have come." He pursed his lips, decorating his beautiful face with in childlike expressión of acknowledgment. "Have you waited a long time?"

He nodded, just barely moving his head.

"A very long time?"

Again, a slight indication in the affirmative.

"I'm sorry you were lonely." It was a peculiar thing to say, but she knew it to be verity. "Are you by yourself?"

He did not move but his eyes flashed in sudden terror. Looking to her side, Helen saw that Joshua and Brian had come up alongside her. Her reaction was swift and decisive.

"Stand back."

"I can't see it," Joshua whispered, craning his neck. "What does it –?"

"Him," Helen corrected. "Him."

"I'm sorry –"

She spoke over his apology. "He's... a youth."

"A child? Teenager?" This, from Brian.

"No. At least I don't think so. A young man." Inclining her upper torso forward so she could have a better look without actually moving her feet, Helen squinted at the face. "If I can judge him by our standards, I'd guess he is about twenty. But I could be off by ten years, either way."

I could be off by light years.

"Does he speak English?"

"He appears to understand me," she hedged. Noting that the alien's terror had increased during this exchange, Helen held her hand up, then waved it cautiously, taking care not to make any sudden motion which might scare their host. Modulating her voice, she addressed her own companions, but never did she take her eyes from *him.*

"Please. Will you stand back? Out of sight, at least."

They did not argue for there was no disobeying her command. When she felt their presence go, both the Earth woman and the star traveler breathed a simultaneous sigh of relief.

"Is that better?" she asked, grinning in satisfaction. A barely perceivable nod of his head indicated assent. "I'm glad, too," she confessed. "Two's company, four is a crowd."

He frowned, tiny furrow marks lining his brow. His lips moved but she did not catch the words.

"Say again, please," she requested. "Repeat what you said. If you speak slowly and clearly, I will try and understand you."

Rather than reply, the man-boy held up three fingers, using his thumb to hold down his pinkie.

"Three," Helen identified. He nodded, then watched her with curious, intense eyes, waiting to see if the light would dawn. When it did, her face exploded into radiant sunshine. "I said it wrong, didn't I? *Three* is company but five is a crowd. There is you and I and Teddy Bear. We are the three."

Tiny mewing noises accompanied his genuine pleasure.

"Thank you for correcting me." He grinned and Helen felt tears welling at the corners of her eyes. "It *was* you, wasn't it? You who I heard calling me from so far away." His smile widened. With a shaky hand, he pointed a finger at her.

"Yes. Me," she acknowledged. "How did you find me?"

Drawing back his hand, he pointed to his head.

"Through your mind?"

Yes, she read.

"Can you speak? Do you communicate with verbal – spoken language?"

Yes, again.

"Will you talk to me?"

I am afraid.

He was transmitting more clearly, almost as though he had the ability to talk without moving his lips or vibrating sounds across his larynx.

"Please do not be afraid. I am your friend. Do you know the meaning of 'friend'? Does that have significance to you?" When he made no response, she remembered the teddy bear. It was still held firmly to her breast. She held out the little animal, caressing its furry brown ears before shifting her gaze back. "Companion. Friend."

His expression, hesitant at first, softened. With another soft mewing, he held out his arms. She reached forward and handed him the bear.

"Here you are. It's hard to be separated from a beloved companion, isn't it?"

He nodded emphatically, rubbing the fur, first with, then against the grain. Droplets of moisture rolled down her cheeks.

"I found him by the chair. Is that were you sit?" Cradling the bear under his arm, so its face stared up into his, he nodded. "You heard us come, so you hid." Another confirmation.

"We did not mean to frighten you."

He shrugged, then returned his attention to the companion. From behind her, Helen could just see, out of the corner of her eye, Joshua inching closer.

"Ask him who runs the ship," he requested in a low undertone.

"Little one," she tried, "are you alone here?"

The alien, who was remarkably human looking, underscoring their close bonds of physiognomy, stared at her without comprehension.

"Do you have other companions? Ones who talk to you?"

His face finally registered understanding. His head bobbed with innocent simplicity.

"Where are they?" His look turned blank. "Are they here, with you? Behind you?" No reply. "In another part of the ship? Hiding? Like you were hiding?"

A frown was all the answer she received.

"Are they afraid?"

This time, he pouted. Helen responded by smiling.

"They are *not* afraid." This, she deduced instantly, was the correct assumption. "I think I'd be a little afraid if strangers came onto my ship."

Releasing his tight grip on the bear, the diminutive ship's captain wiggled the pointer finger of his left hand, twice in her direction, twice in his.

"We are not strangers, are we? Not you and I. We know each other. We've been talking for some time, now, haven't we?"

Yes, she read. *That is good.*

"Very good. I... feel as though I know you."

Me, too. And then, more quietly, *Just a little.*

"Now, we'll have a chance to talk, face-to-face. Is that good?"

Yes. No. I think so. I don't know.

Before he could panic, Helen held her hands up, palms outward.

"It's all right. Slowly. We don't have to hurry, do we?" His confusion persisted. "Will you take my hand? Will you come out, so we can sit on the couch together? Like friends?"

His eyes snaked around her, toward the space she presumed Joshua and Brian occupied.

"Would you like me to ask them to go?"

A moment's consideration, and then *Yes.*

"Joshua. Brian. Please leave this room."

"No, Helen," Terry protested, having anticipated her request. "We don't know anything about him. It's too dangerous."

"He will not hurt me."

"You don't know that."

"I know it." His silence did not indicate acceptance. "It's my life. I choose to do with it what I will. Just as you take chances, so do I. I have never tried to stop you from facing a dangerous situation."

"Because what I do determines the well-being of the ship."

"And the crew," she completed. "What you have done is no more or no less than risk your life. That is your duty. This is mine. I ask you again: go away. Go to some other part of the ship."

"All right, Helen. Call if you need us." It was Brian who spoke. He had overruled the captain. Now it was up to the commanding officer to obey or not. The decision was his.

"You're sure you're in no danger?"

"As certain as I've ever been of anything in my life."

"And you'll call – signal us – if something goes wrong?"

"I will."

She did not give him her word. That would have been beneath contempt. She had said all she was going to. Like her mute space man, he would have to accept what he had been given.

"We'll leave." The statement was begrudged. "There has to be others. He can't operate this ship by himself."

"When you find them," she agreed, "then *you* call *me.*"

It was her little secret: hers and Teddy's companion. They would never call, because there was no one else to find.

"Leave your communicator open."

"Good-bye, Captain Terry."

The statement had more finality than either of them anticipated. With a slight bending of his shoulders, Joshua moved away, Brother Brian trailing behind. In a moment, they disappeared from the room.

As though they had never been.

CHAPTER 18

"They won't come back until I call them," Helen explained, extending her hand. "They are friends, but it is better you and I are alone for now. Isn't that right?"

Yes.

"Will you take my hand?"

Creeping forward as though his feet had rollers on them rather than toes, the alien stared quizzically at her offering. With his mouth rounding into an "O," he hesitantly held out his own, close, but near enough to touch.

"Please," she invited.

The conflict warring inside him was tremendous, but greater than fear was dire curiosity. With a joyousness she had not anticipated, the alien, by definition rather than fact, suddenly grabbed her fingers, engulfing them in his own. With wondrous delight he explored the digits, eyes wide as twin moons. His left hand joined his right, rolling over her skin with minute care, absorbing the warmth and softness. Reciprocating with joy, Helen basked in his amazement.

"I am like you," she stated.

"Yes!" he cried aloud, the word so startling her she nearly withdrew in shock. "Yes. You are like me! I never knew."

With an exclamation of sheer delight, he ran his hands up her arm, feeling the bone and muscle, then touching himself, to compare tactile sensations.

"Like me. Just like me! How can this be?" he continued.

"Perhaps we share a common origin."

"Like me. Like me." His fingers reached her shoulder, then eagerly sought her face, running over the contours of her chin, lips, nose, then tousling her hair. "Like me!"

Helen Fitzgerald was all motherhood, all femininity, all humanity; she was friend, companion; a teddy bear with blood coursing through arteries and veins.

She was like him.

Leaping in tremendous excitement, he grasped her, shook her, then began his explorations anew, rubbing her flesh, patting her stomach, then stooping down so he could examine her legs. There was no sensuality to his touch, only pure, absolute wonder.

She was glad the others had gone. The thought, she realized, was not as pure as she would like to have imagined. Alone with this strange creature, she could revel in his joy, delight in his astonishment, taking each new step as an exploration, more pristine than pure spring water. Were Joshua or Brian to watch, their observations would be tainted by distrust.

And jealousy, Helen acknowledged, suddenly laughing as the lightness of her alien's touch tickled her. There was no room for the baser emotions aboard this ship. Like its owner, nothing worldly should ever be allowed to enter.

In all her life, she had never before come face-to-face with innocence.

"Sit in your chair," she advised, finally laughing at his playfulness. He followed her glance, then, perhaps reading her mind over the spoken word, pranced away, making a hop, skip and jump before arriving at the furniture.

"You – sit," he commanded in a stern, authoritative tone of voice she had not anticipated.

"And if I don't?" came the challenge. His expression changed so rapidly there was no time to analyze the myriad emotions. What finally settled over his features, however, was incomprehension.

"You. Sit," he repeated.

In his world, then, there was no disobedience? It was a staggering thought.

"All right." Agreement was easy. After positioning herself on the couch, she patted the seat of the chair.

"You. Sit." He complied readily, placing his hands before him in the manner of a school child, then waited expectedly. Having no knowledge of what came next, she was at a loss. "Tell me about yourself," came the slow, deliberate testing of the waters.

"Tell me about yourself," he faithfully repeated, astutely capturing the subtle nuisances of her speech. Helen's first instinct was to respond before she more correctly interpreted his repetition.

Her mind whirled with possibilities but only one stood out. Directing her face toward his, as she would if speaking to a student, she said, "My name is Helen. Helen Fitzgerald."

"My name is Helen. Helen Fitzgerald," he supplied, copying not only her intonation but her inflection.

It could not be that he had parroted her previous statements without understanding, for he had appropriately responded to other questions. It was, therefore, she determined, his position in the chair which had altered the situation. Without being precisely sure why, she rose and took him by the hand. When they were both standing, she repositioned him, then pressed against his shoulders, so that he sat on the couch and she in the chair. His reaction was immediate.

"I am your mother," he stated with soft, loving tones. "I am your father." As her throat constricted, Helen's eyes were magnetically pulled toward the discs on the table. "We love you," he continued, placing great emphasis on the word "love."

There was only one thing for Helen to say and she articulated the sentiment with precisely the same emotion, but with the stress on the last word. "I love you."

"I *love* you. I love *you.*"

He was learning his lesson. Unlike a blank page, however, he was already well versed in the meaning of what he said. Of that, she would have staked her soul.

She pointed to herself. "Helen."

"Helen."

"Helen. I am called 'Helen.' What are you called?" A sad look of puzzlement overcame him. His head shook slowly. He had no appropriate response. "What do you call yourself?"

Again, a blank. She indicated the stuffed toy. "What is his name?"

His face filled with pleasure. "Teddy Bear."

"Helen," she pursued, again indicating herself. "Teddy Bear." She nodded toward him. "What does Teddy Bear call you?"

That finally made sense. "Star Bright." It was not the name which surprised her as much as it was his pronunciation. "Star Bright," with stress on the second syllable.

"Star *Bright.*" It was not until she repeated it herself, that it came to her. "Star bright, star light, first star I see tonight."

"Wish I may, wish I might, have this wish I wish tonight," he completed with the reverence of a prayer.

Yea, though I walk through the valley of the shadow of death, I will fear no evil.

"Yes!" she agreed, clapping her hands. "You know that rhyme! You are Star Bright."

"Star Bright," he joyously repeated. "Helen. Teddy Bear. Star Bright."

She began to cry and did not know why. Seeing her tears, Star Bright burst out weeping. Flailing his arms wide, he first hugged himself then mashed the small bear into his chest. Before she could react, his sobs transmuted into torturous wails.

"No, it's all right. It's all right, Star Bright. I-am-here. I-won't-leave-you."

He did not respond, as though he had inexplicably gone deaf. Without fully comprehending his sorrow, Helen threw her arms around him as she would a baby, pulling him near, rubbing his head with her hand, soothing his trembling shoulders. "I love you, Star Bright."

The statement had the opposite effect of her intention. His voice deepened into a howl of agony. Extricating himself from her grasp, he pounded on his chest then slipped off the couch onto the floor, rolling over and over with grief.

Don't touch him, she warned herself, angry at the mistake she had inadvertently committed. *He won't understand. He doesn't understand that sentence the way I meant it. To him, it means separation.*

Why she felt that way, she did not know and had no time to analyze.

"'Star bright, star light. First star I see tonight.' Say it with me. 'Star Bright. Star light. First star I see tonight.'"

"'Wish I may, wish I might, have this wish I wish tonight," he gasped, tears rolling down his face.

"That's right. It's a poem; a rhyme. It has your name in it. Star Bright. It's all right. Everything is all right. Helen," she repeated carefully. "Teddy Bear. Star Bright."

"Helen," he sniffed, daring to relax his tensed, cramped muscles. "Teddy Bear. Star Bright."

"I'm so sorry I upset you. Come sit beside me."

He was just rising to his knees when Terry and Hardy burst into the room, their faces a mask of fury. In his hand, Joshua held a laser.

"What's going on? We heard –"

It was problematic who reacted first: Star Bright, who cried, then raced behind his wall, or Helen, who rose to meet the enemy, fists clenched.

"Go back! Go away! Who called you?" she spat, eyes blazing.

"We heard someone screaming –"

"Crying, you bastard! For God's sake, have you lost so much humanity you no longer recognize the sound of misery?"

He did a double-take, then stepped back, mouth agape, eyes haunted by her accusation. "Helen, I –"

"Back, both of you. Go away."

Brian hurried to place himself out of her immediate path, but Joshua retreated no more than a foot before holding ground.

"Calm down," he began, putting into his voice the measured tones of command. "I can see you're upset –"

"You're damned right I'm upset. A weapon, for Christ's sake. In your hand. Are you that afraid?"

"Frightened for you."

She did not want to believe him. Were it within her power, she would banish them to *Target,* where they would be safely away – not from Star Bright, but from her. Their presence crowded her, made her skin crawl, as though they were the aliens and Star Bright her fondest friend.

Because she did not possess the ability to whisk them away, Helen swallowed her anger, forcing herself, at the same time, to put herself in their places. The act was distasteful but necessary, and within it, she found calm.

"I'm sorry. I really am. Forgive me." With an up-and-down motion of her hand, she bade them hold their positions while she checked their host. Seeing her brought instant relief to his face.

"Stay put," she admonished him. "I'll be with you in a moment."

Seeing that he comprehended, Helen drew closer, stroked Teddy Bear between the ears then winked. For half a second she almost believed it winked back.

Motioning they sit on the couch, her companions obeyed. She joined them, leaving the chair conspicuously empty. Because she had assumed control of the situation, the men waited for her to guide the conversation.

"What have you discovered?" she asked.

"This ship is incredibly complex; far beyond any technology I'm familiar with," Terry began. "His engines are as small as personal computers, yet they appear to have ten times the power and efficiency of our cruiser."

The awe in his voice allowed her to relax. Sitting back against the soft material, Helen crossed her legs in the attitude of one who has scored a great victory. It was not against them so much as a reaffirmation of her own feelings.

"Are they difficult to operate?"

Terry jerked his shoulder with a noncommittal gesture. Unlike her, he was perched at the edge of the couch, his posture suggesting restlessness, or pent-up energy.

"I wouldn't attempt to run them without bringing Jingles over."

If he meant that as a cloaked opportunity for her to offer the invitation, he was disappointed.

"Would he understand them?"

"I doubt it. Not without serious study. And even then –" He stared at his fingers a moment, then clasped them together. "I can't say." With effort he turned his head to meet Helen's eyes. "Its 'gears and pinion wheels' are quite a bit different than we're accustomed to seeing."

She grinned because he tried to put her at ease. The gesture was as timely as necessary.

"And you found no one else?"

"No. You didn't expect us to?"

"I didn't know... I wasn't sure. Not until we boarded her. And then I was sure."

Rubbing his ear lobe with exaggerated energy, Brian finally took up the thread.

"How does he run this ship by himself?"

"I don't know that."

Leaning back, the minister flattened himself against the couch so he could stare at Helen between the gap left by the captain's forward position.

"*Is* he a child?"

The question had more behind it than she could fully assess.

"No."

"Is he human?"

This was harder to answer. She rolled over the question, trying to decide whether it were poison or safe to consume.

"If, by human you mean, was he born on Earth, then no. I don't know from where he originated. If you're asking for a generality, is he human-like, then the answer is yes. He's clearly humanoid. I imagine he eats, sleeps, thinks, functions very much as we do."

"You were able to communicate with him? Make him understand you?"

"Yes."

"In English?"

"Yes."

"How is that?"

"I didn't have time to ask him."

"But you will?"

"Of course. Why wouldn't I?"

"And you'll tell us?"

This time, it was Joshua who spoke.

"I have nothing to hide. Nor does Star Bright, I imagine."

This revelation finally prompted the captain to change positions. Without being comfortable enough to lean back against his shoulders, he stood and resettled himself on the armrest beside her.

"Star Bright?"

"Star *Bright,*" she corrected his emphasis.

"Is that your name for him, or his name for himself?"

It was as obvious as the nose on her face, and she intuitively understood Joshua had already inferred where the name originated. She made it easy for him, however, by repeating the child's rhyme.

> "Star bright, star light,
> first star I see tonight.
> Wish I may, wish I might,
> Have this wish I wish tonight."

"But that's... an Earth poem," he softly protested. "We're a long way from there."

"I know."

"How could he –?"

Reaching out, Helen placed a hand on his. Touching him that way, she realized how thin he had become; how the veins protruded from the skin, the roughness of his knuckles. There was a sadness there, as if he were slowly disintegrating beneath her fingers.

"He is not from Earth. His ancestors did not spawn from our oceans." Leaning closer, for she felt the absolute need to be near him, Helen rested her cheek on his arm. "Was he made in the image of God?" A smile lingered over her face. "That depends upon what you think God looks like."

"Don't look at me," Brian offered, although neither were. "I personally think of 'God' as a sort of amorphous, shimmering energy."

She appreciated the comment and moved her other arm, so that she could rest it on Brian's thigh, so that the three of them were linked by physicality.

"If he's not a child, how long has he been out here?" Joshua spoke into her ear.

"I'll ask him but I don't think he'll know the answer. I have a feeling time isn't the same for him as it is for us."

"You mean he could be very old? Ancient?"

"More that way than the opposite."

"And yet he seemed, from the little I saw of him, so... immature."

"Lonely, Josh," she immediately corrected. "Ungodly alone."

"You mean, it's affected his mind?"

This finally prompted her to break contact. With a surge of energy, Helen got to her feet, then paced the small confines of the den, purposely avoiding the invisible barrier between the living space and the bridge.

"No. I don't think he's ever seen, or at least touched, another living soul before."

"How can that be? He must have had parents; come from someplace populated with his own kind. Sailing out here in space, surely he's had contact with other life forms."

"Contact?" She appeared to consider the possibility, but she already knew the answer. "Mentally; probably. Maybe even visually. I don't know what kind of equipment he has; scanners, or probes. He may have the ability to 'see' into other ships. But physical contact? No."

"Did he tell you that?"

Helen paused in her exaggerated movements to shake away the idea.

"He might have, had not you two come bursting onto the scene like avenging angels."

"I like that," Brian decided, flipping her a grin. "So. When are we – that is to say, *you* – going to find out more? And while you're interviewing him for the *Target Chronicle,* ask if he has anything remotely resembling crumpets. Tea. Jam and butter, too, while you're at it."

Terry was not in the mood to add to Hardy's flippancy, but the statement carried its point.

"How does he live? You thought he ate and drank as we do. What sort of hydroponics does this ship have? Recycling? We may be able to learn a great deal from him."

"We may," she hesitantly agreed. "If he stays near us long enough for us to find out."

She broached a point neither had considered.

"What do you mean? Is he planning on departing so soon? He was the one who –"

Holding up her hands, Helen stopped him. For some reason, the resonance of his voice was giving her a headache. Compared to Star Bright, it sounded sharp, cutting, as though English were not her first language, either.

"Please. No more." He quieted abruptly, but the frown on his face betrayed a growing concern. "I don't know what his plans are. I have no idea. But I don't want to force him into anything."

She had put in words the idea none of them had fully translated, yet each knew in their heart had been lurking there from the beginning.

We may be able to learn a great deal from him.

Learn? Or steal?

Where did the survival of seventeen take precedence over the uninterrupted existence of one?

Brian was the first to find his tongue.

"No one said anything about force. If he's as lonely as you think, then he may enjoy our company. He may crave it."

"He may."

"Be careful, Helen," he continued, shifting positions but remaining on the couch so his words would not have the effect of intimidation by height. "Don't make decisions for him. What you think you know and what is actually true may be two different things. We're still not entirely certain he's harmless."

"Don't play devil's advocate for him," she retorted, indicating the captain.

"I'm not. I'm just asking you to be careful. I've already sensed a bond between you two. You're overly protective of him."

The hair on the back of her neck rose in righteous indignation.

"And you're too damned eager to exploit him."

"I said nothing of the kind," Brian protested, rubbing the flat of his palm over the arm rest. And then guiltily, "I was kidding about the crumpets."

"No, you weren't. I don't blame you. But the rest...." She let her thoughts trail off, uncertain now, whether she was jumping to conclusions, or if her suspicions were justified. "I'm sorry. Let's all back off. Shall we?"

"Back off is exactly what we should do," Brian agreed, the edge in his voice creeping in over his training. "Go back to *Target;* take a breath. Try and sort things out. We're under a lot of pressure, here, and it's affecting our thinking."

It was the one point Helen had not taken into consideration. The idea of separation now was staggering.

"I meant pull away emotionally; not physically."

"You don't want to leave?"

The quickness of Joshua's question startled her, for she was unprepared for it.

"No. I mean... not without saying good-bye."

The latter was a concession, a hurried, confused triteness which came to her because all the other thoughts swirling in her mind were far too complex to express.

Let alone understand.

"No one said we're going to rush off."

Crossing to her, Joshua easily engulfed her in his arms, allowing his own body heat to seep into hers. Contrary to the laws of physics, it had the effect of cooling them off, which was exactly what he hoped.

Nor was he unaware that Star Bright, the man-child alien, on the space craft so technically advanced it had the effect of rendering them children, had crept forward and was astutely observing them from the clandestine cover of his tunnel.

She's mine, Star Bright.

She doesn't need you.

Any more than I need you.

Lying, he had learned in the past six months, was tantamount to command.

Had the good brother been reading the captain's thoughts, he might have kindly amended the last thought to *obfuscating the truth was tantamount to survival.*

And survival, as they were learning, was the name of the game.

CHAPTER 19

"Star Bright," Helen began, reaching out a hand to him. "Will you come out and talk with us?" It was difficult to know whether he understood the request. She would not force the issue. "Captain Terry and Reverend Hardy want to go back to our ship. They want me to go with them. But... we don't want you to fly away."

He made a low, inhuman noise which was neither a growl nor a whimper.

"We want to be your friend. We want to get to know you. May we come back? Later?"

The answer was long in coming. He flinched, contorted his face, then began trembling.

Go? Go?

"Captain Terry has duties to perform. There are others, like us, on *Target.* They are worried. We need to... reassure them. To tell them everything is all right. You might have been..." She raised her arms, indicating a creature of great height, "a monster." Changing the inflection of her voice to one of exaggerated levity, Helen added, "some terrible creature who wants to eat us."

Responding to the comic way in which she transformed her face, he finally nodded.

I have seen such monsters. They are very scary.

"Yes. They are. You don't want the others to worry, do you?"

She comprehended that he was reading more of her mind than was her intent, but there was no help for it. Nor did she question why he chose to communicate to her telepathically, rather than answer verbally, as she spoke to him.

He did not want "the others" to overhear.

No. I do not want them to worry.

The sentence was carefully uttered, using her own words rather than rephrasing them into ones he would have chosen himself.

But if you go away, you will never come back.

The abruptness of the warning caught Helen off guard. There was no way of telling from his expression whether he meant it as a threat, or was merely transmitting his own fear of being abandoned.

The cords of her heartstrings strummed with a willing accompaniment. There was much at stake, much which needed to be resolved. Unwittingly, she had become the intermediary between want and need.

"Would you like me to stay here? With you? So we can talk?"

Yes.

"Then I will send the others away. But first you must promise me two things."

I am listening.

Not a childish promise nor a man's negotiating tactic. She would have to continually remind herself she was dealing with a life form who was both and neither.

"One: that you will not take me away without my permission. I will tell you truth: our ship is badly crippled. If you fly away with me aboard, they cannot follow."

You have the Skip.

The statement was startling. She had no way of assessing his full knowledge of them and their capacities.

"That is true. But the Skip is not as fast as your ship. And it has limited range."

What is the second condition?

"That you allow Captain Terry and Brother Brian back aboard. At some later time."

With some of the others?

That thought had been at the forefront of her mind. She nodded.

"Yes. Our chief engineer. Would it be all right for him to look at your ship? We have never seen anything like it before. We could learn from it – ideas which might help us repair our own."

I will consider.

"But you will not take me away without my permission?"

That, I would never do.

"And not hurt me? He will ask," she added, uncertain whether it was necessary.

I will not hurt you.

She had almost turned away to impart her news when the thought struck her. Seeking Star Bright's eyes, she demanded, *Could you?*

"Yes."

They had reversed the situation. Her question was transmitted through the air and his verbalized. Helen shivered, but not from fright.

"I will tell them."

Helen returned to the bridge where Joshua and Brian awaited. They had abandoned their exploration for the moment. Their intent now was to escape. She sensed more trepidation from them than that which lay dormant in herself.

"I'm staying."

"No! I won't allow it." Crossing to her, Terry grabbed her by the arm. "You're coming with us."

"No, Josh."

"What did he tell you? What did he say that changed your mind? What trick –?"

"No trick." Her heart pounded with the enormity of her decision and with her attempt to make them see its necessity. "Not forever," she hastened to explain. "For an hour; or a day and night. Let me be alone with him."

"Too dangerous," he growled, fingers tightening around her arms.

"He won't hurt me."

"We don't know that."

"I know it."

Suddenly releasing her, Terry stomped away, the lines in his neck distended in poorly disguised anger.

"You're letting yourself get carried away. He's not a – a child, Helen. He's no one for you to mother!"

Her fury instantly superseded his, and the new danger became indignation.

"How dare you say that to me, when you would take this ship in an instant and be gone? It's what you've always wanted – you said so. To fly a Rover around space by yourself, exploring the universe, communing with the stars. What I want is a hell of a lot more –"

Brian interceded by placing himself physically between them. The intrusion was as unwelcome as it was necessary.

"Whoa, kids. You're letting your personal feelings stand in the way of logic. Let's discuss this rationally, shall we?"

Terry was not to be pacified.

"I'm the captain. I make the decisions. I'm not opening this up to a vote. *Your* advice, if I remember correctly," he darkly added. "I decide what's best for the welfare of the ship and the crew. And I say it's too dangerous to leave her here."

"This is outside your prerogative, Captain," Helen retorted. "I'm a scientist; a researcher. That's my role aboard your ship. I'm a civilian –"

"Not any more. Encounter changed all that."

"Joshua. Helen. Listen to me!" They faced off, two opposing combatants, with Brian the unwelcome interloper. "Let's get our facts straight. Helen, you told Star Bright we were leaving. What did he say? How did he react?"

"He didn't want me to go."

"Did he threaten you? Indicate that he would leave?"

"I made him promise to stay. I'm in no danger from him."

"We don't know that, Helen," Joshua pleaded, abruptly losing the command in his voice. "He's an unknown. A... random element."

"Precisely. Star Bright is our link with the universe. There's so much we can learn from him; if only we handle the situation correctly. He's not used to people," she pleaded. "If I go now, it will appear as though we're abandoning him. Logic doesn't rule emotion, Brian," she continued, the words pouring from her heart. "We're not dealing with machines but with a lonely, confused, frightened soul."

"One whose emotional capacity we have no way of gauging," the captain protested. "You don't know what he might do to you."

"No. I don't," she evenly admitted. "But I'm willing to take the chance. For the greater good," she added.

"And because?" he asked, sensing more she had not said.

"I feel sorry for him. He communicated with me, Joshua. From the stars. He reached out in his great loneliness and touched me. I'm not unmoved. He's had other contacts... ones which were less than friendly. He's taking more of a risk than I am."

"How do you know this?"

She did not know it; she knew only what she had felt on an instinctual level.

"Monsters," came the whispered reply.

"Monsters?"

Helen nodded.

I have seen such monsters. They are very scary.

"Trust me. I am in no danger. I want to do this."

I must.

It was Brian who finally broke the stalemate. Without usurping Joshua's leadership, he crossed to Helen and embraced her. In no way concerned that his intentions would be misinterpreted, he kissed her on both cheeks, then briefly on the lips.

"Wouldn't want you to think of me in any paternal way," he joked as they parted.

"Never have," she happily agreed.

"We'll wait in the Skip," Joshua abruptly decided. "That way –"

"You will display a complete lack of faith," she finished for him, opting to use a Brian word, rather than one she would have employed. "It won't do. You must go back to *Target.*"

Or ruin everything.

"What will you eat? Where will you sleep?"

Inadvertently, he gave her the edge she was hoping for.

"Oh, I'll dine on pheasant-under-glass and repose in his bed."

"All right! I'm going." He threw up his hands in defeat. "But I don't like it."

"Thank you, Josh." She meant it, not insensitive to the plight he was in. "I appreciate you worrying about me. It means a great deal. We... have a history," she completed. "What time is it?"

Still back on "history," he had no answer. None of them wore chronometers. "I'll have to check."

"It doesn't matter. Give me a day – twenty-four hours. If I need you before then, I'll communicate with you."

"Can you? How? We don't know whether this ship has the capacity."

It was a good point; one she had not considered.

"Wait here and I'll ask."

Leaving them at a midway point between being poised for flight and rooted to the spot, Helen slipped behind Star Bright's protective wall.

"Do you have a radio aboard ship? A means of communicating with *Target* by speech?" He mouthed the word *yes.* "I told Captain Terry I would call if I needed anything. And that I would report back in a day. Is that acceptable?"

"I will show you how to work the communications."

"Then it's agreed; I will stay with you. I want to stay," she added with sincerity. "You and I and Teddy; we have much to talk about, don't we?"

He nodded wonderingly, as if he had not thought beyond the point of keeping her aboard.

"Fine. They're going now. Back to the ship. Do you know what this means?" she continued, giving him a thumbs-up. The alien frowned, then raised his eyebrows in puzzlement. "It signifies everything is all right; something is good. That we've won."

A smile flickered over his face. Hesitantly, Star Bright held up his own thumbs, stared uncomprehendingly at then a moment, then imitated the up-and-down motion she had used.

"Which hand?" he softly inquired.

"Either."

"Does using two hands make it even greater?"

Choking back a surge of emotion, she nodded, then matched him by returning the two-thumbs up gesture.

"Yup."

"Yup," he repeated, rolling the unfamiliar slang over his tongue and finding it to his taste.

Returning to her companions, Helen imparted the information, then waved to them as they turned their backs on her. She didn't follow them to the debarkation area, aware that to do so would only evoke further trouble. As though sharing the same thought, both men departed quickly to avoid unintended consequences.

Her initial concern that she would feel lonely without them dissipated almost immediately. Instead, her heart pounded with anticipation at being left alone aboard the alien space craft and it was with no small amazement that she wondered whether this was how Joshua had felt when she and he had spent time alone on the small Rover he had hired for their private holiday.

To navigate through the stars, responsible to no one, choosing a course and a destination on the whims of fancy. It was an exhilarating idea. One, she discovered, which brought her closer to him than she had ever felt before. Yet, juxtaposed with that thought was the realization his life's ambition had been to serve as captain of a star cruiser, the diametric opposite of "sailing the Seven Galaxies" as a nomad.

With a shiver of awe, Helen abandoned the idea of comparing herself with him and whatever she might have confessed vanished with the moment.

Crossing back into the den, she called with new joy, "They're gone, Star Bright. You can come out, now."

She heard him shuffle through the narrow opening, then saw him, standing alone, Teddy Bear held to his chest, his large, dark eyes quizzical, yet lit by excitement.

Alone, and yet not alone.

Two beings from worlds apart, coming together in friendship.

She had not conquered the Unknown. She had become a part of it.

"Will you show me your ship?"

"You want to see it?"

"Very much. It want to become familiar with it."

"Why?"

"Because I feel you everywhere. That gives me the sense of being at home."

"Home," he intoned, gently stroking the small bear's ears. "It is my home."

"Yes."

"And your ship – you call it *Target?*" he asked, stepping further away from his hiding place. "That is your home?"

"No, not exactly. It doesn't belong to me."

"To him?"

"It doesn't belong to Captain Terry, either. He serves aboard her as captain; the person who makes the decisions on where she goes and what the crew does. It's owned by the civilization which sent us out into space."

"Why are you here?"

There was only one answer.

"To meet you."

A spontaneous grin of pure joy split his radiant features.

"To meet me. I am glad you have come."

"So am I."

"I will show you my ship. You call it a 'ship'?" he added for confirmation.

"Yes. What do you call it?"

He tried for a word or an expression, then tapped his fingers against his companion. "Here. I call it Here."

"Here," she repeated. "And so it is. Here. Where we are. I like that."

"I like you," he whispered.

With a hesitancy born of unfamiliarity, Star Bright held out one of Teddy's paws. She accepted it, grasping the stuffed arm as tenderly as though she were accepting an invitation to dance. Taking the other paw in his own grasp, they walked, the small, silent friend suspended between them, linking both their identities into one common universe.

"This is this," he began, as they started their journey in the bridge.

"We call it the bridge; the command center."

"Yes," Star Bright agreed. "I have sensed that." Sitting in the left-hand side of the two dual chairs, his fingers played lovingly over the controls.

Helen watched him, fully cognizant of the fact he did not actually touch the keyboards, but rather pantomimed the motions.

"May I sit beside you?"

He nodded agreement and she settled beside him, in the right-hand chair.

"It was constructed for two," she observed carefully, least she tread on painful ground. "Yet you are one. Or two," she added, indicating Teddy.

"Two. Yes, I am two." But then he remembered. With a flourish as gracious as a cavalier of olde, he plunked Teddy Bear into her lap. "Now I am three."

"Now," Helen corrected with equal grace, "we are three."

"Three." He worked the equation out in his mind until he fully comprehended its significance. "Yes. Three. Star Bright and Teddy and ... Helen."

It was the first time he had attempted to articulate her name on his own, without imitating her. She listened carefully as he spoke, agreeing with him as the word passed his lips.

"Helen. Helen Fitzgerald."

"That – is your name?"

"Helen Marie Fitzgerald. 'Helen' was the name chosen for me my mother and father. I don't know why they chose it. I suppose they just liked it. 'Marie' was my mother's name. Marie O'Donoghue. So my middle name came from her. 'Fitzgerald' was my father's surname. When my mother married him, she became Marie Fitzgerald. Do you understand?"

"No," he smiled, content just to hear her talk.

"And you are Star Bright. From the poem."

"Yes."

Leaning back in the command chair, she rocked herself a moment, delighting in the feel of the soft material, the confining, yet non-restricting form of the seat.

"How is it your parents named you 'Star Bright'?" When he turned away, she thought she had hurt him. But those were not his emotions. "What were your parent's names?" she asked.

The reply was prompt and happy.

"Mama and Papa."

"Mama and Papa," she repeated. "No others?"

"Should there be others?"

"No," she demurred, then quietly requested, "Can you show me on a star chart, where they came from?"

Star Bright appeared to listen to voices in his head before giving any indication he understood her question. Drawing up a map on this screen, he pointed to a star cluster. "Helen," he slowly articulated, and she comprehended his reticence stemmed from the fact he was unaccustomed to verbalizing his thoughts. "They may have come from here. Not" he rapidly corrected, "the *Here* where we are, but the here where they were."

Studying the grouping, she has hard-pressed to place it. That it was not the Milky Way Galaxy, however, she readily grasped.

"Which one?"

"This one... I think. But I do not know."

"What is it called?"

"'There,'" came the prompt answer. "I have no other word for it."

As goose bumps crawled along her spine, she studied the configuration.

"When did you leave that planet?"

"When," he repeated. And then, "When?"

"When you were a child? An infant?" Star Bright shook his head, unfamiliar with the concept. "A baby? As small as Teddy Bear?"

"I am what I am."

"But surely you were smaller?"

Again, the repetition.

"Smaller."

Words failed him.

A horror of suspicion added a chill to her wonder.

"They put you on this ship? Alone?"

"Alone. I have always been alone. With Teddy."

"Always?"

"No," he demurred, changing his mind and brightening. "I am not alone."

"You have Teddy, but –"

"Come. They are here."

"They? Your parents?"

He smiled, the light of it melting her essence into softening butter.

"Yes."

"Aboard ship?"

"They are with me."

"May I meet them?"

Two ideas worked simultaneously in her mind, the primary one being that she had psychically searched the ship and sensed no other presence. If her mental exploration proved inaccurate and she neglected to sense them, that placed her entire foundation of trust in herself in doubt. Less, significantly, it also meant Joshua and Brian had overlooked their presence. Neither would be pleased to know they had been fooled, which would heighten their own suspicions.

Working to steady her voice, she asked, "Will you introduce me?"

"You want... to see them?"

Detecting the hope and pride in his voice she readily agreed.

"Yes. Please."

"Then I will show you."

Without waiting, he jumped from his chair, scurrying back into the den. Before she arrived, he had taken one of the discs – the ones she had identified as being special – and placed it into the computer. Instantly, the image of a woman appeared on screen.

Not totally human in appearance but lacking any alien features Helen could identify to explain her impression, she radiated youth, giving the impression of an age in her mid-twenties. Strikingly beautiful by any standards, her hair was dark and shiny, her eyes bright and filled with a radiance of love. Even in the seconds she had to absorb the image there was no mistaking her resemblance to the being at Helen's side.

Seated on the same couch upon which her distant audience now viewed her, like Star Bright, she was dressed in a long, flowing tunic. Around her waist was a slim golden belt. Her hands were folded before her and she spoke to the camera as though to a human being, reaching out through time to impart her message.

In her hands she held a slim book. While the words were not apparent on the screen, Helen could see there were pictures as well as printed text. The mother read from it, but from the ease of her recitation, it was clear she knew the content by heart.

> "'Star Bright, star light.
> First star I see tonight.
> Wish I may, wish I might,
> Have this wish I wish tonight.'"

"My beloved child," the woman on the screen continued, departing from the text, "I am with you always. Whenever you close your eyes and think of me, I shall be there with you."

She resumed reading.

"'The Owl and the Pussy-cat went to sea
in a beautiful pea green boat,
They took some honey, and plenty of money,
wrapped in a five pound note.
The Owl looked up to the stars above,
and sang to a small guitar,
'O lovely Pussy! O Pussy my love,
What a beautiful Pussy you are,
You are,
You are!
what a beautiful Pussy you are!'"

"I thought," Star Bright whispered, freezing the image, "that you might be Pussy. But you are Helen." His words were tenderly spoken, puzzled, yet not disappointed. When she met his gaze, she smiled tenderly, completing another stanza for him.

"'Pussy said to the Owl, 'You elegant fowl!
How charmingly sweet you sing!
O, let us be married! too long have we tarried:
But what shall we do for a ring?'
They sailed away, for a year and a day,
To the land where the Bong-tree grows
And there in a wood a Piggy-wig stood
With a ring at the end of his nose,
His nose,
His nose,
With a ring at the end of his nose.'"

"Yes," she continued, hardly daring to believe, "I thought once, not so very long ago, that you were the Owl."

"You *know,*" he whispered in awe, his irises expanded to gigantic proportions. "But how do you know?"

"It is... an Earth rhyme. Or, so I thought. One I memorized in childhood. Like you," she gently concluded. "How is it these poems have transcended space? You are not from Earth."

"And you are not from There," he reverently intoned. "But you know." And then, with more certainty, "I knew you would know."

"How?"

"When I cast my mind out... I found yours. I found the... poems inside it."

It was inexplicable. But Helen did not need a more definitive answer. It was decreed their two paths should meet; destined by a higher power that she and Star Bright, the lonely, lost alien, would sit, side by side, reciting the words of a child's rhyme, penned two centuries before either were born.

Brian Hardy would not question Destiny.

Joshua Terry would spurn it.

These were the differences which made up the vastness of the Universe.

CHAPTER 20

Not one extraneous word was spoken on the short trip back to *Target*. Captain Terry informed the bridge that Helen Fitzgerald would be remaining behind to "interrogate the alien," and that the Skip should be refueled and made ready to launch at a moment's notice. Nothing else.

Those members of the crew off duty, or those whose duty dictated they meet the shuttle, were assembled outside the hanger as they arrived. Whatever curiosity they had was kept to a minimum as Paula issued the order to keep the welcoming celebrations to a minimum.

"Whatever we need to know, we'll be told. Ask no questions."

The instructions were sufficient for most, but not all. Before she had time to do more than salute the returning party and confirm Fitzgerald's absence, Jingles pushed his way past her, confronting the captain with wild gesticulations.

"Did you have a look at the engines? How does he run? What fuel source? How many crew?" The run-on sentence might have taken him to Andromeda had not Terry silenced him with a growl.

"I'll make a full report. I don't have any answers."

Abandoning military protocol, the engineer dared restrain him by placing a hand on his arm.

"I will get a chance to review the schematics, won't I? I want to go over there – see for myself. That will be allowed, won't it?" Seeing the scowl, he added a "sir" to the end of the sentence, but failed to release Terry's arm, desperate to be certain the captain understood what was at stake. He need not have bothered.

"Yes. You'll get a chance to inspect the mechanism; to ask your questions."

It was a promise he had no right to make. Brian shuddered, then lowered his shoulder, using it as a wedge to pass through the crowd. He made no attempt to speak, which Paula interpreted as meaning neither he nor Joshua had come away from the alien ship with their own curiosity satisfied.

"Welcome back, sir," she spoke to break the silence. Belatedly, she added, "I assume decontamination procedures won't be required?"

His look, which might have seared a less stalwart crewman, merely deflected off her armor.

"No."

Signaling she come with him, he marched through the chamber, pausing only briefly to ensure himself Porteous was carrying out his orders to have the shuttle prepared for a second voyage. She followed at a respectful distance, only closing the gap from necessity as they entered the roundabout.

"Bridge."

Impatient at the slow upward progress, he drummed his fingers against the wall, then abruptly deceased the telltale action, balling his hand into a fist. When the doors finally parted, he was the first out. Janice Miles sat at the com. She was dismissed by a sweeping gesture, which he mitigated only slightly by adding, "I'll take over. Thank you."

Saluting, she hurried into the empty lift, the look of concern on her face unappreciated. It was his place to put her at her ease, but he had not. Burbone would speak to her later, in private, reassuring her the fault lay in the circumstances, not her performance.

Ordinarily, the new commander would not have confronted her superior officer, for it was his prerogative to remain silent. As his second in command, however, she could ill afford him the luxury of sulking. Waiting until he had settled himself into the captain's chair, she decided it was not his plan to dictate the log, either for her benefit or the official record. That forced her to speak.

"I would like to hear it."

Snapping his head around, their eyes locked in combat. When she failed to back down from the staring contest, his authority shriveled, forcing him to reevaluate his behavior. He found it wanting, but was loath to abandon it.

"One alien; humanoid. Dr. Fitzgerald, apparently, was able to communicate with it. She remained behind to debrief it."

"It posed no threat to us?" she inquired, using the pronoun he had adopted.

Slapping his hand against the armrest, he bit off a tart rejoinder, then flung himself up, crossing to the navigation console, where he altered the magnification on the small Rover-type craft.

"Would I have left her if I thought so?"

"You might have."

Her statement caught him off guard. Conflicting emotions ran across his face, finally settling on resignation. Paula pitied him and did not know why.

"My apologies for being abrupt."

"There is nothing to forgive, sir. But I do need to know."

"Ask Brian."

"Professor Hardy will tell me what he saw and interpreted; I wish to have your briefing."

He had created a monster in his own image.

"One alien. No tangible threat. No weapons we were able to locate; Jingles will give us a definitive answer on engine capacity, after he's had a chance to go over the ship."

"What sort of alien?"

"A lonely one," he spat, before regretting his choice of words. Paula gave no indication she read in them more than he intended to convey, allowing him to recant. "I don't know. He's alone; Helen spoke to him in private. Apparently he's unused to companionship. Brian and I made him uncomfortable. He's... a child. Or gives that impression."

"What about the ship?"

Joshua sighed, returning his attention to the viewscreen. His eyes danced with anticipation, while short tufts of hair around his temples ruffled as though he were flying through the air and not ship-bound aboard a derelict vessel.

"It was awesome."

Paula drew closer, her attention peeked. As he expressed his sentiment, she read his lips and by the time he repeated it, they had unintentionally synchronized themselves.

Awesome.

"It's a self-contained world – bigger inside than it appears from the outside," he continued, leaving her behind in his rush to explain. "Two levels, the command center on the upper. We already know it has fantastic speed – and maneuverability. The bridge," he swept on, straining forward to stare through his own viewscreen as if it had the power to transport him through space, "is designed for two pilots."

Tearing away from his make-believe journey, Terry bit his lower lip, hoping pain would serve to erase the undissolved images. With the descent to reality, his jaw set as his eyes hardened.

"The craft may be entirely computer operated; either that, or the alien is more sophisticated than he appears. It was difficult to gauge."

Creeping up behind him, Burbone braced herself for the next question.

"How did Fitzgerald react?"

"She... has a rapport with him. My word," he lamely added. "She... picked up his thoughts from space; received them, whatever you want to call it. That relationship carried over into their physical confrontation."

Confrontation. Another word of his own choosing. Paula didn't have to be a divinator to know it was not the one Helen would have used.

"So. This creature was the one she was expecting."

Terry grunted in resignation, although the fact should have held more reassurance than it did.

"Yes. But for all I know, 'Star Bright' might have corrupted her mind –"

"Star Bright?"

"That's what he calls himself."

"An interesting name," Paula observed, anticipating his next action by stepping back.

Waving his arms with gesticulations meant to convey theatricality, he made certain the act was interpreted as non-threatening.

"Everything about him is 'interesting,' but none of it makes any sense. He's too pat, too... perfect." He did not continue until his back was to her. "He's a boy and a man, with a child's charm and a lover's sensuality. He's both elfin and handsome. Every woman's dream."

"Not mine," she replied, but in an undertone he was free to ignore. To her surprise, he did not. Turning back, he stated gratefully at her with an expression she could not quite fathom.

"All right. Thank you for that. But he's Helen's – as though some malignant force had probed her mind, assembling all the elements of a fantasy into one living, breathing – humanoid being. 'Star Bright' – a name, taken from a wish. If you'd seen him, you'd know what I mean."

"Perhaps I do," she guardedly admitted. "We all have our dreams; our secret lovers." And then abruptly, "What does yours represent?"

"What do you mean?" he queried, caught unawares by the question.

"Just this: how do you know you saw what Helen did? Or that Brian's alien was the same as yours? Consider what you've told me." She began a slow walk around the inner circle of the bridge, speaking as she moved. "You said it. He's too pat, too perfect, as though he were not real but imagination. You may be right."

"I'm listening."

Paula felt his mind digest her words, prompting her to walk more deliberately as if her movements were tied in with her reasoning process.

"There is much we don't know about space. This creature, whatever it is, is only one being. Let's assume for sake of argument, it truly is weaponless.

But mark: I said weaponless, not defenseless. It may be a predator, but not in any sense we understand. We have superiority of numbers; aboard *Target* are lasers which could blast his ship out of space."

Pausing by the helm position, Paula absently ran her hand over the controls. "In a one-on-one confrontation, and even without the ability to maneuver, we have a very good chance of winning a battle. So this alien disguises itself, so that in a manner of speaking, we're disarmed. It probes our minds – creating an outward visage calculated to put the three of you at your ease by reading your thoughts and transformed itself into a non-aggressive image. Helen finds an elf-like lover. You find a ship so precisely like your dreams you're more interested in exploring it than listening to the story of how and why this creature came into our sector.

"Brian – who knows what he wants? Perhaps he'll discover the True Cross aboard the ship. Or proof of God's existence. Jingles: he'll find engines so technically superior to ours, he'll lose himself. While all of this is going on, the alien strengthens its control by intoxication. Before we can stop it, it's taken over."

"That's a staggering thought," the captain admitted, re-crossing the bridge to his command chair where he could reason less emotionally.

"I've done no more than draw out your suspicions to a logical conclusion," Paula admitted, asserting her own authority by placing herself at the helm.

"Then if what you say is true, Helen is in danger."

Slowly shaking her head, Paula dismissed the idea.

"Not now; not yet. I seriously doubt it will make any overt moves until we've all been subjected to its brain washing. If, in fact, that's its intent."

"How do we fight this insidious attack?"

"I don't know. And I could be wrong. Star Bright may be exactly what he seems. But like you, I'm wary."

Terry settled in, letting the cool feel of the position cleanse his mind. It was here, as nowhere in the universe, he could control his emotions.

"If what you're saying is true, we have to be careful. It may be reading our minds at this very moment."

"Perhaps. But let's not accord it too much power. I'm betting it can only completely handle one person at a time – which is why it chose to speak to Dr. Fitzgerald in private."

A gush of exhalation burst from Terry's lips. His hand bobbed vertically over the hand rest.

"That would explain why he wanted Helen to remain behind," Joshua pursued, alternately substituting "him" for "it" as the spirit moved him. "Get rid of Brian and me and it has the ability to exert total control over her. Once she's convinced of his sincerity and good will, he has recruited a very powerful ally."

"One, you, of all people, find hard to alienate."

The accusation stung and he flinched.

"Correct."

Swiveling in her chair, Paula assumed a more formal attitude.

"I don't mean to imply a slur against your command judgment, Captain. But she is a..."

"Weakness," he graciously finished for her. "You're right. She is. I love her. But more than that, I respect her judgment. I find it hard to argue against her."

"More so now that we're all thrown in such close contact with one another. You can't avoid her. We have to work in tandem or acrimony spreads to the rest of the crew. I know what a responsibility that is. I've... seen it."

Hanging his head in shame, Joshua mentally dissected the joints of his fingers.

"None of us are what we were," he whispered.

Dr. Young will be here soon, she mentally countered.

"We all need hope. We all need a sense of normalcy. Your relationship with Helen hearkens back to a better time. It's a stability we all crave. Even those of us who have no right to be part of it."

As the blush on his face faded, he raised his eyes.

"If we can't trust what we see and feel, we're prone to make a mistake. Were I to recall Helen, that would give Star Bright a chance to concentrate on someone else. Find another weak link. Brian," he suggested, nodding thoughtfully. "Or Jingles. Or me. We're all susceptible." Narrowing his eyes, he studied the young woman across from him. "What about you? What dream do you have which he could exploit?"

Pulling back sharply, Paula rotated the chair so that she presented no more than her profile.

"I don't know," she hesitantly began. Yet it would be unjust not to answer. "Command, I suppose. As long as I can remember, I've dreamed of commanding a space cruiser. Yet, I'm as close to that as I probably ever will be. As close to it as I want to be *now,"* she firmly underscored. "I would never seek command over you, Captain Terry. I don't wish to assume your position."

"I understand," he began but she cut him off.

"I have no dream if that means your death. Or your resignation. Or even if you were to take that 'Rover' craft and fly off into space. I think, sir, I am as content as I ever shall be."

He considered her confession carefully, for within it was the seeds of salvation.

"That makes you the perfect 'weapon' to use against him. If there truly is nothing he can tempt you with, you're the one who has to make the final determination whether Star Bright is what he says he is, or if he's attempting to deceive us by mind control."

"There may be others," she protested. He shook his head. "Who doesn't have dreams?"

This finally prompted her to move the chair so they were once again facing each other.

"Let's ask them."

"Explain."

"The crew. We'll put it to them: now, before Helen returns, or any of us go back to the ship. Establish a baseline, so we'll know."

Realization burst upon him with a chill of certainty.

"Exactly right. But we must do so in a way they won't suspect... question our motives. Asking them what they dream is a peculiar action, you know."

"Then we'll have to give them some excuse; not the truth, but some plausible reason why we're asking."

Both rose simultaneously and began pacing, hands behind their backs. Paula went counter-clockwise, he clock-wise. With their heads bowed and deep in thought, they came upon one another unexpectedly, one-hundred and thirty degrees from the command chair.

"We can make it a contest," she tried. "Whoever comes up with the most creative dream gets – a chance to visit the spaceship."

"No. First, that would prompt them to lie – to create grandiose fantasies. Second, we'd have to honor our pledge to the winner. That's not something I'm sure we'll be able to do. If nothing else," he honestly added, "it's not our right to invite ourselves aboard. We did so once, but that was under extraordinary circumstances; before we were certain it was inhabited. We can't do that again."

Shaking his hand in the air with the attitude, if not the precise frame of mind of an auctioneer, he tried his idea on her.

"We need an accomplice; a third party."

"An innocent bystander," she more adroitly described his unintentional co-conspirator. Joshua grinned.

"Nicely put." Leaning back against the communications console, he carefully considered. "We've talked about publishing news bulletins via the computer network –"

"A gossip rag," Paula identified. "Items for trade, services to render –"

His smile widened.

"All right. What if we ask one of the crew to start it – Janice Miles comes to mind. She's not only a technology specialist, she'll be happy to volunteer."

"That's because you made her a lieutenant," Paula observed, gripping the back of the empty communications chair, the way an instructor might confront an ensign on a matter of protocol.

"I made you a commander and look what I got," he groused good humoredly, responding to the challenge with an observation of his own.

"An intentional co-conspirator. I think she's an excellent choice," came the approval from one so recently in the position she had physically "cross-examined."

"She can pose our question to the crew without raising eyebrows. And the prize – something to make every one want to participate."

"One of the candy bars. Or their choice from the 'grab bag.'"

"That's it!" he cried, clapping his hands together. "Let's get on it. Once we know what they dream, we can check it against any further observations they may make. Let's make it..." He considered rapidly. "Five 'hits' out of thirty-three. Brian wants tea and crumpets; Star Bright delivers them. LaTanya Carson wants paints and brushes for her art work; Star Bright finds an artist's kit aboard his ship. Katherine Bacce craves a recording of a certain obscure Earth band; Star Bright finds it among his collection. Hernando Diaz wants to be transported to a green planet; Star Bright possesses the ability to transport his mind there for a week of R&R."

"Then you won't count yours or Helen's desires in the equation?"

The expression on his face registered, *Not unless we need them to make up the five,* but he failed to say so. At this juncture, that would have been cheating.

"With a time frame," Paula reminded him, accepting his silence for what it was worth. "How long is Helen to be gone?"

"Twenty-four hours. At least, that's what she asked for."

"We'll need the crew's replies before then. By lunchtime tomorrow. Make it seven bells. That's eleven o'clock."

He raised his hands and she slapped them.

The gesture of camaraderie served in lieu of black slapping, which was generally exchanged between men, or an embrace, the exclusive realm of lovers.

CHAPTER 21

"This is not hydroponics," Helen gasped, her hand instinctively rising to her lips in a subconscious gesture of wonder. "It's a faerie kingdom!"

Abandoning her guide, she raced, with childlike enthusiasm into the vast expanse, crying with delight as a branch of an outstretched bush tickled her arm. Pausing to examine it, she rubbed her fingers over a velvety green leaf, reverently imbibing the tangy undercurrent of citrus and raisin.

She thought she was prepared for any marvel this magic vessel could produce; she thought she was immune from the simultaneous sensations of shock and wonder, but in that, Helen had erred on the side of the angels. Abandoning one mysterious plant for another, she flew from case to case, laughing, then crying, her tears a commingling of profuse emotions.

"Look! A flower!" The whiteness of its pristine beauty took her breath away. Without a thought of picking it, Helen bent closer, pressing the entire stem toward where her heart lay. The change of position had the effect of subtly altering the flower's appearance, so that, with close proximity, it shone a fluorescent pink.

"How?" and then, "Look, Star Bright! Did you see?"

Shyly accepting her praise, he slid nearer, his own eyes shining with enthusiasm.

"It is my favorite," he whispered.

"What do you call it?"

"Pretty," he explained. *"Changeable.* Watch this."

Drawing up the corner of his tunic, he directed it toward another flower. In a moment the white had turned to gold.

"Again," Helen begged, spinning around the room. "There," she indicated, pointing toward a small, reddish tool. Responding to her plea, he touched the instrument to a third bloom. Before her eyes, the pedals miraculously assumed a pinkish tint.

"A chameleon plant! How wonderful. How long will it hold the color?"

"Until we walk away. You will never see it change," he added with a knowing grin. "I have tried." Puffing out his chest, he intended to convey great prowess. "It is a game we play. I turn the flowers into yellow and blue and red and wait. Like this." Hurrying to a small stool, Star Bright perched himself atop it. "Once I waited for a..." He groped for words. "A long time." Spreading his arms, he attempted to explain by a physical demonstration.

"All the time my eyes were open, it stayed the same. And then I fell asleep. When I awoke, it was white, again." Dropping his eyes, he shook his head. "I have never won."

"But that never stopped you from playing, did it?" she accurately guessed, imagining herself in the same position.

"Never!" he avowed with pride.

"And you never cared because a game is meant to be enjoyed, rather than beaten." Crossing to him, chills ran down her spine. "A game is meant to be fun; for both parties. You and the plant: it knows, Star Bright. It's a tease, isn't it? A way of asserting its own sensitivity. My God, this is communion."

He waited until Helen stood before him then popped up, leaping up and down, his padded slippers making soft thumping noises on the floor. "Look!"

Making a graceful pirouette, Helen grasped the transformation. Remaining on tiptoe, she quivered in delight. "White. It's reverted to its basic coloration."

"You took your eyes off it; and blocked me, so I could not see. And so, it has won."

"You won! You won!" she bragged, as if the verdant leaves and white flowers were her child, placing together scrabbled letters to make a high-scoring word. There was no sense of competition, no disappointment in her own "failure." "If only I had time, I would play with *Pretty* for one thousand days and nights. And never win!" she finished, rising on tiptoe. "And never wanting to. Or do you suppose," she hurried on, words running into one another so that her sentence came out one long exclamation, "it would let us win just once? To keep us honest?"

"No," he smiled, correctly divining her intent. "It knows we are 'honest.' But it might... to keep us playing."

"Yes. You have said it right. Better than I. No cheating here. Who would ever want to?"

Maintaining her tiptoe stature, Helen pranced down the aisle, lost in the wonderland of living fantasy.

"Beauty," she intoned with reverence. Turning back to him, they nearly collided, for he had also followed on the balls of his feet, silently pantomiming her movements. "My world isn't devoid of color," she continued, steadying herself against him with the form of one dancer playing off another. "It isn't living color, but the hues and configurations have... meaning."

Shaking her head, she sought a more accurate description.

"Significance. Everything in my life has to have purpose." Her voice dropped as the disparity of their worlds shook her foundations. "Red for alert; symbols in green. Blue for emphasis; black backgrounds. All coordinated yet none of it real. Symmetry for the sake of form and convenience. None of it to... love."

As her shoulders slumped, Helen found herself placing more of her weight against his supple body. "You have captured – no," came the awed correction. "You have instilled the essence of life in *Here,* Star Bright."

"And you have not, in yours?" he asked, but she flew away from him, unable, for the moment, to abandon exploration for theology. "What is this one called?"

With the emphasis on "this one," she meant, "this one, and this one, and this one," and "I must have it all, because it is breathtaking and wondrous, and because you have shared it with me."

"Grew," he promptly responded, swelling with pride at her obvious admiration.

"The leaves – they're so dark; almost the absence of color. The opposite of *Pretty.* And yet it has its own beauty. What do you call it?" she demanded, hands on her hips, challenging him to deny her assertion.

Figuratively accepting her dare, Star Bright scratched his head, displacing little tufts of hair.

"As Pretty," he suddenly announced, figuratively countering her move and sending them both into gales of laughter.

Encompassing the dark-leafed plant with her two arms, Helen high-stepped with her legs.

> "'There were two *black*birds sitting on a hill,
> one named Jack, and the other Jill;
> Fly away, Jack – fly away Jill,
> Come again, Jack – come again, Jill.'"

Eagerly grabbing her by the arm, Star Bright literally dragged Helen toward another grouping. The green vegetation, reminiscent of holly, was overloaded with iridescent scarlet berries. Placing her hand over a cluster, he bade she pick one.

"Are you sure?"

They seemed too perfect to disturb. With his reassurance, she tugged on the plump fruit. To her consternation, it did not budge. Stealing a sideways glance at her host, Helen noted his eyes squinted in mischief. Casting her mind back to a recent and similar situation, she cleared her throat and addressed the plant.

"Friend –" But that was not enough. To its human caretaker, she demanded, "What is its name?" He was ready for her.

"Grow."

"Friend *Grow,* may I have one of your berries?"

This time when she attempted to pluck the marble-sized berry it nearly rolled off into her hand. Six more followed in suit, until she possessed a handful of treasure. Star Bright inched closer, aglow with private joy.

"Now, tell me: what do you do with them? Shall I pop one in my mouth?"

She had given him the cue he was seeking. Crinkling his nose, Star Bright simultaneously raised an eyebrow.

> "'Cross Patch, draw the latch,
> Sit by the fire and spin;
> Take a cup and drink it up,
> Then call your neighbor in.'"

"You make a beverage from it," she easily deduced, her astonishment at his rhyming no less great than the wonder of the foliage which required permission before giving up its fruit. "Show me, please."

"They go in there."

Following his gaze, she noted a peculiarly shaped, silver-chromed piece of equipment. Domed on the top, several small, cone-like containers sat at the corners.

"Drop them there," he indicated. Following his instruction, Helen dolled the berries, one-by-one, inside the furthest of the four inverted triangles. When her hand was safely away, Star Bright touched a key pad. Immediately, an arc of orange light, in the shape of a horseshoe, leapt across the inside. The contents glowed, then snapped, turning a darker, cranberry red.

"A food processor," she identified, the tone of her voice reflecting *Target's* own critical need for such a working apparatus.

Once the berries were properly roasted, the cone rose of its own accord, rotated on its axis, then was deposited in the next. A low, whirring noise alerted her to the fact they were being ground. Her mouth watered as a sharp, tangy aroma stimulated her taste buds.

Hardly daring to believe the minor miracle, Helen pressed her face close to the third cone as the powder was automatically measured into in.

"Hot," Star Bright warned, but she was not to be put off. Steam filled the chamber as her head whirled. Deprivation, and the mental fortitude of preparing herself for a lifetime of being without any sort of flavorful hot beverage elicited a low moan of pleasure.

Gently brushing past her in acknowledgment, Star Bright opened a recessed cabinet. Inside were placed two mugs, side-by-side, so their handles touched. Removing the decorated cups, upon which were depicted golden shooting stars against a bluish-black background, he offered them for inspection.

"Mama and Papa's," he identified. "But now they are used by Teddy and me. He will not mind if you drink from his," came the humble explanation. *He* has had his *jaba* today."

"Are you sure? I wouldn't want to –"

Winking gaily, Star Bright pantomimed drinking from both mugs to indicate it was he who actually drank from both, then filled them to the brim. There was just enough for two.

Accepting the royal nectar, Helen blew on it, then touched her mug to his before bringing it to her lips. Breathing in through mouth and nose, she inhaled deeply, eyes misting with memory.

"Oh, my God. Coffee."

Almost afraid to drink, not for fear of being disappointed, but from the very real expectation of gulping the entire contents in one swallow, she sipped. An explosion of intensity filled her being. The flavor was intense, yet not overwhelming, reminiscent of coffee, with an aftertaste of cinnamon and chocolate.

"Wonderful," she sighed, wrapping herself around the experience. "You can't possibly know what this means to me. We've had so few luxuries on *Target.*"

"Drink more," he urged, sampling his own with new respect.

"Please don't rush me. This a treat I wish to savor."

His face fell into sadness as he cradled the mug to his breast.

"Why, companion Helen? Why is this?"

Compressing her lips, she stared into his luminous orbs, hesitant to bring sorrow to this moment of proud accomplishment, yet compelled by obligation to share her grief.

"Our ship – *Target* – inadvertently struck a ribbon of dark matter. Surely you saw the damage as you approached. Much of it was destroyed. Many men and women perished." Hanging her head, the old horror revisited itself upon her as she reflected upon her own good fortune to have survived.

"We lost most of our food stores and all the equipment needed to prepare it." As she shuddered, Star Bright glanced across at Teddy, then toward the discs in his den, identifying with her hurt. "It was a very great tragedy. Terrible sadness," she reiterated, employing an expression she knew he would understand.

"I am... so sorry for your loss."

"Thank you, little one. Your sympathy touches my heart," she replied, fully comprehending, without elaboration, that he, too, had suffered loss. This mutual emotion bonded her to him as nothing else could have. "Every day has been a struggle to survive – to live aboard our crippled vessel. The strain has been horrific."

Reaching out, Star Bright extended his hand, palm upward. When she nodded, he guided her back into the den. Indicating she sit, he retrieved Teddy, offering the bear a taste of jaba before returning his attention to their guest.

"Tell me," he pleaded. "About the...." He struggled for the word. "Perish."

Curling her shoulders inward, Helen hesitated, uncertain of her ability or the actual extent of his knowledge. "How much do you already know?" she began slowly, gauging her grief against his expression. "How much have you discovered?" His look of genuine puzzlement caused her to clarify, in a more gentle tone, "From your long range scanners? Or by reading my mind?"

Star Bright analyzed her request, eyebrows knitting in concentration. When he began to speak, however, his head rolled slowly like a pendulum.

"*You* were my only interest. You. I felt your mind crying out." His lips mouthed another sentence, but as she indicated he verbalize it, he lifted his hands a foot over his lap and waved them horizontally through the air. "I cried with you. I felt..." Again he groped for the word and came up with only "sad."

Leaning closer, until their noses almost rubbed, she tried to extract, through a form of mind meld, exactly what he meant.

"But I was not sad, Star Bright. Not when I first encountered your thoughts. I was...." Now it was her turn to search the heavens for the right expression. "Lonely. And confused." Memories crowded in, combining past with present until she was no longer certain just what she had been experiencing in the Observatory.

"Joshua and I... we are... like this." Holding out her right hand, Helen crossed her pointer and index fingers. "Close. We are bound to one another." She waited until the little alien had copied her action, then she touched his chest at the level of his heart. "Here."

"Bound," he repeated. Behind fluttering eyelids he sought the definition. "Tied."

"Emotionally. We care about one another." Leaning back, she sighed, training her eyes overhead on the low ceiling. Had she discovered clouds above her, she would have tried to clarify her own emotions from the tales they told. Being deprived of such aid, however, she was forced to draw on the peculiar swirls and indentations of the peculiar building material.

How, or if, they altered her sensations she couldn't have said.

"It's been so difficult; so very hard. A great pressure is exerted on us all. We fight to live. Every day, it seems, we face a new obstacle; an even greater challenge than the day before. Such adversity has altered our perceptions."

Bringing the cup to her lips, she drank the hot liquid, finding its taste had altered, so that it no longer resembled coffee, but another beverage unknown to her. As surprising as the fact was, she was even more pleased by the distinction.

"You would think – convention has it," she rearranged her thoughts, "that tragedy would bring us closer together. We struggle together; we have the same goals. We need one another more than ever." Putting the cup down on the floor, her shoulders sagged. "I do love him. I will always love him. But I feel I no longer know him. I think I was seeking an answer to that puzzle when I first felt you. Does that make sense?" she concluded, finally turning back to meet his penetrating stare.

"Lonely," he whispered. "I felt loneliness."

"Yes. That, certainly."

"But more." Touching her on the forehead, he smiled. The gentleness of his concern washed a soothing temperature through her which the coffee had only begun to stir. "You, too. The stars."

It was a revelation she only dared acknowledge in private.

"Yes. Me, too. But not as he sees them. Not as an end in themselves, but as a conduit to other lives. Yours, for instance. I am a communicator. I want to know... to bring together. I want to touch the warmth of life; Joshua seeks its coldness."

"I came for you."

"I know." Taking his hand, Helen brought it to her lips and kissed it. His reaction was so immediate it nearly took her breath away.

"Let me show you."

He picked up one of the treasured discs. As she waved him permission, he placed it in the computer. Immediately a face appeared on the screen.

Holding her breath, Helen found herself transfixed. It was Mama. Her first impression was that of the young woman she had seen previously, when she recited the poems of her own childhood. Looking more closely, however, Helen witnessed the image slowly alter. Lines by her eyes developed, while the beginning of wrinkles showed across her hands. Her hair, so dark on first glance, subtly assumed a shade of grey, so that the Earth woman realized the alien must be older, in her forties or early fifties, to judge by her own standards.

It was the vitality, the energy surrounding Mama that had previously hidden the telltale signs of age. Or more aptly, Helen corrected herself, the glow in her eyes, so much like Star Bright's that obfuscated her appearance.

The woman was sitting on a couch; the very one from which Helen now watched her. In her hands was a paper-bound book, filled with pictures. As in the previous scene, she was reciting from the text, although her eyes never strayed to the page, for she had the words memorized.

Her voice had a musical cadence, sweet, tender, loving. While Helen didn't understand the language, she readily recognized the poem. It was one her own mother had recited to her so many years ago.

> "'Here's A, B, C, D, E, F and G,
> H, I, J, K, L, M, N, O, and P,
> Q, R, S, T, U, V, W, X, Y, and Z;
> And here is good mama, who knows
> This is the fount whence learning flows.'"

She found herself repeating it, letter by letter, word by word. As she did, the woman's words magically transformed into English, so by the time the melody was complete, their voices were synchronized.

"How?" she intoned, wonder clouding her brain. "How?"

Star Bright pointed to a panel on the controls. As he waved his hand over it, the woman began again. This time, she completed the child's lesson in her native tongue.

"You did that? You have the ability to change languages at will?" A chill of awe swept over her skin, finally settling in her breast. "A universal translator?"

While he was unfamiliar with the expression, he comprehended the intent.

"Yes."

"I have been working on just such a device, but yours is so far in advance of mine. I am... stunned." Touching the console, she shuddered from unbridled respect. "Wonderful!" Swallowing a mouthful of saliva, she turned to her companion. "They left this for you?"

He hesitantly shook his head.

"No. I made it."

"You! How?"

Tapping her temple, he pointed back at the screen.

"From your mind I learned the words. I gave them to Mama. So she would sound like you."

Blinking away tears, Helen stared at the woman's image, so like his own.

"She's beautiful. You have her eyes." He did not understand. "She's your mother – mama. Heredity. She gave you... you inherited her face. Look." She indicated the image he had frozen in time. "Look at her eyes. The curve of the brow; the lips. So delicate. Can't see yourself in her?"

"I see mama," he slowly reiterated.

"Her name, Star Bright? What was her name?"

"Mama."

"And papa? Do you have papa's image?"

With the eagerness of one so long alone, who has never shared a secret, Star Bright brought another visage to the screen.

"Papa," he identified.

Before her, transcending space, was a man, more alive on the disc than any dozen men of her acquaintance. He also was dark haired and youthful appearing, forcing Helen to concentrate to decipher the signs of age, as she had done with Mama. Like his wife's, the husband's eyes were a deep brown, intense and intelligent, with an otherworldliness which inspired her.

His nose was sharper, his cheekbones more prominent, although it was clear he was of the same race. The man was clean shaven, with a cleft in his chin and a wide, eager smile. His hair was short and neatly combed. She did not have to try her imagination to know that the length of Star Bright's hair was a combination of his parent's.

Like Mama, Papa was speaking to an unseen camera, in words foreign to her ears.

"Let me understand him," she begged. Star Bright immediately altered the transmission so that he spoke in English.

"... care for the plants so they will sustain you. You must pick only what you need; the rest will regenerate themselves, so you will never be hungry." Moving away, the camera followed him, panning into the hydroponics area. "Watch me." He reached over the low glass to extract a plant. Taking it to the food processor, he placed it inside. As she had witnessed when Star Bright roasted the beans, an arc of orange light jumped out over the food. "You may combine what you prepare to vary your diet."

When the food was cooked, he took it out and set it on a plate. Bringing it back with him to a table, he sat and held up utensils. "Fork. Knife. Watch me." He cut the vegetable, which had radically altered shape, into bite sized portions. Bringing a taste to his mouth, he demonstrated mastication. "Chew slowly. Carefully."

"Chew slowly. Carefully," Star Bright repeated, a child at his lessons. A reverence of a different nature slowly crept down Helen's spine, nearly depriving her of her ability to breath.

"He's teaching you."

"Papa," he acknowledged, which was not a confirmation of her words, but rather a pronouncement of ownership.

Helen would have watched it all, from start to finish, but time was precious and she felt it slipping away. She also understood there were others, equally, or more impatient than she. Prying eyes, probing minds. They could not see what she saw; their brain waves were limited to processing the energy synapsed within their skulls. When next she accosted the crew of *Target,* Helen would have to have answers.

Satisfying herself was not a luxury in which she dared indulge.

"How old were you when they...?" *When they what? When they died? When they went away?* She did not know for a fact Star Bright's parents had perished. Or even that they had left the ship. They might still be aboard, in some form of suspended animation.

If she had ever held it, Helen abruptly dismissed the idea that the two people she had just viewed on the screen were alive and functioning aboard the *Here.* Terry and Hardy had found no trace of others. Yet well beyond their limited exploration, she confirmed within herself that Star Bright was alone.

And had been that way for a very long time.

Not in the way she was, but in some fashion which bound them together. She could not be mistaken. Helen Fitzgerald was a communicator, and that message she had received without a shadow of a doubt.

"How old were you when they were no more," she lamely finished. *Died* seemed too harsh a word and *abandoned you* too cruel.

Raising a hand to his head, the little alien patted himself, then stroked his chin before crossing his arms and making a rocking motion, imitating the actions a mother made with a newborn.

"No," she gasped, refusing to believe. "You couldn't have been an infant." He gave no indication of comprehending her denial. "Show me your earliest tape. Please," she added. "I would like to see it."

"See it? You would like to see it?" Beyond his expectation was a hopefulness which nearly tore her asunder.

"Yes."

Reversing her conviction of the moment before that she had no time, Helen made a command decision. As the only member of *Target* aboard the alien ship, that meant she was the ranking officer, and therefore dictated her own actions. She would get answers, but to questions *she* wanted answered.

Reaching for another of his most cherished discs, Star Bright deposited it in the player. Without realizing she was doing so, Helen moved closer to him, until their thighs touched. As the picture clarified, she found herself clasping his hand.

There was "Mama and Papa Star Bright," sitting side-by-side, their own hands clasped in a loving embrace. They were seated on the bridge, in the dual command chairs, their backs to the viewscreen. Both were staring down at something out of frame, below the level of their knees.

"There is so much we want to say to you," Papa began, face contorted in misery. "So much we had hoped to explain as you grew. You are the child of our love; an expression of the deep regard we hold for one another. We meant to be a family; to raise you among the stars."

He looked to her, to his wife, his voice breaking. She nodded, forcing a smile to her face as both turned toward the camera. Her fingers tightened around his.

"Your mama and papa want you to know how much we love you. That nothing but tragedy would ever take us from you. We are making these recordings now so you will know what we look like – so you will have an image of us to hold in your heart."

Tears began flowing down Mama's eyes and her shoulders shook. As Papa reached out to comfort her, the scene abruptly ended. When the tape resumed, both had composed themselves. They were still on the bridge, although what was visible of the background had subtly altered, indicating the passage of time.

"There was an accident; a terrible mistake. Mama and I were exposed to a very bad form of radiation. It will take us away from you. There is nothing we can do to stop the progress of the disease." He cleared his throat and stared down. "While we have many advanced medicines aboard ship, we have nothing to cure us. Believe me when I say we tried."

As he faltered, Mama resumed the narrative.

"Our journey through space was meant for three. Now, you must make it alone. Papa and I have reprogrammed the ship to care for your needs. You will be fed and cleaned. When you cry, a tape will play, so you can hear our voices, see our faces. Though you will say your first words, take your first steps without us, you will live."

This time when the scene altered, the transition was smoother, less obvious. They had taken more care, editing the tape at this point, Helen deduced, her mind a whirl of tortured emotions.

"You must live, for life is precious. Grow to adulthood, our beloved son. Be a brave explorer. Seek the wonders of space as we chose to do; meet alien races. Embrace them as your brothers and sisters, for we are all one family. Learn to communicate with them. Perhaps one day, some culture will adopt you, take you to their planet. Stay or leave as you choose, beloved, for you are a child of the universe. Go where your heart takes you. You are free."

"Cherish your freedom, son. Never impose constriction on others, nor allow them to restrain you. This ship is yours. She is your passport to eternity. She is your home, your world. Within her, you have been cherished and will cherish. Be safe, be kind, be wondrous, for that is the true meaning of existence."

Glancing to her side, Helen watched as Star Bright mouthed the words, so long memorized, so completely cherished.

"Do you remember them?" she whispered, hardly daring to interrupt his prayer.

"They are there," he indicated, pointing to the screen.

"Touching them? Feeling them hug you in return? Do you recall their kisses on your brow?"

He shook his head. The pain was so acute, Helen threw her arms around him, bestowing his face with the tenderness so long deprived this solitary creature of the stars.

"Look," he said when she had reluctantly withdrawn. It took almost more courage than she possessed to follow his command.

On the screen, the two parents who would never live to witness the development of their baby, picked up a small bundle, wrapped in a yellow, silken blanket. Gently pulling back the hood, they revealed the countenance of the infant.

Star Bright was no more than six months old, with a stock of long, dark hair covering his eyes. As Mama pushed the locks away, she rubbed the diminutive nose, then allowed the grasping fingers to encircle her own. It was a gesture Helen had observed in Star Bright, as he clutched Teddy Bear. The similarity was heart rending.

Mama cradled the baby in her arms, then passed him tenderly to Papa, who repeated the same rocking motion. As the baby smiled, he caressed the ears, then waved his hand over the infant's face in blessing.

"We are never gone from you; remember that. We live in another dimension; one you cannot see. But we will watch and guide you. Grow up and find love. That is our wish for you."

"Do not join us quickly," Mama added, overcome by emotion. "Or we will have done a terrible thing, leaving our planet for the vastness of space. We wanted to share it with you: now, you must discover it on your own."

As she wept, the recording stopped.

"I remember," Star Bright said, eyes glued to the frozen image.

"You remember them holding you? But you were so small –"

"I remember *that,*" he persisted and she understood. He "remembered" the image; the words. He had relived it ten thousand times in his mind. But the feel of a warm, living body did not exist in his memory. Hers had been the first touch he could call his own.

Restraining the impulse to engulf him in an embrace for Mama and Papa, Helen wiped her eyes, then steadied her resolve. She had the beginning. She would have the end.

The middle would fill in itself.

"Show me the last tape."

Sniffling back his own tears, Star Bright made a quick, practiced manipulation on the player. She did not doubt he could find any scene, any segment, any individual word at the touch of a button.

"There," he said.

There, she thought. *As opposed to* Here.

They, the dying, distraught parents, cheated out of a life with their child, out of their own futures, had recorded their last voyage for his posterity.

One dual-sized coffin sat in the cargo bay, the one Helen recognized. It was the same chamber through which she had entered. Markings, similar to those outside the ship, but bright and fresh, were etched on the sides. She would remember the cuneiform and translate it.

Later.

As they watched, the bay doors parted. There was no sound. Seemingly by magic, the box containing the bodies of two loving souls was elevated up and catapulted into space. It drifted away, out into the pitch blackness of another, less transitory existence. The doors sealed behind it. In the background came the faint hiss of compression as the room refilled with air.

Their last breath.

CHAPTER 22

"Thank you. You've done good work."

Janice Miles finished the last of the adjustments to the computer, tightened the connections, then nodded. While she would not have said so, receiving a compliment from the captain meant the world to her. Not a military person by trade, she had adapted readily to the new world Encounter had literally propelled her into.

"You're welcome, sir. My pleasure." Noting his eyes were on the screen, she tried a smile. "Cross training has its advantages. Not only am I a lieutenant, I'm also a technology specialist."

Leaning back in his chair, Joshua rubbed his eyes, allowing himself the luxury of enjoying the relief afforded him by the pressure. He rocked back and forth as he spoke, using the muscles in his thighs, rather than the springs in the chair, as propulsion.

"In this era of specialization, I think we've gone back and rediscovered the wheel. Too many people, each with their own separate knowledge. It's a wonder we can communicate at all. What we've achieved here bears serious consideration throughout the so-called civilized planets. Sharing what we know and learning from others is a tremendous equalizer."

Ceasing his activity, he slowly lowered his hands. "It creates a commonality I hadn't realized we'd lost." Pointing to the desk, he continued, "Where'd you scrounge the computer from?"

"Can't take credit for that. We have dozens of units we're not using. Encounter corrupted or wiped out all of the programing. I never thought we'd be able to repair them, but Maurice and I worked together and were able to make several workable. What we discovered tied in with the intraship communications, so we actually achieved a dual breakthrough. It's still a work in progress, but as I've reported, there's hope we may eventually reestablish all the bridge consoles. We've already proven it works on those designed into the Captain's chair. As you said, sir, we reinvented the wheel by combining different modalities."

"Brilliant work."

"Even Jingles admitted he couldn't run this ship without us."

"Nice to know he's changed his mind," came the less than enthusiastic reply. "And the security systems?"

"We've had less success with them. Especially the voice recognition in the roundabouts. Rather than a repetition of what happened to you, Helen felt it more prudent to deactivate them until we were certain we could correct the problems. The same with the computers. We eliminated the need for retina identification."

"Yes, thank you. She discussed it with me and I agreed. And the ship's newsletter? How is it coming along?"

"The generic copy comes up in this file; the responses to the contest are in this one. You can chose to listen to the responses, or have them displayed visually, your choice. Let me show you."

While he was familiar with the technique, Terry took a peculiar pleasure being instructed in basic computer use.

"Once you access the file, your choices are indicated here. The computer backs itself up automatically, and the files you erase are sent to a separate holding area. You have to erase them twice for them to be permanently eradicated."

"I see."

Scrolling his eyes down the column, he noted with satisfaction that fifteen of the crewmembers had responded to the first "contest."

"Never underestimate the power of treats," he observed.

"Nor of morale, sir. That was a good idea, asking us what we dreamed. I think it had a tremendously cathartic effect... expressing ourselves like that."

"Then, I'm glad."

"I think we ought to publish the responses; not just the winning entry. That way, we can all get to know one another."

"You're right," he decided, mentally assigning that task to the future, when all danger from the alien was past.

"But Dr. Fitzgerald – she didn't have a chance to participate. She might feel cheated, sir. No one wants to lose out on a chance to win some candy."

He smiled, but it was for her benefit alone.

"Helen will have her opportunity."

"And you, too, Captain. Your name is missing."

Frowning at the oversight, he finally cleared his throat in a dismissal.

"No fair, asking me to play. I'm the judge."

"Then next time," Janice decided for him, "Let someone else be the judge."

Letting a trace of genuine emotion into his face, he waved her away.

"I have work to do. But I'll consider it."

"Yes, sir. Good day."

"Good day."

When the sliding door had closed behind her, Terry turned his full attention to the dream file. Listening to the innermost hopes and wishes of his crew was not the type of labor to which he was accustomed and he needed the proper frame of mind. Sipping from a thermal cup of hot water, *Target's* substitute for tea, he blew on the liquid, then drank it slowly while selecting the first name.

"My fantasy, if that's what I have to call it," Jingle's voice began, hesitantly at first, then picking up steam, "is to retire from this damned service and make my living as a minstrel."

Terry's hand went instinctively toward the controls, tempted to turn off the recording. Suddenly, he did not want to hear what his chief engineer had to say. Asking him to bare his soul for the promise of a reward seemed petty and dishonest. It was not the fact he planned on withholding the candy, for he had every intention of awarding it. Rather, it was Terry's certain knowledge that he preferred anonymity over confession which turned his stomach.

All of his previous feelings of camaraderie and communication soured. Although the "contest" had been designed with a tactical purpose, he didn't want to know what Jingles wished; he didn't feel capable of carrying that burden of secret knowledge. It was enough to know the man was capable of handling his duties. What he harbored in his soul was private and extraneous.

It was with some horror that Joshua Terry realized he had fallen, or rather been molded, into a pattern. All those who had gone before: his instructors, mentors, superior officers, had functioned on a purely military level, where trust was earned and identities were judged solely on the basis of how well an individual could be expected to function under stress. While they might have considered it a curiosity to know Mr. Gingleheimer played a musical instrument, that was all it was: a piece of trivia, not a glimpse into the man's soul.

Emulating what he believed to be proper military form, Terry now felt the brunt of his own ignorance. Chief Engineer Gingleheimer was as alien to him as Star Bright. With both, he had adopted a professional decorum, instead of cherishing a personal relationship. That way, neither owed the other any more than loyalty, respect and duty.

Duty.

The word which had framed his existence. One he thought he had understood from infancy. It was disconcerting to know he had been wrong.

Duty entailed more than performing a job to the best of one's ability. It required give, as well as take. Duty was more than the definition of "conduct or action, required by one's occupation or position." It was more than a moral or legal obligation.

Duty was on a higher order than religion.

Or, were they one in the same?

With a snarl at his weakness, he knew he couldn't listen to the recordings alone. Ironically, sharing it with another made the dreams less personal.

Brian was his logical choice for a companion, for the brother understood religion. Of all the personnel aboard *Target,* he was the best qualified to hear confession. He would know how to assimilate the dreams into data, without compromising himself. But Brian wasn't accessible to him. He hadn't been brought into the captain's confidence.

A lack of trust.

Trust.

Another aspect of duty.

Activating the intercom, he spoke in what he hoped was an authoritative, command tone. If his ears did not deceive him, he succeeded.

"Commander Burbone. To the Command Center. Level Two," he added for no particular reason except to be exact.

He would dilute his responsibility by giving half of it to Paula.

Shirking his duty.

Another new concept.

It was going to be a night of them.

Recalling Casey Hanson the bridge, he left him in charge while he retired to the designated headquarters on Level Two. Settling into the room behind the Command Center which functioned as both his private office and personal quarters, he had barely poured another cup of "tea" when Burbone announced herself at the inner door.

"Paula Burbone, sir."

"Come."

She was all business, with a look of anticipation, as her eyes darted to the computer he had activated.

"It's beginning to look as though things are returning to normal," he observed for her benefit.

"Yes, sir," she nodded approvingly. "If the technology specialists can manage to reprogram out long distance scanners and provide more than minimal maneuverability at helm, we'll be farther along than I dreamed possible."

She stopped, considered what she said and then made a slight frown. "On reconsideration, I guess I do dream. Of a fully-functioning ship."

"Be aware of that. Still, that desire is more obvious than what the others may wish for. Let's see what we've got."

Leaning closer, she quickly read the names.

"All of them. I wasn't sure."

"Never underestimate the power of candy."

"I won't," came the serious reply. "It's a lesson. Have you listened to them?"

"No." He suddenly felt awkward and confused. His weakness dug a hurt between his shoulder blades. "I thought we ought to go through them together."

"Thank you, sir. I appreciate the confidence."

Although the original plan had been for her to listen and judge the recordings, she had suspected otherwise, and was, therefore, not surprised at her shared responsibility. As if sensing her thoughts, Joshua's guilt deepened. Leaning back in his chair, he stared from the telltale list to his second in command. "Actually," he began with deliberate slowness, as he frantically tried to form the correct words into a semblance of cognitive thought, "I don't want to listen to them at all."

"Why not?"

"I don't want to know the crew any more than I already do," he blurted, shamed and lessened in his own eyes at the revelation of so heinous a confession. Paula considered a moment, then pursed her lips in mute denial.

"I think you do yourself an injustice. You've misinterpreted your feelings."

"How so?"

"You want to understand them; share with them their lives outside the service. Just not in this way. You've convinced yourself you're spying; delving into regions of their private thoughts you have no right. I don't see it that way."

"How do you view it?"

"First, this exercise was entirely voluntary. No one had to participate if they didn't want to."

"The candy —"

"All right," Paula acquiesced, sitting at his invitation to do so, then placing her left hand on her lap. "That's an inducement. We're all starved for a change of diet. A treat to us is like *Creame bruelle* to a gourmet. But it's hardly a life and death situation. We're talking about a luxury, Captain, not listening to them plead for their lives."

"I don't see the point. They've revealed their inmost thoughts to us."

Her lips tightened as she made a consolatory gesture, confirming for herself that he had already listened to one or several of the submissions. The fact neither surprised nor lessened her appreciation at being summoned to review them.

"The key is that they did so willingly. It's my belief they used the exercise as an excuse to open up about themselves. Share hopes and expectations that would have been inappropriate before Encounter."

"Because of how they've changed?"

The answer was self-evident.

"Because they're lonely."

"I understand, but –"

"No, sir. I don't think you do." Silently asking permission and receiving it, she poured herself a cup of "tea." Staring inside the container, she peered at her own reflection revealed in the clear liquid. "Before Encounter, as you've admitted yourself, the crew was unknown to you on a personal level. Afterwards, when it became apparent our entire existence was very likely limited to those who survived, they see this as a ways and means of rising above anonymity – to become a person in your eyes."

"Is that significant?"

"If you'd stop to consider you'd realize it is. There are only seventeen of us. At the end of our journey, none of us can guess what that number will be. Some will die from accident or in the natural course of events. Others may choose to begin families. But, none of us want a stranger in our midst. That's what you are. If you open yourself to them, they'd like to consider you a friend as well as a commanding officer. Given the chance, they want to like you. And for you to appreciate them."

He made a weak protest, then hitched a shoulder.

"You're correct in saying I've... changed my perspective as regards the crew. Knowing nothing of them beyond their on-board responsibilities left me floundering when it came to assessing them for survival instincts and cross-training. But, that wasn't meant to imply a... friendship."

"Then it's time you expanded your horizons. You look at duty," Paula continued, underscoring the word to which she knew he would relate, "as a one-dimensional concept. Unemotionally. Duty. Four letters, meaning responsibility to the ship and the mission. That's only one aspect. And in the end, the least important."

"You can say that?" he questioned, shocked by her statement. "You? A command officer?"

"Maybe it's because I never finished my training. The hierarchy didn't have time to finish brainwashing me. They didn't mold me into their neat, square hole. I envision 'duty' as pertaining to the welfare of the people under my authority. What is the use of a ship and a mission if we put those concepts before our humanity?"

"I'm different than you are," Joshua protested, physically withdrawing from her. "I... prefer the loneliness of command; the emptiness of space as opposed to –"

"Space is not empty. And neither is command," she corrected, making a point to sip from the cup to slow the pace of the discussion. "That's a fallacy and you know it; a cover-up. Yes, I believe you might prefer to view yourself as the staunch officer who leads his ship – note, I didn't say crew – through the uncharted vastness of the universe, standing alone through adversity and triumph. Yet, when that image failed you – when, I dare say you failed yourself and considered resigning your responsibilities – you didn't learn from the lesson."

Placing her right hand over her left as a means of conveying adaptability, she stared at him with defiance.

"You've changed. We've all changed. How many times have we said that to one another? In your moments of despair you've expressed a desire to leave the service and explore the galaxy from the confines of a small Rover craft; one that you could fly through the uncharted regions, making discoveries you'll harbor within yourself without ever sharing. Perhaps that's always been your plan, but I consider it as ingenuous as it is unrealistic. You failed to take into consideration the time would come when you needed companionship. Someone with whom you could express your wonder."

The fact she was accurately paraphrasing Helen's words struck him with awe.

"No man is an island, Captain Terry. Not even you. That's what these crewmembers – these people –
are trying to tell you, in their own, subtle ways. 'Here I am. I'm more than a rank and a face. I have wishes, dreams. Let me tell you, in the hope that one day you'll share with me, so we can go beyond duty.'"

"Is that what you really think?"

"Yes. Just as I think one day you *will* share with them. Willingly and with an open heart. No one writes a novel without the ultimate hope someone will read it. No one creates a life without ever once wanting to share it. You've locked yourself up in a very small universe, Captain Terry. You let no one in – not even the woman you profess to love."

"I do love her," he objected, feeling the anger of indignation flush his face.

"You're jealous and possessive. You're also comfortable with a relationship that has gone nowhere. How long have you been engaged? Five years? That's an ungodly long time. And totally unfair to Helen. You cling to her love, but give her nothing back. You made a commitment, but only half of one. You never consummated it with marriage."

"I was waiting until I became a captain, had my own command –"

"That's a patent falsehood and you know it. What then? You decide to wait until you retire because your job is too dangerous to risk starting a family? Have you ever asked yourself why she was in the Observatory staring out into the stars?"

He hung his head and gave no answer.

"You probably did, but you didn't come up with the right answer," Paula pursued. "She was lonely and she wasn't getting any comfort from you – the one person in the universe she had a right to expect it from. You promised love and fidelity and all the tender emotions which stem from such a vow, yet you withheld them." She paused, then gave it to him straight. "Why did she decide to stay aboard that alien vessel?"

Shaking his leg, Joshua continued to stare at the floor.

"Because she could communicate with him – with Star Bright. She's a communicator," he quietly added.

"Because," Paula corrected, "she was lonely and you were too wrapped up in yourself."

Looking up sharply, Joshua bit the underside of his lip, then averted his head, revealing no more than his profile.

"Do you think Helen is in danger?"

The answer was terse and without artifice.

"Yes."

When Joshua looked back, his eyes reflected deep pools of light. Angling his face closer, Paula depicted the tiny characters of the alphabet, reflected from the computer screen into his irises.

"From the alien?"

"From you." Leaving the statement hang, she indicated the computer. "I suggest we go through the submissions. We wouldn't want to disappoint anyone. They're all eagerly awaiting your judgment."

But he was not quite through. Grabbing for her right hand, forgetting, in his anger, there was no wrist attached to the limb, his fingers, poised to wrap around bone and flesh, contracted in a spasm. She waited until he had regained his composure, before commenting.

"A better judgment than that, sir. Who shall we start with? I see you have Chief Engineer Gingleheimer highlighted. As good a candidate as any."

Calmly reaching out with her functional left hand, she opened the audio file and played it. It ran from the beginning.

"My fantasy, if that's what I have to call it, is to retire from this damned service and make my living as a minstrel. I've always wanted to play the flute, or any reed instrument. They appeal to me. Music is alive. You never know where it's going to take you. Every time I pick up my instrument, it's a new experience. I feel as though I'm flying outside my body."

"I suppose," he sighed, "that's why I love my engines so much. They hum; they make music. They fly me when I can't fly myself. I play music for them, sometimes, when I'm alone." He paused so long Paula nearly fast forwarded the recording before the voice continued. It was lower this time, less reflective and more laden with condemnation.

"I keep thinking that if I was playing music before we struck that damned ribbon of floating death, we might have avoided it, somehow. I know that won't make any sense to you, but to me, it's as tangible as life itself. I'm sorry, Captain. I know this admission won't win me anything, and I wasn't intending to say it. I don't know why I did. Just grade me on the first part, all right?"

The transmission ended. Joshua's nostrils distended.

"You see why I didn't want to listen to these alone?"

Paula responded by placing the stump of her right arm on his hand.

"I'm glad you called me."

Rubbing his eyes, he then stroked his chin thoughtfully. "Really?" She nodded. "You wanted to hear what he had to say?"

"Yes."

"Why? It wasn't his fault. He's entirely blameless."

"But knowing how he feels is significant. It has bearing on how he performs his *duty*." Joshua shuddered at her word as she hoped he would.

"And how he regards you. If he didn't respect your personal integrity, he would never have said anything."

"I... didn't know."

"And now you do."

"What do I do with it?"

"Store it away. Keep it in your heart. Remember it. Use it."

"When?"

She backed off, running her tongue under her front teeth.

"You'll know when. When your command instinct tells you that you need an extra effort from him; the performance of some deed of extraordinary heroism. When he says what you're asking is impossible."

"I don't know if I have that skill."

"If Jingles didn't think you did, he wouldn't have given you the edge." She waited a beat, then finished the thought. "It's also an introduction to something else. An invitation to friendship. One day when we've been on this ship forever and a day and life has devolved into a dull routine, go down to Engineering and ask him to play for you. See if that doesn't add new meaning to your existence. And his, too."

Reaching past her, Terry highlighted the next name. She understood that was his way of expressing appreciation.

"My fantasy dream," Lamar Porteous began, "is to cross-train as a Skip pilot." His voice took on the tinge of surprise. "I never knew I wanted that; I was never interested before all this happened. But I've been giving the idea a lot of thought; studying the shuttles in my spare time. I know it takes a lot of training, but I'm willing to learn. I always thought Skip pilots were aloof; maybe better than we were.

"They looked down on us in Security and we always sort of dismissed them as being creatures with four heads. You know what I mean? Different. Then when all that happened with Hank and Tim, I got to thinking. They *were* creatures with four heads. They grew too big for themselves. I don't want to be like them, but I do want to test myself: be at the forefront of danger. I think I can handle it.

"Anyway, that's my dream. I don't know if that's exactly what you wanted to hear and I guess I didn't know how else to tell you. Anyway, even if I don't win, I've told you. S.O. Porteous, out."

Joshua and Paula both blew air into their cheeks, saw what the other was doing and grinned.

"This is going to be harder to judge than I thought."

"Good thing we have a large candy jar. And an ulterior motive for this exercise. Captain."

"Thank you. Commander."

Brian Hardy's was the next name on the list. Joshua was tempted to skip his, for he thought he already knew what the brother had to say. Were he alone, he would have. But Paula's presence forbade such cowardice.

"This is Brian Hardy," the voice identified itself. "Also known as Brother Brian and a host of less flattering nicknames, none of which I shall repeat now, but all, in some fashion, rather well deserved. I've had many dreams in my life. I suppose you could say I've grown out of some and abandoned others as wisdom, maturity or practicality got in their way.

"More than once I've dreamed of being one of Christ's disciples; of defending Him at Calgary, but you know all about that, so I won't bore you with the details." He made an effort to chuckle, but the effort cost him and the transmission stopped before resuming. The time bar on the computer registered the lapse of half an hour. *One bell,* Joshua absently determined.

For whom the bell tolls.

And then, more bitterly, *Dr. Young will be here soon.* His fantasy for the moment became a sudden case of deafness, for which he would have traded all the candy in the universe.

"I've been considering the possibility of 'playing' Jesus," Brian droned on, although Joshua knew he was not articulating in a low, monotonous murmur at all, but that was how he needed to interpret it. "Of preaching to the masses; standing on the Mount; changing water to wine; finding agony and forgiveness on the Cross. But I never was a very good actor and never mind.

"We are talking about dreams. I guess I always dreamed about being a prestidigitator, a seer, a reader of tea leaves and palms. You know I have the talent. At least you ought to, because I foretold your future," came the slightly accusatory threat. "I imagined myself being eagerly sought after. 'Tell us the future, Brother,' people would plead, and I would. 'Tell me whether I'm going to have a girl or a boy,' by hanging a coin, suspended by a stick over the swollen womb.

"'Make rain, Brother, with your witching twig.' 'Make a puppy come out of your hat'; 'produce a rabbit,' 'tell us about the end of the world.'"

"That's what I used to think about. Until I was faced with the very real consequences of possessing knowledge no one was meant to have. Sounds trite, doesn't it? I used to think so. I used to think if I had the knowledge of the sure and future, I would know how to use it. If it were there for me to read, then I was meant to possess it. You know all the trivial and true rationale.

"All that's changed. I don't want to know the future. I don't want to foretell it. I don't even want to make magic puppies. My dream now, is to be a lonely hermit on some distant world. Will I preach the Gospel to the unenlightened? I don't know anymore. I just need to be alone with my thoughts; somewhere other than here. Eat bread and water and think through how I lost my dreams and maybe try and discover why I abandoned my faith.

"I don't think that qualifies me for a prize. I don't even think I want one. Sorry."

The voice metaphorically clicked off. Casting a sidelong glance at Paula, Joshua saw she, too, was experiencing a throbbing in her temples. They said nothing. There was nothing to say.

Dreams, they realized, did not always live up to their billing.

The two listened to the rest, pausing occasionally to refill their tea mug, or to stretch their legs. Idle conversation was kept to a minimum. The marathon seemed to last hours, though did it not. During the elapsing minutes they heard about the accent of tall mountain peaks, wind-swept prairies dotted with windmills and sheep; promotions within the Service and assignments to other star cruisers.

Several of the crew spoke of their dreams of rescue, naming names of friends or relatives who would brave the distances and meteor showers to save them. Some dreams were short and to the point, while others elaborated in great detail about banquets, libations and frenzied dancing. A handful spoke in hushed tones of being reunited with husbands, wives and children, speaking their names in voices normally reserved for funeral orations.

Paula Burbone's was the last entry. When they came to it, Joshua questioningly raised an eyebrow.

"Go ahead. Listen to it. As I said earlier, in reflection, I confess I do have a dream. It's necessary I be included. I'm no different than the rest of the crew."

"Yes," he softly disagreed. "You are."

Nevertheless, he played the recording with trepidation, not sure he would be able to cope with her dream.

Paula's voice was calm, controlled and distant, giving the impression she had sat across the room from her computer while dictating. At one point the tape faded, making him think she had averted her face. But he would not have bet a candy jar on either of his observations.

"Someone once told me his dream was to soar through space on a small Rover craft, communing with the stars. I've thought a lot about that, comparing it to a life I had chosen for myself. Since I was young, I wanted to serve aboard an exploratory ship; a star cruiser like *Target*. I envisioned myself performing deeds of heroism; making life and death decisions. Coming to the attention of the higher-ups, being promoted.

"In my dreams I faced countless challenges: warlike aliens; negotiating difficult peace treaties; handling mutiny aboard ship, holding lonely vigil on the bridge while crewmembers were consigned to the deep. I fought hand-to-hand battles, walked the empty terrain of newly evolving planets, made friends with my officers, watched them live and love and die and retire and be promoted away. I experienced joy, heartbreak, exhilaration, sadness, loss.

"On occasion, I even envisioned my own death – always young, vital; usually tragic and greatly lamented. I've had a lot of time in these last months to reconsider my dreams. To reevaluate the practicality as well as the desirability of those fantasies. Nowhere did I find them wanting. A bit childish, perhaps," her voice admitted, half with embarrassment, half from wonder. "As Brother Brian would say, one has to be careful what one wishes for, least it come true.

"Words from a wise man but not always accurate, for I did get my dream and I have no regrets. This is what I've waited for all my life. I am a commander aboard a star cruiser. I've faced challenges beyond my wildest expectations. Buried friends. Achieved the recognition of my superior. Before me may be the opportunity to walk on virgin soil; to confront alien life forms so different than I, that the basis for communication has to be through the integrity of the heart, rather than with words or symbols.

"I've learned that the 'unknown' means exactly that: a concept so pervasive, the imagination cannot scratch the surface. I've made friends with people so unlike me they once seemed alien. I've lost a hand and learned to accept tragedy. I've been hungry and fantasied about a candy jar.

"I've changed and watched others change. Yet through it all, I've come to the realization nothing has changed. We're still the same people we always were. Space is still there. Challenges come from unexpected sources. The stars are as distant – and as close – as they ever were.

"I'm living my dream. No regrets. If I had to add a fantasy element to it, in order to qualify for the prize, I guess it would be that we go on forever. I guess that qualifies."

The recording ended. Staring down at himself, Joshua realized his uniform shirt was soaked in perspiration, yet the room temperature was only warm, not hot. He was panting, his breath coming in rapid, shallow inhalations.

"I've taken mental notes," Paula continued, her voice in real-time sounding oddly different than it had in retrospect, though she had only recorded her thoughts the hour before. "We can reference them, should the occasion arise."

"Thank you," he acknowledged, finding it difficult to concentrate on the present, for he was only partly there. The rest of him was enmeshed in an aspect of his own personal dream, spoken by a woman's voice.

"I think we've got what we needed," Terry finally concluded.

"Yes," Burbone agreed. "

And then some.

It might be said they were now well-armed against the alien's powers.

On the other hand, there was an equal likelihood they had been disarmed.

CHAPTER 23

"Target to spaceship, come in, please." He waited less than the requisite ten seconds before repeating his summons. *"Target* to Dr. Fitzgerald. This is Captain Terry. Over."

He heard the channel open and then a fumbling in the background before Helen spoke. Relief flooded over him like calm before the storm.

"This is Helen, Joshua." She did not bother attempting to copy his military verbiage.

"Your time is up. I'm coming over to get you." He had not meant to say that; the words had spilled out the moment she spoke. "It's not my fault," he murmured, knowing perfectly well it was.

"What was that last, Joshua? I didn't catch it."

"I'm sorry." Which would have to stand for more than in-articulation. "How are you?"

"I'm fine. Everything is all right."

"Permission to come aboard."

He could hear her talking in the background to Star Bright.

"Permission granted."

"Helen, I'd like to bring Jingles over. And Commander Burbone. There's so much we can learn, I would hate to miss the opportunity to have them inspect the ship. They won't touch anything without permission," he added.

"You and Jingles and Paula?"

"That is correct. Will the ship hold five people?"

"Stand by." Helen clicked off the channel. She did not have to turn and face Star Bright, for he was standing within a half meter of her. "You heard?" she asked from politeness. He nodded. "Will the ship hold five people?"

"Yes."

"Without being overloaded? You're certain?"

"I am."

"That answers the second part of his question. The first was, do you want to invite the captain and two of his officers aboard?"

"Why... do they wish to come?" he asked, gently reaching out a hand to her for support.

"Captain Terry said there is a great deal they can learn from you. Your technology is far in advance of ours. Particularly in hydroponics. If we could discover why your plants grow with such wonderful perfusion, we might be able to apply it to our own." Squeezing his fingers, she touched his cheek. "You remember, I told you we were hungry. That we were having a great deal of trouble; our hybrids aren't thriving. Our need is critical."

"So many," he began, shying away. "So close. I am not..." He faltered, losing his grip on language.

"You're not used to being in such close proximity to people. I understand. But you've met Captain Terry. He won't hurt you."

"And the others?"

"I can vouch for them, as well. Commander Burbone is a woman. Like me."

"Not like you!" he pouted, shaking his head in absolute denial. Helen relented, pressing her hands together in acquiescence.

"All right. Not like me. But she is a woman, as I am. She is quiet and polite. And Star Bright," Helen added, just remembering. "Paula was hurt in the accident that nearly destroyed the ship. She lost her right hand."

Staring down at his own hand, his lips trembled.

"I am sorry."

"Thank you. It would be appropriate for you to say that to her."

Sniffing away his emotions, he tried to present a brave front to her.

"And the other?"

"Jingles is our chief engineer; the man who operates our engines. What he learns from the construction of your ship may aid us in repairing our own. As it is, we have very limited power and even less maneuverability. We can travel, but only very slowly. Without repairing the ship, we can never get home; never hope to find a habitable planet on which we can settle."

"How... long will they stay?"

"Until you tell them to leave. It is your ship, Star Bright. It is against our code of ethics to force our will on another."

The corners of his eyes narrowed.

"Even if such force might mean your own survival?"

Helen stiffened her shoulders and faced him with brutal honesty.

"That's a subject I explicitly addressed with Captain Terry."

Star Bright was quick to respond.

"You were not of the – same minds, is the expression?"

"We were and we weren't. But I dare say we were, and the initial disagreement was in a problem with semantics. Captain Terry has given me his sacred word no harm will come to you or your ship. I believe him."

He surprised her by his rapid assessment.

"Yet, you say your need is critical. I deem it likely he will do much to save *his* crew."

Without offering any outside show of agreement of his emphasis, she debated the point.

"It will never come to that." Her fingers, which had not relinquished their hold, tightened. "In this case, his *duty* is to you."

This time, Star Bright pulled away, clearly intimidated by the prospect of entertaining so many aliens.

"What do *you* want?" he whispered, panting rapidly.

She had not expected him to put her on the spot and this time the conflict registered on her face.

"I trust Joshua Terry with my life. He and I... we're engaged to be married. That means in our eyes we are one. If he feels it's necessary for him to bring Engineer Jingles and Commander Burbone with him, then I defer to his judgment."

Her reassurance did not convince him. Detaching himself from her restraint, Star Bright retreated behind the command chairs.

"So many. Please. So many. I am afraid of their thoughts."

"Please be more specific," she requested, although in the asking she already divined the answer.

"The thoughts of others. Alien thoughts disturbing what has been only mine and Mama and Papa and Teddy's. They may... dissolve them. And then, I will be alone. For ever and ever. Amen."

Her response was immediate and subjective.

"Yes, little one. That touches me here," she continued, placing a hand on her heart. "Then, three is too many. Will you allow two to come aboard?"

"Which two?" he piteously whimpered.

"Your choice."

Moving further back, Star Bright slid to the side of the command chairs, placing them between himself and his guest.

"I am afraid of that one."

"Of whom? Of Jingles, the engineer?"

"No. Of the other."

"Of Paula?"

Raising his head, Star Bright stared wildly around the bridge as though suddenly discovering himself in a strange place, devoid of comfort and solace. Instinctively reaching out, Helen attempted to hug him, but he dodged aside, pointing instead toward the viewscreen. As words failed, he whimpered, creating a low, hopeless sound of fear and betrayal, reminiscent of a tiny bear cub caught in a cruel, inhuman trap.

Before she could react to his terror, he madly spun the command chair before darting away. Pausing to control the seat as well as her frayed nerves, she took in a ragged breath before crossing unerringly into the den. Star Bright was not there, vanished as surely as the streaking tail of a comet.

A visual examination of the room failed to reveal his presence. Nor had she thought it would. He had gone into hiding, behind the partition where she had first discovered his diminutive form. Unlike their first encounter, however, she could not lure him out by her physical presence. That was the before-time; this was now. They had melded spirits; to make their transformation complete, he must make the overture of reconciliation.

Seating herself on the edge of the couch, Helen pressed her palms together in an attitude of prayer. The muscles across her breastbone jumped in nervous agitation, making her arms shake. Her eyes were dry and tired; a nervous tic developed in one corner, forcing her to rub the affected spot. Pressing her eyeballs deep within their sockets, she let the pressure relax her, unconscious Joshua had performed the same act not very long ago.

Come to me, she willed, not as an order but as a plea. *As you did in the beginning. My mind is open. Tell me because I am your friend.*

"Friend Helen."

The sound of her name and the repetition of her own term of endearment brought solace no physical manifestation ever could. She sensed, rather than observed, his reemergence. Dropping her hands, she looked across at his face and smiled.

"You and I may run from many things, Star Bright, but never from one another. Do you understand?"

"It was Teddy who knew that," he tried, the corner of his mouth dragging downward. "Teddy who has faith."

"You and I both share Teddy Bear's faith. He is brave where we are weak. Will you sit beside me?"

Shuffling out from behind his partition, Star Bright approached, hands clutching the hem of his tunic. Slowly, ever so carefully, he made his way across the short distance to the couch, feet dragging behind like crippled tin soldiers. When he finally stood before her, she bade him sit. His acceptance was the culmination of their friendship.

Without the ability to shed the incipient weakness of her own scare, Helen grasped his arm, allowing the tactile sensation of living warmth to unfreeze her thoughts.

"Star Bright. Star Bright."

"First star I see tonight," he whispered, following through on her unintentional cadence to continue the poem. She nodded in loving recognition.

"If what Captain Terry asks is so frightening, you need not agree."

"But you wish it of me," he sobbed, body wracked by a fit of trembling. She increased the force on his arm.

"If there is any possibility their thoughts will disrupt the peace of this ship, they shall not come."

"I cannot be certain."

Directing a finger toward the center of his head at a point above his nose, Star Bright made her realize he was picking up on thoughts to which she had no access.

"You're reading his mind? You sense hostility?"

It was not beyond probability, yet she did not want to believe it.

"Something," he mouthed, just barely audible.

"Will you tell me?"

"Something," he began again, struggling for the memory. And then abruptly, "Like them."

This time it was an emotion akin to horror which swept over her.

"Like the... monsters?"

"I... have no way to tell you," he faltered. "Too... bad. It was too bad. Dark," he added, although the word did not clarify his intent.

"Oh, dear God." The hackles on the back of Helen's neck rose in indignation. Still, her loyalty ran deep and she could not allow Star Bright's obscure comparison to stand without explanation.

"It would be hard for me to refuse him without knowing more. Will you try and help me see?"

The request exceeded the bonds of his present ability. Lowering his head, he withdrew into himself, arms crossed against his chest. Far away he went, to a place she could only guess. Seconds dragged to minutes before he twitched and came awake. Baring his teeth, not from displeasure but memory, he spoke in a voice of convoluted emotion.

"You will let me touch you?"

"Of course."

She gave an open permission, freely and without stipulation. Whatever it took, whatever was required, she would be a willing participant. That was the salve which healed.

"You will be brave?"

"When I am with you, I cannot be otherwise," she swore, for her strength was in his love.

"Then come with me."

And judge for yourself.

His fingers brushed across her temples with the airy feel of a bird's down. The touch was warm and compelling, not that of a boy's but of a man's. Before she had time to fully assimilate the impression, Helen Fitzgerald was catapulted back into a time and a place not of her own experience.

Two souls merged on a psychic journey down a road only one had traveled.

She/he was sitting on the left bridge chair, looking toward the right. Teddy Bear, little furry companion, was seated next to them in the opposite seat, its bright, shiny eyes reflecting objects from the viewscreen. The images were so vividly depicted, the interloper could identify the stars by name. It was a familiar, comforting reality.

"Megamus; Pastia; Kalia."

The words were poetry, the celestial bodies so far away and yet so close. Passing friends in the vastness of the universe.

She felt hungry. It was time to eat. In another minute, after Teddy had finished his inspection of space, they would go to the den for food. An array of eatables filled her consciousness. She imagined preparing a tray of good things, familiar tastes. Her mouth watered. Hers was a quiet hunger, a pleasant sensation. A drink of something cool; a plate filled with purple berries.

Mantarry.

She could taste the sweetness. Teddy Bear especially liked Mantarry.

Inside her mouth she rolled around the firm, smooth texture of the tiny fruit, warming it from body heat. In a moment the skin would dissolve, releasing a galaxy of flavors like a sunburst.

Good.

There were other choices, as well. Tender bluish leaves, crisp and crunchy. In her mind's ear she heard the mastication, cracking and popping.

Smile.

Dinner time was a pleasant time, a time of peace and rejuvenation.

Music filled her head. A sonata of sound. She swayed gently to the rhythm.

Happy.

Teddy Bear blinked. He had no eyelids and was incapable of independent motion, but this was a familiar realization. The stars disappeared.

Curiosity.

Slowly, for there was no hurry, her eyes turned from the black orbs to the window. Megamus, Pastia, Kalia winked out. Not gone, but now of secondary interest. Something was moving across the screen. Coming toward her, approaching. A ship.

Wonder.

No recognition. Something new, something unknown. Pressing closer to the window, not to better visualize but to experience newness. Bright colors, flashing with intensity. Crimson, vermilion, exploding-nova yellow. Heart beating faster. Noises, coming from the radio. Alien sounds.

Calling.

Mouth agape, fingers tingling. Listen. Translate. Try and understand. Syllables, consonants, vowels, unfamiliar enunciations.

Creatures like me.

Open a channel, hunger forgotten. "Hello?" And then, "Hello!"

"XXX." And then, *"XXXXX."*

Untranslatable.

Foreign. New poetry. Different music. A taste of strangeness. Tensile striations of thoughts and ideas.

"Welcome."

More speaking. More *"XXXXing."*

Concentrate.

Coming closer.

A glance at Teddy Bear. Nod in approval. Excitement so vast it encompass the cabin with joy. Sensors indicating life forms. Many. Still coming closer.

Sharing the universe.

A novel idea.

I am not alone.

Comprehension off the scale.

Beings of the stars.

"Where do you come from?"

A pause while they translate. They cannot do so. A smile. Teach them as I have been taught. To learn is a great achievement. To grow is the meaning of life.

"XXXX," and then *"XX XXX XXXX."* So easy when you know how, when you have the power. Talk to them in their own language. Peculiar sounds, difficult to pronounce. The tongue sings with its new exercise.

"I am I. Who are you?"

"We are we." Not quite right. *We are Andriens.*

Able to translate, now.

Mama and Papa beside us. Sense their presence. Watching.

Welcome the strangers.

Open our hearts.

Friends.

Why we are here.

"Who are you?" they asked.

"I am I." No, I have said that and they did not understand. "I am... *Here."*

"Who do you represent?"

Questioning. Puzzlement. A peculiar question. How to answer it?

"Teddy Bear."

"What people are those?" Friendly voice. Guarded voice. Suspicious voice.

Not a good answer.

Mama, Papa. What to say?

"I am a star gazer." What was that? Listen to my memory. What would they want me to say? Yes, I hear them. "I mean you no harm. I come in friendship."

"How many are you?"

Surprise. Consternation. How to explain? Never before considered.

One.

Two.

Four.

Which is the correct reply? Want to say the right thing.

"Many, or one."

Will they understand? I am trying to make them see. "Friendly." A good word. Friendly. Friend. "I come in peace." Not a better word, but a good word, too. Peace.

"We are peaceful," they respond.

"I am glad to hear it."

New friends, where before there was only Teddy Bear and me. And Mama and Papa. I am not alone.

Chills.

I want to see what they look like. I want to go among them. I want to – what did Mama say? Exchange gifts. I want to share my universe with them. They are of the stars. I am of the stars. Together, we are of the stars.

Moving with hands so skilled, so honed to the task she/he did not have to think about what they were doing. Scan the ship. Bring it into view. There it is! Yes, the ship. The ship with Andriens. Closer, still.

Fascinating.

A clasp of the hands, then reaching out for Teddy Bear. Hold me. I will hold you. Can you see the ship? So big. So huge! Bigger than ours. As big as anything in the universe. Bright. Dazzling.

Squinting through his eyes, taking in the form of the ship. Not huge, at all. Small. Quite small. Helen was thinking as Star Bright did, forming small, excited sentences, working out the puzzle one, two and three words at a time.

It seemed the most natural way in the world to express herself.

Larger than a Skip but smaller than *Target.* Not the mother ship, perhaps. She heard the sound of "mother" and smiled. Mama. Concentrate. Things were not as they seemed. An explorer craft; or a scout.

Bigger than a bread box. She tried to smile.

A peculiar configuration, vivid coloration. She had never witnessed anything quite like it. She had never heard of the Andriens. The race did not belong to the Consortium, nor had they ever made contact with any known race.

I am far out in space, she reminded herself. *Discovering a new people.*

Star Bright was excited, trembling with anticipation. Within her separate identity, her own eagerness faded into wary skepticism. What were those symbols on the outside of the Andrien vessel?

Think. It was difficult to reason because she was sharing his past within the confines of her present.

Concentrate. Separate yourself from Star Bright. A difficult task to manage. She did not want to do it. He was brightness, joy, innocence. To be as Star Bright was to be a child of space.

She had been like him once.

Experience had taught her harshness; given her skepticism. Where had her unblemished expectations gone?

Down the drain of exposure.

History was its own best teacher. Star Bright had no history. He was writing his own as he went along. Mama and Papa Star Bright had never told him about danger.

They, too, had been innocents.

The Helen Fitzgerald inside the star gazer started to cry. He did not comprehend. His tears were of exhilaration.

Reason. What do those symbols mean? She had seen something like them before; similar. Not the same, but close. Slashes of yellow, intersecting blue, making green where they crossed.

Close only counts in horseshoes.

What was a horseshoe?

She laughed, carried away by the moment. What was a bread box? What function did a drain serve?

Her moment was fading. Fast.

Shared hands working the controls. Closer, now. Kissing cousins. Her mind was in a whirl. He did not know the expression. She felt his nose twitch.

She could not emulate the act.

She was too old. She had lost her childhood.

Lasers.

She was not an expert on spaceship design, but she recognized the outward manifestations. If they came in peace, they arrived with the capacity to conduct war.

Speak softly and carry a big stick.

Trepidation. Warning bells. Time slipping away. One bell equated to half an hour, Earth time. One bell: 12:30. Eight bells: 4:00. Start again. One bell: 4:30. Captain Nguyen. She could not remember who Captain Nguyen was. He did not exist in Star Bright's world.

Confusion.

I want to see what they look like.

Seeing was not always believing.

Probe the inside of the vessel. There were many. One, two, three, four, twelve. *Have a peek. No harm taking a look. Manipulate the controls. What a fantastic ship, little 'Here.' She can do anything.*

Anything but defend herself.

Why am I thinking that? Put aside skepticism.

The bridge; the command center. Two bodies came into view. A gasp of inhaled air.

They look like me!

One head, two arms, a torso, two legs. Lean and dark; dressed in royal purple, with shiny silver piping. Slashes of color across their chests, forming new and bold designs.

"X" marks the spot.

Long, long, long fingers. Moving. Always moving. They talked to themselves by sign language. Fascinating.

If they communicated silently, no one could overhear them.

One, passing commands to another. Dark expressions. Scowling. Tense. They do not know I, we, are friends.

Do I, we, know they are friends? They said so.

Belief is a gift.

One not to be taken lightly.

Closer, still. I want to see their faces. Close in. Bring the image inside 'Here.'

The image, not the being.

Why not? They are friends. They said so. No, they did not. I said that. I said, "I come in friendship." They said, *"We are peaceful."*

Not the same thing.

Is it?

If they are peaceful, then they must be friends. Reason it out. Employ logic.

If they come in peace, why do they have weapons? 'Target' has weapons and those aboard her come in peace.

Weapons mitigate trust.

She would have to remember that. It was a conundrum.

The tall one was issuing orders with his hands. What was he saying? *Observe. I am a communicator. Translate.*

I cannot influence this. This scene is from the past.

Realization came with a horrific blow.

The alien captain looked like Joshua Terry.

No. That is not true. He does not look like Joshua Terry. He feels like him. Authority. The aura of command. Supreme power. No one can defeat me; nothing can fool me. I was trained for this moment. Protect my crew. Curiosity of the alien. Suspicion.

Conquest.

No! He is not like Joshua Terry. There is no humanity.

Helen felt her mind about to overload. Too much data, assimilated too rapidly. *Do not combine the past with the present. Or the future. Concentrate on the now. Help Star Bright.*

You cannot alter what was.

Learn from past tense.

Impossible, when it is "now."

"We invite you and your crew to come aboard."

"Come aboard?" The idea was incomprehensible. Titillating. I/we have never left *Here.* Is it possible? Nothing Mama or Papa taught ever said "go aboard." Remember the tapes. Eyes closed in swirling thoughts. Planets. They spoke of exploring other planets. Reach out. Encompass. Cherish your sameness, honor your differences.

What does Teddy Bear say? Teddy is not talking. Teddy only speaks in my mind.

What to do? So excited. I am not alone.

"Do not bring any weapons, or we will consider that a hostile act."

What is a weapon? What does "hostile" mean?

There is much I do not know. I must learn it all. New concepts.

The commander giving more orders. Sign language. Easily understandable. A child could read it.

Star Bright was not a child.

Or was he? Look at the screen; not into it, at it. See our reflection. What is this? Little fingers, short arms. A baby face. Youth in abundance. I am not the Star Bright of now; I am the Star Bright of then. When was this? How old am I?

What does time mean? I do not understand the question. I am I. I am *Here.*

A round face, crooked teeth, just growing in. Not a toddler, not a man. Ten years old?

A babe in the woods.

Where are "the woods"?

Be careful, Star Bright. They are not what they seem. They have not come in friendship.

More commands with those damned fingers. Silence was not golden. Plotting for a takeover. Plunder.

Space pirates.

The identification was staggering in its simplicity. And even more shockingly came the realization, I/we have no weapons.

I am I and you are you and never the twain shall meet.

If only it were that simple.

> *When I was a little boy, I lived by myself,*
> *And all the bread and cheese and I got put upon a shelf;*
> *The rats and the mice, they made such a strife,*
> *I was forced to go to London to buy me a wife.*
> *The streets were so broad, and the lanes we so narrow,*
> *I was forced to bring my wife home in a wheelbarrow;*
> *The wheelbarrow broke, and my wife had a fall,*
> *And down came the wheelbarrow, wife and all.*

I do not want to go to London. Danger.

What is "danger"? Mama and Papa, bless them, never spoke of danger. They had left the probability of peril in the great wide universe out of the curriculum.

They were the innocents.

Blessed are the peacemakers, for they shall inherit the earth.

What is "the earth"?

A question Helen had no opportunity to answer.

CHAPTER 24

"Surrender!"

The word barked across outer space with the finality of an executioner's command. The child had learned that fire burns, roses have thorns and evil contaminates the majesty of star paths.

Star Bright reacted more quickly than Helen anticipated, the force of his activity nearly severing his mind from hers. She sensed his anger, his disbelief and more acutely, his bitter disappointment.

Not like me.

Here lurched, moving rapidly in some direction she could not immediately place. Up, down, forward, reverse, it did not matter. Away. Get away.

This is the past, she reminded herself, teeth firmly clamped, muscles tensed, eyes riveted to the screen. *He escapes their clutches.*

But what she actually meant was, "We escape their clutches," without the certainty. Altering "what was" had fascinated civilization for eons. Time travel, manipulation of the past was as acute a longing as the need for food and water. Theories abounded as to the feasibility – and morality – of such a concept. Discovering the precise equation, crossing the threshold of a warp in space, had driven scientists and dreamers alike to the brink of madness.

Time existed. Therefore, transmutation of time was possible. Being wrapped up in the present, Helen had only recently encountered the possibility. It was not her field. She was a language expert, a being dedicated to improving the future. Her lack of insight now frightened her, boding both fear and excitement. Going through the Eye of Yesterday. Where would *Target* emerge? They had accepted the challenge. And discovered something Other.

There was no way of knowing whether her participation in the revelation of Star Bright's encounter would alter the outcome. Merely by witnessing the events through his eyes, communicating with him as they relived the experience, she might taint his escape.

Or had, already. Stealing a glance at his unlined, boyish face, the large, luminous orbs, the elf locks of black hair falling across his forehead, the delicately sculptured body not yet grown to manhood, she did not know.

And he had no way of reassuring her.

The little caravan which had once tenderly housed three and one teddy bear and now confined one shape, two consciousness's and one teddy bear, shuddered, raced away from those who would rob its life's pulse. The marauder's vessel was lost from the viewscreen, giving her hope they had outdistanced them. Wrong. In another second it reappeared by the reincarnation of an evil wizard's black magic, close behind. Or in front, or to the side, she could not tell. No matter. They were there, tail of the dog, wings of the bird, Meduca's dual countenance.

Without spatial reality, Helen concentrated on flight, willing *Here* faster, swifter, invisible. Wishing it possessed the power to blow the pursuers to hell and knowing it was an idle hope. Wishes were not horses and they were not riding.

In reality, they were tumbling through space, a freefall, maneuvering away in a zigzag pattern of random flight.

A laser shot emerged from the pirate ship, sailing wide. While the deadly weapon was invisible to the naked eye, she saw it clearly, highlighted as a bluish light on her monitor. Another projectile, this one orange, then a third, more reddish-purple. A rainbow of death. She knew hate.

Star Bright did not harbor such emotion. It was not in his nature. Teddy Bear, clutched to his chest by one slim arm, was equally guileless. They had come in peace and were departing in fear. Brian Hardy would have argued fear was a baser emotion than hate. Helen Fitzgerald would have disagreed. A sentient creature experienced fright; it took a corrupted being to contemplate execution.

Four more shots from the enemy ship, each a different color, more intense than the last, until it seemed to be raining a spectrum of destruction. *Here* was struck and she was catapulted forward, hitting her chin on the console. Fireflies of silver exploded from outside her window. Celestial hail. She waited for the angry buzzing of frozen rain in the form of super-charged energy to pelt the ship, straining her ears, forgetting there were no sounds in a vacuum. But she could not see laser light, either, yet her eyes had registered the blasts as brightly illuminated zigzags.

The gravity controls within *Here* manipulated her shared body, maintaining stability. Panels before her hands sang with flashing lights. Data poured in through outside sensors. She could not read them, had no way of determining whether Star Bright understood the meanings. He was a child, playing an adult's game. No one had taught him the rules. How could he hope to win?

"Surrender, or we will destroy you. You cannot escape." Then laughter, or what she took for macabre humor, emitted as a cruel sound, guttural and rough. She determined, with unmitigated surprise, it might actually be mechanical. In her mind, she rapidly translated the tone and consistency of their transmissions. Perhaps these beings, these creatures of an unknown planet, were mute. They communicated with themselves by sign language.

The point seemed moot, but she could not let it go. Think. Reason. If they had no vocal cords, they had developed some system of audio speech for others they encountered. That was reasonable, even likely. They could not demand capitulation by waving their hands in the air. As she knew from experience, any space travelers expecting to encounter aliens required the ability to make known their wishes.

If they had no larynx, then perhaps they were deaf, as well. Sound would have no meaning for them. Deaf mutes. That might explain the colors of their ship, the arcs of brilliant light from their weapons. They relied on other senses to augment the two they lacked.

Star Bright was not reading her mind, because she did not have one. She was not there. Or was she?

One of the multi-hued laser beams struck target, glancing a blow off the protective shields of *Here*. They might have been designed to deflect meteors, but served admirably in the double duty of fending off enemy blasts.

The ship was hit again. This time, he/she was heaved forward, into the semi-circular panels. Star Bright cried. It was a piteous plea, a child who had injured himself without comprehension of how. Or more importantly, why.

"It's all right, baby," she soothed, her instincts aroused. "The pain will go away."

He glanced at his wound with dull surprise, but it was to Teddy Bear he lavished attention.

"Poor baby, poor baby," he chanted, caressing the toy, then rubbing its nose. With one of Teddy's ears bent back against his chin, he caressed the injured paw, which, incidentally, was where he hurt. The nurturing seemed to help, for as he held the bear out to inspect the damage, the glass eyes were bright and hopeful.

Helen cried for them both.

Her sobs were loud and wracked with fury. Without the physical ability to smash her fist against the perpetrators, she mentally performed the deed, envisioning their faces covered with blood. Not content to let it go at that, she constructed thunder bolts with her fingers, pitching them with a velocity faster than the speed of light.

BANG! Smash! Crash!

Grim was her satisfaction to paint a scene of mass destruction.

"Take that! And that, you evil bastards!" But they could not hear her. They were deaf. Her pique increased proportionately. "Die! Die, you destroyers of innocence!"

No reaction. It was infuriating. She wanted them to hear, to fully comprehend their wickedness and her shared triumph.

"Suffer!"

No reaction. They were going about their business of trying to limit the damage from her strikes. Lights flashed. On, off. Off, on. Red. Scarlet. Purple. Blue.

The colors of pain.

Fingers flew in rapid succession, giving orders, acknowledging orders. Asking questions, answering questions. A puppet show without the voice master. If only she could sever their strings, but she had no weapons – no real lasers with which to blast them out of existence.

An oversight on Mama and Papa's part. How could they have been so negligent?

Because they had been creatures of peace.

Turn the other cheek.

If the universe had been perfect, they would have been the First Citizens.

Here was responding on its own, according to pre-planned instructions. Another shot deflected off the screens. More fingers transmitting data. Her pretend destruction had gone by the board. She had done no damage. The Andriens were out there, closing fast.

Booty is where you find it.

"Damn you!"

They still could not hear.

Star Bright and Teddy Bear huddled in the command seat, too shocked, too frightened, too uninitiated to comprehend evil. Theirs was a world of love and friendship. Violence was unknown, unexperienced, unanticipated.

Into Eden had come the serpent.

The colorful, rainbow ship drew nearer. In all its glory, the vessel was magnificent, radiating hues of such intensity they rattled her senses.

Beauty was in the eye of the beholder. In a universe where white was good and black was bad, they had shattered the color barrier.

"No! You can't do this!" Helen was so close to the viewscreen, she could feel the intensity of her own hot breath. It stung her like a slap in the face. She recoiled, but not far enough. "You cannot have him!"

Inanely, her mind recalled a second idiomatic phrase.

If a tree falls in the forest and no one hears it, does it make a noise?

"Yes!" she shrieked. "It does."

Order out of chaos.

Deaf mutes. If her surmise were correct, the Andreins could neither speak nor hear. What, then, was alien to them? What might they fail to comprehend? What could be used as a weapon, which was no weapon?

Sound waves.

The velocity of noise. The effect of the stimulation of receptors.

They might have a defense against lasers and conventional weapons, but they would never have encountered masses of sound waves. There was no sound in space.

A creature might be deaf, but that did not mitigate the fact sound existed. They had aboard their ship a translator, for sending and receiving speech. She/he would overload it, short-circuit the mechanism. Explode it.

Sound. Sound. Sound.

Star Bright opened the channel of his radio. He began to speak. The words were not important. The sound was. When he received no response, he adjusted the gain. Open. A high pitched squeal emitted from the equipment. His words boomed out across the emptiness.

Still no answer but the bombardment ceased. Teddy Bear began to talk through Star Bright's mouth. He was asking why they were doing this; why had they frightened him? Why had they hurt him?

No reply. Try and reach these people who were like him but not like him. Play Mama and Papa's tape. Perhaps they would understand that. He ran into the den, turned on the player. More sound.

The ship sang with noise.

Music. Mama had said music was the universal constant. Play music. Star Bright activated a console. Strains of beautifully played notes emerged. Turn it up. Let them hear. Music soothed the soul.

The interior walls of *Here* vibrated with noise. Papa was reading a passage from a book. Mama was demonstrating how to use the dehydrator. A symphony was performing a magnificently arranged orchestration.

Teddy Bear was sobbing.

Sound waves shot through space, surrounding, encompassing, wrapping itself around the enemy ship. There was no protection from a weapon which was not a weapon. Inside, the Andriens were holding their hands over their faces. One by one they fell to the floor, writhing in incomprehensible agony. The vessel began to waiver, then break apart.

Chards of metal outer casing broke away, floating into space. All directed forward motion ceased. Colors began to fade, losing their luster. Blue turned to black, yellow to white, green to ashen grey, ironically proving the point of a delineation between good and evil.

White hat, black hat.

Grey for the in-between.

Grey for death.

The alien ship was disintegrating. Helen might have looked at the final explosion but she did not. She was staring down at Teddy Bear. He was staring up at her.

Teddy Bear had won a great victory and he did not even know it.

Or perhaps it had been Mama and Papa's triumph after all.

CHAPTER 25

Green. Green was the color. It dominated the viewscreen.

Green for living things.

The planet was a small one by Earth standards, barely larger than the moon. It hung suspended in space like a ball dangling from a Christmas tree.

Star Bright did not make the analogy but Helen Fitzgerald did. For the youthful alien, the massive profusion of green represented hydroponics gone mad.

It was another time, another place. Gone were the acute memories of the Andriens, the horror, the fear. Even the tears had dried on Teddy's face, wiped away by countless head pats, endless rubs behind the ears. The experience with the space pirates had been muted but not forgotten. As Star Bright/Helen examined the images coming in from the sensors, it was with a combination of awe and skepticism.

She read from his thoughts that *Here* had passed innumerable planets but never one quite like this. The verdant hues attracted him as though they were powerful magnets and he a mass of iron shavings in the form of a boy.

Time had passed. Of that, Helen was certain. Star Bright was no longer a child but a youth. Stealing a look at his reflection, she guessed his age to be fourteen or fifteen. His nose had sharpened into one more closely resembling that of an adult's; his chin had strengthened, his eyes grown more piercing, but no less inquisitive.

Muscles had developed along the line of his shoulders, while those in his arms moved seamlessly and without effort, proving a glimpse of his agility and grace. His legs were longer, his thighs hardened from exercise.

His attire, too, had changed. He now wore a long-sleeved tunic of muted burnt-orange, reaching a foot beyond his waist. Beneath it were dark trousers. On his feet we wore soft, form-fitting boots without heels. His glossy, soft brown hair fell in casual disarray about his neck. The elf locks, short, pointed peaks on his brow, which had been so distinctive in his childhood, remained. No facial hair grew on his cheeks or lip, nor did any shadow of beard stain his countenance. Thinking back, which was truly reaching into the future, Helen could not recall seeing any in the adult, either. He either took great care to remove it, or his species did not grow mustaches and beards.

Teddy Bear was in his accustomed place beside Star Bright in the right hand command chair. He was positioned so that his eyes could take in the unveiling spectre.

"Look." The youth pointed toward the monitor. "It's beautiful." His voice was reverent, filled with pleasure. "I wonder what it's like, to be among so many plants? To have them tower above us?" He grinned, then winked at his silent companion. "I will have to lift you over my head to pick the berries."

Teddy seemed to consider the proposal. It was a wonder to him, as well.

"Shall we get closer?"

The co-pilot did not reply and his quietness was taken for an affirmative.

Working the controls with a simplicity of movement indicating he had become one with his vessel, Star Bright aligned the ship for orbit. In a matter of moments, the tall trees and green-bedecked mountains jumped into closer proximity. So near, Helen felt tempted to reach out a hand and pluck the blades of unkempt, waving grasses.

It had been a long time for her, too, she realized with a start. Two years aboard *Target,* and before that, long travels in space. Conferences in over-developed cities, or service on barren mining planets had robbed her of nature. Seeing the wonderland now, her eyes misted.

Without effort, she could conjure images of waterfalls, sparkling sunlight on rippling water. The cool breezes of early morning giving way to the warm intensity of a natural sun, then reluctantly fading to the inviting coolness of evening. The scent of fresh flowers, the intensity of mulch-dark soil, heat-baked rock. A longing she had never known before stirred in her breast, which was partly hers and partly his.

To walk on solid ground; to run until exhausted, then to flop down and roll like a cat in the waving grasses. To wake to the sound of birds chirping, and go to sleep to the lullaby of the Man in the Moon.

"Yes," she whispered in awed tones. "Let us go closer."

Her need became an ache, then a pain, then a physical stabbing. Too long deprived of natural gravity, imprisoned within the confines of a ship, she wanted to rediscover her roots on this green, alien home.

Reaching to his right, Star Bright scooped up Teddy, whooshing him in the air like a bird. His chuckles of delight were music to her soul.

A flash of light, the curl of smoke and her enthusiasm checked the way a cinch tightened around the underbelly of a horse. In her excitement, she had overlooked the fact the planet might be inhabited. Tears of disappointment stung her face. She did not want to share this paradise. She wanted it for herself. And for her two friends. They deserved the solitude, the unrestrained freedom of being the first to populate Emerald.

Emerald. The name came spontaneously to her mind. Green, and as precious as a jewel. Surely the planet must have a proper designation, but she did not know it. They were well beyond where her civilization had traveled. By rights, therefore, it was her prerogative to name it. She and Star Bright and Teddy Bear were the explorers, the discovers. They could call it anything they wished.

"What do you think?" she asked in her mind. "Emerald. Or would you prefer we name it after you? Star Bright. Or, the Bear Planet?" He did not answer because she was not there in time, only in memory. The realization saddened Helen before she dismissed it.

Emerald.

That would suit. The Emerald Planet.

"Go away," she wished away the unseen inhabitants. "Leave us in peace."

It was an errant hope, a child's fantasy. She was not ashamed of herself. In the presence of wonder, she would be the child. There was no one to tell her no.

"Whoosh. Whoosh." Teddy was flying across the cabin, his short, stuffed arms extended into wings, his button nose to the breeze, his fur ruffled by the gentle passage of air. Whoosh, whoosh.

Clasping her hands together in joy, Helen moved her head from side to side, taking in at one moment the anticipation of her companions, and in the other, the towering, beckoning life below them. Shoulder-to-shoulder-to-shoulder, she would show them what it was like to climb hills, tumble down into valleys, squat by a fire, race like the wind.

"How can we get down there?" she asked, but Star Bright already knew the answer, and in his knowing she comprehended. The transporter. No, that was her word, not his.

The space bubble.

"Space bubble."

Helen ran the words over in her mind, translating from his thoughts. She could envision Papa explaining about the space bubble. He was on the vid screen, down in the boarding area. He was smiling kindly. Papa, she knew, was a kind man. He always smiled.

Almost always, but she did not want to remember the times when he was not smiling.

"The space bubble," Star Bright was repeating. "An envelope of protection. You activate it in this manner." Helen mentally fast-forwarded through the technicalities. She was in a hurry. "Once inside it, you have oxygen and life support. Nothing outside can penetrate the shield. You control your destination by preprogramming it to deliver you where you wish. To another ship. To the surface of a planet. Or with your mind," he added. She was well past that addendum.

"Yes," she cried. "That is what I want."

Papa demonstrated. Before her eyes, he was slowly encapsulated by a sheen of transparent film. A bubble. She smiled. A man in a soap bubble.

There was Mama. She approached, placing a hand on the shimmerous glow. It did not penetrate. Papa reached out, placing the flat of his palm against the interior wall. They touched but did not touch.

"I can hear her and feel her but within the bubble, she cannot reach me. Watch."

Mama stepped away, leaving the room. With a hiss of decompression the exterior bay door opened. Papa floated outside, the camera following his forward progression. He waved. Helen waved back.

How she loved this man she had never known.

Papa was good. Papa was kind. Papa and Mama knew everything there was to know.

Except how to save themselves. But that was a thought for another time.

Outside the space craft, Papa floated, suspended in his bubble. He maneuvered up, down, to the sides. In a flash, he disappeared. Helen gasped, then sang for joy when he suddenly reappeared around the other side of the ship. She waved again. He waved back. Beside her, Star Bright was emulating their actions.

"Papa in a bubble!"

Too precious for words.

"You can do anything you want in the bubble," he was explaining. "Check the outside of the ship. Make repairs." His hand extended, the perimeters of the protection following him, altering from an oval, growing arms. He touched the side of the space craft. Without sound, she could sense the delicate impact.

Then, suddenly, Mama was beside him. Their bubbles brushed against one another's. They grinned. No harm from contact, only a gentle encounter in space.

Helen Fitzgerald, through the eyes of a child, watched as two grown adults played in deep space. They frolicked, spinning upside down, shooting across the screen like stars, dancing on their heads. Poetry in motion. It was a lesson and a game, a time for study and a time for fun.

Off they went, buzzing around the universe, so far away she could not see them, then unexpectedly so close she could almost feel their breath. Mama reached out and caught a floating speck of dust. From her hand emerged a separate, tiny bubble. In went the space dust. Gathering rocks for a collection. Extracting samples for scientific research.

The miniscule bubble stuck to her larger one. She did not have to bother carrying it. Papa found another fragment and made a bubble of his own. If they stayed out long enough, they could make a sand castle of bubbles.

The scene changed; time dissolved. There were three bubbles, now, two large, one small. Star Bright in a bubble. Baby Star Bright, so tiny, a miniature person. Mama and Papa tossed him like a ball, from one pair of protective hands to the other. He yelped in delight. A game in space. He bounced and tumbled and spun, his little arms reaching out, making small indentations in his soap bubble. His feet kicked. More indentations in his playhouse.

"Baby, baby, baby," Mama crooned. The baby laughed, then was plucked from the vastness and embraced by loving arms. Noses rubbed through the film, then baby was flung away, floating, drifting, exploring a universe of which he was born to be a part.

Baby, baby, baby. The far off reflection of light danced on his bubble, making him appear as though he were a walking, talking asteroid.

Star Bright.

Off to get him, bring him back. Time to go inside. Baby crying. Helen crying with him. Her own mother would have called it "making memories."

Inside, as the room pressurized, the film disintegrated, melting away into nothingness. Were she a bird, she might have been molting. The baby, which she was and was not, reached out a fist, pointing back toward space. "More," it conveyed. "Take us back."

"Another time," Mama promised. There was no conviction in her avowal. The recording stopped.

So. It was possible to go to the planet in a space bubble. They could play with one another on the way down. That sounded like fun. It had been a long time, she realized, since she had played a game for amusement.

Pat a cake, pat a cake,
Baker's man!
So I do, master, as fast as I can.
Pat it, and prick it,
And mark it with T,
And then it will serve
For Tommy and me.

Although she could hardly hope he would agree, Helen cried, "Let's go down to the planet. In a space bubble. You and me and Teddy." Peculiarly, Star Bright responded as though Helen had actually spoken the words.

"Let us go down to the planet. In a space bubble. Me and Teddy."

He did not include her in his invitation but she did not mind. He could not be expected to ask a lady he had never met.

Wrapping the bear in a soft flannel baby shirt Helen presumed he had outgrown, Star Bright descended to the bay area. With well-practiced motions, he set the controls then waited as the pliable covering surrounded him. Teddy shared his bubble. There was no sense letting him go by himself. He might get lost.

As the cargo door opened, Helen felt herself being whisked into space. The sensation was not unlike flying, or being levitated on a magic carpet.

"Away we go!"

It was not "good bye" to *Here,* but rather, "I'll see you later. We're off on a great adventure!" Helen and Teddy waved, so the ship would not feel lonely.

Then it was down and around and sailing through blackness, always with the Emerald Planet in sight, growing nearer and nearer, the intensity of its lush green foliage beckoning them on. Beyond it, nearly obscured by the growing profusion of color drifted the moon, a captured chunk of round rock, nearly an eighth the size of Emerald. There were others, Helen saw, even smaller.

A bevy of moons. She smiled. What was the game? Marbles.

They descended through the fleecy, fluffy, cottony clouds, ethereal puffs of cotton candy, the top sides white, the undersides a reflected blue.

Blue for atmosphere. Azure for water. It was going to be a wonderful place to frolic.

Slowly now, careful to avoid the tops of trees. She could almost feel the tips tickling her toes. Branches and leaves; sprouting buds, emerging flowers. Spring. A time of renewal. She wondered if the planet had seasons. Summer, fall, winter, spring. They had arrived at the perfect moment.

There was no imperfect time.

Mountains in the distance, vales before them, rolling hills, meadows of waving grasses. Verdure of a variety and intensity she had never before observed: pale and dark, yellowish-green fading into wheat, forest green and pine needles, veins of darker hues, stems of royal red, blistering brown, eggplant purple. Round leaves like pocket coins, square leaves reminding her of checkerboards; triangular leaves set on twigs, ready to soar into flight. Star-burst yellow flowers, entangled vines a kilometer long, snaking roots making cross-crosses the way lines on a playing field were set. Random abandonment, abstract art.

Turning her eyes inward, she observed the boy beside her. His eyes were wide, the whites a purity of surprise, the brown irises deep with excitement, the pupils contracted in the bright sunlight. "Beautiful," she whispered.

"Beautiful," he repeated.

Reaching out a hand, he maneuvered the bubble. Lower, then across the field, skimming the land, then higher as the plain rose into a hill. "I missed that lesson," she mused. "He can control his movements from inside the bubble."

Pegasus, with wings. A unicorn with saddle and bridle. It was all too wonderful.

They skipped like stones over a pond, striking land, then rising above, twirling and spinning, first one direction and then another. North, south, east, west, the points of the compass, and everywhere something new to see, to absorb, to dance around.

She had no way of knowing whether the air was breathable and did not care. It had to be. That was the only answer allowed.

"Let us get out of the bubble and walk on the ground."

Teddy seemed to be thinking the same thing, for his left foot twitched. "I am impatient to play, to run, to set my toes down on soil for the first time. What it is like, Star Bright?"

"I do not know." She had forgotten he had never before set foot on a planet. It seemed a terrible shame.

"Will I be able to stand upright?"

A grin and then, "Just as you do at home."

"Where is my chair and when can I eat?"

"Patience, little one."

Patience, little one. How many times, Helen wondered, had Mama and Papa admonished their child with just such an admonition?

> *Patience, little one, you will grow.*
> *Patience, little one, you will learn to walk.*
> *Patience, little one, you will absorb all there is to know.*
> *Patience, little one, you will meet someone with whom you can*

talk.

She was a poet and didn't know it.

There they were. Just ahead. They came out of nowhere. She had not seen them emerge from the underbrush where they had been hiding. People. Clothed in skins or furs or some type of rudimentary cloth. Long, disheveled hair, sun-darkened skin with a purplish tint.

Angry eyes. Clubs in their hands.

They were waving, shouting words she did not understand.

"Go away, evil spirit!"

She did not have to be a translator to understand.

One picked up a rock and threw it. Another, lips curled back in defiance, charged with a stick. A third cowered. A fourth beat its chest.

More emerged from the foliage, staring at the apparition. They jumped in rhythm which might have been a dance, or a spell, or the evoking of a charm, then dashed away to hide.

Raving. Curses.

Devil. Bad.

You are not welcome here. This is our emerald isle.

Leave before we kill you.

Rocks, bouncing off the protective shield; sticks striking the bubble, inflicting no damage. None as virulent as those which had been achieved by threats.

"We cannot land here, Teddy. They do not want us. We do not belong."

We do not belong anywhere.

Rising up, over the trees, into the clouds, beyond the atmosphere. High, higher, highest. No welcome for the weary. Moving away, the magic fading, the distant moons dark and depressing. No sunset, no moon rise.

> Lady bug, lady bug,
> Fly away home,
> Your house is on fire,
> Your children will burn.

Return to *Here,* open the bay, float in, heart heavy. Let the bubble dissolve like melting ice cream.

They are not like me.

No one is like me.

March to the bridge, a tin soldier, set the controls.

> Pat a cake, pat a cake,
> Baker's man!
> So I do, master, as fast as I can.
> Pat it, and prick it,
> And mark it with T,
> And then it will serve,
> *Just for Teddy and me.*

CHAPTER 26

Helen was shaking. She could not control her emotions. No matter the reasoning that she was a mature woman, capable of handling stress on many different levels, this was beyond her capacity to endure.

Too much had been asked of her, too much demanded after the breakup of *Target.* Adding tragedy and heartbreak of an innocent being was more than intolerable.

"All right," she whispered, wrapping her arms around Star Bright in an effort to ward away memories, rather than danger. "I understand."

What she understood was the face of the Andrien leader, revealing hatred, glowing like burst ions; his haughty assumption of superiority and conquest, transcending time and space. He was not Joshua Terry, yet she had made the connection, just as had Star Bright. It was unfair and unjust. Worse, she felt a traitor in her own eyes.

Yet, it was not to be denied.

"I will... ask him."

Helen's first impulse had been to say, "I will tell him – do not come aboard," but that was not her right. In a moment of betrayal, she was not even certain he would obey the command. Like the pirate, he had might on his side. The thought constricted her windpipe, causing her to cough and loosen her muscles before continuing.

"You will permit Paula and Jingles to come aboard?"

Employing their first names was a ploy – not for the benefit of her companion, who had no negative connotations of "commander" and "chief engineer," but to fool herself. Using first names made them sound less threatening, less... alien.

"If that is what you wish."

His reply, so innocently offered, tore into her already shattered psyche. While he had years, a decade or more, to assuage the horrors of attack and rejection, those emotions were as alive in her as simmering embers. By the simple act of sharing, Helen Fitzgerald had changed allegiances.

No, she sharply corrected herself. *Not changed. I am the middle ground, the ambassador between two disjointed worlds.* With the best interests of both sides on her conscience, she was the neutral negotiator. Paula and

Jingles would not harm Star Bright. They wished only to learn from the technology inherent in his ship. For the benefit of their own kind.

Joshua would want more. He would seek a deeper understanding of her little alien. Helen did not want to share.

Neutrality, she decided, was a double-edged sword.

"Swords" having nothing whatsoever to do with ambassadors.

Returning on wobbly legs to the bridge, Helen activated communications. Lowering her head, she spoke softly in the direction of the concealed microphone. "Joshua – Captain Terry. It is I. Helen."

"Yes, Helen," came the sharp, immediate response. "Are you all right? What is your situation?"

Through her awkward pronouncement he had read worry, confusion, and misinterpreted. The fault was hers. Shame was added to the emotions burdening her essence.

Running her hand through her hair, which she erratically thought must be mussed, she forced a smile to her face.

"I'm fine." Explanations died on her lips. She should try and explain, make him see what she had experienced. Strength failed and she found it difficult to understand why. Her temples throbbed as a wave of vertigo passed through her head, forcing her to close her eyes until it passed.

"Request permission to come aboard."

Gone was the friendliness, the concern, replaced by his command tone.

One thousand excuses floated through her mind, all of them true and all equally false. The best policy was honesty. Truth had always been the mark of her character. If he had been beside her, she would have grasped his arms, stared into his eyes, attempted to merge her feelings with his. But he was not beside her and might have been a dozen parsecs distant.

Remember the times we were separated, she tersely ordered herself. *While he was aboard ship and I on some distant planet. The long hours we talked, Josh of his duties. Of what he had seen. Remember the stories he told. The myriad rock formations he had discovered on Yetten.* 'One of them reminded me of you,' he had whispered. 'It was beautiful; a pale, crystalline, nearly transparent figure of a woman. I called it Helen.' And then he had grinned, knowing she would infer from his expression the ribbing he had taken from the other officers. It had been a good time, a shared secret; a period when she had loved him more than she had ever thought possible.

Remember telling him about the conference on Brottin III. Her frustrations in seating the delegates. 'As much as things change, they always stay the same,' he had joked. 'Try a little bluster. Throw out your chest; make a statement.'

'What statement, exactly, do you want me to make?' she had challenged back and they had both laughed.

They had not talked after that for nearly six months, and when they spoke again, they had forgotten Yetten and Brottin III.

"Remember the good times."

"What was that?" Joshua queried. "I didn't copy, Helen. Repeat."

She had not meant to articulate out loud. Her hand tightened into a fist.

"Star Bright extends an invitation to Commander Burbone and Chief Engineer Gingleheimer."

"Very good. I'll see you directly."

"Not you, Captain. You are to remain on the Skip."

Silence. Was he angry? Hurt? Surprised? She thought she ought to care. Muffled sounds in the background. He was speaking to someone, his head averted from communications, so as not to be overheard.

"Very well. Stand by to receive two visitors."

She had guessed wrong. He had accepted the limits of the invitation without question. They would have a reckoning, but not here, not now. She did not look forward to it. It would entail more lies. She was not what she had been.

They had all changed.

"Do you wish to meet them in the cargo bay?" Helen asked, disengaging communications and turning toward Star Bright and Teddy, who had noiselessly joined her. "They are your visitors, after all." She hesitated, then bit the inside of her lower lip. "Visitors" had been Joshua's word and she had subconsciously reused it.

"Do I – do I have to go?"

Hiding behind Teddy Bear, his arms clutching the toy as though it were a shield, she shook her head, then slowly lifted her eyes, so that they finally met his.

"I hope... I haven't done the wrong thing."

"You couldn't!" he blurted, then unexpectedly blushed and tweaked Teddy's ear. She inferred it was Mr. Bear's fault that Star Bright had confessed his inner feelings.

"I'm afraid, Teddy, that I have been known – on occasion – to let my temper or my emotions get the better of my common sense. But in this case," she continued, summoning her inner strength, "I think we can welcome our visitors with open arms. They are my friends," she added. "Just as I trust Joshua with my life, I trust them with yours."

It was not only a step she had to take, but a path she wanted to travel. They were of her, and she was of them. To deny that was to abandon her home on *Target*.

"Then I trust them... Helen, for you are my friend. The first I have ever had."

She knew that as well as the fact she could not allow herself to be carried away by the moment. There was too much at stake, not all of it emotional.

That was the road less traveled.

"Will you come with me?"

"No."

"Is it all right if I greet them?"

Turning his head to the side, then taking a step out of the overhead light, so that she viewed him in profiled shadow, Star Bright appeared more alien to her, less human. With his hair falling in bangs across his brow, the peaks, for the moment, dissolved into a straight line, his ears taking on a slightly pointed shape. Elfin. With boots curled at the tips and a pointed cap with silver bells, he might have belonged to the family of faerie.

"Go," he dismissed her with a slight bow. She was almost to the door when he spoke again. "You will come back, won't you?" On her kindly stare he added, "You won't stay with them?"

Clasping her hands together, palms inward, she made a rapid determination.

"Give me Teddy. I will introduce him to the new arrivals. Once he has made their acquaintance and I have shown them around the ship, he and I will both return. That way, you will be sure."

The idea of parting with his companion, even for so short a time as an introduction and a tour, was torturous. Stroking his fingers lightly across the bear's body from toe to chest, he appeared to study the way the fur stood on end before making his decision.

"All right."

Crossing back, Helen accepted his gift, then spontaneously placed a kiss on Star Bright's brow.

"To seal the bargain," she whispered, then scurried away before either had the chance to change their mind.

Helen arrived in the bay moments before Paula and Jingles reached the outer port. Once admitting them, she sealed the compartment, then expertly let out the oxygen and altered the gravity. Without hesitation the two crewmembers from *Target* floated in. Neither reacted as the door slid shut behind them. Holding onto stabilizing bars, they readjusted easily as the chamber refilled with air.

Crossing the threshold, Helen hesitated then held out her arms to Paula, who gave no indication of removing her helmet.

"It's all right," the hostess advised, noting her reluctance to accept the normalcy afforded them. "You'll find the environment aboard *Here* remarkably similar to that which we are accustomed."

Though she spoke the word naturally, the "we" felt awkward, out of place. Although she had been gone only 24 hours, Helen had experienced years of lifetime through Star Bright's eyes. Without awareness until this moment, she knew now that knowledge was not only power, it meant separation.

Glossing over the sensation of dissociation, she continued hurriedly, "Welcome aboard."

Jingles' hand went spontaneously to the lock at the junction of the suit and headgear, but Paula held him back with a curt shake of her head. Extending a hand which Helen first thought was for her, Burbone manipulated the controls on her sleeve, testing the atmosphere. Not until the quality had been ascertained did she give the thumbs-up to disengage their suits.

Catching Helen's eye, Paula was more than ready with an explanation.

"Things are not always what they seem. It's always best to be safe."

"You're absolutely right. Things are not always what they seem, Lieutenant Tolbray," Helen replied, referring to the name plate on Paula's helmet. The commander did a double-take before putting the remark in context.

"Indeed... Helen." While the familiarity in using the woman's first name was apparent, the tone said, rather, "Dr. Fitzgerald." Unfastening her suit, she peered past the inner door without bothering to disguise her curiosity. "Where is the alien – our host. Star Bright?"

Wondering if she had erred on several counts, the communicator debated before holding forth the second resident of *Here*.

"Star Bright remained on the bridge. This is Teddy Bear. He bids all who enter as friends welcome."

It was Jingles who took the initiative. With a delighted cry, he made a polite bow.

"Pleased to make your acquaintance, Master Bear." Without any indication at awkwardness at addressing a little stuffed toy, he reached inside his shirt, retrieving a small package. "A present for you." Offering the roll of candy, he grinned as Helen extended Teddy's arm, grasping the gift between her hand and his. "I won it," Jingles explained, "in a contest. Never won anything before in my life. It may not be much to look at, but to me, it's priceless."

"Thank you," Helen accepted, flustered and pleased. "The magnitude of your generosity is greatly appreciated." Stealing a sidelong glance at Paula, the commander shook her head. She had not thought to bring a welcoming present.

"On behalf of Captain Terry and the crew of *Target,* we thank you for the generosity of inviting us aboard. I hope this is the beginning of a fair exchange of ideas and technology."

Nonplused, for Helen would have expected Paula to offer a gift and Jingles to make a perfunctory statement, she took a step back before extending her hand.

"Let us show you around."

The chief engineering's trip was a short one. As they passed the engine room, he grunted in pleasure, planting his feet firmly on the deck, indicating he would go no further.

"Mr. Bear," he began, while politely maintaining eye contact with Helen. "This is where my heart lies. I beg you to release me from the tour, so that I may stick my nose in your jar of honey."

While Teddy did not grasp the significance of the phrase, Helen did. Not without misgivings, for she was suddenly loath to be left alone with the former ensign, she could not refuse his request, so graciously expressed.

"Be our guest."

Moving on tip-toe so as not to disrupt the delicate machinery, Jingles pressed himself through the narrow opening and disappeared. His sighs of contentment were clearly heard by all his listeners as he settled himself carefully before the engines.

"Shall we go on?" Paula requested, directing her sentence at she who had become, not her equal, but her subordinate. While far from rude, Helen shuddered.

"With pleasure."

Hoping her voice did not betray her conflicting emotions, Helen led the way into the lift and upward to the bridge. As the doors parted, she was inordinately relieved to observe Star Bright had absented himself.

Suddenly, she did not want to introduce him; did not want to expose the small alien to the prying eyes of Paula Burbone. In less than five minutes, the commander had gone from friend to enemy.

The were no rational explanations for Helen's suspicions, yet she couldn't convince herself the officer was who she said she was. The irrational idea had begun in the reception area when she noticed the wrong name on the helmet. By itself, the fact should not have disturbed her, for she understood Paula would not have had a spacesuit of her own. The impression had become highlighted by the curious exchange of identities during Jingles' presentation of his gift. Now, she could easily believe that Joshua Terry had assumed her body shape in order to board the ship. Either that, or he had so thoroughly brought Paula over to his side that she thought, acted and felt precisely as he.

Which was another question, entirely. Why would she consider Joshua the enemy?

Contrary to expectations, Paula did no more than glance around the bridge before shifting her attention beyond.

"I would like to see the hydroponics unit, if I might."

This entailed crossing the command center and the den, something Helen had hoped to postpone. Comprehending the importance of the request, however, she nodded.

"Certainly. Follow me."

Paula's excited grunt of surprise at seeing the vast outlay of hydroponic equipment and the profusion of varied plants should have reassured Helen, but did not. Nothing the commander said or did would put her at ease. There was something wrong; a latent sense of disjointedness which prevented her from relaxing.

"All of this!" Paula remarked in wonder, apparently oblivious to her shipmate's suspicions. "There must be twenty or thirty different species here. And growing in such abundance!" Spinning around, it was with difficulty she met Helen's eyes. "I presume these are all eatable. Do you know their names and purposes?"

"No. I'm afraid I don't. That," she pointed aimlessly, "is processed into a hot beverage; very much like coffee."

"What luxury! What I wouldn't give to bring back coffee to the crew."

"There isn't enough," Helen sharply objected. "Keep in mind what you see here feeds the master of this vessel. It was meant to sustain him, and him alone."

Paula's right eye twitched but her expression didn't alter.

"Of course. What I meant was, if he could spare some plant clippings, we could grow our own on *Target.*" Without waiting for a reply, she turned her back, then stooped over, peering through the semi-translucent housing material.

"Or, if we could learn what he uses to feed his plants, that would be a great benefit. Possibly, we could duplicate it. As you know, our need for nutrients is critical. And in very short supply. What we can learn here may save our lives."

She made no attempt to underscore her statement, yet Helen took it for a threat.

As though she had responded in the affirmative, Paula continued, the implication being, they were on the same wave length. "I'm not an engineer or a botanist, but I can see he has a system of extracting oxygen from the growing plants. Very sophisticated. No wonder he is able to maintain life support. Everything has more than one function."

Positioning herself away from the speaker, Helen demurred.

"I'm afraid I haven't had time to discuss the technicalities with Star Bright."

Paula's eye twitched a second time before she placed the stump of her right arm atop the tank. It was an attempt at soliciting a shared remembrance of suffering, and only partially successful.

"What have you been talking about?"

Whatever she gained by her call to solidarity was lost by the interrogative.

Caught off guard by the abrupt change in subject, Helen tried an endearing smile. Without realizing it, the expression was one she would have given Joshua, were he in Paula's place.

"Getting to know one another," she faltered. "He's been alone all his life. My presence here is a ... wonder to him. And a danger," she menacingly added. "I must be careful not to tread too hard, or too fast. If he's going to help us, we must first establish a bond of trust and friendship." Looking down, she gently stroked Teddy behind the ears. "He has been... much abused."

Straightening from her post of observation, Paula matched her cautious expression.

"Explain what you mean."

While it was not her intent to touch the companion, Helen withdrew Teddy from her easy reach.

"I'll make a report out for Captain Terry."

"Of course you will," Commander Burbone agreed, her tone assuming a more formal exchange. Helen recoiled. "Is there anything Star Bright requires from us? We haven't much to spare, but I would like to consider our intercourse of mutual benefit."

Helen bristled at Paula's word choice. As a scientist who made her living in the field of communication, she was acutely sensitive to language. While "intercourse" was not inappropriate, it held a dual connotation she resented.

"Friendship," she retorted more angrily than intended. "Trust. An exchange of civilizations." Stepping away, Helen placed a row of hydroponic units between herself and the officer. "I think the greatest gift we have to offer is the belief there are friendly races in space. Those who come in peace," she meaningfully emphasized. "Those who will respect the rights of others."

Paula followed Helen, unwilling to let the separation stand. Her face was calm, her demeanor relaxed, but her eyes burned with an intensity belying body language.

"That," she began evenly, as though reciting a well-rehearsed speech, "is the one abiding tenet of our mission. Our code of honor; one we all swear by. It's written in the constitution of the United Planet Earth – as well as the International Space Federation. To break such an oath goes against all we believe." Helen gave no indication of having processed the information. "Why do you suppose we would break it here?"

"I do not," Helen countered. Her denial held no more emotion than Paula's assertion. Paula continued as though it had.

"I have never met him – this alien creature. Will I have the opportunity of presenting my compliments?"

"I don't know. Perhaps. It's up to him."

"I understand he's shy; and as you infer, he has good reason. I respect that." Paula began walking, taking in rapidly all she passed, as though cramming for an examination. Helen followed, as she knew she must. "Tell me. What does he look like?" No description was forthcoming. "It would help me prepare myself, when I have the honor of making his acquaintance."

"Surely Captain Terry told you –"

Paula stopped so fast, Helen almost bumped her. She awkwardly retreated.

"As a matter of fact, we had very little time to discuss details. I would appreciate you describing Star Bright to me. Now."

It was a military command and Helen resented it. Her civilian status, only recently altered, caused her to rebel at the demand. Before Encounter, Paula had been no more than an ensign, an officer-in-training. As a department head and acknowledged expert in her own field, Helen had always considered herself apart from the crew. It was not in her nature to submit when her authority was questioned. Without being transparent, she hoped, she withdrew Teddy behind her back.

"Why do you want to know?"

"I've already explained."

Paula began moving again, but this time, Helen failed to follow. The commander was thus forced to complete an entire circuit around hydroponics before coming up on the other woman's back.

"Would you accept the fact that I'm curious?" Silence was denial. Paula easily slipped into an accommodating tone of comradeship. "Encountering alien life is one of the reasons I went to space; why I was so pleased to have been assigned to *Target*. Exploration and discovery; the assimilation of cultures. The opportunity to communicate with unlike beings. Surely, you can understand."

"If Star Bright makes his presence known, you will see him then."

Paula extended a hand, resting it on Helen's shoulder. She turned slowly, allowing each to search the other's expression.

"Please. It's important to me."

"Why?"

There was no easy explanation for Paula to offer. To confess her suspicion that Star Bright was presenting a different face to each crewman would only serve to put Helen on guard. It would also destroy any chance she had of receiving an honest answer. Three days ago, Paula Burbone would have trusted the doctor of language and letters with her life. But not at the moment.

"Because I asked you to."

"And who are you, to make such a demand?"

Joshua Terry would have replied, *Your commanding officer,* and possibly received an answer. Paula instinctively understood the same would not hold true for her. It was a mark against Helen she would not easily forgive.

"Someone entrusted with the safety of *Target* and sixteen crewmembers."

Helen's grip on Teddy tightened.

"They are in no danger."

It was her training and her instinct for command which prompted the commander to relent.

"Please understand my position. You've been gifted with the alien's friendship. As our representative, you've been privy to his thoughts, his experiences. We have not. We are in a very vulnerable position. It's difficult to take appearances on face value. I'm asking you, as a member of *Target,* to help me understand *Here's* captain. That way, I can report back that all is right." Helen wavered, torn between two worlds. "Your friends need reassurance. Their lives may hang in the balance. Captain Terry was denied permission to board. How do you think they reacted to that?"

Nearly crushed with the weight of responsibility, Helen pivoted, simultaneously drawing the stuffed bear in front of her. Paula's brows knit a moment as she feared losing Helen. This was no longer a confrontation. She didn't want to battle the woman on military grounds, or arcane protocol. Their lives *were* at stake. What she had asked was not unreasonable. If Paula were denied here, then it was Helen's loyalty she would question, more than the alien's "humanness."

"I don't know."

"Put yourself in their place... Helen. Turn around. Look at me. Please."

Helen didn't want to be drawn back. While she realized her sense of protectiveness was acute, that failed to mitigate its sway over her. Her own trust had invariably been weakened by the revelation of Star Bright's betrayals.

Beyond the dual experiences she had witnessed through his eyes was her own guilty knowledge of Mankind's history of treachery. Oaths and high-sounding promises to the contrary, when pushed to the brink of destruction, they would fight like demons.

The hard, cruel fact was that *Target* held the very real potential to be a death ship. Even if they maintained environment, it would not sustain them forever. Eventually, they would have to find a planet upon which to settle, or be rescued. If neither of those scenarios transpired, their outlook was grim.

And that didn't even touch upon the more pressing need to produce more food. Harvesting radishes and sprouts was only a means to an end, not an end by themselves. The genetically-altered soy plants were their only true hope of immediate survival.

Against her advice but not her common sense, the nutritional tablets had been sacrificed for the greater good. That had been the one judgment Terry feared most, yet when confronted with the choice, he had opted to play God.

How much easier would his decision be when deciding between his crew and one defenseless alien?

Where it in her power, Helen Fitzgerald would see to it that it never came to that.

Slowly, and with the trepidation felt when facing an unknown menace, she confronted Paula. As Helen turned, she inadvertently brushed against an outcropping stem. The leaves rustled gently. In other circumstances, the action might have served to restore normalcy.

Instead, the awareness of being surrounded by plants of unknown species only exacerbated the separation between them. To mitigate the damage they both felt, Paula ran her fingers over one of the leaves, hoping, by tactile sensation, to make it less strange.

"Tell me what he looks like. That cannot be construed as divulging a confidence."

"This is how I appear," Star Bright announced, slipping noiselessly to the fore of the hydroponics area. His unexpected arrival caused Helen to gasp in surprise. Unable to suppress her first instinct, she ran toward him, thrusting Teddy into his arms. Accepting the tiny companion, he followed Helen's lead by placing the animal behind his back. His action indicated to Paula that he had either been watching them, or in some manner divined her action and copied it. The action did not lessen her suspicion the alien could read minds.

Nor did it alleviate her concern to observe Helen's reaction. Without words, she had affectionately placed herself by Star Bright's side.

All other considerations would be based on that one action.

"I am very pleased to make your acquaintance, Captain Star Bright," Paula began, rapidly scrutinizing his features while attempting to store away first impressions. They would be what mattered: what she would compare with Joshua Terry's. If the alien were manipulating their minds, subtly altering his appearance to project an image on innocence unique to each individual, this might be the only test they had to prove it.

Extending the stump of her right hand, the commander approached cautiously, hoping her own defenseless appendage would compel him to touch her. The fact Helen's arms grasped solid flesh was no proof her own experience would be similar. Just as they had speculated he could only fully control one mind at a time, so, too, perhaps, he was limited in his ability to project a tangible body.

"My name is Paula Burbone. I am the commander of the space cruiser *Target.*"

"She is second in command – under Captain Terry," Helen elucidated, the words spilling eagerly from her lips. "In his absence, she is the superior officer; it is to Paula he goes when he seeks military advice. They... occupy the bridge together."

Without acknowledging Paula's gesture, Star Bright stared curiously at the stranger. His eyes wide and eager, he compared what he saw to Helen. Then, with his head nodding slowly, he performed a gentle rolling motion with his hands, encircling them without touching.

"I welcome you."

There was nothing in his demeanor to indicate a reluctance to touch her, yet his greeting was patently non-physical. Rebuffed, Paula drew nearer, an expression of shame on her face not entirely intentional.

"I hope I didn't offend you."

Holding back her right hand, she offered the left.

"Offend?" he questioned, cringing more from the accusation than the proffered sign of good will.

"She wants to shake hands with you," Helen rapidly explained, gently grasping his hand in hers. "It's a way of expressing friendship."

"Offend?" he repeated, eyes riveted toward Paula's missing hand.

"Commander Burbone was injured when *Target came into contact with dark matter.* Hurt. Her arm was crushed. She lost her fingers in the accident. They couldn't be saved."

"Offend?" he reiterated a third time, before delicately withdrawing Teddy from his protective hiding place. Blinking away moisture from his eyes, he stared at the bear's small paws, conspicuously devoid of fingers. "Look, Commander," he demonstrated, gently bobbing the companion's two good arms. "Teddy Bear has no fingers. He does not offend me. He is," he gravely concluded, "as he should be."

Confused and embarrassed, yet afraid to abandon her opportunity, Paula re-extended her disfigured arm.

"Then will you shake hands with me?"

He complied immediately, but not in the manner she expected. Extending Teddy's paw, he delicately touched it to Paula's stump.

"I do so, gladly."

"You honor me," she replied, reacting with regret she could barely feel the light touch of fur.

Looking sadly at Helen, he sought an appropriate answer.

"Say, in return, she honors you by her visit."

With a smile of joy, he repeated the words, "You honor me with your visit," then cradled the bear beneath his arm.

Feeling the moment slip away, Paula dropped the arm to her side, then thought better of it and pointed beyond them.

"Will you show me your command center?" His eyes were slow in focusing. "Is it designed for two?"

"Yes," he thoughtfully agreed. Without moving toward the bridge, Star Bright sketched in the air, marking out two seats, then roughly filling in the controls and viewscreen. "I sit in one chair now and Teddy in the other."

"So I understand."

His eyes narrowed in concentration, then abruptly he held Teddy up to eye level. Tapping the companion on the nose, then blinking to simulate the proper response, he glared up sharply.

"But your – bridge – what you call the bridge – it is not like mine."

"No. It's not." It was Paula who answered and her attention was keen. "How do you know this?"

Rather than reply, he answered her question with another.

"Tell me. How is it different?"

The commander's first instinct was to repeat her own query, for how he answered was imperative to her making the proper judgment concerning his abilities. If Helen had alluded to the differences, described *Target's* bridge in limited detail, than his knowledge was appropriate. If she hadn't, however, then he had obtained the information in another way.

By reading their minds.

A creature who could translate thought might also possess the ability to plant suggestions, create scenes which, in reality, did not exist. By presenting the impression of a Rover-type craft, inhabited by a sole occupant, and himself as harmless, he could first charm and then disarm them.

Burbone's predicament was dual-edged. She must not put him on his guard and at all costs, she had to placate Helen. Making her choose sides would infinitely complicate their situation.

To say nothing of placing Joshua Terry in the very dire predicament of having to decide between the woman he loved and his own crew.

Because no ready solution arose, Paula opted for a different tract.

"There hadn't been time for me to properly examine your ship. If you will show me the bridge, I'll be in a better position to answer."

Not being privy to Paula's suspicions, Helen was eager to respond. With Star Bright's approval, she offered the invitation.

"We passed through it briefly. Will you come with me?"

Leading the way, she guided the woman who shared with her a common heritage through the den and into the bridge. Star Bright and Teddy followed at a respectful, not quite standoffish distance.

"Here," Helen began, warming to her task. "The two co-pilots sit in these chairs. The controls can be operated from either position. This is the main viewscreen. I'm sorry I don't know more. I expect the panels make more sense to you than they do to me."

She meant her statement to be taken as a compliment, but Paula accepted it as no more than simple logic.

"I' like to study it," she decided, settling into the seat on the right. Her hands hovered above, but did not touch, the instruments. They were, she decided, well beyond her power to grasp without a proper education of the working components.

What could a pilot do from this position? Scan the universe? Detect signs of life in other galaxies? Chart the trajectory of meteors? Activate a weapons system so powerful it could destroy the entire population of a planet?

"Will you teach me, Star Bright?" Leaning closer to the instrumentation, she attempted to interpret the indecipherable characters marking the panels.

Paula sensed him come up behind her but did not turn around. Her attention, for all practical purposes, was concentrated on the unfamiliar mechanisms.

Tucking Teddy Bear under his arm, the little alien stared into the screen which revealed, to his intense orbs, the reflection of Paula Burbone. He shook his head slowly, from right to left. His voice, when he spoke, was angry.

"I will teach you nothing."

Paula had not expected so negative a denial. Twisting in the chair, she saw him shoot his free hand up, motioning her to stand. She complied with his order, placing the command seats between her and the ship's owner. If he were to make an aggressive move, distance would give her a precious second to prepare her defenses.

"Leave," he commanded, baring his teeth. The action served to make him appear older, stronger. Gone was his veneer of innocence, replaced by that of a well-trained soldier defending his fort.

Perhaps it was an alternation in the lighting, or her own rapidly evolving evaluation, but there seemed to be grey around his temples, lines underscoring his eyes. He might be ancient, with a score of centuries to his credit. The stuffed toy under his arm could be no more than a ploy, an evil deception. Or possibly the outer casing for some sort of malignant creature dwelling within.

"If I have inadvertently offended you –"

"Star Bright, what is it?" Helen cried, overlapping Paula's apology. When she placed a hand on his shoulder he didn't flinch.

"I want her off my ship."

Startled and unable to cope with his abrupt change of mood, Helen sought Paula's eyes, silently pleading. *No trouble,* she begged. *Do as he says.* To Paula's arched eyebrow, she could only shrug a simple *I don't know.*

The commander acknowledged the captain's right with a curt bow.

"And my engineer?"

Star Bright hesitated, a look of confused innocence returning to his face. His eyes shifted from the two command chairs to Helen, then down to the stuffed toy. When he replied, he did not look up.

"Take him with you." Then awkwardly, "Please," and a more reticent, "Thank you."

Stiffening her shoulders, Burbone took a step away, then directed her piercing gaze at Helen.

"And you coming with us?"

"Back to *Target?"*

"That's what I meant."

Helen put a hand to her face, patted her lips in a nervous gesture, then demurred.

"No."

"I think you should."

Thrusting Teddy Bear out, the way an attacker would a sword, Star Bright stepped between them.

"She stays here."

Paula did not react, though her stomach muscles tightened to fend off the physical blow which never came.

"She belongs with her own people. Captain Terry is waiting for her."

A momentary cracking of his resolve, the shadow of a doubt, then his lower lip thrust out defiantly.

"He will wait longer."

"Go," Helen begged. "I'll be all right." As her former ship-bound companion raised her arms, prefatory to touching and possibly forcing her away, Helen cried, "I want to stay!"

Paula didn't have to ask, *Of your own free will?* She wouldn't have believed the answer.

CHAPTER 27

They watched on the viewscreen as the two humans, Commander Paula Burbone and Chief Engineer Jingles Gingleheimer departed. Star Bright operated the decompression from the bridge. He did not speak as the humans tested the stability of their environment before floating into space.

Not until they were safely inside the distant Skip did the little alien let out an unexpected shriek. The wail reverberated off the walls, nearly knocking Helen Fitzgerald from her feet.

Captain Terry was waiting for his crew as they arrived in the Skip. Without prior communication of their return, he suspected the worst. Noting the anxiety on his features, Paula made a placating gesture with her hand, then placed a finger to her lips.

"We had a wonderful time, sir. The ship is marvelous. His hydroponics unit is simply amazing; growing plants of every description. I can't wait to tell you all about it. Back on *Target.*"

"Very good. Mr. Gingleheimer," he continued, addressing the engineer. "I'll expect a full report from you, as well."

"I don't know that I can make one," Jingles began, but was as quickly silenced. With a disconcerted shrug, he followed the others into the cramped cabin. "It was amazing, really. A treat for me; better than candy," he grinned. "I only began my examination. I didn't even determine what he uses for fuel." The "he" in this case referring to the engines, rather than the pilot. "But it's incredibly efficient. No waste at all. The ions are all recycled into other forms of energy."

"That's the start of a report, thank you. Set yourself in place. Burbone, you co-pilot."

"Yes, sir."

Other than the technical jargon required to maneuver the shuttle on the return flight, no further words were spoken.

As before, there was a welcoming committee to greet them in the receiving bay. Paula responded to the eager faces by smiling and waving, as though she had just returned from an exploratory journey of many months.

"Thank you," she beamed good-humoredly, following Terry as he made his way through the throng. "We'll have a shipwide meeting soon; I want you all to experience what I've seen."

"Did you bring any plant samples back with you?" Janice Miles eagerly inquired, pushing her way through the well-wishers. "Did you learn any new methods of hydroponics?"

"Nothing specific, but I assure you, there's much for us to study."

"No tea?" Brian lightly inquired. Neither Joshua nor Paula had seen him come up. As usual, he seemed to appear by magic.

"Helen did say something about coffee; and it wouldn't surprise me in the least if there were green tea, as well," Paula responded. Brian tugged on his ear lobe, then fussed with his nose.

"Well. I'd like to hear all about it."

His words, casually intoned, indicated he was not fooled by the showmanship, and wished to be taken into confidence. Joshua hesitated, clearly torn, then finally relented.

"Yes. Well, come along, then. The rest of you," he continued, moving his arm in an arc across his body, "back to work."

"Where's Dr. Fitzgerald?"

"Why didn't you bring Helen back with you?"

Surprisingly, it was Jingles who responded.

"She's staying behind to teach him English. That way, he'll better be able to explain to us what he knows."

Neither of the two top officers could have come up with a more plausible explanation. Caught off guard at his insight, then questioning whether it was actually wistful thinking, Paula led Joshua and Brian into the roundabout. The door slid shut behind them, then began its arduous upward trip.

It was her decision to stop at Level Two. The first off, she led the group into one of the unoccupied computer rooms. As they each paced off their own private space, Paula activated a series of controls, filling the chamber with loud, discordant static. Only then did she feel safe to speak.

"I believe we were correct, Captain," came the initial pronouncement. "He can read our minds."

"What?" Brian protested, but was waved to silence. He would have to fill himself in as they went along. As if expecting as much, he leaned back against a console, legs expanded at a thirty degree angle.

"And I do believe our 'Star Bright' is not what he seems." She indicated the static with a desultory motion of her right stump.

"Tell me."

"First, he didn't want you aboard. You've already seen him; you and I would most certainly exchange notes about our observations. Second, I don't believe he would have presented himself to me at all, were it not for my outright request."

"He wasn't there when you arrived?"

"No. Jingles never saw him at all. Helen gave me the 'tour.' It was sketchy, at best."

"Was she holding something back?"

This time, the answer was less forthright.

"I don't think so. I think she told me everything she knew – about the ship."

"But not about Star Bright."

It was not a question.

"No. When I asked her what he looked like, she wouldn't answer me."

"Why not?" Brian demanded, his reasoning taking him only so far. On Joshua's exasperated look, which shouted *guilty* to an experienced observer, the cleric was willing to concede and forgive. "All right," he slowly began, giving all three time to settle down. "You've already made some suppositions, to which I wasn't privy."

"We didn't want –" Paula began, but he eased her conscience by repositioning himself in a chair, arms striking the hand-rests with a dull plop.

"I'm not asking for explanations as to why I was omitted. You had your reasons. But I'm here, now. If I'm to be any help at all, I must have the background. You suspect Helen of some... complicity?"

"Not a willful one." This time, it was the captain who began. Helen was his responsibility on many levels. "This alien –"

He faltered and Brian filled in the name. "Star Bright."

"The facts don't appear to correlate with what we've heard and what we've seen."

Scratching himself on the chest, Hardy rapidly attempted to put two and two together.

"You think... what? The question about our fantasies. That was a test, or a –?"

"Fact gathering," Paula resumed for Terry.

They waited while he tried to solve the puzzle.

"Fantasies... dreams." He snapped his fingers as his equation equaled four. Which, he would have been the first to concede, was only correct in certain well-defined dimensions. "You surmise Star Bright can probe our thoughts and make us see what we want to? You think Helen has been taken in by what she perceives to be a lost and lonely soul?" The pair nodded. "Why?"

The responsibility again fell to the captain.

"First, he chose to communicate to her through space. That proves he can send and receive thought transmissions. It doesn't take a great jump in logic to believe he can probe a person's thoughts, and thus manipulate himself into anything he senses is agreeable to his intended victim."

"Maybe not a great jump, but certainly a leap," Brian hedged.

"Second," Terry continued, beginning a slow revolution around the room. To offset his action, Paula sat down. "Everything is too pat, too... perfect. Let's start with his ship."

"All right," came the agreeable noncommittal.

"In my wildest dreams, I couldn't construct anything which appealed more to me. It's a self-contained world. In a vessel like that, a man could explore the universe to his heart's content."

"But isn't that exactly what Star Bright is doing?" Brian abruptly stood up and exchanged one chair for another. "You're not the only being who has wishes like that, Josh. We have no reason to assume others – Star Bright included – don't have the same goals... desires. He may be exactly what he seems – a space explorer."

"But he's not like me. He's a... child," Terry began. He was interrupted by both Brian and Paula, reacting simultaneously in the negative. Quickly glancing at one another, the cleric gave way.

"He appears young, or youthful, but I saw his face change... age. At least I thought I did," Paula added for the sake of honesty. "And if I hadn't, I still wouldn't classify him as an innocent. There's too much behind his eyes."

Holding out his hand, Joshua indicated his agreement before indicating he would continue.

"Let's take this one step at a time. Brian, you were with me on the first trip. Describe what you saw."

A sudden itch caused the man of the cloth to bend over and scratch the back of his calf. His listeners presumed he was stalling for time, which was incorrect.

"Five-foot seven, wavy dark hair, inquisitive and frightened brown eyes. Slightly built. Helen deduced he had never experienced physical contact with another being. I thought that plausible."

"Doesn't that stretch your powers of reasoning?"

"Common sense, perhaps," Hardy objected. "But there is so much we don't know. His planet was at war and his parents sent their infant away, for safety's sake. Or he was born in space and the adult crew perished. Before they died, the ship was programmed to care for him until he was big enough and skilled enough to do it for himself."

"You're guessing." Brian shrugged. "What kind of a ship can do that?"

Brian was quick to answer.

"One which is a self-contained world. Your expression," he added, finally straightening. Terry was unconvinced. He confronted his second in command. "Your turn. What did you observe?"

More reticent than her captain, Paula was loath to concede her suspicions.

"The same physical characteristics as Brian describes. I would go so far as to call him handsome. Left alone with Helen, I could easily see why she would respond to him. His demeanor is... childlike but not childish. The teddy bear. The soft speech; the apparent lack of guile." Her voice hardened. "But hardly a galaxy-weary traveler. He's suspicious, over cautious. When I asked for an explanation of the bridge controls, he grew angry, as if there were much he didn't wish us to learn."

"Perhaps you put your request badly," Hardy suggested. "The wrong tone of voice... or possibly he suspected your motives were more dangerous than curious."

"If he did, then he divined it from reading my mind."

Brian blinked, wondering if she realized the admission behind that statement. Apparently the captain picked up on it, for his denial was forceful.

"He had no intention of explaining."

"Which means," the cleric pursued, "Either *you're* reading *Star Bright's* mind, or you've jumped to an unsubstantiated conclusion. One more emotional than factual."

"How would you explain it?" Terry demanded, eyes piercing the other's face with an assault Brian knew he could not maintain.

"You're jealous. You have been from the first. Once you discovered Helen's attachment – profoundly expanded, once contact was made aboard ship – you've been looking for an excuse to turn every nuance into a negative connotation."

Joshua was less angry than he anticipated. Oddly, having it out in the open served to lessen the impact.

"Perhaps that's true." Joshua stared down at his hands. "But I don't believe my command judgment has been affected. The alien links psychically to Helen, then maneuvers his craft here. He refuses to communicate openly with the rest of us. We board his ship and only Helen is allowed to speak with him."

"You see her as our weak link?"

"Yes. Or, rather, the most manipulative one. She's easy to bring over to his side. Far easier than myself or Paula."

"What about me?"

"You're looking for God," Joshua bitterly scoffed, feeling Brian slip away. "Maybe you think he's closer to it than we are."

"Maybe he is."

"And maybe he's just looking for a quick way to conquer us. Maybe his world isn't as 'self-contained' as we think. Maybe he needs something from us – something we might be reticent to part with."

"Such as?"

Terry snorted through his nose.

"Anything. Chemicals in our body. Components of our life support system. Maybe he can suck the thoughts and emotions from our brains and put them on a disc, to keep himself amused."

Brian considered the explanation before addressing Paula.

"What about you?"

"I think the captain has valid points."

"And you don't think jealousy is affecting his judgment?"

"No."

"Elaborate, please."

Unlike the two men, Burbone was not one to put up a pretense of relaxation. Lifting up her right hand, where the healed flesh clearly revealed her stump, she stared at the philosopher with calm, unemotional eyes.

"The crew, were they to meet the alien, might feel predisposed to trust. He has an engaging air about him. But I don't feel it."

"What did you experience?"

She found the sentiment easy to put into words.

"The same thing you might, were you to confront the lone representative of a species claiming to be divine."

"And that is?"

"Distrust."

"Go on," Brian urged by wiggling his fingers and according her the probability.

"I believe he is far more advanced than Helen suspects. She wants to accept him at face value."

"That's her nature."

"Granted. The captain and I are more prone toward suspicion. Perhaps I *was* thinking about what we could do with his ship, had we the knowledge to fly it. Not consciously, but deep inside my mind, I was considering..."

She hesitated. Terry stared at her a moment in guilty complicity, for he knew where she was going. Brian remained curiously implacable, perhaps fearing any interruption would prevent the confession from being verbalized.

"Using *Here* to scout the solar system. It has maneuverability, speed and a seemingly unlimited fuel supply. Something our own Skips don't have. Aboard that ship, we could search for a planet with atmosphere; use its sensors to detect where food grows in abundance. We could even navigate it back to Earth, or close enough to communicate our plight to Fleet Command. If they had all the facts, we would eventually be rescued."

"And if you were Star Bright, wouldn't you have taken offense?" Brian was compelled to point out.

"I couldn't have," Paula darkly observed. *"I* can't read minds. I wouldn't have taken my reactions as anything more than what they were – simple wonder at the complexities of an alien vessel."

"And you don't think your body language – your expression – might have been transparent to someone in an obviously vulnerable position? We outnumber him by a considerable margin, you know."

"No."

Brian threw up his hands, which was a gesture calculated to concede the point.

"We've come to a standstill. Where do we go from here? That is why we've gathered, isn't it? Are you plotting a takeover? Some sort of aggressive action?"

"I want Helen off that ship," Terry growled.

"To order that, you stand a very good chance of losing whatever help or knowledge we may glean from Star Bright."

"I'm willing to take that chance."

"Are you? I don't think you are."

Terry slapped his hand against his thigh, then abandoned his position for one which placed him above the questioner. Leaning over, he pressed his face to Brian's.

"Maybe you're right. Maybe the needs of *sixteen,*" he gritted, in veiled reference to the loss of one crewwoman, "do take precedence over one."

Hardy counted to five before answering.

"That's against everything you believe."

"Like you," Joshua angrily snarled, "my beliefs have changed in the last six months."

It was a low blow and the cleric flinched.

"So far as to abandon every canon you hold sacred?"

"I hope it doesn't come to that."

Brian moved away to give himself breathing room.

"I hope not. Because I won't support you."

Terry's face reddened but he couldn't abandon his position, no matter how suddenly and unexpectedly it had come upon him.

"Life aboard this ship is tenuous, at best. We survive day-to-day by the skin of our teeth. One set-back, one minor disaster and we're dead. Have you considered that?"

"Every day."

"I have a duty to my crew."

"You also have a larger responsibility to the civilization you represent."

"Even over death?"

Silence grew into a pall before they responded.

"That's a decision I can't make for you."

"You're the one who wanted me to become a dictator. Or have you forgotten?" Terry persisted, closing the gap between them a second time.

"No. But my position then pertained to absolute control of this crew. It had nothing to do with beings outside that sphere."

"You can't make that distinction."

Terry's warning was terse and angry. The line had been drawn in the sand. There was nothing Brian could achieve by crossing it. He wasn't even sure he had the courage to, even if he had seen an advantage. He was not, after all, a martyr.

"We're under a lot of pressure," he began, hoping that by backing away he could defuse the situation. "For my part, I apologize."

Since Paula would say nothing, it was up to Terry to offer a counter point. One he was hesitant to make, for his blood ran hot. Yet, like the mystic who went under the guise of a minister, he saw no point going for the throat.

"That's all right. We got off track."

"If you'll forgive an old man, let me repeat back what you've said, to be certain I understand."

He was not an old man by any standards. Paula guessed he had used that particular expression since childhood. And gotten away with it, for he was one who had been born old.

"Please do," she agreed, for now it was the captain's turn to go mute.

"You're suspicious of this alien because he doesn't seem to be what he claims to be; or at least what we surmise him to be." Paula nodded. "You're going under the assumption he can read minds and possibly manipulate what others see. His ulterior motive for doing this is to obtain something we possess and that he needs." At the conclusion, neither of his listeners spoke. The static, used to block unwelcome listeners, swelled to gigantic proportions. To counter it, Brian raised his voice.

"Why has he – why has Star Bright – tried so hard to endear himself to Helen?"

"She's on his ship," Burbone began. "For the moment, she's a willing hostage."

"He might have kept the captain and me aboard," the minister tried, now making an effort to modulate his voice. "Or you and Jingles. But he didn't. On the contrary. He made a point of dismissing us."

"We don't know what weapons he has. Perhaps his powers of mind manipulation are his sole strength. He may not be able to control more than one at a time."

"Or," the captain interjected, "he hopes that by convincing her of his plight, she'll intercede for him. Plead his case."

"Not if he wanted chemicals from our bodies," Brian concluded for the absent woman, making it apparent she deserved more credit than they seemed willing to give.

"All right! That was just a thought," Joshua exploded. "Of course she wouldn't sacrifice any of us for him. But if he needed something else... supplies, or some equipment necessary to our... comfort," he faltered, choosing it over "survival." "Then, she might ask."

"And if she convinces you, you make a favorable decision." Brian performed a private countdown, starting with the pointer finger and working to the pinkie. "That makes sense. I think it's a viable suspicion. So what do we do about it?"

"Bring her back."

Paula's abrupt decision startled both Joshua and Brian.

"If she doesn't want to come?"

"I order her to return. She can't disobey a direct command from her superior."

It was then Hardy finally understood the difference between a civilian and a military mind. As worlds went, they were galaxies apart.

Helen Fitzgerald might possibly respond to Joshua Terry's personal request, but he doubted very seriously she was bound by the same rationale to obey his dictate on the grounds of obedience to orders.

If the two men had been alone, he would have said as much. But with Paula present, he would get nowhere.

"What if she agrees? Then what? Star Bright activates his ship and flies away. Gone." He snapped his fingers for effect. "Just like that."

"I won't trade Helen for a goddamned hydroponics unit!" Terry swore. The growl underneath his breath had not been absorbed into the walls before he added, "There are other ways."

They had come full circle. For once, the mediator had discovered no common ground.

Brian rose slowly, working out the kinks in his too-long stationary muscles before strolling toward the door. He paused two feet away so as not to activate the electric eye.

"This is where I leave you. If you want my opinion, seek me out. Otherwise, you know where I stand. I'm sorry."

He waited, but a look between Paula and Joshua convinced him whatever inroads he may have made were small, indeed. With a small sigh of resignation, he crept away, like fog, in the night.

Not even his shadow, nor a shadow of his faith, remained behind.

CHAPTER 28

The delights spread on the table should have sharpened the appetite of a hungry woman, but with the sudden, terse departure of Paula and Jingles, Helen's interest in food had diminished to the point of nonexistence. Staring with a fixed gaze at the banquet Star Bright had so lovingly prepared, her guilt and the desire to please finally forced her to select an eating utensil. The heft of the two-pronged fork was oddly off balance. Catching Star Bright's eye and conveying her dilemma, he took his own, cheerfully demonstrating the purpose.

Spearing it into an overlarge, irregularly shaped slice of orange-brown fruit, he lifted the food without making an attempt to cut it into bite-sized portions. Drawing it toward his mouth, she was astonished to see the *neelie* curl up and inward. By the time he had it properly positioned to eat, the fruit was compact and easily manageable.

"Go ahead," she challenged, not yet ready to believe he could eat what had been, a moment before, so large a serving. He happily complied, chewing carefully, as he had been taught. "But how....?" she questioned, leaning down to more critically examine the *neelie*. Prodding it with her finger, the fruit remained inert. "Is it some property in the fork?"

"Fork," Star Bright repeated, correctly identifying her word with the utensil. "Yes. It is the fork."

"Does it... communicate with the fruit?" The concept was staggering. "Does the *neelie*... want to be eaten?"

"Of course. That is its – you would say 'purpose'?" Helen nodded. Leaning back in his chair, the little alien directed his attention toward hydroponics. "Everything there has a sense of purpose. A need. And an...." Again, he struggled to explain the concept. "Appreciation. It is a symbiotic relationship." She started, for that was precisely the word which had come to mind. "We – the plants and I – are living things. We take care of one another. I tend to their needs and they feed me."

"They understand?"

He frowned, then hesitantly replaced the fork on the table.

"Why should they not, friend Helen?"

To rationalize plants were a lower order of life seemed superfluous and in grave error. Copying his example, she touched her fork to the fruit then ate the compacted portion. The flavor was subtle and sweet, similar to a melon, yet of a more substantial texture. She swallowed the bite easily, luxuriating in the smooth, satisfying way it slipped down her throat.

Seeing she would eat, Star Bright offered a morsel to Teddy before taking another for himself. When Helen did not follow suit, he "fed" the bear a second time before returning the food to his plate.

"You do not like it?" The hurt in his voice was tangible and sorrowful.

"Very much; more than I can say."

"You are not hungry?"

"I'm starving," came the retort, so sharp and biting Helen withdrew from her own statement in shock. Reaching out to mitigate the damage, she gently wiped Teddy's chin, the only one of the three who might be considered "stuffed."

"I'm so sorry," she apologized, abandoning any further attempt at eating. "I didn't mean to raise my voice. Nor refuse your wonderful repast. I... don't know what's the matter with me. My mind is wandering."

Tapping his finger thoughtfully at the indentation of his lip, Star Bright considered, then activated the small monitor by his hand. The blank screen instantly metamorphosed into that of *Target*. He considered the image a long moment before holding out a shaky hand.

"That is where your thoughts are."

"Yes," she agreed, struck with dull horror at the image of the crippled ship. Contrasting it to her first sight of *Target,* years ago, vast and awesome in its symmetrical majesty, what she beheld now was a horrific tangle of mismatched parts. With a third the vessel cruelly severed and destroyed, the remainder hung in space, a blackened and pitted remnant. It was almost beyond the power of grim reality to fathom any form of life existing within.

Although she had previously viewed *Target* from the Skip on two separate occasions, both had been brief and her attention divided. Aboard *Here,* separated by time, distance and safety, she fully grasped how "home" had altered.

"My God," she exclaimed, caught between physical repulsion and heightened sensitivity. "How did any of us survive?"

Following the direction of her eyes, Star Bright shivered. Inadvertently, death had come calling aboard his little ship.

"There," he indicated, his hand wavering from deep-rooted pathos. "Is that where contact occurred?"

She nodded, afraid to acknowledge the truth for fear the remainder of *Target* would disintegrate upon verbalizing the truth of its actual condition.

"Encounter occurred without warning. We were caught totally off-guard. I shall never forget the...." Closing her lids, she searched in vain for an appropriate description. "The... suddenness." Her shoulders drooped. "The noise; a screeching, eerie keening of twisted, tortured metal. Almost as though the ship had an awareness it was fatally struck."

Waving a cupped hand in front of her face, Helen attempted to grasp the incomprehensible.

"Darkness." Her head jerked up, pupils distended. "An expectation of the walls caving inward – or being sucked outward. Of knowing, with every fiber of your being, the next second you would lose gravity; strike your head on the ceiling. Even though it didn't happen, I can feel the atmosphere leaking away." Her fingers clenched into a fist. "Of trying to breathe and finding you can't."

Stifling a scream, she threw up her hands in a futile attempt to protect her head. Responding in horror to her plight, Star Bright quickly altered the view, his fingers trembling over familiar keys. When the ship was no longer visible he dared look back at her. The paleness of her complexion brought a cry to his own lips, pursed into an oval, silent shriek.

"No! Bring it back!" came the frantic command. "If I can't see it, I won't believe it's there."

Although his instincts warned him otherwise, he did as he was told. Her hand shot out, resting on the monitor. Had the instrument not been so well placed, it would have been torn apart from the strength of her grip.

"I'm sorry, I'm sorry," she cooed, talking to *Target* and Star Bright and Joshua Terry and all those who had perished in one simultaneous apology. "Forgive me."

"It is there," he promised. "Still there."

"Yes," she agreed, finally able to say the word. "But what it is and what it was.... Horrible."

"We will leave it on the screen; for safekeeping. So you will know. But come away," he pleaded, attempting to disengage her stiff and unyielding fingers. "We will... sit amongst the plants. They will sing to you. You can hold Teddy," he offered as his last and best gift. "He will comfort you."

She choked on his love, swallowed the wrong way, then coughed, her body wracked by so great an upheaval that it took her long minutes to recover. "Teddy," she whispered, the only thing she knew to say. "Little

Teddy." As tears streamed from her eyes, Helen clasped the bear, adding to its plump body her own reservoir of misery.

Without the power of locomotion, the beloved stuffed toy seemed to settle into her hands, small tufts of fur overlapping the edges of her fingers.

Hold me tight, the round, bright, yellow irises conveyed to the communicator. *For I have been down this path before. Draw strength from my resiliency. No matter how you feel, you are not alone.*

Teddy was Mama and Papa, consoling their child. He was Joshua Terry, rising from his knees to whisper "I love you." He was Star Bright, offering the gift of unreserved affection. He was Helen Fitzgerald, discovering depths of strength she never knew she had. He was Brian Hardy's conceptualization of God, all wise and wondrous.

"I am better now," she said, drying a tear with the back of her hand, then pausing to contemplate the sad smile which had slipped onto her face. "Let me show you my ship." If she had said, "Let me reveal to you my universe," the sentence could not have been more all-encompassing.

"There. That's where we brushed across what we believe to be a floating ribbon of dark matter. It cut us in thirds; severing off the starboard side." Removing a hand from Teddy, she made a curt, cutting motion with her second and third fingers. Her voice steadied. She was speaking of the past. Teddy had reminded her. "The devastation was unthinkable. We lost the storage areas, food preparation, hydroponics; crew's quarters. Everything." No, that was wrong. "Not everything," she corrected, forcing the bitterness away.

"This part of the ship... the part that... survived. There was great damage. Sick Bay, where we treated those in need of medical care, gone. Parts of Engineering... damaged beyond repair. Here – and here," she indicated, forcing herself to touch the screen with the type of reverence reserved for the dying. "The bridge; Level Two where the technology units were housed. And here – level Four. That's all which is left. And yet," she forced herself on, losing the veneer of control, "it is large for our needs as we are few."

Star Bright twitched, his glance going instinctively toward Teddy.

"There was great suffering?"

He spoke so softly she had to replay the sentence over in her mind to make the translation. A low moan arose in her throat; the kind of sound a lost and lonely bear cub might make.

"Tragedy to a degree I never imagined possible," Helen admitted, clasping a hand to her throat, then distractedly slipping her fingers beneath the collar. "I have no way of expressing the – suddenness of it all." Her voice hardened on "suddenness," then trailed off. "One moment everything was normal and the next – our world had shattered. Nothing was ever to be the same. Ever. No matter how much we wanted it."

Gripping Teddy's paws together, Star Bright seemed to fade into a shimmering translucence before slowly re-solidifying his shape. While Helen knew on a subconscious level the effect was a trick of her overwrought senses, the transformation was startling. Not jarring, but rather, the stirring of a vortex of ideas, half real, half transposed from faerie tales.

"I feel your pain," he explained to her questioning eyes. "There are times... when space is still, I hear Mama and Papa call to me. Then I know they are still with me, but not... *Here.*"

Her blue eyes opened in shared belief as a chill, emotional instead of temporal, swept over her.

"In the Observatory... where I first felt you – I experienced the same phenomenon. My friends – my... dead friends... spoke to me. Or a trip they had taken outside the ship. 'We just returned from a spacewalk.' 'You should have come.' Did you miss us very much?' Star Bright," she cried, biting her lower lip until blood flowed, "why did I live? Why was I spared when so many others died?"

He knew the answer, but it had to come from Mr. Bear.

"Because we needed you."

She had known that was the answer; known it from the first moment Star Bright sang to her. And for longer than that. Much longer. Since the moment her dear, sweet mother had read a cradled infant *Mother Goose.*

"I took a spacewalk, didn't I? In a sort of a way. With you. To the Emerald Planet. You invited me and I came. And the others – those others," she indicated with a trembling hand, pointing at *Target,* "missed me very much."

"Does that mean..." he sobbed, burying his head in Teddy's fur, "that you will go back to them?"

"It means," she clarified, wiping his wet cheeks, "that I am *of* them."

"You could be... of us," he whispered, without moving his lips.

"I am, already. You know that. You knew it all along."

"For how long did I know it, friend Helen?"

"For as long as I did; our mothers, who did not know it, told us when we were wee."

"Wee," he repeated, slowly holding out his fingers. "It rhymes with thee."

"Yes, baby," she agreed. "Thee. You, and I... and Teddy and Joshua." Touching a control on the key pad, Helen magnified the crippled ship.

"'I had a little husband no bigger than my thumb,
I put him in a pint pot, and then I bid him drum;
I bought a little handkerchief to wipe his little nose,
And a pair of little garters to tie his little hose.'"

Placing her own thumb by the image, Helen playfully wiggled it.

"Joshua Thumb," she softly intoned. "He, too, knows Mother Goose. Who could believe?"

Because he could believe, Star Bright nodded. Yet it was without joy.

"If you and I are two and he is one, why does he...." Star Bright put his own thumb up to the screen, as near as it was far. "Why is he... sad with me? Is that how you would say it?"

She didn't know, and in not knowing, her belief wavered.

"He's confused. Here," she indicated by touching her head, "and here." Her hand lowered toward her heart.

"Will he ever be... 'friend Josh-u-a?'"

It was the first time Star Bright had ever pronounced Terry's first name. Hearing it in the peculiar, otherworldly pronunciation, the three syllables sounded oddly reassuring.

"He must be."

With spontaneous affection, Helen soothed Star Bright's cheek. It was not the gesture of an adult soothing a child, nor that of a woman responding to a man, but couched deep within that grey area amorphously encapsulated under the heading of "friendship."

She did not expect him to respond, but he did, quickly and anxiously bringing his own nose to hers, then gently touching, flesh to flesh.

"Try this," she suggested, kissing him a second time. Anxiety transformed to puzzlement, then questioning wonder.

"Mama and Papa... they touched noses," he began.

"As a gesture of affection for a baby. But I'm sure they also kissed one another on the face and lips. They... simply did not think to show you on the images they left. A pity," she sighed. Slowly, she brought her hand to her mouth, simultaneously touching nose and lips. She kissed her fingers, then directed it toward him.

Star Bright leaned forward, staring intently at her mouth from an angle not possible for him to achieve while watching a non-interactive video. Holding her unresisting hand in his, he pushed it back toward her face. She obligingly kissed it. "Now," he encouraged, pantomiming her own action of a moment before. Helen obligingly blew the kiss to him.

"What do you call it?" came the urgent demand.

"A kiss. And this," she demonstrated a second time, "is called 'blowing a kiss.'"

"A-kiss."

The brief remark was spoken as a single word, rather than two distinct sounds.

"The word is 'kiss,'" came the correction from the language master. "The 'a' is a prefatory article of speech.

"Mama and Papa... they did this? I never knew. I.... I have made a mistake."

"Because you couldn't see the entire action," Helen elucidated. "You thought she was rubbing her nose. As I would have," she added quickly before continuing. "Where I originate, a parent kisses a child; two friends kiss after a separation as a way of saying 'I missed you.' People in love kiss to signify the special bond between them. And because it is pleasurable," came the added touch.

"This I know." Star Bright blew her a kiss, then grabbed Teddy, duplicating the gesticulation. "But this..." he continued, brushing his lips against her cheek, "I do not. What is the difference? You will tell me, please?"

"Of course I will. You kiss physically when you are near someone." Plucking Teddy from him, Helen kissed the bear on the delicately stitched mouth. "You blow a kiss to a person from whom you are at a distance." Holding out the companion at arm's length, Helen blew him a kiss. "You have no word for such an act in your language? Or perhaps your people don't kiss in the same way."

Without answering, Star Bright stooped over, rapidly shuffling the small discs so tenderly stored by the couch. Finding the one he sought, he placed it in the machine, then scanned forward until finding the correct place.

Mama's soft, shimmering image materialized on the screen. She was staring down into a tiny cradle, obviously speaking to her baby. "I love you," she cooed, then carefully brought a finger to her mouth, puckered her lips, made the appropriate sound, then reached out her hand toward the unseen infant. Minute shivers spread over the watcher's body as realization came to him. "So that," he whispered, "is blowing a kiss."

"You never saw anyone touch lips to lips. I'm so sorry, baby. That never occurred to me."

Tapping him lightly on the shoulder to draw his attention back, Helen bent over and kissed him again, this time on the cheek, taking care to impress her lips on his warm flesh.

"That is a kiss between friends."

"And the other? The kiss between two people in love?" he demanded, squirming in his seat.

The demonstration was neither painful nor begrudged. With her hand on the back of his silky hair, Helen held him steady while moving her own face near. With a slight incline of her jaw so as to avoid his nose, she pressed her lips to his. When he responded, she intensified the act, only releasing him after they had held the affection for a long moment.

The tinges of red on his cheeks and the tips of her ears was not lost on the Earth woman.

"Three types of kiss," Star Bright gushed, eyes wide. "All so very different."

"Yes. Three." She was not unconscious of the significance of the number. "Three types, used to express love." Bouncing on the padding of the couch, his body language implored her to continue. "A mother blows a kiss to her child to express maternal affection. She also kisses his cheek or his brow or his lips, or his fingers," she laughed, carried away by the intensity of Mama's emotion. "Had you been in her arms, she would have kissed you that way."

Helen duplicated her words by kissing him in all the designated spots. The color of his skin heightened.

"May the baby kiss her in return?"

"Babies don't usually have that ability," she teased, ruffling his hair. "They're too small. But as they grow older, they learn how. Kiss me, and see."

Star Bright eagerly kissed her body in exactly the same order she had kissed him. Little chuckles emerged from his expressed joy.

"Did she do that to me?"

"Most certainly. And so did Papa. I'm sorry they never thought to capture those moments for you."

"And when I got bigger, I would kiss them back?"

"You would."

"Because I love them."

"Exactly right."

Bouncing again, he kicked his feet into the air.

"Who are the people you would kiss?" he demanded, eager to have his mind expanded with new and fantastic knowledge.

"Friends from whom I have been separated. I would kiss Brian or Paula," she responded, taking care to mention names to whom he could put faces.

"And it means you love them?"

"Love is many things. Love for a child is different than love of a friend. But, yes, I do love them. Kissing them would be a way of saying 'I care about you.'"

His brows knit together at the revelation.

"Brian and Paula... they are your friends?"

"They are."

"Tell me the meaning of 'friends'."

"Individuals you trust. Those whose company you enjoy. Brian and Paula and I have things in common; subjects we like to discuss among ourselves."

"Who else is your friend?" he challenged, and she understood the implication. But it was not the moment to meet it.

"You are my friend," came the reply, instead.

The little space wanderer's head flew back at the intensity of the revelation. While he had used the word before, never had it carried with it such significance. "I?" And then, more forcefully, "I am your friend!"

"As you have called me," she confessed, awed by the way her own intensity flared.

"You are! You are!" Grabbing Teddy Bear, Star Bright squeezed the animal, then kissed him on the nose, repeating with cheeks, brow, hands and toes until he was squealing with delight. "We have a friend! Teddy Bear, we have a friend!"

"And I have two friends," Helen countered. "You and Teddy. I am twice blessed."

"It is a miracle," Star Bright choked, tears running down his face. "A blessing."

"And you learned a new word. In my line of work, that, too, is a great thing."

"Kiss! A kiss! Blowing a kiss! I am three times blessed!"

"Yes, you are," she cried, engulfing the two newest admissions to her universe. *And God willing,* she concluded, bowing her head with reverence and hope, *one day we will be many friends.*

Against the backdrop of the crippled star cruiser *Target,* it was one small baby step forward.

Chapter 29

He could have accosted her in the crew's mess, for he saw her go in there, but what Joshua Terry had to impart was not food for round-table discussion. He therefore bided his time until her meal period was up. Fortunately for his purposes, she came out alone.

"Lieutenant Miles, may I speak to you a moment?" The request was couched in the veneer of civilization. He could as easily have demanded, "I must speak with you on a matter of urgency," but did not.

Her response, in either case, was the same.

"Certainly, sir."

There was no conference room and the Observatory was off-limits for personal reasons. That left his quarters behind the Command Center.

She followed him without a further word. The walk was a short one. Per previous orders, Jingles was waiting for them at the door, an air of expectant uncertainty permeating from his pores.

Terry entered first, the other two following. The door sealed behind them. Brian Hardy, who occupied the area as his personal space when not otherwise in use, was conspicuously absent.

"Be seated."

Both complied, leaving the engineer's chair which Terry had received as a gift, for the captain. He assumed it with the air of one unaccustomed to extravagance.

Straightening his back, the captain met and held the gaze of each before speaking.

"I've asked you both here to impart some confidential information. Mr. Jingles, you have spoken for the crew in the past. Lieutenant Miles, after myself, Commander Burbone and the chief engineer, you're the ranking officer aboard *Target.*"

His hands, pressed against his knees, were flat and motionless. It required considerable effort to flex them. "We're facing a crisis: one which requires I solicit your... input."

Input.

Opinion.

Vote.

The words were not interchangeable. They understood the terms.

"Is it about the alien, sir?"

It was Jingles who breached the silence.

Rather than reply directly to the question, Terry reached across his body for a report he had set out beside his computer. While his eyes appeared to scan the text, his officers inferred he was searching for words, rather than data.

"You're aware a decision was made concerning the disbursement of the nutritional tablets. Instead of the routine issuance of three, the number was reduced to two. With the explanation we had misinterpreted the instructions." He paused, letting them draw their own inferences. "The plants in Hydroponics were dying from lack of proper nutrients. There was only one source of food with which to try and sustain them."

Jingles sucked air in between his front teeth, then bit his lower lip. Color rose into his cheeks. Janice leaned forward, then changed her mind and pressed backward in an attitude of concern.

"Yes," she admitted guardedly. "We... came to that conclusion."

Sensing she had more to say, he motioned her to continue.

"Go on."

"When the tablets were first discovered, we were each given our own private bottle. The wording was quite specific: take one of each color together. There were three colors."

The statement was not something neither he, Brian or Helen had taken into consideration. Hearing their mistake now caused him to wince.

"I weighed the consequences of reducing rations against the very real probability of losing our one hope of keeping those hybrids viable. Without them, we could hardly expect to become self-sufficient."

Jingles glowered, not at the captain, but at the chair he sat in, as though blaming himself for parting with it.

"Why are you telling us this now?"

His words were tight and emotional. Running one fingernail beneath the other, Terry's training forbade him from breaking eye contact. Nor was it a time for excuses, although, on a personal level, he would have appreciated the opportunity.

"Initial results were positive."

"If you're looking for our approval —"

The captain terminated the sentence with a harsh stiffening of his fingers.

"I am not. You are here to be informed the experiment has ultimately proven a failure."

The blow was vicious and unexpected.

"Can you be more specific, sir?" Janice inquired, her own voice both deadened and sharpened by the revelation.

"Our initial assessment is that the tablets didn't contain sufficient vitamins and minerals to nurture the plants. Or, that they varied too greatly in proportion to what the plants required."

"Are they... lost beyond saving?"

Had Miles phrased her question, "Are they lost without redemption?" he would not have altered his reply.

"Unknown. But the situation is dire."

Jingles reverted to his former thought.

"Are you asking us to support your initial decision, or have you come to us to make peace?"

"Neither. What's done can't be undone. For that, I accept full responsibility."

"Then, the issue," Miles calmly supplied, "is uncomplicated. Merely announce to the crew you're rescinding the cut rations and are resuming the normal supply."

"I can't do that."

"Why not? We have enough tablets for sixteen years. Not a pleasant prospect from a gastronomic perspective but hardly dire," she concluded, using his word.

"There was... a miscalculation. Entirely," he confessed, "on my shoulders."

Jingles squirmed in his seat, leaving it to Miles to ask, "How so, sir?"

She expected something trivial: a looming expiration date which might be of some significance but hardly *dire*. A miscount, depriving them of a year or two in which to find a planet that could sustain them, but hardly bringing them to the point of imminent starvation.

"The containers stored in the brig were incorrectly labeled."

That proved the death knell. Both officers shuddered.

"How many?" Jingles found voice to ask.

"For the sake of clarity, all that remained in storage."

"Leaving us... how long before the supply of tablets runs out?"

"Less than two months."

"You have more to say, sir," Miles bravely spoke. "We're here to listen."

Terry's reply was ready, for he had formulated it one-thousand times over the past hour.

"One alternative is to prepare for death. We accept the inevitability of starvation, while trying everything in our power to overcome what appears, at this moment, to be our fate."

Jingles made a disparaging noise in his throat.

"Trying to save those miserable plants was a mistake. How many tablets were wasted?"

Janice Miles bowed her head.

"You spared the rest of us from having to be involved." She spoke for the crew and her statement was unhesitant and uncompromising. "You acted within your means, and within the scope of your command, which all of us acknowledge. I believe, in that instance, you acted for the greater good." Leaning forward, she added, "God help us." Before either could approve or rebuff her words, she continued the thread. "Please continue."

Joshua nodded, his eyes the steely blue of a storm at sea.

"Second option: we solicit the aid of Star Bright. His technology is far in advance of ours. If he can't save our food source, then we request he supply us with sufficient plants or cuttings to replace those we've lost."

"Is he likely to agree to that... demand?"

Substituting Terry's word of "request" for "demand," was deliberate, opening the way for him to finish his countdown. He did so with conviction.

"Assuming he's unwilling or unable to comply, we confiscate what we need from his ship – without permission."

The silence was prolonged and damning.

"Well," Janice began, leaning back and closing her eyes in the attitude of one who has heard more than she wanted. "I did have to ask."

Before the statement was completed, Jingles stood, fists clenched, arms held upward and toward his chest, in the stance of a boxer. As his complexion turned from pinkish to a blotched scarlet, he appeared, for all the universe, to represent a defeated pugilist, down for the count but not out. Though his action was clearly deliberate and self-contained, Terry's first instinct was to back away.

The damage, when it came, was not physical, but emotional. Instead of reaching out, the engineer spasmed, a huge expulsion of air from his inner fabric tearing from between clenched teeth. Staggering from his own blow, he attempted to right himself by huffing inward. His chest heaved laboriously, then his arms flailed as the red of his face seemed to transform from mere coloration to liquid. Beneath swollen eyelids, tears gushed in unashamed torrents.

"If that last is the decision, I don't ever want to eat again!" Staring around in wild abandonment, he sought his opponent. Though his lips trembled, his words were clear. "Give my portion – what's left of it – to someone else."

Terry felt the figurative punch in his stomach and actually doubled over, before rising helplessly to full height. His own throat constricted in horror at the ghastly apparition before him. In one split second, the engineer he thought he knew enough about became a human being. What that created was an even more horrific picture.

Swallowing his own pulse, which had risen into his throat, he glanced miserably at Janice. Negating his desire, she refused to involve herself. It was not her fight. Nor, for the moment, even her universe.

Abandoning reason, the mainstay of his personality and his command, Terry stripped himself, hurtling forward to wrap his arms around the big man.

"Jingles, I'm sorry. I didn't know... I didn't suspect..." He lost his train of thought. Waves of dizziness blurred his world. *Here, Target,* the room in which he stood dissolved. He was left standing on a mat which could not hold his weight.

What hadn't he known? That his engineer had feelings?

Why hadn't he suspected that Jingles had an empathy so acute he was willing to sacrifice himself to save an alien?

"But on the bridge," the captain tried, grasping madly at straws to re-thread his life. "You were the one who wanted to attack. Use the lasers," he mumbled, uncertain whether to continue, or even if the incident had actually transpired.

Pulling himself free, Jingles wiped his dripping nose on the back of his hand, ignoring the tear tracks. As the whites of his eyes shrunk from their gigantic proportions, he attempted to right the wrong to which he had just been accused.

"Scare him off; that's what I meant. Tickle him under the armpits. Make him think twice about attacking us, if that's what *he* meant. Besides," he added, eyes rolling around in their sockets until it appeared he might faint. "That was before I met Mr. Bear. I knew then it was all right." Jabbing out his finger, he made an erratic circle, then thrust his neck forward, the fighter who could not quit. "Why didn't you?"

Terry's mouth went dry and the pounding in his temples turned into a roar.

Why didn't I? he silently questioned, unconsciously holding up his hands in surrender. This was a bout in which he no longer wished to participate. Without ever knowing why, the odds had been stacked against him.

"Please." It was the first time in his professional career he had ever used such language. His actual ability to employ such a *civilian* word shocked him. Nowhere in "the command book" was "please" ever mentioned. "You've misinterpreted." That gave him firmer footing for it was rational, unemotional. The fact it was also a lie forced his head to hang in shame, a disgrace no captain should endure. "I was only offering options."

His weak defense did not pacify the engineer. With a snarl of contempt and a window of insight greater than the sum of his parts, Jingles sagged.

"You have my answer."

Left without boundaries, Terry floundered, the choices he had outlined floating amorphously before his face. Death hovered over his head, close enough to touch. It was a frightening spectre.

"I... just wanted you to be aware.... To know the truth. It's ugly." But not as ugly as his own opinion of himself. His misjudgment was on the scale of Encounter. "You've spoken for the crew in the past," he finished without conviction, at a loss to comprehend how it had all gone so wrong.

Gingleheimer's body melted into a puddle of misery. He would not be drawn back. He and Joshua Terry had reached the count of ten.

"No, sir," he negated, waving an arm-like appendage in the air. "I speak for myself. All of me. And if I'm two or three times the size of everyone else, I speak for all three of me. That's three portions you can give to someone else."

"Believe me," Joshua tried, shrieking inside for release. "There's no thought of that —"

The engineer cut him off with a blunt thrust of his suddenly leaden eyes.

"I've got work to do." For a moment those same eyes flared with the spark of a dying star. "The food processor. I promised you I'd make it work."

With a desultory wave which might have been taken for a farewell, Jingles turned his shrunken body on the small gathering and shuffled away, head hung low. With his departure flew his spirit, the remnant of a man starved to death. The pall, as the life he attributed to "Mr. Bear," was palpable.

Captain Joshua Terry silently abraded Father Brian Hardy. It was he who had said he ought to get to know his crew on a more personal level.

With knowledge came added responsibility.

Insight, like death, had its ugly side.

Equally affected, but on a different plain than her commanding officer, Janice Miles wrung her hands. Returning to the scene like the Ghost of Christmas Past, her present was offered with the condition of complicity.

"You know he was right." Spoken with contrition, she stepped toward him, respectful and awed. "I don't know what else to say to you." He shrugged, barely understanding. "You're a good man, faced with confronting a dire reality. If it makes any difference, I forgive you."

Her sympathy staggered him. Losing his balance, Terry tripped, nearly falling into her. Waving off her assistance, for he dared not be touched, least he shatter into star dust, he crept to her recently vacated chair, perching precariously on the edge.

Moments slipped away. Grasping what he had left the way a condemned man willed the second hand of a clock to stop, he repositioned himself, spreading his legs for better balance. He hung, like *Target,* half viable, the rest shattered into nothingness.

Language failed him. He struggled, finally resorting to the one word which had already taken such a toll.

"Tell me. Please. Janice. What does life mean to you?"

He had to know. It was a galaxy apart from wanting to know.

Janice stepped closer to the form on the chair. Her lips pursed, not because she had no answer, but to prolong the moment. If survival were ebbing away, she would cherish both the good and the difficult times.

"Life is better that the alternative." It was not a *carte blanche* and he accepted the statement as such.

"Which is?"

"Death."

Reaching out a hand, he rested it very lightly on her arm.

"But that was exactly what we were speaking of. I made a mistake.... miscalculated. Explain, please, life's value... to you."

Glancing around the room, she took pleasure in the simple, familiar surroundings: a makeshift bed upon which to repose; a pillow, for resting the head. The computer, an old and well-cherished companion of a former existence. The form and substance of Joshua Terry, a man like any other. Yet not, she realized, like any other, for in being a captain, he was separate from the rest.

"I think, sir, what you wish to ask is what existence means to you."

"Perhaps I do," he conceded, wondering himself.

"Then I will speak for you, as though I were your conscience. Shall I?" He bade her continue with a slight bow of his head, which is all he dared move for fear of breaking.

"To have meaning, life must have hope. A chance beyond bare subsistence level. It must have goals, challenges. It must have rewards to offset the tragedies. You've seen too much suffering: you anticipate the worst. Your optimism has been muted by the inexplicable. There are some things in the universe even a star cruiser captain can't influence." Janice paused, then lifted her eyes upward, drawing inspiration from limits beyond the room. "I pity you."

"Pity me?" The idea was incomprehensible. Following her gaze, he stared upward. What he saw was the ceiling tile. To place his mind beyond required more effort than he felt he could give. Sensing his dilemma while doubting his reticence, for she knew he would have given anything to see beyond the narrow confines of "here," Janice riveted her face toward his.

"You wanted us to condone the taking of life to save others. We could not."

Reaching out her free arm, she attached herself to him, so that they were connected, arm to arm. He continued to look above himself and she was glad.

"Sacrificing the starboard side and those who stood no legitimate chance of survival – of having a meaningful life – was horrible, but contained within that decision was the element of mercy. To needlessly prolong life where no hope exists is not kind, but cruel. I believe in your heart, you understood that."

Finally breaking contact, Janice pressed her hands together so that the flats of her palms touched in an attitude of prayer. In this, he did not copy her. Nor had she expected him to. It was enough that his hand curled inward, missing her touch. For that, too, she was happy. It was an inroad she had made for another.

Without experience or expectation, Janice Miles had become his voice of reason. Just as he had trusted her once by promoting her to lieutenant, she felt the present obligation keenly. It was another step forward in her own development and within that awareness was pride.

"I want to live as much as the next person; I want to be free from fear and worry. I want to love and be loved." Joshua inched closer to her, nodding thoughtfully. "I don't want to fight when I don't have to. I came to space to experience the unknown. Influence it, if you will, with the essence of my personality – of the good within me. If nothing else, I wanted to be part of the greater whole."

His thoughtfulness deepened. Nodding again, he permitted himself the luxury of reexamining the ceiling.

"What you asked Jingles and I was whether we prized our own continued existence over that of Star Bright's. Which represents that greater good? No one wants to die, sir," she continued, gliding seamlessly toward the chair Jingles had once offered as a token of his esteem. "We all like to believe our continued existence has meaning." Revolving the chair, she drew from the action a sort of inspiration. "Balanced against one another, you compel me to weigh right and wrong, hope and fear."

Once the "throne" had completed its three hundred and sixty degree revolution she stopped it so that the unoccupied seat was directed toward the captain.

"You've frightened me. I don't know if I can be more honest than that. Jingles made his decision. Mine is more hesitant, and for that I'm ashamed. But," she said, letting out a deep, audible breath, "if it came down to a confrontation between myself and Star Bright – just the two of us, which is all any of us can rightfully reflect upon – I don't know that I could kill him to save myself. Not," she continued, clearing her throat, "when his only 'crime' has been to arrive in our sphere with a ship full of eatable plants."

Bowing her head, she whispered a silent prayer, then made desultory steps toward the door.

"I said I pitied you. Now, I think, perhaps, you know why."

Raising her hand in solemn farewell, which was not "good-bye," but rather, "I will see you later," Janice Miles left him alone with the condemnation of either choice resting heavily on his soul.

The red alert flashed behind his back, opposite the wall Joshua faced. It had flashed so long, he no longer took note. He needed no reminder that disaster was pending.

As Brian would have said, *he wrote the book on that one.*

The confrontation with his engineer and lieutenant had unsettled his mind. What had been clear one moment was disrupted the next. Against the logic of self-preservation, Star Bright had made two more converts. He would like to have believed their motives were purely altruistic, but there was that inside him which prohibited so easy a solution. Rank had its privileges and its obligations. One of those was doubt.

Janice Miles, and not the ceiling beyond which he could not see, had taught him the difference between healthy skepticism and outright denial.

With the walls closing in around him, he had gone to the Observatory. Without activating the viewscreen, he had opted to direct his mind toward the challenge of a game; one on a small, hand-held device, left behind from a time when games were meant to amuse rather than divert.

The task he had set himself was intricate and unforgiving. Whenever his mind wandered, he took a "hit," the sharp, rasping sound of the "score" jarring his concentration back where he wanted it. With a little imagination and some luck, he could lose himself for a minute, or even a "bell."

Maneuvering the spacecraft he was "flying," Terry grunted in concentration, ignoring the rivulets of perspiration creeping down his neck. Craning closer, eyes distended, nostrils flared, he fired the graphic lasers, striking the enemy bearing down on him. His cry of exultation was short-lived. Either he had not channeled enough energy into his weapon, or his aim was off kilter. Before his taut nerves could counter, the ship he was maneuvering sustained a serious blow, it's too realistic image disintegrating before his eyes, fragments of power pods hurtling off the screen. Cursing under his breath, he bore down, snarling with anger.

Punching in a new set of directions, the vessel reappeared.

"All right, you bastard," he warned, gritting his teeth, as his flying fingers responded to the challenge. "I'll get you this time!"

Beyond his limited world, Joshua Terry should have seen the reflected glow of the Red Alert disappear, as a body moved between the wall and himself, but he was too absorbed in countermeasures. The voice, therefore, when it spoke, shocked him more than if he had been physically struck.

"Have you accorded *Here* that much power that you can't avoid blasts from its weapons?"

The question was neither unfriendly nor accusatory, but rather, tinged with sadness. It was that emotion and no other which prompted him to truthfulness.

"I'm not fighting Star Bright."

"Who, then?" Paula asked, disentangling herself from the darkness where she had been concealed for at least an hour.

Terry had not suspected her presence, but had no thought to rebuke her for spying. In her place, he might have reasoned the captain had disappeared to fight his private devils, and needed help to conquer hell.

"Not a 'who.' A 'what.'"

Twisting his shoulders to the left, Joshua granted her access to the screen. What was revealed took a moment to assimilate.

"Encounter."

"The Ribbon," she developed, verbally spelling the word with a capital "R."

"My private obsession. The game was easy to design: one huge strip of dark matter floating in space. Our sensors don't detect it. The only indication I have is from manual observation."

He reset the game and began again. Paula crept nearer so she stood directly behind him.

"But, it wasn't visible. It didn't move, either," she continued, watching as the ribbon extended one end of its octopus-like tentacles toward the starboard side of *Target*.

"It does in my game. The challenge is time: how much am I allotted to identify, react and respond."

"What's the answer?"

"It changes with every game. I don't know."

As she watched, transfixed by the sight of the dark matter, he maneuvered the ship to port. Paula's stomach heaved from the powerful imaginary force. On the screen, the ribbon, seemingly endowed with life and intelligence, responded as though it had second sight, rubbing its outer edge across the ship. In a split second the computer screen turned black, temporarily obliterating the picture.

"How much damage?" she whispered, this time experiencing an acute phantom pain in her right hand.

Joshua checked the data, then ran a quick calculation.

"Obliteration."

"You killed us?"

Her shocked innocence curiously rejuvenated his lagging spirits.

"Yes."

Paula digested the information, then made a low grunt.

"I guess that means you lose."

He noted the reversal from "us" to "you," and his expression brightened.

"I've lost every game so far." Leaning back, he reconstructed the picture, so that *Target* once again rested complete and intact in the foreground.

"I programmed in the data from the bridge – that which survived," he added, almost cheerfully. "I'm trying to calculate what, if any chance we had for escape."

"But, you've given it super powers; ones it didn't possess," she protested.

He looked up and caught her eyes. Matching his with her own, stare for stare, they probed deep inside the other's consciousness.

"I'm trying to teach myself to see using my third eye."

"By developing psychic vision?"

"If you like. I've decided that's the difference between a living, sentient being and a mechanical one. We can both learn from our mistakes, we both have the ability to calculate strategy and react against unanticipated counters, but I don't believe a machine can add extra sensory perceptions to its repertoire. Therefore, to win, I must look beyond my five senses."

"Is that possible? I'm aware some people possess ESP to an extraordinary degree. But, is it something that can be cultivated?"

He immediately picked up on her word choice before she had a change to amend it.

"More chance of that than us growing hybrid plants in hydroponics."

"I think we can learn to be adept at both."

He continued as though she hadn't spoken.

"I had a discussion about the subject with Brian. I forget now what he called it, but his rating is quite high. And he had a system whereby he tested himself against other people."

"You mean, tried to read their minds?"

"Not only that, but attempted to influence their thoughts."

"How successful was he?" she inquired in an interested but guarded tone.

"He-wouldn't-tell-me."

"Which implies he had positive results."

"Knowing Brian, it means he didn't want to tell me," Joshua reiterated more firmly. "He likes to think of himself as a mystery man."

"What it means to me is that he didn't want to frighten you. Knowing what we think about Star Bright, he might have brought that up."

"He couldn't. Because that would mean we could use him as a weapon. Something Jingles and Miles both rebuffed, by the way."

"Rebuffed?"

"They handed me my head. Or, if you prefer, they accused me in so many words as having no conscience. Or, of betraying it. Something I hadn't expected."

"Then, they were brainwashed."

He hesitated, clearly torn, before confessing, "I don't think so. And if they were, Star Bright tried his hand at me through them."

"And succeeded?"

The bluntness of the question did not surprise him as much as he might have thought.

"I'm not at the stage to say."

Rather than argue out a point she had no way of winning – or, if determining if there was a win-loss ratio, she glanced back at the game in his hand.

"You've been playing for over an hour. How far have you gotten?"

"That it's entirely possible we experienced the best possible outcome. By being unaware of it and thus taking no action, it didn't sense us and therefore it did no more than react the way matter and anti-matter would do in nature. It destroyed that part of the ship which came in contact with it, but no more."

"And if we had seen it but failed to correctly identify it – and having no idea how far it extended – we might have tried aggressive action. To blast our way through it. Or, take the chance to moving into its sphere and having the entire ship destroyed."

"Yes. I might have chosen either option."

She stiffened in indignation.

"No, sir. You would not have."

He scowled in annoyance.

"I won't allow you to judge me in hindsight."

"I wouldn't think of it, sir. I was judging *Captain Nguyen.* As you're no doubt aware, he was in command when Encounter took place."

His face blanched in extreme consternation.

"Yes. No..." A hand went to his face. "I had forgotten."

"I thought you might have."

"He's been dead so long and so much has happened...."

"It's best to keep things in perspective, Captain Terry."

His lips moved wordlessly before his head thrust back in wonder. For a moment, Paula thought he was going to laugh.

"We tend to overlook the obvious, don't we? How quickly we adapt to new situations."

Wiggling his fingers, Terry motioned her closer, his mood considerably altered. This time, she was all too eager to comply.

"Call it a game, if you will," he pursued, overlooking the fact that was his term, "but I've used it as a diversion. While I've been reconstructing Encounter, the back of my mind has been on Star Bright."

"It's like dreaming," Paula acknowledged. "We sleep to free our thoughts from waking distractions."

He nodded, interlacing his fingers then bending them backwards, stopping just short of cracking his knuckles.

"Like this game, I needed to see the situation in an entirely different way. I still believe you and I were correct in our initial determination, but it's blinded us to a far more simple solution."

"Tell me."

"We've been to his ship. It's time we invited him to ours."

Paula did not know whether he expected her to counter the proposal, and his expression gave no indication. She therefore took it upon herself to be his game-advisor.

"If he starts manipulating the minds of the crew, we're in serious trouble."

"That... candy jar may already be open," he hedged, without elaboration. "On the other hand, you and I and some of the other crew might reasonably be expected to physically overwhelm him, if we determine that's our only course of action."

"All right. How do we approach it?"

"The same way we would, were *Target* at full strength. We treat him like visiting royalty."

"You've been talking to Brian."

"No." He smiled sadly. "But I suppose it might be how he'd express it. And not without merit."

"He's a better strategist than he knows."

"Now we've insulted him."

Joshua grinned for Brian's benefit, then directed his attention away from the monitor and toward the nearest observation screen. Activating it, he manipulated the outboard cameras to focus on *Here*.

"If Star Bright is what he says he is – if he is what Helen believes – he can't help but be moved by our plight. Then, if it's within his power, he'll offer to help us."

"And if it isn't?"

"We counter our bet – the same way a player uses computer prompts to beat that same computer at chess. While the 'prince' is being given the Grant Tour, several of us will be on *Here* – trying to learn as much as we can without hindrance from its recently departed occupant."

"And in position to take what we need, if he refuses?"

Just as there was no concept of betrayal in Paula's voice, so, too, there was no definitive answer to her question.

For that reason, he didn't answer it.

His silence was enough. They were not really playing a game. Survival was all or nothing.

Chapter 30

Jingles, Janice, Brian, Paula and those of the crew not on duty gathered in the mess, the air of hesitant expectancy suspended over them. They had been summoned together at the behest of Captain Terry for a conference. Of the assembled twelve, ten were eager to hear what Joshua had to say and two were not.

Moving apart from the others, the two conspirators who assumed they knew the purpose of the meeting, hung their heads in guilty complicity. Standing in front of a large holograph of Mars, they might have been the only two survivors of a lost expedition.

"I wish he hadn't requested my presence," Jingles growled. "I don't want to be here."

Turning sideways, his shadow cast an eerie apparition across the barren landscape. Moving to accommodate him, her shadow joined his, transformed, by a trick of light, into a nebulous Martian.

"Neither do I. But I think it's our duty to express our feelings, if we're asked."

The engineer shook his head, running his fingers absently along the nooks and vales of the alien landscape.

"He's not going to *ask* anything. He's going to lay it on the line." Indicating the others, he shivered miserably. "I don't know them. I don't know *people*. I'm not a person; not really. Not like they are."

"Then what are you?" she gently probed.

"I'm a flesh and bone engine. Right now, I wish I were made of components and circuits."

"No, you don't. And I'm glad you're not," she shyly added.

"I don't think the same way as the others. I didn't want to know about the plants," he added in an undertone.

"I did," Janice blurted, surprised by her vehemence. Jingles amazed her by pressing his nose closer to hers. It was a non-threatening gesture of confrontation and tortured confession.

"Why?"

"Because our situation aboard ship has altered. It's no longer a military mission. We're no longer defenders of the furthest reaches of our civilization. Or even explorers, for that matter. I'm not sure Captain Terry fully understands the change, but maybe he's beginning to."

Reaching out, she touched Jingles' face. Her shadow, imitating her motion, seemed to be casting a blessing.

"You and I and the rest of us have the moral right to decide our own fate. I admired you so greatly when you told the captain you didn't want to eat again. That was the bravest testimony I've ever witnessed."

He was so taken aback by her avowal, his eyes shut in humble concentration and patent emotion.

"I don't know what got into me. It wasn't bravery. It was...."

"Yes, it was," she concluded over his painful grope for the proper explanation. "And I'm glad you're not an engine."

Trying to backtrack, he nearly bit his tongue.

"I know what I am. And I know what I'm not."

"You know what people say you are. And I say you're beautiful."

Before he could withdraw in horrified denial, Joshua Terry made his appearance. Unlike their previous confrontation, he appeared taller, more relaxed. Taking Jingles' hand, Janice moved him closer to the front, leaving behind them, in the holograph, the promise of life on a barren planet.

They settled beside Paula Burbone, purposely choosing her out from the crowd. Without proof, Janice sensed the young woman had been watching them. If they were to stand united, she and Jingles would encompass the entire crew, not only the converted.

For her part, Paula seemed to appreciate the gesture. Nodding pleasantly toward them, she made a point of smiling. Their radiance warmed her, evoking a curiosity and a longing, long buried. Without the ability to ask for an explanation, she absorbed the gentleness before directing her attention toward the front.

"Thank you for joining me," the commanding officer began, voice measured and even, instilling in those gathered a peculiar sense of hope. "I want to ask all of you to participate in a very important project."

Janice and Jingles exchanged glances, their expressions conveying to one another the silent understanding Terry was not going to discuss the situation in Hydroponics. For the moment, they breathed a sigh of relief.

Moments, they seemed to say, *which made life worth living.*

Moments which might become hours and grow into days.

Without knowing why, the phantom pain in Paula's hand dissipated.

"As you're aware," Terry explained, "several of us have boarded the alien's ship. Now it's time to extend the same courtesy to Star Bright."

If Brian had not been crowded against the others, he might have fallen over backward.

"We don't have much to offer in the way of amenities, but what gift we can bestow is companionship. Star Bright has never encountered beings like himself – he's lived alone his entire life. I'd like to expose him to people; let him observe how we function together as a cohesive unit."

Making a point of directing his line of vision toward Jingles and Janice, Terry kindly added, "When one of us falters, another picks him up. Our strength is in unity; the pooling our talents." Reading his engineer's face, the captain added, "And in having the courage to correct one another's mistakes."

"Discovering our humanity," Jingles supplemented, his face red from ear to ear. Shocking himself by the admission, the man who was not made of components and circuits ducked behind Janice Miles, the technology specialist-turned first lieutenant, thus acknowledging she, too, was greater than the sum of her parts.

Without fully divining the exchange, Father Hardy glowed with shared enthusiasm.

"I think that's a wonderful idea."

Whether he meant the invitation or the acknowledgement was problematic, for the crew cheered, their own excitement mounting. As Maurice Kincaid thumped Brian on the back, others raised their hands in salute to Jingles.

Bashfully waving back, Jingles attempted to divert attention from himself.

"Tell us more," he pleaded. "Will he come?"

"I don't know," Joshua admitted, assuming a sobering countenance. Moving through the throng, the captain settled himself in the middle, making it easier for contact. "I hope so." Reaching across Leonard Broderick's body, he rested a hand on Brian's shoulder.

"I want you to act as host. Show him the ship; introduce him to the crew. Let's not overwhelm him. Take it slowly. Katherine," he continued, picking Bacce, one of his former security officers, while taking the unusual step of addressing her by her first name. "See to it we have a small meal of sprouts from Hydroponics prepared. Here, in the crew's mess. An informal gathering, where you can share stories with him. Tell him about yourselves. Of all the knowledge Star Bright possesses, family histories are most lacking."

"Even the sad ones, sir? Our... losses?" Her voice broke. Joshua allowed a moment to pass before nodding. "You and Morris," he stressed, using the man's preferred pronunciation of his first name, "let Star Bright see us through your eyes. Can you do that?"

"Yes, sir," Kincaid responded, paled but suddenly eager at the prospect. "None of us have... dared think too much... of the past. I'd like to do that. Share... memories."

"Thank you. And Jingles. Will you give him a tour of the engine room?"

The big man considered, eyes flashing. When he spoke, however, his answer caught the captain off guard.

"Aye. I'd like to show him the' boys.' But, sir?"

Terry stiffened, mitigating his answer with forced calmness. "Yes?"

"I'd like Star Bright to sit in the big chair; my throne. But I... don't have it, anymore."

Tension dissipated as the captain's face split with a huge grin.

"I'll let you borrow it, if I'm sure it will be returned."

It was the perfect answer and the crew cheered. Blushing again, the engineer attempted to hide behind Janice.

"As to that," he mumbled into her hair while addressing Terry, "I think you've earned it."

Staggered by the enormity of the compliment, Terry rose and took a step toward the door, as if the weight of it were too much to bear.

"Let's get to it. We haven't much time."

He was almost to the door when the question came from the back of the room. His ear was not acute enough to identify the speaker.

"How much *time* do we have?"

The question was vague enough to be innocent, and astute enough to be damning. Terry stiffened but did not lose his smile.

"Time, like most things is relative. We have what we have. Thank you."

He did not need to stress the importance of this mission. Whether the speaker knew of the grim conditions in Hydroponics or not, their life hung by a tread. Star Bright was not only to be their guest, he was the key to life, itself. That much was obvious to even the most unenlightened.

It was Paula who sealed the pact.

"Let the preparations begin."

Conditions accepted.

The small Skip hung suspended in space outside *Here,* a very tiny speck in the vastness of the universe. The crew had not announced their arrival, although the two aboard the larger vessel had watched their progress with trepidation. When the signal came to open communications, it had been Helen who responded.

Steeling for a confrontation, what she saw took her breath away. The eyes of the man on the monitor sparkled with nova-like intensity, while his countenance radiated with the type of boyish impishness she had not witnessed in years. Leaning closer, hand to the monitor, she attempted to discern a screen or filter which would have created the effect. When none was readily apparent, she quizzically examined the face of her companion.

Star Bright, aware of her silent interrogative, shrugged his shoulders then ruffled Teddy's fur, a mute denial of their complicity.

Dreading to waste a precious moment of this seeming transformation, Helen resumed her interrogation, wishing to instill the speaker's essence into her being.

"I have a proposition to put to you," Joshua was saying. "In private. Will you come aboard the Skip?"

The little bear whined a low protest, but Helen shook him off. Joshua's question had not been an order, but a request. Covering the microphone, she attempted to explain her feelings to her companions.

"Something important has happened. I need to understand."

Leaving her hand on the screen to maintain the link she dare not break, Helen leaned closer. "What is it, Joshua?"

"Please. The question I want to put to you must be expressed in person. It will only take a moment. If, afterwards, you choose to return to *Here,* I will not stop you. In fact," he added sincerely, "I would encourage it."

Star Bright snuffled. She reached out a hand, engulfing his in hers.

"It's all right. I trust him. If he says I can return, then I will."

"Go away?"

"Not so far. Only to the Skip. You can see it," she demonstrated, nodding toward the monitor.

"What does he want?"

"I don't know. But I must go. He said it was important. Only a moment," she concluded with tenderness.

"I will miss you."

The tone, so reminiscent of Mama and Papa tugged at her heartstrings. He was so much their child, the product of their goodness, their most delicate emotions.

"I'll miss you, too. But you can watch me go – and return. I'll wave at you," she grinned. "Like this." Gently detaching herself from his arm, she raised her hand, then swept it in a friendly arc. "You can wave back. Try it, now."

He imitated her action, attempting to summon bravery from his frightened mind.

"That's it! Exactly."

"I will be alone."

"You will never be alone again," she promised with absolute conviction. "You and I will always be together, wherever we are."

"But this..." he began, faltering for the proper words. Brushing his hand across her cheek, he shivered, then brought it to his own face. "No one to touch."

"You have Teddy. Hold onto him while I'm gone."

"He... cannot kiss," Star Bright protested, tears welling in his eyes.

"You can kiss him," she amended. "And I will blow you a kiss from space. How is that? When I come back, I'll kiss you. Promise."

"How?" he pouted.

Helen laughed. The answer was simple.

"In as many ways as you want. And as many times as you want."

"As a baby, or as a friend? Or, as two people in love?"

She had readily comprehended what he meant without the reiteration.

"That, sir," she teased, "is an impertinent question."

"What does that mean?"

"I will explain it when I get back."

Rotating in her chair, Helen addressed the computer screen.

"Yes, Josh. I'll come. Under your conditions."

"Very good. I'll expect you. And Helen.... I love you." He grinned, a wide, toothy expression of innocent emotion. She happily returned it.

"I love you, too."

Disengaging the open channel, the woman from Earth stood, then remained in that position as the alien, born in space, baby-stepped close to her.

"I am hurting," he whispered, hand to his chest in sad confusion.

"Love can hurt. But it is also the most wonderful emotion in the universe."

"That, too, you will have to tell me when you return."

"With bells on my toes." Glancing down at her feet, Helen wiggled them. "That means, with a smile on my face."

He accepted the explanation without comment, then bravely squared his shoulders.

"You will go in the bubble?"

"The bubble? Me? Travel to the Skip in a bubble?"

It was an offer, the only gift he had; his only manner of expressing love.

"Will you?"

"And how will I get back?"

"I will program it so that it stays near you... that you can summon it back when you are ready. I can do that," he promised, holding Teddy out as an example. "It will dissolve when you arrive, but will return at your summons. If you do not take too long," he added, not as a warning but as a plea.

"Then I will be honored to accept your proposal."

The unusualness of her expression washed over Helen like a warm shower. Making a low bow, she held out her hand. Star Bright hesitated, before offering Teddy's paw. Accepting it gracefully, the three began their short trek to the bay.

Following his direction, Helen stood apart as Star Bright and Mr. Bear manipulated the controls. Without realizing what was happening, she found herself encased in a transparent, oval-shaped spacesuit. Lacking all trapping of traditional protection, she felt both naked and exhilarated.

"I feel so light and airy," she demonstrated, waving her arms in the air.

"You cannot fly, yet, but you will," her friend promised, stepping back and then sealing her inside the decompression area. In a moment her wildly rotating eyes took in the alteration of the color indicators. The atmosphere was gone and she was literally functioning inside a bubble.

"Now what?" she called, her attention drawn to the outside door as it slowly crawled apart.

"You can fly!"

Taking Star Bright at his word, for there was no fear in her, Helen launched herself outside. In the span of time it took for her rapidly pounding heart to beat twice, she was floating, unattached and free.

"I can fly, I can fly, I can fly!" she shouted, raising and lowering her arms the way a delicately sculptured song bird would maneuver through the air.

"What the hell is going on?" Captain Joshua Terry of the space cruiser *Target* screamed at his view screen. "Jesus Christ, she's out there without a suit!" Only the firm grip of Brian Hardy restrained him from leaping toward their own bay and his own spacesuit.

"Easy, boy. She's alive; she's moving. Look at her!"

Forcing Terry back to the monitor, they stared in dumb disbelief as Helen Fitzgerald bounced and danced her way toward them. She could not see what they saw, nor did it occur to her they might worry, never having been introduced to the space bubble. She waved in their direction, then, remembering another obligation, spun back to face *Here*.

With her hand to her lips, Helen blew Star Bright a kiss.

"I love you," he whispered back, raising Teddy's paw to the bear's own lips. Making the sacred noise which he would never forget, were he and his companion destined to live forever, the pair blew back a kiss.

"Move toward the Skip and I will guide you," he continued in a louder voice. She obeyed. In less than five minutes found herself inside the boarding area.

"Stand by to pressurize," came Paula Burbone's officious voice. Helen relaxed, waiting for the atmosphere to reenter the room, then raised a hand in greeting as Joshua entered. To her surprise, she noted a thin film on her arm, which rapidly evaporated as he hurried to meet her.

"Where's your space suit?" he demanded after embracing her in his arms. "What was that thing you were wearing?"

"A bubble," she replied, happily meeting his lips with her own. He was long in breaking off the welcome. By the time he finished, Brian and Paula had joined them.

"Good to have you home again," the minister stated, bouncing on his toes in pure joy. "I must say, when you're gone, the place has an empty feel to it."

"Thank you. I missed you all. But it really hasn't been that long. Has it?" she finished, starting up into Joshua's wet eyes.

"Forever," was his determination.

"You scared the heebie jeebees out of us," Brian continued. "When we first saw you, I had to restrain this one from going out and rescuing you."

Helen jerked back, guilt transparent on her face.

"I'm so sorry. I should have realized how it would look," she tried, attempting a grin. "With all this concern over telepathy, I somehow presumed you would read my mind." Tapping herself lightly on the arm, she indicated where the transparent film rested. "The bubble is Star Bright's equivalent of our space suit," she lamely concluded, furtively wondering how much damage she had done her own cause.

"How did you know how to operate it?" It was Paula's turn. "Did you train in it? How do you manipulate the controls? And what happened to it?" she demanded, looking around for the remnants of the suit.

"I don't really know; I'm not sure whether Star Bright actually directed me, or if I came on my own. Or a bit of both. And it dissolved. But it will come back – when I'm ready to return." In her excitement, she did not notice the crestfallen expressions of her companions. "Now, please tell me what it was you wanted."

"Come on. Let's go into the cabin and sit down."

With Paula leading and Joshua pulling up the rear, the four went into the more comfortable but equally crowded cabin. The captain indicated Helen and Burbone sit it the two command seats while he and Hardy crouched in the narrow confines behind them.

"Helen, we've given this situation considerable thought." Looking from one to the other, she failed to decipher their expressions.

"Situation? You mean, Star Bright?"

"Yes; Star Bright." His prepared text evaporated as surely as the alien's spacesuit. Thus unprotected, he was forced to forge ahead, unconsciously reverting to a more formal, and thus less compelling, explanation. It stood her on guard.

"And our own position, as well. *Target's* mission. I'm afraid we've been negligent. We've been too preoccupied with ourselves to make him a proper welcome."

"I've tried to explain that," Helen interpolated between his breaths.

"I'm sure you have," he agreed, leaning forward to be closer. The mental feedback he received through the open barriers of his mind transmitted the fact she was Helen Fitzgerald but nothing could hide the fact she had metamorphosed, altered in ways he could not fathom. It almost felt as though she were no longer human, but had somehow absorbed so much alien-ness from Star Bright that not only had her personality mutated, her body had changed as well.

This observation was not dissimilar to the one Helen had experienced with Paula on *Here*. As it had with her, the change tied his tongue.

"And we appreciate that," Paula resumed for her commanding officer. "But now it's our turn."

"What do you mean?" Helen queried, aware of the tension but not the reason for Joshua's silence. To her, their companionship was natural and familiar. More so, in fact, for her experiences aboard *Here* had sharpened her delineation of duty.

"We want to give him a proper introduction to us and to our ship. If we understand correctly, he's never been on another vessel before. We think it's high time he was given a tour of an 'alien ship.'"

"Think of the wonder, Helen," Brian hurried on, acutely eager to carry the point. "Never to have set foot on foreign soil. And while *Target* isn't exactly Earth, we are its representatives. What a chance for him to expand his horizons."

This was the moment Helen had been waiting for; what she had anticipated from the first contact with Star Bright. Yet offered now, under these circumstances, her suspicions were aroused. The invitation itself was logical, but its very appropriateness lacked emotion. Where she had expected joy, two of her three companions offered no more than restrained expectation. Only Brian exhibited Terry's earlier enthusiasm, and he was to be trusted only for his non-military status.

A moment before, Helen believed duty had strengthened her ties with Joshua. Doubt ate through the apple of her eye like a worm.

"Wonder is an interesting word, Brian," she cautiously began. "That Star Bright should be exposed to the wonder of our ship is without question. But I *wonder* at the timing. And the rationale which brought you to this unexpected invitation."

Changing positions, Helen straightened her back, placing her feet firmly on the floor. If this were to be a command conference and not the social gathering she expected, she would treat it accordingly.

"Captain Terry?"

Joshua's mind flashed back to the Crew's Mess and the pains he had taken to employ first names, rather than surnames. It had been a giant step forward for him. Helen's sudden use of formality rocked his moorings.

She had used her powers of divination to attack the weakest link and he knew it. If, in fact, his sense of powerlessness stemmed from the belief Star Bright would refuse the invitation, this was the moment to defend the offer. If jealousy were the true reason behind his lukewarm stance, an open admission would not only place Helen on the defensive, it might finally clear the air between them.

Conversely, if his reticence arose from the consequences of facing those measures deemed necessary to counter other, more far-reaching refusals, he was placing himself in the untenable situation of alienating himself from everyone.

A man was not an island, and a ship's captain was no exception. Whatever his reasoning, neither his command nor his life could survive being ostracized aboard *Target*.

Were that to occur, he would have only one recourse: strand Star Bright aboard his own ship and steal *Here* for himself. To his shame, the idea was not without appeal.

Chapter 31

They were waiting for his response: Paula, sitting in her the co-pilot's chair, back straight, left hand clenched over right. Brian, flattened against the wall, eyes alternately wandering from his friends to the ceiling, never alighting long enough to get a fix on any one object. Helen, a combination of the two, searching faces while rolling her thumbs over interlaced fingers. Joshua's foot nervously moving back and forth to the tempo of un-orchestrated breathing.

The silence grew ominous. Paula changed position, glancing down to stare at her stump. As she brushed her hand over a rough edge of skin, Brian shifted weight from one leg to the other, inadvertently bumping her. His *sotto voce,* "I'm sorry," went unacknowledged. Prefatory to reacting to either, Joshua tensed his muscles, then as suddenly relaxed them. Only Helen remained resolute, content with the posture she had adopted.

"I wonder," Terry began, taking care to couch his words as a request, "if you two would mind moving as far away to the back as possible so Helen and I may speak privately to one another."

Paula immediately responded, rising gracefully to her feet. She expected Brian to follow, but he delayed his action, conspicuously tugging on the cuffs of his sleeves.

"I'd just as soon stay." His open denial came as a bombshell. Before Terry could reach him with a shove, Hardy unexpectedly winked. That action stifled any contact between the two men.

"Helen," the reverend continued, engaging her with an endearing smile, "I'm used to speaking for the higher ups. Whether or not I adequately express their opinions is a matter of supposition. I hope so," he added, scratching his nose. "In this case, of course, Captain Terry is that authority and I don't claim to voice his opinion. But the others aboard *Target* – your friends – would like you to know how much we want to befriend Star Bright. Don't question the sincerity of their invitation. We mean him no harm. We want to help, but we're also... *starved* for his companionship.

"We need to know we have something to offer, if only ourselves. You should have seen how Leo Broderick responded to the chance of having someone to share his wife and child with."

Helen's head bobbed with the awe of that realization.

"We want to hear Star Bright's stories and share our own. Jingles has agreed to play his flute. Let's remember why we're here."

Overcome by the sentiment, Helen raised a fist into the air, the moral equivalent of blowing a kiss to a lonely soul.

"Yes! I will ask him. When would you like him to come?"

Caught between two worlds, yet nearly overcome by her own expectations of fully encountering that which was strange and wondrous, the twenty-four year old commander-in-training touched her crippled arm to that of Helen's intact one.

"He must come," Paula pleaded. "As soon as he will."

Staggered by the seeming reversal of roles, and hardly daring to believe, Helen leaned forward.

"You... wish it, too? Why?"

Although her question was blunt, it conveyed no harm. None was taken as Paula raised her right arm.

"Something I witnessed." She did not elaborate and Helen did not press. "It made me think. Call it a hope."

Spontaneously reaching out, Helen brought Paula's arm to her face. Tenderly pressing her lips to it, she wrapped the stump inside her hands, bringing the woman beside her.

"God bless us all, Paula," she cried, nodding toward Brian, who grinned and bounced. "He shall come! And Josh," she continued, glowing with shared affection. "Make me believe it's your wish, as well."

Grasping his hand, she immediately regretted the action, for it was cold and clammy. Helen's sharp intake of breath caused him to pull away, but there was no mistaking the pain the action caused him. With downturned mouth and lowered head he quickly attempted to mitigate his body's betrayal.

"Ask him.... With my... blessing."

Discovering himself unaccountably in Paula's position, he buried the offending hand between his thigh and interior wall.

"I'll open a channel," Paula eagerly volunteered, but it was Helen's turn to disappoint by waving her down.

"No. He won't be responsive to an invitation like that. It's something I have to broach in person. Or he'll be suspicious," she underscored. "He'll think you're holding me here; keeping me from him. Not unless I go back of my own free will, will he ever consider leaving his ship."

"Yes. Go back." Joshua's pronouncement startled his listeners. "That's the right thing to do."

Brian clapped his hands, then straightened as far as he could, leaning toward Paula.

"Come on," he urged. "These two have some serious kissing to do, and as much as I'd like to stay and watch, you're too young."

Her pout caught him by surprise, but her follow-through of grasping him by the hair and dragging his face toward hers came close to buckling his knees.

"I'm not too young and you're not too old," she warned. "Star Bright is coming. We can give him a story to remember."

Without ever knowing it, the strange little alien and the teddy bear toy had found a new friend. If they were the line between hope and despair, then Paula Burbone had leapt over it in a somersault. Had Jingles had been present, he would have played a flute accompaniment.

Neither Joshua nor Helen were sure whether Paula pulled Brian away, or if he ran to escape her clutches. Either way, their playfulness should have eased the tension, but in that it failed.

Ordinarily, Helen would have snuggled into his arms, but the remembrance of his corpse-like hand stayed that action. He was sick, but he wouldn't say how. That frightened her.

"You're not getting enough sleep," she began, then let the words die. While undoubtedly true, such a statement was no more than the social equivalent of telling him he looked like hell. "I *will* try and convince him, Josh. Not only because I think Star Bright would benefit from exposure to our people, but for you."

"Why for me? As you heard – and saw for yourself – it's the crew who is looking forward to his arrival."

"But not you?" Helen asked, putting aside her objection of the previous moment to move closer to him. Scrutinizing his haggard expression, the grey hairs streaked through his sideburns, she discerned, but could not identify the conflict warring within. "What's happened? Something in the past twenty-four hours has changed you."

"Yes," he agreed, the haunting image of Jingles' tear-stained face dancing tauntingly before him. Rather than sit beside her, he stepped as far away as the cramped confines afforded.

"It's something they instruct future officers in at the Academy, but I'm only just realizing can't be taught," he began, placing a hand on the back of the chair.

"And that is?" she asked, twisting to see him.

"Values." His lips curled around the word as he trust it from himself into the open area of the room. "Personal tenets; standards of conduct. We can make all the rules we want, but in the end, no two people ever feel exactly the same way about anything."

Crossing in front of her, Joshua started her by his vehemence. "What it truly comes down to is who makes the ultimate decisions."

"Those we make for ourselves," Helen began, but his bitter laughter belied her protest.

"Not really. Not on the larger issues of life and death. Those are always made by others. Consider," he clarified, holding up his index finger. "Aboard ship, we may all be equal as human beings, but it's not a democracy. No one votes. As captain, I make the final determination on everything from how much we eat to when to take aggressive – or passive – action. I decided to destroy the starboard side; I went after the mutineers and killed them. Ultimately, there was no way for them to stop me and consequently they died."

He held up a second finger.

"I decided Star Bright was a threat and acted accordingly. I have now *decided* my original position may have been in error – or at least partially so. And so I've determined to change course – in a figurative way," he added, bitterness running deep. "Inasmuch as *Target* itself is crippled. No one else has a say."

Steeling herself by taking in a deep breath, Helen's eyes narrowed. While limiting her vision, the act sharpened her sight.

"Joshua, without knowing precisely what's occurred, I can tell you more than you know yourself."

"Do so," he urged, in what might have been sarcasm. Undaunted, Helen stood, forcing him to move back a step or accept the close proximity of their bodies. He hesitated, then retreated as far as the inner wall would allow.

"You're maturing."

His reaction was immediate and violent. Jerking back his head, he tensed himself for a physical confrontation, although he had taken care to avoid such by previously moving back.

"What?"

Helen licked her lips, giving herself a second to search for precisely the diplomatic phrase she sought.

"You've been thrown out of your safe, comfortable sphere. You've been looking in from the outside for so long, you've forgotten you've never fledged."

"What does that mean?"

"Your entire adult life has been as a subordinate. While you've certainly taken command responsibility, it was always under the responsibility of a ranking officer. While your entire career from cadet to commander has been one of... taking chances – at least to the degree you've shared your experiences with me – in the final analysis, you've never been free to make the *ultimate* decisions. Encounter irrevocably altered that. Within the last six months you've been thrown into the position of captain. That sacred attainment you longed for so badly."

"We've discussed this," he began but she cut him off.

"You've been forced to make decisions. Some of them were wrong. Although you find that hard to accept, no one is right all the time. You debated resignation; to abdicate your responsibilities, yet in each instance those under your command have seen the situations differently than you. You should have learned something from that, but you didn't. You've kept to yourself. Yes, you've occasionally sought the opinion of others, but in the end, you went your own way."

"On the whole, I'd agree with that."

"Feeling no remorse. Shall I tell you why?"

"I can't prohibit you."

"Because your idea of being a captain isn't based on what you know to be right and true, but from what you've observed in other officers. Take George Nguyen, for example. At one point you told me how much you admired him. He stood for what the military service deemed a competent leader. Perhaps he was, but he lacked what you have: emotion. He played by the book; he took no chances. His duty was toward the completion of an assignment. I find it interesting that when the inhabitants of CO-49-B refused to accept the nutritional tablets, his response was to stow them. Not because they might be used elsewhere to good advantage but from the fact they were expensive and he would be chastised for losing so valuable a cargo."

"My response was to send them out an airlock," he stubbornly protested.

"Yes. As you relayed it, that was your response to him. It was what he expected and what you supplied. Had you been in command, I seriously doubt that would have been your first thought. Or, your second. Or, your third."

"You give me too much credit."

"When left to your own devices, you have the... sentience to correct your mistakes. You abandoned a pregnant cat, then found you couldn't live with the consequences and went after her. Captain Nguyen wouldn't have taken her in, in the first place."

Awkwardly shifting his shoulders, he shook his head.

"I'm missing the point."

"Because you understood what it took to be a successful career officer, you expected others to follow suit. Without having been there and having no idea what actually happened – your suspicions to the contrary – you reached a Captain Nguyen decision. Some aggression against Star Bright and possibly against me. I don't need to know who stood up to you, but it must have been devastating. Not Paula and not Brian. Two others whom you expected to support you. They spit in your eye. You not only failed them, they failed you. Unthinkable, and yet it had to be thought. That pushed you out of your military role."

He waited a long beat before challenging, "Into what?"

"I don't know. Neither do you."

His lip curled into a sneer.

"That's not an answer, it's an evasion."

"All right, you were rebuffed in your plans. That required you to recalculate, which you did. The same way Artificial Intelligence does: by calculating the odds on what's required. Not to accede to their wishes, but to bring them around to yours. And, for the sake of your heart, I'll add with just enough wiggle-room for you to go the other way."

"You're accusing me of lying to them."

"I'm afraid I am. You proposed this visit which you were perfectly aware they'd jump at. More than that, they'd be excited, eager, even joyous. Because they don't view Star Bright the way you do. They actually believed your words of encouragement because that's actually what they wanted from you, their captain. To be the steadfast voice of moral authority. Never suspecting you were using them as pawns and this visit as a trap. Or, I should I say a diversion? While he was here being regaled with stories of wives and children and impossible rescues and planets to land on, you either planned to subdue him and take over his ship, or less aggressively, to visit his ship and steal whatever it is you think can help us survive."

She finished with a flourish, out of breath and sick to her inner fiber.

He held out his hands, but she had already finished what she had to say.

"Helen."

She was ready.

"Yes?"

"If Star Bright doesn't help us, we're going to die. Starve. The plants in Hydroponics are not going to survive."

While such news should have devastated her, it did not.

"I'm sorry."

Her casualness was a blow of another sort.

"Is that all you can say?"

"We tried."

Joshua shook his head, then leaned against the bulkhead in an attitude of a long-distance runner at the starting block.

"Not good enough."

She understood the tacit threat against Star Bright.

"The personal choice is yours, captain. You can be George Nguyen and take what you need by force, or you can finally be Joshua Terry."

"And who is he?"

"The man who acknowledged a terrible mistake and went in search of a stray cat. The man I fell in love with."

"You said you would never forgive me."

"Like you, Joshua, I've changed. I'm maturing, too."

Helen stared at him with a peculiar expression, half pity, half compassion, then finally smiled. She did not intend for it to be deceiving, but behind it was the image of Joshua Terry alone on the bridge with no one else beside him.

"If you decide to sacrifice honor and integrity, eventually you'll discover life is not worth *any* price. You're just finding out what others 'lesser than you' already know." She gravely nodded. "Whether you rejoin the human race or not depends on what you value most. But be warned: if you chose incorrectly, you walk alone."

Helen crossed to him, but the fight had not gone out of his eyes.

"I just told you. Weren't you listening? If Star Bright doesn't help us, we're not going to make it."

"So, you wanted me to intercede for you – carry that burden on my shoulders? Plead our case? Ask him to sacrifice his own life for ours?"

"It doesn't have to be that drastic," he began, moving sideways, but she interrupted.

"You don't know that. Perhaps he has only enough food for two – himself and Teddy. There's a very real possibility giving us new plants and the nourishment to sustain them will ultimately cause his own demise. How altruistic should he be?"

"You tell me. You know him best."

Hands akimbo, Helen demurred.

"I'm not going to ask him that. He owes me nothing. If there's an obligation, the debt is on my end. *You* ask him, Captain Terry. But when you do, I should think carefully beforehand. What have you, or Brian, or Paula, for that matter, done for him? You've been overly suspicious, doubting, aggressive. You've come across more as..." She groped for the proper expression and found it. "Marauding pirates, than as a loving, wondrous people. He looks upon you as a familiar enemy. Can you say otherwise?"

The question was daunting.

"I've only acted in a manner best calculated to protect my crew."

"Spoken like Captain Nguyen. Congratulations."

"Helen," he pleaded, flinching from her accusation, then extending his arms. "We're going to die."

"Weigh that against what Star Bright has to lose. Then try being humble. Or not," she added, pushing past him for the door. "I just pray it's Joshua Terry who worships the purity of space that makes the ultimate decision." She paused as his arms dropped listlessly to his side. "If Star Bright agrees to come, and I'm not going to pressure him, I'll see you back on *Target.*" No answer. "He will undoubtedly wish to travel to the ship in a bubble. So will I. It's perfectly safe. Will you be there to greet us?"

As though the gravity in the room had been immeasurably lowered, Captain Terry stood, taking a moment to acclimate himself to the change in atmosphere. The air, too, must have thinned, for his chest heaved with strenuous effort.

"Yes. Of course. It's my duty."

"Make it your pleasure," she concluded in parting and then thought, but did not say, *You'll be amazed at how easy it is.*

With a wave, she was gone.

The receiving bay aboard *Here* held the form of one small alien. As the door opened and Helen floated inside, he quivered with anticipation. The bubble around her had barely dissolved before Star Bright flew into her arms.

"You came back!" he joyously exclaimed.

"I told you I would."

They tenderly embraced before stepped back toward the small bear who sat on a ledge carefully appraising the pair. Grasping the companion in the crook of his arm, Star Bright hesitated, then raised his eyes.

"I doubted, but Teddy believed."

"I had to bring your bubble back. Didn't I?"

He started to correct her, then caught the glint of a smile. The tease did not stop him from completing the explanation, however.

"No. As I told you, the protective force eventually wears away. Though you summon it, it is gone and must then be replenished from the ship. The only loss to me would be your absence."

She nodded slowly as comprehension came, then crossed to them, so that her next question was spoken at close proximity..

"What did you do while I was gone?"

"I watched the Skip," he replied, eyes wide with truthfulness.

"What did you see?"

"I saw you go in and I saw you come out."

Helen considered, but she was not through with her questioning.

"Did you hear what Joshua had to say?"

He frowned, then cast a sideways glance at Bear.

"That would have been –"

"Spying," she finished for him.

"A betrayal," he agreed.

"Let's go inside and I'll tell you what they had to say."

He did not speak again until the door had parted and they were on their way to the bridge.

"You will not tell me everything you spoke about."

His insight was precise.

"Most of what we discussed has no pertinence to you."

"I want to know," Star Bright suddenly demanded, stopping in the corridor so she could not pass. The action was not meant to be threatening, but rather a decisive exclamation to his sentence.

"Why?" Helen asked.

"I want to know everything about you."

It was a child's request, but not a childish one. Taking a step back, Helen changed her mind, activating a side door to a room she had not before seen.

"What's in here?"

"Don't go in there," he protested, then as quickly withdrew his order with a shamed, embarrassed expression. "That is Mama and Papa's room."

Making a small bow, he bade her enter. "I cannot expect you to share with me, if I do not share with you."

Stopping at the entranceway, she put a hand on the wall.

"I won't go in if it upsets you."

"No, Helen," he gallantly apologized. "I was wrong to stop you. They would like you to go in."

"Thank you."

Inside was a spacious bedroom. It was much like suites she had seen on luxury transports. A large, double bed was placed toward the rear wall. No wardrobes were present, leading her to assume they were recessed into the walls. A couch and two chairs were set beside a large viewscreen. The floor itself was designed of a colorful, interlocking tile, which, she noted upon entering, gave the impression, if not the fact, of spring and softness.

The walls were a pale green, offset by streaks of dark verdure, swirling, like ivy, up and across the panels. Craning her neck upward, Helen gasped at the ceiling. A constantly moving panorama of shimmering, amorphous clouds simulated a planet's sky.

"At night, the sky darkens and you can see the stars," Mama and Papa's offspring explained. "It can be programmed from what you see here to simulate the sector of space we are currently occupying, or changed to any planet."

"Is this your native sky?"

"I do not know," he confessed. "It was not labeled as such. I wondered...."

"And the walls?" she continued, noting a subtle alteration of the shapes and hues surrounding them.

"Those, too. They can look like barren planet surfaces, vast plains, sweeping mountains, tall trees, oceans, bubbling volcanic surfaces. I have looked at them all, but I always leave them the way I found them."

"Because this is how they left it."

"Yes."

"Which is your favorite?" she asked, crossing the room. On impulse, Helen reached out a hand and touched the ivy-like leaves. Had she not known better, she would have sworn her fingers actually rubbed plant life.

"None of them. My favorites are on the top." He pointed upward. "Space. That is what I know. Where I feel at home."

"But they knew what life was like on a planet. They once lived on land."

"They spoke of it. In some of their stories they told. They did not miss it, and I do not miss what I never knew."

"But you should have the opportunity of visiting such places," she protested, sitting on the bed. It had a delightful rolling motion, almost like sitting on the sea.

"Before I thought I would, but not now." Star Bright came and sat beside her, tenderly running his hand over the coverlet.

"Because you have been unwelcome. But there are many places you would be greeted with great joy." Before he could argue, she hurried on. "What Captain Terry wanted to ask was whether you would accept an invitation to visit *Target*. To be given a tour of the ship; meet the crew. They wish to share their life stories with you. And hear yours, in return."

His face reflected surprise, but she could not be certain whether it was genuine or not.

"I? Go to your ship? Away from *Here?*"

"They're asking you to visit. As a friend. Not to stay," she hastened to reassure him. "But to spend some time with creatures similar to yourself."

"And Teddy Bear? Was he invited?"

"Not specifically, but I will gladly extend the invitation to include him."

Star Bright bounced on the bed, sending tiny ripples across the surface.

"No," he demurred. "He would *not* like to go. There are none like *him* aboard *Target.*"

"And you?"

"Do you wish it?"

Helen would have preferred he not ask that question. It tore at the roots of her doubt.

"You wanted to know what Joshua and I spoke about," she began, instead. "What we discussed was deeply personal. That means, it pertains to he and I, alone. He's frightened, because he questions his own judgment. Much has happened to change him since Encounter. He's learning how to assimilate being a captain into his humanity. It is not an easy thing to do."

"Why is it not easy, friend Helen?"

That was more difficult to answer.

"He has been trained to preserve life at all costs. Life – physical existence – is the one continuation of which we can be sure. He must now go beyond that belief to question the right and wrong of certain actions."

"About me?" Star Bright whispered in so low and hurt a tone she could do no more than nod. "I have done this to him. It was not my intention."

"I know someone who would say a higher power put Joshua Terry in this position. Perhaps he's right."

"I only wanted to... touch you. To share a moment of your life."

Helen reached across and took his hand.

"I'm grateful you did. Meeting you has been the most awe-inspiring event in my life. Besides, it was I who called you, wasn't it?"

Star Bright hesitated, then stretched upward to more closely observe the cloud formations on the ceiling.

"You were seeking," he hesitantly began. "It was I who heard."

"You came for me and I love you for it. I will never fully comprehend the sacrifice you made in contacting me. It was a trust of such magnitude, I am..." There was only one word to use, although she had so recently applied it to another. "Humbled."

"You are not like the others."

With a sigh of resignation, Helen followed his gaze toward the upper regions.

"Yes. I am. I am exactly like them. I have my fears, my doubts. Tragedy has mutated who and what I am. I discovered anger inside myself; even fury. I resent being helpless. I want to fight back; strike out at what has hurt me."

"Not in the same way."

Her guilt was onerous.

"I can't agree. I'm no more than a civilian – an advisor, if you will. I don't make the decisions. Perhaps if I did, I would be exactly like *him.*"

"What will he do?"

Helen averted her gaze from so lofty a scene, for she did feel equal to it.

"I honestly don't know."

"Will he harm me?"

The most apparent reply came easily to her lips.

"Our species holds that all life is precious – to be cherished and respected. That, I believe, is the message our crew gave Captain Terry. The ultimate reason they chose space as their avocation: to reach out and touch alien beings like yourself. To greet them with friendship and dignity."

"He did not expect such a reaction from them?" Star Bright probed, easily seeing through her evasion. Helen grimaced, not awed yet unhappily surprised by his perception. Placing a hand to her head, she restlessly massaged her ear, reliving her discussion with Joshua over values. *No,* she corrected herself, kneading harder. *Humanity.* He had proposed some course of action and had morality thrown in his teeth.

But that, too, was incorrect. Not thrown: one or more of his confidants had draped their own cloak of beliefs at his feet, and he had stooped to pick them up. Who had it been? Brian? No, Joshua had defenses for whatever the minister might say. It had come from an unexpected source. Someone he anticipated would agree with his plan.

Paula? Again, she was implausible. Her statements in the Skip had caught him entirely off guard. Helen had dismissed both once and did so, again.

Running her mind over the possibilities, only one name stood out from the rest. Jingles. Mr. Gingleheimer had cracked the captain's shell with the kind of tenderness only a strong, powerful man possessed.

Joshua had retrieved Jingles cloak but he had not wrapped it around his shoulders. That, she hoped, would come later.

"He's a better man than he thinks he is," she stated with conviction, turning to Star Bright. But as Jingles discovered, offering peace was not the same thing as having it unconditionally accepted.

"Will he harm me?"

Star Bright's face was calm. His patience, for the moment, was untried. He had asked and he would wait for an answer.

Having the grace of time, Helen leaned back, resting her head on the bed. Allowing her eyes to flutter shut, it was easy to place herself beside Joshua. At another time and in another sector of the universe, the room might have been their bridal chamber.

In a form of astral traveling, Helen rose above her body, then manipulated her third eye to view herself and the man she loved lying side-by-side. The sight of them took her breath away, for while she had been forced by circumstances to acknowledge the passage of time, never before had she witnessed it so clearly.

While unlined and without obvious blemish, their skin bore the marks of age. They were no longer young. Father Time was not their ally but yet another amorphous concept with which to do battle.

Even before Encounter, her window of opportunity for raising a family was closing. While there were many ways for her to conceive and develop a life, the natural process had been the most appealing. After Encounter, it had become her sole option. Yet her eggs were aging, and reaching the period where congenital dangers lurked behind the scenes, like hidden enemies.

Without the technology to correct DNA abnormalities, she – and the man with whom Helen Fitzgerald would conceive that child – were at the mercy of essentiality.

And as she had learned, Mother Nature was not always kind and loving.

Hesitantly abandoning one sphere for another, Helen parted her lids. Star Bright's face was pressed close, his eyes peering inquisitively into hers. An overwhelming emotion of peace washed over her, prickling her flesh with goose bumps. It was the type of singular comfort and the peculiar sense of righteousness stemming from the inner knowledge of being absolutely certain life has purpose and meaning. Her lips curved upward in spontaneous acknowledgment of his grace.

"No, Star Bright. He will not hurt you. And in not doing so, he will determine all our fates."

Realigning her position, Helen sighed then bounced on the mattress.

"Shall I be part of your destiny?" he inquired, accurately exhaling as she had done, and thus reminding her of how acutely vulnerable he was to outside influences.

"Mine, and all of *Target's* personnel." Reaching out, Helen allowed him to grasp her fingers and pull her into a sitting posture. The symbolism and his innocent complicity were not lost on her hypersensitive perceptions.

"Joshua and Paula and possibly even Brian believe your technology can save us. What they fail to consider – or care to delve into – is that such a transference of knowledge is a complicated process. It will take time. Time," she concluded, finally meeting his gaze, *"they don't have."*

Star Bright's guileless eyes met hers with silent acknowledgment.

"How do you know?" he whispered. "Are you reading my mind?"

"Perhaps I'm reading Teddy's," she countered, reaching out and taking the stuffed companion from his arms. "Teddy Bear is growing restless. He thinks it would be best if you departed soon. There are places you must be," she added, leaving off on an obscure note she saw no point in clarifying.

"I think you speak truth."

"I won't ask you to stay long. A day, or a week – before the stars summon you back among them. If there is anything safely you can do in that time, I beg you to do so. They may put the request badly, but trust me when I say their need is great. Overlook their trepidation and take pity on their plight."

Star Bright sighed again, a gesture she knew he would keep until the end of his days. It was a peculiar gift to bestow upon an impressionable life form.

"I do not know them... but I will listen to what they ask. I have never before been confronted with..." He groped for the word. "Sacrifice. Mama and Papa did not speak of it, yet I believe such would be their wish. It is so hard," he sighed a third time, "to know what one does not know."

Helen shivered as realization struck. That was another "gift" she had presented to the little alien: suffering, for the sake of another. As presents went, it was a dubious acquisition.

Star Bright jiggled on the gently flowing mattress.

"I would like to think I have... friends in the universe."

"You will always have one."

It was an awesome concept, expanding his horizons with limitless possibilities. With it came much responsibility. Nudging her with his nose, Star Bright breathed softly into her face.

"I am greatly frightened."

On a bed which might have been, but was not, her bridal chamber, Helen Fitzgerald contemplated love.

"We are all greatly frightened."

It was a difficult statement to follow through on. She fleetingly wondered what Jingles would say, and then she recalled Paula, teasing Brian on the Skip. Perhaps none of them were as old as they thought they were.

Just as the universe was constantly expanding, so too were their lives. There were always lessons to be learned, new concepts assimilated. Some of them even held the potential for great wonder.

Star Bright was a child of the universe. As with Joshua and Helen, he, too, was growing up.

"I will go with you to *Target.*"

Across the room, the simulated ivy, which too had a life of its own, rustled gently against the wall. Like computer games, whispering spirits of departed friends and Mama and Papa, it seemed to realize the value of the final frontier – discovering humanity in the least likely places.

Chapter 32

Teddy Bear sat on the right-hand command chair, paws placed outward in a position of readiness. His glass eyes were trained on the viewscreen, upon which hovered the image of the star cruiser *Target*. With a little effort, Helen could see the crippled ship reflected in those two bright orbs.

On the panel just beyond the monitor, a bowl of fruit and fresh bread had been set, so that he might not go hungry in their absence. *Mantarry,*

Helen remembered, was his favorite food. She also knew Teddy would not eat while they were gone. Fasting, too, was a form of sacrifice.

At another time, she might have considered the gift a waste. With her own people starving, a bowl of berries might save a life. Yet there was no reprimand or loss. No gesture of love, she was learning, was ever wasted.

Nor did she have to ask again if Star Bright might prefer to take his friend with him on the journey. She understood a part of him had to be left behind, safeguarding *Here* from the unknown. And keeping his seat warm.

"Why don't you put some music on, to keep him company?" she asked, instead.

"No. Whatever I played I would never listen to again," he responded. She accepted the logic.

Shoving aside her vague doubts of betrayal, Helen followed him to the bay. Gone was her jovial mood of only hours before, when she was to travel through space in a protective bubble. His nervousness, she supposed, was affecting her. That was the easiest and most obvious explanation, and kept her thoughts from darker concerns.

"I'll stay by your side," she had promised Star Bright. "I will never leave you alone for a moment while we're on *Target.*"

"He will not like that," her friend had responded, and she knew it for truth.

"He understands the conditions."

The terms between she and Joshua had been unspoken. That he would uphold them, however, was a tacit promise less binding than either's acceptance of "Will you marry me?"

"Ready."

Helen gave a thumb's up, then suddenly laughed as he copied her gesture.

"Why have I amused you? Have I done something wrong?"

It was the tension-breaker they needed. Helen pounded on her chest, simulating great prowess.

"Me. The 'great communicator'; author of the universal translator, yet I pass along an 'all's well' with body language."

"You taught me," Star Bright bragged, copying the action from memory. "In an… exchange of ideas. Just as your people wish me to teach them. That is good. But, you did not explain the significance."

Her dumbfounded expression made him grin.

"We'll ask Teddy when we get back. I'm sure he'll know. It probably has something to do with extracting a paw from a jar of honey. And as to that, you will just have to wait for an explanation."

"Is it a good one?" he hopefully inquired.

"The best," she promised as the liquid film of the protective bubble spun upward around her. When he, too, had been sheathed in translucence, they emerged together, close enough to touch. "But I'll give you a hint. It's about a bear named Winnie the Pooh and a little boy called Christopher Robin. They get in a lot of mischief."

"I like the sound of that."

"I thought you would."

As thoughts went, it was a much better way to begin a journey than with long faces and uncertain expectations.

Held within was also the promise they would return.

A red carpet, procured from Who Knows Where, the country bordering the Land of Nod, had been set out in the receiving chamber. Jingles played a rendition of a Calopien marching tune on his flute. Sheafs of a cloth-like material, rolled together, then pulled outward and serrated to resemble palm leaves, were flourished by the crew.

Captain Terry, attired in a uniform reconfigured to reflect his promotion in rank, met them at the door. Saluting him with arms held at right angles, fingers interlaced in the recognized greeting of peace, he gracefully dipped his head in welcome.

"Enter as guest," he invited the wide-eyed alien.

"I come in peace," Star Bright countered, clasping his hands together, then remembering his lesson and offering the thumbs up. Brian Hardy, at Terry's side, immediately reciprocated.

"Good to have you aboard. Let me introduce myself again. I am affectionately called Brother Brian. I serve as minister and cultural liaison aboard *Target*. You have met Captain Terry and Commander Burbone."

Paula extending the stump of her right arm.

"I offer you my own, personal token of welcome."

Star Bright obligingly touched the pink flesh with his open palm. It was the first time they had touched and incidentally obliterated her doubt of his corporeal stability.

"You are most kind."

Sneaking a glance at Helen, she nodded approvingly, then steered him through the passageway created by eager bodies.

"This is our crew," she introduced as they passed. A hand was extended; others jammed in, close but respectfully.

"Lamar Porteous, security officer, sir. Cross-training for a little bit of everything else." Pushing back a strand of reddish hair, he uncovered a forehead of freckles. Star Bright pulled back in shock, then bounced on the balls of his feet exactly as Brian was doing.

"Spots!"

"Freckles," Lamar proudly explained. "I've heard it said the more freckles a person has, the more intelligent he is."

"His father told him that," Katherine Bacce kidded, poking Lamar in the side. "He had a mess of them."

"A mess?" Star Bright exclaimed, eagerly demanding an explanation.

"A whole lot."

"'Mess,' is slang," Helen clarified, caught in the exuberance, then giving permission for him to touch the "spotted" skin. Star Bright did so with profound appreciation.

"Do they... rub off?" he asked, glancing at his clean hand.

"No –"

"They sure do," Katherine overlapped. "Since this voyage began, he's lost more than half. Which directly relates to his drop in brain power."

"Freckles are a personal characteristic; inherited from a parent or grandparent. In the same way as hair color or eye shade."

"Oh. Wonderful. I did not know. Already, I am learning new... ideas."

"Come on, now. Stand back," Brian urged, attempting to clear the path which had shrunken to a vague, meandering trail. "Everyone will get their turn."

"The 'mess' of you," the guest reiterated, excited to use his new word. "I am... humbled by your outpouring of... friendship."

Sensing him shake at the magnitude of the sensory input, Helen easily slipped her hand in his, guiding him ahead of the crowd.

"Where shall we go?" she asked Joshua, craning her head upward as he joined them at the head of the parade.

"Wherever he wishes." Then, to Star Bright, "Would you like a tour of the ship, or would you prefer a moment of privacy to compose yourself?"

The question was more than he could answer, so Helen replied for him.

"The bridge, I think, and then Level Two."

"As you say."

With a surreptitious glance at Burbone, he guided the procession down the corridor and into the roundabout. Brian squeaked in, just as the door slid shut.

"Bridge," came the verbal command. The elevator lurched, then began its slow trek upward. Star Bright stared with wonder at the conveyance, prompting the captain to explain. "Before we struck the dark matter, there were thirty-six working lifts. Most were destroyed or rendered useless by Encounter. Those that survived operate at below the normal standard. This particular roundabout is the only one that reaches the bridge."

The points of Star Bright's eyebrows touched as he considered the implications.

"Having but one elevator to such a critical area appears...." He searched for a way to express his thought. "Dangerous. You might have been stranded."

As accurate as the observation was, no one expected him to draw that logical conclusion. Without obvious discomfiture, the commanding officer tapped the lift wall.

"You're absolutely correct." Spoken without suspicion, he succeeded in quelling doubts. "In fact, it's a design flaw," he emphasized, having found the descriptive word Star Bright missed. "I've given considerable thought to the problem."

Rather than accept the explanation, the alien pressed him. Taking them both in, Helen was struck by the fact of their disparate appearances. Terry was a head taller, with sharp, chiseled features, while Star Bright's smooth, gently curved face and short stature made him appear as only half grown. The wisdom and experience in their eyes were a match, however, canceling any advantage one might have had over the other.

"What did you conclude?"

As the only woman present, Helen began to speak, hoping her intervention would lesson any tension stemming from this unexpected critique, but Joshua motioned her to silence, signifying he was comfortable with his answer.

"*Target* was designed by engineers primarily as a vessel of exploration – not war. Her mission is one of non-aggression. While there is the capacity for defensive counter-measures, she is not truly constructed for battle."

The roundabout temporarily ceased its upward progression, shuddered, then resumed the climb.

"That is a good answer." Star Bright's head bobbed eagerly. "One to which I can relate." Repeating Terry's gesture, he tapped the wall, listening to the hollow reverberation. "To smaller space crafts, however, *Target* appears – overwhelming. It is the largest ship I have ever encountered. Were I to have come upon it unprepared, I might have taken it for a... conqueror."

"That," Joshua quickly responded, placing a hand on Helen's arm, "is why we have so distinguished a linguist aboard. One well-versed in conveying our peaceful intent."

Meant as both a compliment and an end to the discussion, he was taken back by Star Bright's adamant rebuttal.

"It is not enough. One person cannot speak for the whole. Nor can words alone be trusted."

Fearing an open confrontation, Brian casually slipped between the two parties.

"But I'm sure you've found our Helen a more than adequate representative of our species."

"I have found her," Star Bright articulated, "unique." After making eye contact with Hardy, he seemed content to let the matter rest. "Going to the top." While the word was not new to him, its use in context with assertion was. "It is so... peculiar for me to think of moving upward three levels. My world is only two. This is exciting."

Reaching the bridge, the passengers held back, allowing Terry the right of first exit. Smiling graciously, he swept out his arm, in the custom of good manners.

"Honored guest and lady, first."

Because she knew he was remembering her admonition to knock before entering a foreign environment, Helen winked before rapping her knuckles lightly on the lift frame. Her action stimulated Star Bright, for he bound forward with unbridled enthusiasm.

"So big!" the stranger gasped, awed by the enormity of the oval space. Dancing around on tiptoe, he spun in a circular motion, attempting to absorb the undreamt-of sights. "How many are here?"

"If we were functioning with a full contingent, there would be between eight and twelve. The captain sits in the central chair," Joshua directed. "That way, he has a three-hundred and sixty degree view. The second in command – that was my position before I assumed the captaincy – sits there. To the right of the main viewscreen is the helmsman and beside him, the navigator.

"Beyond those stations, as you follow around the command center, sits the data processor, the astronomer and the communications officer. To the left is the engineer, if so required. Other areas function for a science officer and whatever technical crew might be required at any given time."

"He means me," Brian elucidated.

"And me," Helen completed. "If we encounter life forms which do not understand our language, then it becomes my place to work out a method of communication."

"That is very important," Star Bright gushed, greatly impressed. "Show me where you are placed."

"Here," Helen demonstrated, crossing to a station to the left rear of the captain's chair. He inched along behind, hesitantly touching the panel she used.

"So far back. You should be toward the front," came his protest, spoken in an undertone of respect.

"Sit down," Brian offered, coming up behind them. "With your permission, of course," he addressed to Helen.

"Certainly."

"I dare not."

"Please do. I would be honored."

It was only the pleading of her avowal which finally prompted Star Bright to sit. Placed in her position, he breathed in the air belonging to her, then reverently swiped his palm across the console.

"So much responsibility."

"I'm seldom needed," she demurred.

"That's because Dr. Fitzgerald is developing a system which allows us to translate many forms of speech into English," Brian clarified for her. "Without it, we would have a great deal of difficulty communicating our peaceful intentions. Just as your people must have done, Star Bright," he concluded, resting his hand on the chair back. "You speak English flawlessly."

Looking up over his shoulder, the youthful alien smiled tenderly.

"When I first became aware of Helen, I – used her thoughts to teach me. It was...." He struggled for the word. "An excitement for me. Or perhaps I mean to say it was a challenge," he abruptly amended. "An... exercise."

"Why do you say that?" Joshua thoughtfully inquired, moving up beside Helen.

"There are some species which do not wish to be friendly. Speaking with them is not interpreted as a peaceful act."

Rotating slowly in Helen's chair, he gave the console a final scrutiny before averting his eyes. There was in the gesture a finality, bespeaking both a hello and a good-bye. From that moment, he never again let his eyes rest there. Instead, he focused them on the wide viewscreen.

"In my travels, I have 'discovered' many species, some as divergent to... us... as to defy belief. Others were similar in body shape; some, perhaps in temperament."

Without reacting, Helen absorbed the statement, realizing that with only limited contact he had grasped words and concepts not verbalized.

"Did you ever attempt to contact any of them?" Brian asked, perching himself on the workstation, then busying himself adjusting controls that were, he might have presumed, still nonfunctional from Encounter.

Star Bright waited so long it appeared he would not answer.

It became Helen's turn.

"Hailed them? Spoke directly to them?"

"Once. You know," he whispered.

"And the other times? Did you contact them psychically? The way you did Helen?" It was Joshua who wanted to know. Without intending, he leaned forward, straining to hear the answer, however quietly enunciated.

His effort was wasted as the questioned did not respond.

"I have found," he chose to articulate, instead, "it is better to leave well enough alone. What is your expression? Non-intervention. It is not easy to guess from the external design of a ship what is meant," he concluded, clasping his hands together.

"But they might have become friends," the cleric objected.

"Or the opposite."

Terry had had enough of the interchange between veiled meanings.

"What do you consider us?"

Slowly unlocking his fingers from the display of peace, Star Bright swept them across the vista of represented space. Immediately the scene changed. Different stars filled the void.

"What do you wish me to consider you?"

It was difficult for any of the three viewers to interpret Star Bright's intent. Or, whether he actually caused the screen to change. Repairs on the bridge had not been completed. It was doubtful but not inconceivable to believe the movement of his hand had only appeared to affect what they saw.

The question lingered too long unanswered for any to assume responsibility for replying to his interrogative. Instead, Helen opted for a complete change.

"Why don't we go to Level Two? Star Bright, do you feel up to spending some time with the crew?"

"I believe I do," came the gracious response. Meeting her eyes with a calm, steady gaze, he held it a moment, then smiled. The radiance she read there was as genuine as her trust she held in those waiting below.

"Good. It's very exciting for us to have a new face aboard," she continued, taking his hand. Gliding effortlessly across the floor, he followed, as though they were only whole when attached. "Very few of our crewmembers actually have the opportunity of greeting guests. This will be a first for them."

"Why is that?"

"It's a quirk of human nature," Hardy explained for her as he trailed behind. "We wish to introduce our alien guests to what our star command considers the 'best and brightest specimens.' That includes ranking officers, heads of select departments. Unwittingly, of course, what we do is reveal only the 'safe' side of our nature. Those trained in diplomacy. What we leave out are the individuals; those who represent a more accurate cross-section of humanity. Coming, Captain?"

The three were in the roundabout by the time he finished. The captain curtly replied in the negative, but the expression on his face softened the denial.

"I think I'll remain here awhile; at least until I'm relieved. I hope you find the party we have planned for you enjoyable, Star Bright."

The "Thank you" was lost as the elevator closed behind the words.

Decorating Level Two had become something of a priority for the crew, and the anticipated arrival of the stranger proved no exception. A banner, pieced together with squares of multi-colored cloth proclaimed, "Welcome!" while computer-generated images of Earth had been affixed to the walls. The impression was one of pride as much as aesthetic value.

All stood as Star Bright entered. Eyes wide with the wonder of it all, he looked first at the images of the blue planet, then slowly, as though he dared not take it in all at once, he viewed the crew. Each, in their turn smiled, or made a small bow or raised a hand in greeting. When he had completed the circuit, he turned to Helen, seemingly exchanging a thought with her. When she nodded, it became obvious to those of the crew carefully dissecting his actions, he was, in fact, capable of reading minds.

More certain of his action after receiving confirmation, Star Bright smiled and gave them the thumps-up. They responded with sheers and yips of "Hurray!"

"Here, Captain Star Bright," Jingles offered, indicating the borrowed chair at the head of the table. "The place of honor is for you."

He did not miss the significance of the title bestowed on him or the regal chair Jingles offered.

"I do not feel... fine accepting such an honor. Let Helen sit there."

"No," she quickly demurred. "It's a gift for you."

Studying the throne, he quietly held up his hands.

"It belongs to him."

It required a moment for her to register his statement.

"You mean Captain Terry?"

"I do."

Jingles stepped forward, nearer, but not close enough to touch the little alien.

"It was mine, Captain Star Bright. While it's true I did give it to Captain Terry, I've been... missing it. I'm a big man and it fits me just right. But, you're the baby bear, and it's big enough for you to play in."

Ignorant of the reference, Star Bright frowned.

"Teddy is the bear –"

Helen chuckled in genuine amusement.

"Jingles is speaking of an Earth story. A children's bedtime tale, of the type Mama and Papa read to you. It's called 'Goldilocks and the Three Bears.' In this house live three bears: a Papa and a Mamma and a baby bear and their furniture was designed to fit their bodies. Papa's was the biggest, Mama's was middle-sized and Baby's was the smallest. What Jingles is alluding to is that being the child, Baby Bear, liked to pretend he was big and sit in Papa's chair."

"And when he did," Jingles finished the translation for her, "he *was* the Papa Bear. So, having you sit in my chair makes you more important than all of us. Meaning," he grinned, showing a profusion of teeth, "you outrank us, which is proper for an invited guest."

Star Bright tried to digest the story.

"Why does Papa Bear outrank Mama Bear?"

Having anticipated his question, Helen was quick with her answer.

"Because in Jingles' story, Joshua Terry figuratively becomes Mama Bear."

The crew laughed and clapped.

Star Bright still didn't quite understand.

"You wish me to outrank Captain Terry?"

"You, sir," Jingles bowed, "are the senior officer, having been a captain longer than he has."

"If that is so, then I shall sit there."

He snuggled into the throne, placed his hands on the armrests and savored the feeling of power.

"I like this," he agreeably acknowledged before raising his hand in an imperious gesture and waving it around the circle of those standing around the table. "But, it is not right. I wish my... new friends to be equal. I therefore declare that while we are here, we are all the same. No one outranks the other."

"And Mama Bear?" Helen teased.

"Since he is not here, he may maintain his rank as... not senior captain." More laughter followed his pronouncement. "But, explain, please. What of 'Goldilocks' from the title. Where does this bear fit into the story?"

"Goldilocks wasn't a bear. She was a little girl; a human," Helen tried. "She was out in the woods – a forest of trees. You understand?" He nodded. "She was tired and hungry and she saw the house of the Three Bears so she went inside. They weren't home, so she ate their porridge – their meal – and slept in Baby Bear's bed."

"Without asking permission?"

"She was very young and didn't know any better. When the bears come home, she awakens, is frightened and runs away."

"In the version I know," Lamar Porteous laughed, "the bears follow and eat her instead of their porridge."

"That isn't how it goes," Helen protested in annoyance. "She ran away, promising to be a good girl from then on," but Star Bright pounced on the first ending.

"Do not tell what is not true, Friend Helen," he corrected. "You must always speak truth to me. The bears ate her."

Suddenly very frightened, Helen tried a reassuring smile.

"There are many endings to the story. It's a fable, actually. I gave you the one I prefer."

"Then, say that, so I make up my own mind."

"I apologize. I always tell you the truth, but if there are multiple interpretations, I'll make every attempt to explain them to you."

Stepping forward, Janice Miles broke the conversation by holding out a clear-sided container.

"This is our treat jar," she explained, easily and with enthusiasm. "It's filled with candy. We wish you to take from it whatever you wish."

Star Bright looked to Helen for an explanation.

"Candy. Sweets. A pleasant taste very much appreciated by humans. Somewhat similar to mantarry."

"Then, I will take one for Teddy Bear." He reached into the jar, selected one the color of his own berries and wrapped it in his hand. After a second, he nodded. "I understand. 'Sweet.' Yes, Teddy may like this. He thanks you."

Disappointed he had not eaten it, LaTanya Carson was the next to offer a treat.

"Here, Star Bright, is some radish sprouts we've grown in hydroponics. They haven't made radishes, but the leaves are tangy. They're the first we've harvested. We want you to try them."

If the candy proved odd to him, the sprouts appeared far stranger. Running his palm over the small plate, his fingers vibrated from the sensations received.

"What are you doing, Star Bright?" Winston Rey asked.

"They are talking to me. Did you not know they are alive?"

"Alive, yes, but... they don't talk to us."

"What do you do with them?"

"We eat them. For food."

"They do not understand this. It has never been explained to them. That is not right." He pushed the plate away. "I will not eat them."

The rejection of so precious a gift and the reason for the denial dampened the spirits of those around him. Before the situation could deteriorate further, Brian stepped forward.

"What we'd like to do, Star Bright, if you've no objection, is to share some of our personal stories with you. As a means of teaching you about Earth and Earth people."

"Yes," he responded with a sharper agreement than anticipated. "Tell me about yourself."

Surprised and ill-prepared, Brian shook his head.

"The others –"

"I want to hear your story. Speak about Brian Hardy."

"Yes, Brian," Helen encouraged in a tone not to be disobeyed. "Tell all of us about yourself."

"Oh," he dismissed. "I have all sorts of stories, but none are fit for innocent ears."

"I will have them," Star Bright insisted. "They sound interesting. All of us," he suddenly decided, "would like to hear not-innocent stories."

"In that case, I'll have to think of some."

"Sit. And regale us."

The use of the word he had not previously used and had never heard, caused the smile to slip from Brian's face. He sat and slipped into a casual posture.

"Once upon a time –"

"No! I do not wish a 'fable.' Speak truth."

"I was being facetious. I apologize."

"And do not use words you think I do not know for the sake of... amusement."

The shock on Brian's face was all too apparent. Rapidly recalculating, he strove to find an appropriate tale. Finding his literary bag of tricks empty, his heart started racing and his breath came quickly and rapidly.

"Please. Call on someone else."

"I think this is some of your stage presence, Dr. Hardy. Come. Helen tells me you are amusing. Tell us about the drink of water you refused the fallen man. Who was he? Someone of little importance?"

Brian's eyes narrowed in fury as his fists clenched.

"If you're reading my mind you know who He is. And, it never happened."

Star Bright arched an eyebrow.

"Never?"

"Never to *me!*" Brian screamed. "I placed myself in an historical event where I had no right to be. I was testing myself – to see if I had the courage to withstand the Roman soldiers – and what would surely happen to me."

"What would that be?"

There was no innocence in the question.

"Ridicule; harsh judgment. A loss of status."

"Surely, more than that," the listener encouraged.

"A sword between the ribs! Yes; that's what I feared."

"That would be too quick. The soldiers were in a playful mood. They asked for the crowd to free one and they demanded Barabbas. That left an empty... what is it you call it? A cross." He smiled in remembrance. "Room for one more. Up you go, Brother Brian. Nails through your palms and nails through your feet. But, no broken bones. That is significant, is it, not?"

Hands over his ears, Brian cried, "I'm not listening."

"But, you are. You hear every word I say. What then, man of God? You are beside the Son, sharing His agony. And if the soldiers shout, 'Which one?' again, do you not beg to hear, 'Give us Brian!'"

"No! No!" yet he meant, "Yes! Yes!"

"And they listen. Why not? They have done this before. Your toga is not worth casting dice for. So, they let you down and you lie in the dirt? To die, Father Hardy? Nay. To wait. You know the time where others do not. Three days. Mary will come. The stone will be thrown back. The Son shall emerge, not dead and not alive, but reborn into ethereal filaments that He can make whole to prove his Resurrection to the Doubters. Mary arrives but the stone does not move. There is no glorious appearance. She goes away weeping, leaving you behind. You, who now know the awful truth."

Standing on shaky legs, face red, tears streaming down his face, Brian Hardy waved a fist at Star Bright.

"It wasn't like that!"

"No. You are correct. It was not like that. But, I was not recounting events as they were. I was telling the tale with which you torture yourself. Oh, yea of little faith," he mocked.

"Bastard —"

"No!" Leonard Broderick startled them with his demand. Attention turned in his direction. "I don't want to hear Brother Brian's story. I want to hear one of my own. It's said among us you can do anything. That's why the Captain asked us what we dreamed."

"Did he?"

"To present you with a list — of what we wanted. So you can make miracles."

Stunned by the incorrect interpretation he, and at least some of the crew had put on their test, Paula tried to contain him.

"No, Leonard. That wasn't the reason. It was a simple exercise in imagination; a game. We were trying to cheer you up by offering a treat. No one was to lose. You all won. A piece of candy," she stressed.

"But, look," Star Bright interrupted, holding up the candy he had saved for Teddy. "Perhaps he is more right than any of you know. For, I have 'won' the treat without even playing the game. And all of you have lost."

Pursuing his original thought, Leonard shoved the candy jar toward the head of the table.

"Take it all. None of us will care. Just use your power. Tell me of my wife and daughter. Let me speak with them. They must think us dead." He wiped his nose, then smeared his face by running the back of his hand over his eyes. "Alert the Space Command. Give them our coordinates. Explain what happened. Encounter. We're crippled. Tell them to send a rescue ship."

"Stop!" Helen ordered. "Enough of this. I don't know what 'game' you played, but you've been misled. Star Bright doesn't have these powers."

"He does! He does! Help us! We're so alone."

The accusation both shocked and dismayed those gathered for a party which had disintegrated before their eyes. While there was no way to salvage the moment, Brian put an end to whatever chance they had by stepping forward. Face as ashen as Broderick's was red, he waved a fist at the two standing apart from the others.

"What powers do you have, Star Bright?" he demanded.

Helen took responsibility for replying in his stead.

"Powers, you better hope to God he doesn't have, Dr. Hardy, because you'd be the first he used them on. On my recommendation."

His hands went out in a threatening gesture. Star Bright copied his exact position, appearing small and helpless against the larger, full-grown man. Physical intimidation was not to carry the fight, however, because a shove in Brian's direction sent him flying across the room. Falling at Janice Miles' feet, she hurriedly stooped to check him.

"He's dead."

Everyone in the room turned to stone.

Chapter 33

Jingles recovered faster than anyone else. Pushing his large body between the prone man and the officer, he put a hand to Brian's carotid.

"No. He's not. He's just stunned."

Grabbing the cleric by his shoulders, he got him to his feet. As blood and oxygen returned to his face, Brian struggled with the engineer, who did not let him go.

"Damn you," he cursed, upsetting the crew more than if he had actually risen from the dead. "I knew it. You do have powers. Ones greater than Helen led us to believe." He glowered at her before turning back to the alien. "What sort of energy did you harness to fling me away like that?"

Star Bright started at him a long beat before finally blinking.

"No power. You came into my sphere and I held my hands out, pushing you back. It was that overmatching your forward progression which caused you to propel backwards." He turned to his companion, tears welling in his eyes. "I have never harmed a living creature and now your people have placed me in a position to do bad. Momma and Papa will never forgive me."

Brian stomped to draw attention back upon himself.

"You read my mind. Pulled the shame of that incident from the depths of my soul. Captain Terry is right; you're not what you seem. What other strange attributes do you possess? Have you corrupted Helen's mind? Made her see you as quiet and gentle when you're nothing more than a wolf in sheep's clothing?"

For a moment, his statement elicited confusion in the creature so addressed, diverting him from his moral agony.

"What does that mean? A wolf in sheep's clothing?"

"Oh, for God's sake," Brian shot back, curling his lips upward to reveal teeth.

As confused as the rest, for she hadn't seen Star Bright touch Hardy, Helen held up her hands for patience. Instinct warned her to address the question rather than go back to the flying minister.

"Another fable from long ago. A wolf is a four-legged predator that hunts defenseless animals called sheep for food. In order to lure one of the gullible ones toward him, he wrapped himself in a sheepskin to make him appear to be a sheep so the flock wouldn't sense danger. Thus, the expression conveys the idea of deceit and trickery."

He appeared to comprehend the idea slowly.

"I am accused of being a wolf? Of wanting to eat you?"

"Of being worse than that," Brian snapped.

"Shut up! Paula, take him out of here." The communicator complied without protest. When they were gone, Helen faced the crew. "I'm sorry. This is my fault." To Star Bright," she added, "I apologize to you, too."

He began to shake.

"I was trying to be like him. I thought that was… expected. That I not appear strange to you." He moved his head from side to side. "I cannot read minds; I can only feel what is there on the surface and translate it. I thought… it was what he wanted. A game. I see now I was in error. The same way your Joshua Terry was when he doubted me. He doubted you, too. His game was meant to see how far I could… deceive. To see if I have… tricked you into seeing only that I wish you to envision. It is…" He struggled for the word. "Sad."

"Yes, Star Bright. It is. Worse than sad; it's tragic because by doing so he has destroyed any chance we have of befriending you as a group. Of...asking you to help us."

The alien was not ready to address her open plea.

"It was not a nice way. He may think of me as a wolf, but you are not a... gullible sheep. I have not lied to you."

"I never doubted."

"Then, you must be a wolf, too."

"Neither one of us are wolves."

His left arm curled upward in the position it might be, were he cuddling Teddy Bear.

"Then, what are we?"

"Two like souls on a ship filled with aliens."

"No." Both turned to stare at Jingles, who had almost been forgotten in the melee. Pushing his way forward, he held out both hands, palms up. "I'm hardly one to speak for the crew because I've gone through my... wolf period, too. There was a time when I thought only of myself and my two technicians. I stole food. I was found out and I regretted my action. I lied to Captain Terry...." His hands started trembling but he refused to drop them. "To cover my misdeed. And then, I believed my lie which maybe was only partly a lie. I've had a long time in the solitary confinement of my mind to consider. My actions; the actions of the others. I've had to judge what life means to me and by doing that, I discovered who I really was. Not an engine, but a very fragile and... sad human being."

Knotting his fingers together, he scanned the faces watching him. "Joshua Terry thinks because he's the captain it's up to him to save us. He's wrong. It's up to each of us to save one another – including him. And to forgive when we see the frailty in others. Brian Handy isn't a wolf, either, Mr. Star Bright. He's a man who feels he has let not only himself but the entire ship down. Before you came, he was our 'magic man.' Maybe even a little bit of a god; or one gifted with extraordinary blessings bestowed by God. Too much has happened for him to believe that, now, and he feels hollowed-out inside."

Moving closer to Star Bright and Helen, he hesitated, waiting to see if he, too, were to be propelled backward. When neither made an aggressive move, he pursued his speech. "We wanted this party to go so well. We were so excited. Had we stopped to examine it, we could have seen this coming. Not because you weren't welcome: because we invited you for the wrong reason."

"I have divined that," Star Bright sadly acknowledged.

"Instead of offering an unconditional friendship, each of us wanted something from you. We sought answers: a planet we could settle on; the news from… Earth. Redemption from real and imagined sins. A solution that would repair our ship. We hoped you'd have some way to save our plants, or share with us some of yours." His head bowed. "I don't have the right to apologize for everyone, but for myself, I beg your forgiveness." He swallowed, trying to re-discover his voice. "Just once, before you go, I'd like to play my flute for you."

"Yes," Star Bright agreed. Not in answer, but an acknowledgment time was running out. "I must go." Arms going slack and legs weakening, he fought to stay on his feet. "But, before I do, I should like to see your hydroponics." Reaching out his hands, he took one of Helen's and one of Jingles. "Perhaps that is why I was summoned here. For them. Why I was drawn across space."

"Not the only reason," Helen corrected with a firmness of one who was making a mental journey around a circle. "But, I think now isn't the time. We should go back to *Here*. Teddy Bear is getting lonely."

His eyes lowered for a moment before he replied.

"He is not lonely." Before she could argue, he began to sway, then tottered over. If she hadn't been holding his hand he would have fallen.

"This is too much for him," she cried. "Please, Jingles, help," she cried, struggling to hold him. Grabbing an arm, the engineer attempted to draw Star Bright away, but he struggled, finally freeing himself from their grip.

"Hydroponics; I will see the plants."

Shooting Jingles a tortured look, Helen tried to dissuade the little alien, but he fought her, forging ahead of them. The crew cleared a path and he left the doomed party room with the colorful streamers and the candy jar bearing mute testimony to its failure, and stumbled down the corridor.

"Get Captain Terry," she ordered to any who might respond, and then, somewhat confusedly, "Where is he? And Paula. Bring her. We need help."

Star Bright responded by jerking away, eyes rolling around in their sockets.

"Plants! Plants!" he called in a pitiful voice. "Where are you?" Although Hydroponics wasn't labeled, Star Bright's heightened senses alerted him to what lay behind closed doors. Heading down the corridor, his face contorted in agony. "No. No! I am the magic man. I have been brought here to help. Let me go!"

Because their credulity was no less great than the others, his two companions followed, shimmering with an awesome expectation of fear and hope. Oblivious to their needs, Star Bright threw out his arms, compelled by the madness of the moment, to engulf this new and terrible challenge. The wild gleam of his eyes, copied from a character resurrected from a long ago first edition that may once have belonged to another crewmember, gone mad but not forgotten, was too similar to ignore.

"My God!" Helen screamed, pushing those who might come closer to the man-monster, shaped, so it was written, in God's image, away from her with a physical shove. "Get Joshua! Bring him down here. This has gone terribly wrong."

Lamar Porteous, who had followed close behind, hesitated then took it upon himself to follow the order, leaving the Earth woman who had rescinded her title as a language expert, and the Earth man who had confessed his origins were not circuits and metals, along the abandoned star child, crossing into the greenhouse where they were suddenly alone with the languishing plants.

Turning one way and then the other in miserable confusion, Star Bright moaned, then put his hands to his ears.

"Too loud; the cries for help, too loud."

Tempted to rip his hands down, tear at his flesh and drag him away from the impending disaster, Helen could not, for even she believed she could hear the dying gasps of wilted cuttings and shriveled root systems.

Not unlike the desolate outlay of what had once been Sick Bay II, Hydroponics was a deserted battlefield, strewn with the remnants of defeat. Standing like bookends at opposite ends of an uneven contest, an appalling carnage of turgorless "soldiers" spread themselves out from behind misted glass. The gulf of emotion spanning the three people was little more hopeful.

Star Bright did not dally from social mores, nor did he stand on ceremony. With a semi-articulate cry of strangulation, he raced around the rows, pausing, on occasion to stare through a partition; at others, rushing by so fast he could have detected no more than a blur.

"Wrong, wrong, all wrong."

"Stop," Helen pleaded, attempting to intercept and impede his forward progress, then abandoning her efforts as useless, instinctively aware he was too upset, too agitated to listen. "Tell me what's wrong, then," she continued, hoping, at least, to drain his energy by picking his brain.

She only served to heighten his frustration. Coming to a screeching halt no more than two meters from her, he extended his fingers. They were not directed at her, but rather toward his own mouth, as though he needed to drag the proper phrases from his throat.

What he said, however, came out garbled, twisted, incoherent, the syllables running together in a series of high- and low-pitched utterances. It was only after identifying the language that she expelled a breath.

"Speak English. I can't understand you. English." For a moment he failed to translate her foreign words Shaking his head in frustrated agony, he repeated the same sequence.

"Haka. Holar watto."

"Take your time. You're speaking in your own language. I haven't learned enough of it to understand."

Contorting himself into the shape of a pretzel, Star Bright twisted and struggled with his sentences, failing to rediscover their common ground.

"Perhaps if we go outside –" she suggested, trying and failing to draw his attention away, yet he was in a fit, or more precisely, a state of shock. The input was too great, the responsibility, the cries of his own mind drowning out maturity, refashioning Star Bright into a five-year-old again, with no one to help him.

"Me-le-grann."

"Come with me, please. Into the corridor. Away from all this."

Grabbing him by the elbow, Helen attempted to bodily drag him from Hydroponics. He squirted away, bones turning to shapeless masses beneath her touch. With her own temples throbbing from explosive pressure, she released him, screaming the two words she knew they held in common.

"Teddy Bear!"

The key partially unlocked his rampaging train of thought. His tongue, cloven to the roof of his mouth, reformed, converting his energy waves into articulate syllables.

"Teddy Bear."

"Yes," came the hurried repetition. "Teddy Bear. I am Helen. You are Star Bright."

Deflated by the snapping sinews, Star Bright sagged away, dropped into a squatting position, then flopped to the floor on hands and knees. She would have raised him, but for the sudden reappearance of Brian Hardy. Her silent plea for help was quickly negated.

"Leave him alone to work through this," the minister warned, calmer, now, and frightfully aware of the consequences intervention might bring.

"Joshua?"

His lips pursed in guilt before admitting failure.

"He wasn't on the bridge. Porteous couldn't find him."

"Wabba."

Star Bright crawled on the floor, but not, as she supposed, as an adult regressed to infancy, but as a man seeking first to understand himself before transmitting a monumental discovery onto others.

"Sauris re-lenton." And then a cry, for what was and what is, in both past and present tense. "Help me."

Raising a hand from the floor he held it out in supplication. Stepping beyond Helen, Brian offered his assistance, hoisting the alien to his feet.

"Steady, now."

Star Bright wavered, swayed forward but halted his fall before tumbling toward the minister.

"Help me."

"Not physically, Brian," Helen urgently warned, all too aware of what the consequences might be. "Star Bright, what are you looking for?"

The words had not returned. He was forced back to their former meeting place.

"Teddy Bear."

"He isn't here; you left him –"

She was waved off with an abrupt sweep of his elongated palm through the air. Then, just as urgently, he beckoned with that same hand.

"Teddy Bear."

Brian's fingers snapped.

"Not Teddy Bear, the toy. Teddy Bear the concept. Quickly," he urged. "What does 'Teddy Bear' mean?"

"Companionship," she ruminated. "Friendship. Mitigation of loneliness. Star Bright and Teddy Bear."

"Two," Hardy pursued. "The number two. Two times –"

She had it.

"No. It's love!" He's looking for love!"

"What?"

Casting about, she skipped through the long, straight rows, seeking some physical manifestation of emotion. Her eyes lit on the object at the exact moment Star Bright saw it.

By definition, the little potted plant could hardly be construed as "love." More closely resembling a weed than a flower, the multi-pointed green leaves with a thin, twisted stem sat buried in a container the size of a coffee cup. One roundish, purple head similar to that of a thistle, thrust boldly upward.

Set apart from the carefully cultivated plants, it served as a lone desk decoration for the technicians pulling long shifts in Hydroponics. Cradling the plant to his chest, Star Bright finally managed to form a grin on his otherwise twisted features.

"Love," he repeated in precisely Helen's intonation. Language reasserted itself in his brain, soothing the troubled grey mass of turbulent activity. "I see it, now."

Standing under the pale ceiling light, his flesh appeared chalky and moist with dew. But like the purple flower, his eyes sparkled like gems.

"Sit down," she urged, but he was still too restless to comply. Holding his treasure as a shield, Star Bright began a slow retracing of his infant steps, Helen and Brian following at a respectful, almost wondrous distance.

"What you are missing here –" he continued slowly, articulating the words with the delicate precision of a horticulturist.

"Tell us."

"It is what I felt in... this ship when I first arrived... and could not express. It is all around me. Very strong... stronger here."

"What?"

His eyebrows pointed downward toward his nose, accurately reflecting the curvature of his thin, delicate lips.

"A lack of love. No patience. Only... anger."

"Please," Brian pleaded, a lump forming in his throat. "Explain to us. We need to hear this."

Star Bright stared at Helen, pleading with her for confirmation. She nodded mutely, having lost her powers of speech as he regained his.

"Those people... the crew. The one called 'Broderick'." Star Bright brought the plant to his forehead, drawing from it the concept he wished to express. "He is like you, but not like you. He cannot help himself. His heart is heavy. He suffers and you cannot help him."

"Yes...."

"Because you cannot ease his misery, you blame yourselves, and in so doing, you are angry. You anger is directed outward." He thrust the plant toward Brian, who did not accept it. "You have put aside your love because of failure. There are others. You," he indicated, staring at the minister. "You are hurt. You cry inwardly and blame yourself for... lost dreams. Just as your friends have turned away, you... seek an outward cause for your misery. God is to blame. You have turned it backwards. And so you accuse one another of changing. Where once you were one, now you are separate. Everything has become a symbol of your impending deaths."

It was impossible to deny and equally difficult to accept. Brian balled his fist, then just as quickly, released it.

Spinning away on the balls of his feet, Star Bright plucked a leaf from one of the genetically altered plants, running the back of it across his upper lip.

"These plants; you do not love them. They are not living things to you, but food which will not grow. You... hate them. You sacrificed what little you had to help them and your gift was unappreciated. The plants did not thrive."

"It can't be that easy –" Brian protested, wiping his palms on his trousers.

"You," Star Bright accused. "A man of God. I know of God. God is love. You have lost your magic because you have abandoned love."

"What... do you mean?" the minister hesitatingly asked, face stained with shame. Within his question was impotent denial which would not protect him from the alien who "knew God."

"In here; Hydroponics. I felt it but could not say." Star Bright again placed a hand to his temple. "So strong. Too much for me to repeat. I lost my words. I needed to find... mercy? Or, do you say beauty? A... reaching out in kindness. This," he avowed, letting the leaf fall unceremoniously to the deck, then holding forth the purple thistle. "You cannot eat it. It has no function but to be... pretty. It is – innocent. It stands by itself. It does not belong here," he boldly concluded.

"That's LaTanya's plant," Helen correctly identified. "She's an artist. Before Encounter. I suppose she brought it in here because...." She failed to finish, for the truth was painfully apparent.

"To keep her company in a harsh new – environment," he concluded for her. "Because it spoke to her of other times. She asked nothing more of it than that it grow and so it did. This is a beautiful thing; a flower."

"Yes. It is." Helen swallowed bile, feeling the acid burn all the way down her throat.

"Are you saying our plants can't grow because we hate them?" Brian queried, nervously moving away from the tanks as though fearful of an attack.

"That is an answer."

"But there's more to it than that," Hardy protested, playing the devil's advocate because that was his inclination if not his nature. To display his bravery, he took a willful step closer to the plants a moment ago he had feared.

"Horticulture," Star Bright agreed. "The ways and means of making plants thrive. That, I can help you with. But the nurturing – the acknowledgment plants are living beings with a sentience of their own. As alien to you as I am, perhaps, but real and true. You must acknowledge a kinship with them. A shared commonality. You must not take without thanking; to offer assurance of their value to the universe. That communion must come from within your... souls. Without it, you have no... humanity. And do not deserve your place here, among the stars."

Returning the weed to the desk, he sighed, then bowed his head. "You attack, rather than heal. You confront your problems as though they were enemies. The same way," he continued, staring upward through the ceiling, toward the unseen bridge, "you met me. Not as a friend, but as a means of taking that which you need.

"Among yourselves, you wondered why I did not greet you when first you hailed my ship. Why I chose to hide. Why I made contact with Helen Fitzgerald." Her name, spoken so oddly, sent a shiver down the backs of his petitioners. "She, alone among you, was not seeking to extract, but only to give. I discovered her mind in space and found a like being. A... lonely human being. She came to me as friend. You," he concluded, staring at Brian, "came in fear and distrust. In my place, would you have greeted the... soldiers from *Target?*"

"No," he admitted, hollowed to the core of his being. "I beg your forgiveness."

The answer rang with condemnation.

"It is too late."

And so they knew it to be.

Chapter 34

The bubble began forming around the slim shape of the alien before either human realized the significance. It grew like a shimmering rind, beginning from a point near his chest, then expanding outward, simultaneously reaching the top of his head and the tips of his feet.

It was not until the edges sealed that Helen cried.

"No! You can't leave!"

His smile, distorted by the translucence of the film which reflected the muted colors of their surroundings, appeared distant, as though he were already separated by an insurmountable space.

"I cannot, or I may not?"

Struck by the pointed question, Helen recoiled. Looking around the room for some foundation with which to link herself, she found nothing.

"Take me back with you."

To her, Star Bright's smile seemed to fade, although for the second observer, it transformed his face into a radiance of godlike proportions.

"You belong here. With your own kind."

"But I promised. I want to go back. Where," she concluded in a stronger tone, "I am loved for who and what I am."

"I release you," he warned, raising a hand to his lips, the bubble spontaneously altering shape to accommodate his action.

"I don't want to be let go. I want to go with you and Teddy."

"For how long?"

It was a question she was not prepared to answer. Star Bright sympathetically nodded.

"You have a home here. To abandon it means leaving behind all you know. He, whom you cherish above all others."

Helen had not forgotten Joshua, but to hear him described in that way caught her unawares. Turning to Brian, she grabbed him by the arms, shaking the older man with force.

"Where is he? Why isn't he here?"

"I don't know."

"I know."

Star Bright's bold statement sent shivers down her back. Gasping with horror, she redirected her attention toward the alien.

"Where?"

"It has something to do with a paw in a honey jar."

Innocent visions of a stuffed brown bear with sticky amber honey dripping from his hand-stitched nose were quickly replaced by those of a marauding space pirate in the guise of Joshua Terry.

"No! I won't believe that!" And then, weaker and with resignation, "How do you know this?"

"Teddy Bear told me."

"Is Joshua there – aboard your ship? Without permission? You must be mistaken. Please, Brian," she begged, tugging on his uniform. "He went to his quarters; or he has joined the others for the party. Tell me he hasn't gone to *Here."*

"I can't."

"You knew! You knew and you didn't try to stop him," she accused, face livid with betrayal.

"I didn't know."

Once Star Bright had disappeared, Helen shook herself away and raced from the room, directing her path toward her own quarters. There, amid the few personal items she possessed and which would never again offer the security of "home," she activated the small personal monitor. Redirecting the images toward the outside of *Target,* she scanned space, finally honing in on the Skip. It was in temporary orbit around *Here.*

"You devil!" she cursed, spittle flying from her lips. "How could you have done this to me?"

There was no answer, for unlike Star Bright, she had no power to communicate with him through the medium of a stuffed teddy bear.

Setting her jaw, Helen switched off the screen. Retracing her steps, she met Brian in the open corridor.

"He's gone to *Here,* hasn't he? By himself or did someone go with him?" She tried to recall who was absent from the party. "I would have suspected Paula, but she's here. To put up a good front? To make ne believe he was still on the bridge?" Her glance turned harder. "Is that what your breakdown was all about? To divert my attention while Joshua savaged Star Bright's ship?"

He crumpled under the accusation, but shook his head in denial.

"No. My – breakdown – was real enough. And if Paula knew, she didn't let on to me."

"We shall see."

Hardly convinced, she closed her eyes and concentrated. Alarmed, Brian demanded, "What are you doing?"

"Summoning the bubble to take me off this miserable ship."

"You can't do that!"

"Why not?"

"Because he won't be expecting you ." She didn't have to ask the cleric to whom the "he" referred. Or where her concern lay. "Please. Stay here. What's between Joshua and Star Bright has to be settled between them."

"No, Dr. Hardy. You're wrong. I am more intimately involved than Captain Terry. And, perhaps, even Star Bright, himself. It started with me and it will continue along the path I choose."

"You're settling yourself up to stand alone."

Her mouth twisted in an awkward smile.

"I'm just realizing I've always been... if not alone, than an outsider." Weighed down by the enormity of the revelation, she fought through the tendrils of the past which still clung to her. "Joshua was wrong, you must realize," she pursued without losing her concentration on summoning the bubble. "He was meant to be here. Among others of his kind. Destined to command. Left alone in space he would go mad. He needs others to perform for. To... protect. Only I can bear ostracism."

Abandoning him to his conscience, she disappeared from sight. That effectively sealed a chapter in both their lives.

He had placed warning devices, but when Star Bright appeared, undetected, on the bridge of his own ship, Captain Terry was not surprised. The alien found the intruder sitting in the command chair. Opposite him was Teddy Bear, exactly where he had been left to guard *Here,* which, in this case, was also *Home.*

"I don't know if I should welcome you, or if you should bestow that honor upon me," the Earthman began. His speech was slow and deliberate. His eyes never shifted from the main viewing monitor, which he had set to pry upon the depths of space.

"Why did you come here, when you knew I would give you what you asked?" Star Bright demanded, fists clenched in yet another Earth gesture he had observed through exposure.

"Because I couldn't be certain."

"There is much knowledge I lack about your race. And an equal amount I am learning." Star Bright picked up his companion and settled down beside Terry. "But of one thing I am certain: you never doubted I would help you."

A silence descended, more impenetrable than total blackness.

Of the three, Teddy Bear appeared the most inclined to talk. And of the select group, he was the only one incapable of speech.

"Are you reading my mind?" came the reluctant, almost disinterested query.

"I do not have to. You wear your thoughts on your sleeve."

Joshua finally tore his eyes from the panorama, a smile twisting its way onto his otherwise taut features.

"An interesting expression. One would be tempted to say an idiomatic Earth phrase. Where did you learn it?"

"From your thoughts." *Which may, or may not have been true.* "She thinks you have betrayed her."

"Helen's correct. I did."

"Why did you do that to her? Because you did not trust her? That is a failing I have observed in your people. You profess honesty and love, yet you betray with impunity."

"Not all of us."

"You speak of Commander Burbone? Why is she not here with you? I divine she is your... right arm."

"She refused to come with me."

"You are alone?"

"Utterly."

"Not by choice."

"No. I'm the only one left with something to gain."

Looking around, Star Bright's nose twitched.

"And yet, you have touched nothing."

"Correct."

"Why is that?"

Terry shrugged, then reached out a hand, adjusting the screen so that another sector of space was revealed.

"Do you know the names of all the stars, or do you make them up as you travel?"

"Neither. I am well beyond the point where my kind explored, so I have no knowledge of what they might be called. Nor has it ever occurred to me to name them."

"Why not? You've made no charts?"

"I have recorded positions but only for my own reference. I have no need for anything more detailed. I will never come this way again."

The conversation was bland and stilted; a parlay between enemies.

"No planet named 'Star Bright'?"

"Star Bright is not my name."

Finally surprised, Joshua drew a small circle on the desk with the tip of his finger before glancing across at his neighbor.

"That's what you told Helen."

"Star Bright is what I call myself. It is not a name so much as a... guess."

"I don't take your reference."

The little alien brought his head back so that it rested on his shoulders. His eyes fluttered shut.

"Of all the information Mama and Papa imparted to me on the discs they left, the one piece of history they forgot to add was my name."

Clearly torn, the captain adjusted positions, shifting his weight, then resting an arm on the support closest to Star Bright.

"Surely they must have called you something," he gently protested.

Rather than reply, *Here's* captain and sole living crewmember reached out, activating a control. Instantly a new scene appeared, this one tempered in time.

Papa sat in the right-hand command position, exactly where Joshua Terry now resided. In his lap he held his child. Cradled under the baby's arm was Teddy Bear. On the screen before them was total blackness. At first Joshua thought the unit was disengaged, but as the adult's hand drew the baby's attention outward, he saw the one gleaming point of light.

> "Star bright, star light,
> first star I see tonight.
> Wish I may, wish I might,
> Have this wish I wish tonight."

Papa continued.

"I wish for you and Teddy Bear a long and happy life. I wish for you to explore the universe, seeking out new life forms, adventure, friendship. I wish for you to be a bearer of peace and knowledge to those less fortunate."

"Star bright, star light," Joshua repeated with an odd inflection.

"Those were the only words they ever repeated. In my ignorance I thought he was calling me by name. It was only as I grew older that I realized he was doing no more than reciting a poem."

"No," Joshua denied. "He was doing much more than that. He was bestowing a blessing upon the head of a very beloved child."

"But not a name."

"Star Bright is a name. A good name; one which does you honor. And which honors your parents. They would approve."

"I have often wondered." Star Bright hugged the bear, then quietly deactivated the recorded image. Another series of stars appeared. "But it is not a name like Helen Fitzgerald. Or Joshua Terry."

"I think if either of us were given the choice, we would have chosen yours," he confessed. "It speaks of wonder."

It was time to move on. Teddy Bear squirmed. Looking across at the seat, unaccustomedly filled by a stranger, Star Bright implored with his eyes.

This time, it was Terry's turn to read minds. Rising gracefully, he vacated the position. Star Bright moved into the captain's seat and restored Mr. Bear to his command chair.

Everything was as it should be, placed in proper perspective. For all practical purposes, the "game" had been restarted. It seemed to require no more than the press of a button to eradicate the events of the past seventy-two hours.

Just as Joshua had placed an intact *Target* before the ribbon of dark matter, to live and relive the tragedy until the story resolved into a different outcome, the allure was to attempt the same strategy now.

Retreat through time, reverse the images, reset the stage.

Joshua and Helen were alone in the Skip, keeping to themselves after the rescue of the engineers. While they were redefining their affection for one another in a bestowal of love in the peaceful womb of the self-contained vessel, she had told him about her other-worldly contact.

"It whispers, 'I am coming. Wait for me,'" she confided. And this time, he answers, *'We will wait for it, together.'"*

Feeling a gentle pressure on his arm, Joshua reluctantly broke his restructuring of the past. Star Bright was staring into his face with wise, old eyes.

"I can help."

Momentarily confused between a past which would never transpire, *Target's* captain worked through his spatial reality.

"With Hydroponics?"

"Yes."

"Then I didn't have to come stealing."

Glancing around the room with wistful sadness, Terry walked slowly toward the corridor leading to the hatch. Shadows settled in the lines of his uniform, giving the impression of antiquity. His feet shuffled. Star Bright spoke to his back.

"If that is why you came, then I have changed my mind."

Ironically, the captain found perverse amusement in the statement. Pausing at the entranceway, he jerked his head and shoulders in a sporadic act of misplaced defiance. For a moment, and the moment was short, his eyes flashed.

"What other reason would I have had?"

Star Bright chose not to answer and Terry resumed his brief journey, his humor faded into resignation. Not until he had placed as much distance as he could between himself and the captain of the *Here* did he offer a small bow.

"I shall take my leave now, sir. With your permission."

"You had no permission to come. Why ask for leave to go?"

"I thought you might expect it."

"Proper protocol from an alien? I think not."

Expecting no less, Terry took his leave. In the dis-embankment chamber where he had left his spacesuit, he watched as Helen Fitzgerald materialized in her bubble. Their eyes met.

Neither had anything to say to the other.

The being, which was neither human, nor inhuman, but in that swirling realm between the two, began his work in Hydroponics. From his bag of magic tricks, he extracted many wondrous potions and mysterious devices.

While the tools and description were unfamiliar, he was not in the mood to dispense clarification. He must do what he could, moving from one plant enclosure to the other.

There was precious little time. The stars were calling. Growing louder. More insistent.

Exactly as friend Helen had psychically divined, although not thoroughly expressed or discussed with either Star Bright or Joshua Terry, *Target's* window of opportunity was rapidly sealing.

Without being able to express herself, for the concept was amorphous, she knew the alien must depart. Already he had tarried too long....

When the idea first came to her, Helen assumed Star Bright's restlessness stemmed from an overdose of exposure. Used to functioning in his own, carefully structured world, the input from too many minds adversely affected him. Unable to filter out the sensory data flowing through his thought patterns, he had grown restive, ill at ease, causing her to fear for his well-being.

Less understandably, but equally within the realm of probability, lay the fact Star Bright required motion to sustain life. Born on a ship, he had been exposed to travel from inception. Never had Mama and Papa stayed their forward progression; never had their son set foot on a planet. Rocked to sleep by the controlled, yet ever-present movement of *Here,* Star Bright learned to crawl, then walk to the hum of passing stars.

Halted on his perpetual journey, without sensing space alter around him, he had changed, grown quieter, less sure of himself. Often, in the hours she shared with him aboard *Here,* preparing the technology he would take to *Target,* she had seen him pause, staring bleakly toward the viewscreen. His muscles trembled as low, mewing sounds escaped compressed lips.

"Soon, Star Bright; soon," she whispered.

"Soon," he agreed, averting his orbs from the summons of the universe. And then, "I must hurry."

It had been a difficult task, deciding how to help, what equipment to take. Consulting his tapes, the ones his parents made, Star Bright scanned the scenes with a rapidity born of desperation. His familiarity with them seemed to have vanished, for he would put one disc in, then replace it almost immediately with another, so that his quest was desultory and confusing.

Rejecting her offer to help, Star Bright then padded away, back bent as if he were fighting an intergalactic dust storm, hands to his head. Just as suddenly, he would leap in the air, twitching with nervous anxiety before disappearing to his engine room, or talking in his native tongue to the plants, growing in such profusion in their water tanks.

Ten minutes, or perhaps half a "bell" later, he would return, more controlled, yet hardly pacified by whatever information he had gleaned from his solitary sojourns.

"We will take this and this," he declared, pointing with abandon at items she could only guess their uses. Finally declaring her assistance unnecessary, he bade her sit on the couch with Teddy while he gathered the material.

On rare occasions he would stop and ask a question, leaving her more at a loss than if he had remained mute.

"Do you eat *tobiaha?"*

"I do not know what that is." And then, hopefully, "We can try."

Or, "Will your plants live in *ghraba?"*

Shaking her head, Helen's only recourse was to smile and nod. "I hope so."

Thrusting out a peculiarly-shaped instrument, curled around itself in a spiraling upward fashioning of metal and brightly-hued translucent material, he had demanded, "Will your people know how to use this?"

"If you show them how."

Which had left Star Bright with a pout and round, "O" shaped lips.

What Helen could do was take his gifts and transport them to the Skip, hovering nearby. Clad in her protective bubble, she wrapped the presents, one-by-one, within her arms, then floated across the short expanse, there to be welcomed by the eager hands of Joshua and Brian and Paula. Thankfully for her, they did not ask the purpose of her inanimate charges, or the flavor of the plants, for she would have had no answer.

Star Bright worked a day and a night without ceasing his activity. Then, on the morning of the second, he had thrown up his hands, declaring with a helpless cry, "Enough."

"All right," she agreed, resting a hand on his shoulder. "Enough." And then, quietly and with infinite gratitude, "I thank you."

As if not understanding the sentiment, he shook off her touch, reverting again to a soft mewing noise before grasping Teddy to his breast. Bestowing a plethora of kisses on the tiny bear's nose, he cried again, then held out his offering.

"Friend, Helen."

"Friend," she avowed, tears welling in her own glassy eyes, so that the three of them might have been toy store displays, temporarily come to life when the clock chimed midnight. "Hurry." And the promise, "I will be with you."

Unexpectedly, Star Bright loosened the fastening over his tunic, carefully slipping Teddy through the belt. "He will go with us."

"I think," she agreed, sadly smiling, "he might like to see *Target.*"

Her assumption had been incorrect.

"I think," Star Bright countered, pouting nervously, "he does not like to be alone."

"We won't be long." And then to assuage his doubts, "No one will come aboard while you are gone. It's safe to leave *Here.* I promise."

For once, her reassurance was unwelcome.

"Do not promise, Helen Fitzgerald, that which is beyond your power to influence. Speak for yourself. That, I have learned." Patting the companion snugly into its holding harness, he stared down, shoulders drooping. "I know they will not come. That is not what I meant. Enough." Raising his head, he smiled, but gone was the aura of childhood. "We will go."

"And I with you." *In the space bubbles.* To *Target.* That was one promise she could keep.

The assistance, or more accurately, the healing of *Target* began in Hydroponics. Jingles met Star Bright and Helen in the receiving bay.

Barely had the bubbles dissolved from around them when he ran to the alien, throwing his arms around him in greeting, his mammoth face beaming with simple joy. As the little alien squeaked, he released the pressure, But just a bit.

"It's all right, Mr. Star Bright," he cajoled, resting a hand, which, in another, would have been restraining, on the little one's shoulder. "I'm giving you a 'bear hug.'" He demonstrated by holding wide his arms, then easily re-wrapping them around Star Bright. "It's meant as a great big, giant welcome."

"Bear hug," Star Bright repeated, letting the warmth of the term soothe his nerves. "That is like a kiss?" he asked, taking care to pronounce the two words with distinction.

Rolling his eyes in jovial good humor, Jingles tightened his grip, then surprised everyone by lifting him off his feet.

"It's better than a kiss! One smack of the lips and it's over. But a bear hug can last forever!" Further shocking his audience, Mr. Gingleheimer carted the astonished visitor away. "Follow us!"

That was how they arrived in Hydroponics – with Star Bright and Teddy suspended a foot off the deck, Helen trailing behind. Not until carefully setting his charge down did Jingles bow and make his departure.

"I'll see you in Engineering," he waved, making good his farewell. "No matter if you can't help me," he added in a whisper. "What's important is that you're here. And you've brought Mr. Teddy"

Before any of them could reply, he was gone, disappeared as completely as though he had been a hologram of himself and not the flesh and blood man. What he was not, however, and never would be again, was the engineer of 'components and circuits' he had professed to be before Encounter.

LaTanya Carson greeted them at the door. Pointing upward, she indicated the new nameplate inscribed over the passageway.

Plant Nursery.

"Enter with love," she invited, stepping back to reveal a stand, placed to the left of the chamber. Upon it sat her purple thistle. "I hope you approve."

"You will not miss it... at your desk?" he inquired, straining to peer beyond the rows of tanks to where she worked.

Carefully shaking her head, the cross-trained technician made a low denial.

"See what I have replaced it with."

Without daring to take his hand, she led the small procession to her desk. Framed in a small handmade protective sheet was a watercolor sketch of Star Bright. With a gulp of air, he bent forward, eyes fixated on his own likeness.

"I painted it, myself. That's what I am – or was," she quickly amended. "An artist. But there isn't any need for my talents, so I've directed my attention to becoming a plant-person. But, then it occurred to me there was room for both, so I set your likeness to canvas. Or, truthfully, I asked Winston Rey to create me something similar I could paint on. He's our resident historian; he remembers the past," she shyly added. "Because there's something timeless about you, I thought he would grasp the significance and make me something appropriate. In exchange, I offered to teach him how to sketch. It's part of our new Project: the R&R board where we exchange skills and services. Do you like it?"

"It is... wondrous. I have never seen myself in – portrait. Look, Teddy," he rattled on, nearly overcome by the magnificence of the artwork. "Do you know who that is?" Lifting the bear from his belt, Star Bright rubbed his nose against the picture. "He knows! He knows!" he cried, doubly joyous. "We thank you."

"At first, I thought to give it to you as a present," LaTanya admitted. "But when I saw it, I knew I must keep it. Here, with the plants. To remind us of our friendship with the universe."

"It is well. I... approve. I will look through my own eyes, which are not my eyes, but those tempered by another. It shall be a way we... keep together. It will make me less lonely."

"Me, too," LaTanya declared. "To know I have a friend like me in space."

"Like me," Star Bright repeated, running the words over on his tongue. Then, in a stronger voice, "Like me. That is a gift." Placing his fingers to his heart, he imbibed the sentiment before turning toward the rows of plants. "Friends. No longer enemies."

Handing Teddy to Helen, he crisscrossed the double room, silently repeating the words to a prayer, before coming to a stop where the hybrid plants were housed. Drawing out one of the planets he had removed from *Here,* Star Bright introduced them, speaking in a language which did not require the services of a communications expert to translate.

Friends. Grow strong and healthy because you are no longer alone.

As the moment passed, Star Bright beckoned Carson. "I will plant mine beside yours. You will keep them close where they will thrive together.

When they are this big," he demonstrated, "harvest the tops. Equally. Thank them as you take what is theirs to offer."

"I will."

"I have prepared food for the plants. Listen." Cocking an ear to one side, he bade her follow his example. "When they ask, feed them. You will know. I shall do the same with your other seedlings; mine and yours. Friendship, Helen," he added, finally meeting her state with a soft smile, "is another gift. And it would not hurt," he finished, returning his eyes to LaTanya, "to give them a 'bear hug.' That, too, is a pleasure – the touching of living things."

"A bear hug," she repeated. "That I'll invite the crew to help me with. We can all benefit from sharing."

"Make it a trade," he boldly requested. "For your 'R&R' board."

She laughed, and Star Bright and Helen and Teddy laughed and together, the sound of their love filled the once loveless chamber, formally known as "Hydroponics."

Engineering was the final stop on their agenda. Jingles met them, directing the alien inside with a flourish and a grin.

"This is my home," he proudly introduced. "The 'boys' have been waiting to meet you. But please, sit. Rest yourself. In my chair." As Star Bright accommodated him, the engineer added quietly, "It's not my chair, really, but it was. I borrowed it back. It's on loan."

"Ah," Star Bright exclaimed, settling his small body down in the giant's chair. "If I were you, I would keep it."

"But I gave it away –"

"Then ask its present owner to trade it back. Offer to… play your flute for him. It will… tame the savage beast in him."

He laughed at his own joke, which Jingles joined.

"That's an idea. If it weren't an insult, I'd say you were becoming more human."

"But it is not an insult," Star Bright decided, resting his hands, palms downward on the armrests. "Not anymore."

With Teddy Bear on his lap, his eyelids fluttered shut. Neither the engineer or his 'boys,' or the language expert bothered his repose. For the moment, time had once more joined their legion of friends.

Chapter 35

Brian Hardy had retired to the Shuttle Bay, where he occasionally held services, and more frequently came to pray. That was not his purpose at the moment, although an omnipresence surrounded him. He was waiting for a late night consultation. When the summons came, he activated the door from the inside, then spoke without first ascertaining with whom he was speaking.

"Come in, Helen."

She entered, holding a mug in her hand. She did not have to ask whether she was disturbing him. Nor, if he were alone.

"Nice visit," she began because preliminaries were her way of life.

"Yes, it was. And very gracious of Star Bright to help with our many problems. I had not expected it."

"Not after Joshua betrayed him." Underlining her statement was the tacit, *betrayed me.*

"Come in. Sit down," Brian invited, tapping the chair beside him.

Rather than complying with the request, she held out the cup.

"I want you to do something for me."

"Anything," he agreed, although like Star Bright, she had come to realize all-encompassing promises held more falsehood than truth. He leaned back, then busied himself with tidying the spotlessly neat table in front of the two seats. Helen indicated the mug.

"Tea leaves. I want you to read my future."

The request placed a wedge between them. Brian shook his head.

"I'm retired from that line of work."

"You can't give it up. It's part of what you are."

"It's a parlor trick; pagan. I'm going back to God."

"Humans have been trying to divine the future for as long as we've existed."

"There's a huge jump between 'wanting' and 'having the ability to obtain'."

She crossed the room and placed a hand on his arm.

"You predicted Joshua's future for him, once. He told me."

Brian snorted in derision at himself and his feeble attempt as casting another's fate.

"I missed that one," he declared. "It was all... in fun. Not meant to be taken seriously. I've... dabbled with what I don't know for too long. Fooled myself," he bitterly admitted. "No more. I'm mending my wicked ways."

"They aren't wicked and you know it. Besides, you have the gift."

"If Man were meant to know the future, we'd all have been given crystal balls."

"And if Man were meant to fly, we'd be born with wings. Take the cup."

He hesitantly held out his hand. In it she placed the mug. Staring down, he ruefully observed the cluster of soggy leaves, taking pains not to catch a glimpse of his own reflection in the watery dregs.

"Where did you get the tea?"

"Mint leaves."

"From *Here?*"

"No. There were some in the cache Captain Terry found in storage. I commandeered them for myself. Call it a theft," she added. "That, too, seems to be inherent in the human race."

"Joshua didn't steal anything from *Here.*"

"I'm not going to argue the letter of the law with you. Intent makes a man guilty. Please. I'm tired. Will you divine my future?"

"It's an inexact science."

"So is life."

"Turn on the desk lamp."

Helen brushed past him, coming close enough to touch. The dim illumination cast no additional light on either Brian or the tea cup. What it did was exacerbate the shadows of two lonely people. As they moved, their dark, substance-less outlines retreated and advanced across the floor and up the walls, giving the impression they were not alone, but in a room full of people.

"What I read here," Brian slowly began, "is the life of a woman. I see past and present courage. Interest; a quest for the unknown. An insatiable need to travel beyond the bounds of..." He hesitated, searching for the right word. "Convention. Your life line is strong, with several branches."

"What does that mean?"

He shrugged. "Children – or close friends. Hard to be sure."

She leaned forward, her shadow dividing into several divergent shapes.

"Go on."

"I see conflict and trial. Look," he indicated, tilting the cup to provide her with a view. Inside, the tea leaves swirled, then resettled. "Here." She could not be certain whether he were manipulating her future or had memorized the amorphous lines, so that altering them was insignificant.

"What else?"

"Love," he quietly stated with the assuredly of a man who no longer understood the concept.

"Love of whom?"

"The love line intercrosses your life line." She might have corrected him by saying "Intersects," but did not, leaving the religious amalgamation intact. "Depth of passion. Separation."

That was the word she had been waiting for. Helen's fingers interlaced in the attitude of one at prayer or meditation.

"And?"

"I'm not sure," he hedged. "The separation may be past, rather than future. You used too many tea leaves," he added with a tired sigh.

"I didn't know there was a specific quantity. Like love, I thought you dealt with it as it came."

"And so you do," came the surprisingly agreeable tone. "Separation and love."

"Where does it lead?"

"Into space."

"Tell me the truth," she spat, suddenly angry.

"I am. See? The way the tea leaves line the side of the cup? Distance."

"Alone?" she relented, pulling back as if the actual idea of reading her future had suddenly become abhorrent.

"No."

"Who am I with?" He did not reply. "Many or one?"

Brian finally lifted his head, offering back the erstwhile crystal ball. His eyes were red-rimmed with fatigue and drawn emotion.

"It's a long line. Thick."

"It curled at the end. What does that mean?"

"You will come back."

She had heard what her heart had already told her. Taking back the cup, Helen swirled the tea leaves until they were irrevocably out of alignment.

"Thank you. Brother. What do I do with the cup, now?"

He smiled ruefully.

"Swallow the contents." On her look he added, "Tea is good for the constitution."

"And tea leaves?"

"Mint is often considered to be an aphrodisiac."

She smiled and it was soft and warm. Bringing the cup to her lips, she drained it dry. In the bottom remained several remnants, stuck to the side. She handed it back.

"And the end?" she indicated.

"We end as we begin."

"You didn't look inside."

"I didn't have to. It was already written. In the stars."

She stood, clasping the cup to her the way Star Bright held Teddy Bear. "Thank you."

"For what? Telling you what you wanted to hear?"

"For being a friend. For loving me. And Joshua." She raised her hand in farewell. "Good night."

"Good-bye, Helen Fitzgerald. Godspeed."

"Star Bright?" Helen was sitting on the edge of her chair. She had drawn it close, so that her face almost touched the monitor. She was alone in the observatory on Level Four.

Back where it all started.

This time, however, they were communicating via a communications link-up rather than through the intangibles of their minds.

"I am here."

It was the first time she had ever seen his face on a monitor. Staring at it now, she could not help but remark to herself how vulnerable he appeared. With her vision limited to a head and shoulders shot, she could not see his companion.

"Where is Teddy?"

Helen thought he started to smile, but the impression was fleeting.

"I have put him to bed."

"He had a hard day. We've all been stressed." Pressing closer still, she put a hand to the screen, palm outward. Star Bright did the same, so that, metaphysically, they touched.

Closing his eyes, the alien bowed his head.

"I miss you," he intoned with so muted an effort it appeared he did not move his lips.

"I miss you, too. What have you been doing?"

For a second he remained frozen in time, then carefully he readjusted the image she received, widening the view. He indicated another monitor.

"Watching images. Of Mama and Papa." He sniffed and did not bother to wipe away the moisture from his eyes. "They did not tell me the whole story," he whimpered in so hushed a voice she had to strain to hear him.

"Tell me the end," she pleaded, listening with her heart rather than her ears.

"Not the end; the middle. They wished me to seek out friendship. Love. They did not tell me how much it would hurt when such ties were severed."

"Perhaps they ultimately meant you to settle down with someone... on their world." It was not an offer, nor a hope, but a simple rendition of fact as she saw it.

"No. Just as they would not have left *Here*. I do not know what their life was like on their native planet, but they were wanderers. Mama and Papa made their choice, and in so doing, made mine. I am where I belong." His face wrinkled. "Here."

"Are you sorry?"

"I am sorry to be alone, where before I was not," he responded, gently sighing. "Yet, they did teach me how to say good-bye," he miserably added, conjuring images of the final departure of two beings he had no remembrance of ever touching.

"There may come a time for that," Helen decided, heart fluttering erratically. "But that time is not now."

Shaking his head, Star Bright pulled away. "Friend Helen, I am going."

Wrapping her arms around the monitor, Helen gave it a bear hug.

"Star Bright, I want to go with you."

Joshua Terry stood on the bridge. Against protocol, he was alone. The captain's chair, the arena where command decisions of life and death were made, was conspicuously empty. He had positioned himself by his old place; the commander's position. From there, he was taking stock of his new world.

Around him flickered multi-colored lights, indicating which equipment was operational. To his right, the three-dimensional depiction of *Target* rotated, presenting the status of the four levels. Much of it was black, absorbing his mood.

He heard the lift before it arrived. In the moments before the door opened, he should have had time to compose himself, but did not. He had done enough orchestrating for one day.

A form stepped out. He did not look toward it. His second sight had already alerted him as to the person's identity.

Neither were in a hurry to speak. When the silence was finally broken, it came in the form of three syllables.

"Joshua."

One word, yet contained within was the essence of all past, present and future considerations.

Without removing his eyes from the hole he had bored through the viewscreen, inflicting damage of a nature unlike Encounter, Terry could sense fright at the pending confrontation. Like the speaker, he was defenseless.

"Helen."

Interlacing her fingers, then setting her jaw, the communicator took a step closer, breaking contact with the electric eye. The doors slid shut. With the effort of hurtling a javelin, Helen blurted her news.

"I'm going. I came to say farewell... for the present."

Craning back his head which was incredibly heavy and awkward to move, he finally met her gaze. It was steady, but not without pity.

"You're going away?"

"Yes."

"Star Bright has asked you?"

"No," she admitted, moving further into the room, but not close enough to touch. The time for nestling close to him had seeped away, like stars, twinkling out. "I offered. He accepted."

He shrugged, but not from acceptance.

"Will you tell me why?"

Reanimating herself, Helen crossed the room, passing directly before his line of vision. She felt his eyes upon her. The look stung.

"There are many ways to answer that. I think I'll start by saying Star Bright is in possession of incredible technology. He has given us some of it; we need more. Even with his ability to translate and interpret into English, the task of combining and correlating his knowledge is extremely complex. I believe I am the only one who can adequately perform it."

Touching, then holding his finger to his nose, Joshua appeared to consider.

"You're sacrificing yourself, then? Leaving your own people – what you know – for life aboard an alien vessel?"

To reply that *Here* was no more alien to her than *Target* would have been redundant. He already knew. She opted for technicality.

"I'm a language specialist; that's my calling. Just as you are a captain. In my place, you, too, would offer to go. For... duty."

Joshua flinched.

"And if you do succeed in preparing manuals – what then? How do you propose getting such information to us?"

"We'll look for you."

A wry expression he made no attempt to conceal flittered crossed his face.

"Where will we be?"

"On *Target*. Or settled on a planet. Or rescued."

"Or dead."

"No. I don't believe that." She paused, then plunged ahead. "Then, there's the factor you just touched upon."

Joshua held his breath. As she began to speak, he exhaled slowly, for it was not what he expected.

"*Here* has the capacity for travel *Target* does not. It may be that he and I discover a habitable planet in our wanderings. We could... transport you there. Or possibly even get close enough to Earth to send a message. Knowing what happened, there may be a chance of rescue."

"Believe what you will," he decided, unable to assimilate either idea with actual probability. Crossing toward Helen, his arms moved upward to embrace her, but he could not complete the ritual, as if physical contact would dissolve them both. "I release you."

"To go?" she demanded, understanding beforehand his true meaning.

"From our engagement."

"You think what I feel for Star Bright is a love greater than you and I possess?"

"I believe it could be."

Stiffening her arms, then hiding them behind her back, military style, Helen shook her head. The action was not denial, but rather acceptance.

"Where is it written a heart can only admit the tender emotion of one other? Nowhere," she answered for him. Continuing her journey of a million light years, she walked a circuit around the bridge, coming to a stop by the captain's chair. By so doing, she discovered an unexpected consolation.

Ironically, that knowledge made it easier to continue.

"I think I have loved Star Bright from the first moment I felt his presence. That... conflict confused me; caused me to behave in a manner unlike myself. Caused me," she emphasized, spinning suddenly to face him, "to doubt you. That was unjust. It was actually me I questioned."

"And yet you were correct – about me." His judgment was harsh. "I reacted out of consternation, rather than friendship. My invitation to the... alien... was a sham. Had it not worked, I was prepared to take what we needed. I betrayed... humanity."

"Yes. You did. But I wonder why." Her statement confused him. Joshua's mouth moved in mute puzzlement, but Helen would not let him speak. "I believe you knew I would go before I did. That I *must* go. We're more alike than we think, Joshua Terry." Drawing in a deep breath, she plunged ahead. "You *sacrificed* my trust to make my decision easier."

He flinched, so that his back was to her.

"Then this is good-bye."

"But not farewell. I've promised to return. And in the meantime, I reaffirm our betrothal. Will you do the same?"

With a quiet sniff of resignation, Joshua held out his arms. She came to him and they embraced, chins resting on one another's shoulders. By doing so, they reset, yet again, the game of life they were living.

Behind them, over the vast viewscreen, blinked the words "Red Alert." In the tension of the preceding days, no one had thought to deactivate the warning.

Her departure would be the reminder.

Helen had forgotten about the bubble. Standing alone in the cargo bay on Level Four, it came back to her, exactly as Star Bright had promised. In one wondrous moment, she was enveloped by the protective film.

Waving her arms upward, the bay doors parted. With a cry of joy and sadness, she floated out and away. And never once looked back.

Star Bright and Teddy Bear were waiting for her on *Here.* As the atmosphere seeped back inside the hatch, they shyly emerged, the smaller thrust out before the larger. As usual, the bear was the braver of the two.

"I did not think you would come," Star Bright began with trepidation.

"And what of Teddy? Surely, he believed," Helen replied, stepping forward.

Glancing down at his companion, the little alien communed with his friend, who was more alive than most endowed with breath. After a protracted pause, Star Bright's head shook in sad resignation. Long locks on his forehead cascaded into naturally-formed points. "Not Teddy, either."

"Then we are all surprised."

"How long will you stay?"

She smiled and it was both sad and happy.

"Until my work is done – and we have explored our hearts, as well as the universe."

"But you *will* leave?"

The answer was automatic.

"Not today, not tomorrow and not the next day. Not for a year and a day. Not until 'Who knows When.' Is that agreeable?"

"It is more than I have a right to expect, friend Helen Fitzgerald." Pronouncing her name gave Star Bright courage. "While we are 'exploring our hearts, as well as the universe,' will you come to love me?"

The reply was unequivocal.

"I will cherish you, as I have no other."

Rubbing the space between Teddy's ears, Star Bright used the act to divert his eyes.

"We already love you."

There was both a childish quality of innocence and an adult's profession of affection to his avowal. Which, peculiarly enough, captured Helen's emotions, as well.

Bowing her head in appreciation, she detected a subtle alteration in his stance as she spoke.

"I thank you."

Removing a small object from the shelf directly behind him, Star Bright held it out for her inspection.

"An image recorder," he identified. "The one Mama and Papa used to chronicle their life for me. Shall you and I use it for the same purpose?"

Behind his question was the unspoken conclusion to his thought: *so that I might have it to keep me company when 'Who knows When' arrives.*

Breathing gently, then having the surprise and satisfaction of seeing him imitate her, Helen refused to acknowledge the poignant future.

"One thing I have learned on *Target,* little one – a lesson you brought home with vivid clarity. We must look at life as a gift and not a burden. Nothing is an enemy before we make it so. Between ourselves, we will use our moments preciously. Just as I pray Joshua and Brian and our friends on *Target* do. So that when we are finally reunited, our bonds will be stronger." Her eyes twinkled in merriment. "Our adventures more grandiose."

Bouncing on the balls of his feet, Star Bright and Teddy Bear led the way outside, into the corridor. Helen followed, her sense of excitement growing into awe.

"Will we exchange great stories?" he inquired in a voice rather growly and grumbly, the way a bear might sound, were he given the gift of articulate speech.

"We will tell tall tales," Helen decided, finally ready to expand their universe into the future, while encompassing all that had gone before. "And exchange poetry and rhymes."

"Whose will be better?"

This time, Helen Fitzgerald laughed.

"We'll have to make it a contest."

Which was as good as promising every hand would draw from the candy jar, and two furry paws would dip into the honey pot.

Joshua Terry was working on his computer when Paula Burbone entered his quarters.

"What are you doing?" she inquired with casual indifference that did not deceive.

"Nothing." The captain swiveled in his chair, effectively blocking curious eyes from reading the words on the screen.

"You'll miss her."

"I miss her already," he admitted before regretting his words. He need not have bothered, for Paula appreciated them.

"You're a good teacher, you know."

Her apparently abrupt change of subject disconcerted him.

"What do you mean?"

Silently asking permission and receiving it, the commander sat opposite him. With her shoulders back, her position was one of formal respect.

"You ask opinions and make judgments. But what you say is not always what you mean. I shall mark that, sir."

To deny her statement would be a lie, but to acknowledge it would be a confession.

"Go on."

"I believed you when you said you would board *Here* and take what we needed, if it were not willingly offered."

"Yes," he agreed, interlacing his fingers, then gazing across at a point against the far wall.

"I was prepared to accept your commands, no matter what my personal feelings were. You were not."

A grin worked its way across his face, going from west to east, or perhaps from north to south, depending upon one's perspective. For like the chronicling of time in minutes and days, direction was a relative thing.

"How can you be so sure?"

"You had an hour; more, before Star Bright arrived, yet you touched nothing. Took nothing."

"How can you be so sure?" he challenged, still avoiding her piercing gaze.

"I read your mind."

An exclamation of surprise, almost a guffaw, escaped the captain. The noise broke his concentration and his eyes met hers, dissolving the distinction between professor and pupil.

"You shouldn't have let her go, thinking the worst of you," Paula added.

This time, he was ready.

"She'll have to read *my* mind."

"And will she?"

"We all seem to be getting pretty good at it," he stated with only a hint of uncertainty.

"She'll come back."

"How do you know?"

"Brian told me."

They had come full circle. Paula stood, stretched, then stifled a yawn.

"Get some sleep," he advised, relaxing back into his chair.

"I will. But not just now. I have... somewhere to go."

"Where?"

"To Engineering. Jingles is holding a private seminar. Top secret. You're not invited."

She had hooked him. He leaned forward, trying to divine her thoughts. Failing in that, he was compelled to ask.

"What about?"

Paula shrugged.

"Star Bright gave him some... ingredients. He's making candy. In the food processor." She grinned. "I volunteered to be a taste tester. Sir."

"Why didn't anyone ask me?"

"It's commonly believed, sir... you judgment is suspect. You'll eat anything."

She meant for him to grin and he did.

"Off with you. Have fun."

It was the first such command he had ever given. God and tea leaves willing, it would not be the last.

"Wait a minute." Joshua stood and hurried toward the door, brushing past her. "When the explosion comes, I want to be safe on the bridge."

His sudden disappearance into the corridor propelled Paula to stare back at his computer. On impulse, she crossed the abandoned room and activated the screen.

Without conscience, Paula Burbone ran a hand across the instrument, bringing back the message Joshua Terry had been composing. Her eyes skimmed the text completely, memorizing the words.

"Helen:

'Your little Meow grieves
When the snow is on the ground,
For the trees have no leaves,
And no berries can be found.

'The air is cold, the tuna is hid,
For Meow here what can be done?
Let's throw around some crumbs of fish,
And then he'll live till snow is gone.'
"Love, Joshua."

She was not familiar with Mother Goose's Melodies. Had she been, she would have recognized a modified text of a very old rhyme. She did not have to be. Opening a channel, she sent the message to *Here,* then closed down the computer.

When the reply came, he would receive it on the bridge.

Star Bright padded past Helen, a tray full of food in his arms.

"Teddy is hungry. Are you ready to eat?"

"Just a moment. Then I'll join you in the den."

With a happy smile, he continued on, leaving her alone in the command center. She would only be a moment.

A moment was all it took to send her message.

"'Dear Meow, are you willing to sell for one shilling
Your ring?' Said Meow, 'I will.'
So they took it away, and were married next day
By the Turkey who lives on the hill.
They dined on mince, and slices of quince,
Which they ate with a runcible spoon;
And hand in hand, on the edge of the sand,

They danced by the light of the moon,
    The moon,
    The moon,
They danced by the light of the moon.'"

When it was sent and received, there was only one more task to perform before she joined Star Bright and Teddy Bear at supper.

Helen blew Joshua a kiss.

The End

GSFE

ALSO BY: S.L.KOTAR AND J.E.GESSLER

"The Hugh Kerr Mystery Series"..

- I   **The Conundrum of the Decapitated Detective**
- II   **The Conundrum of the Absconded Attorney**
- III   **The Conundrum of the Sins of the Fathers**
- IV   **The Conundrum of The Two-Sided Lawyer**
- V   **The Conundrum of the Clueless Counselor**
- VI   **The Conundrum of the Loveless Marriage**
- VII   **The Conundrum of the Executed Defendant**
- VIII **The Conundrum of the Jettisoned Jury**
- IX   **The Conundrum of the Perjured Pigeon**
- X   **The Conundrum of the Haunting Halloween Party**
- XI   **The Conundrum of the Tuneless Tunesmith**
- XII   **The Conundrum of the Meddling Motorcar**
- XIII **The Conundrum of the Blundering Bear**
- XIV **The Conundrum of Shooting Fish in a Barrel**
- XV   **The Conundrum of The Girl with the Emerald Eyes**
- XVI **The Conundrum of The Vanishing Cream**
- XVII **The Conundrum of The Convoluted Confession**
- XVIII **The Conundrum of the Skeleton in the Closet**

    o   **To Be Continued!**

"New Beginnings Series"

- I   **The Believer**
- II   **The Heretic**
- III   **Arrow Song**
- IV   **Peas In A Pod**
- V   **The Agnostics**

"the ReproBate saga"

- I   **Beneath the Rose**
- II   **skull and cRossBones**
- III   **Redefining Bastions**
- IV   **thicker than Blood**
- V   **prioR Battles**
- VI   **Requited Blasphemy**
- VII   **The waR Between**
- VIII **To Richmond or Bust**
- IX   **carrying Battlescars**
- X   **RamBlings**
- XI   **Retrieving Ballast**
- XII   **captain's RB**
- XIII **wondeRous Backdrops**
- XIV **ReproBate**
- XV   **time and tRouBle**
- XVI **the Road Back**
- XVII **oveR the Brink**
-
  - **To be Continued**

"the Hellhole saga"

- I   **First Draw**
- II   **Audition for a Legend**
- III   **Strange Bedfellows**
-

"The Kansas Pirate Series"

- I   **Pirate Treasure**
- II   **Strawberry Fields**
- III   **The Drinking Gourd**

- **Catman**

- **ONE**

- **Shepherd of the Kingdom**

- **Wolf Eyes**

- **I Am the Ship**

- **Blue Moon**

- **Target'd**

- **Star Bright**

Non-Fiction
The Kepi Magazine

- **Volume I and II**
- **Volumes III and IV**

www.ingramcontent.com/pod-product-compliance
Lightning Source LLC
Chambersburg PA
CBHW072105250626
47159CB00007B/2314